BREAKING IN

A NOVEL

TYLER SCHWANKE

BLACK STONE PUBLISHING

Printed in the United States of America

First edition: 2023
ISBN 979-8-200-96079-8
Young Adult Fiction / Thrillers & Suspense / Crime

Version 1

Blackstone Publishing
31 Mistletoe Rd.
Ashland, OR 97520

www.BlackstonePublishing.com

To Tess,
my forever partner in crime

Sadly, the writer is thought disposable here,
Hollywood being the only relay race where you hand
the baton to the next guy . . .
And he shoots you.

—Blake Snyder,
Save the Cat! Strikes Back

PART ONE

THE
LONG
CON

FADE IN:

1

EXT. NEW YORK CITY ALLEY—NIGHT

Feet slap against wet pavement. Clouds of steam puff through manhole covers. An overhead light sputters and goes dead.

A man in a dark alley looks over his shoulder to see if he's being followed, then slows. Pink neon from a diner sign bathes him in light, throwing long shadows against the fragmented red brick behind him. He hugs a duffel bag close to his chest and listens for footsteps, voices, police sirens. The alley is quiet. His breathing is heavy.

He takes off his fedora, kneels down to open the duffel bag. With an anxious hand, he pulls back the zipper. A sound escapes him. He closes his eyes and grinds his teeth. He looks as if he's about to cry, but tears don't come.

He removes a stack of dollar-sized paper cut from newspapers, phone books, and advertisements. He takes out another. His actions are hurried, desperate. It's worse than he feared. He turns the bag over. Stacks upon stacks of paper land on neon-stained cement. He rakes his hands through the pile. It's all fake, not a single authentic piece of currency to be found. It's enough to make a man cry, but still no tears. He gives it a moment. Nothing.

From the front pocket of his trench coat, he pulls out a handgun. He looks it over, inspecting the barrel, then the grip. It looks foreign in his hand, like it's the first time he's ever held a gun. Interesting for a man who shot someone hours ago.

He nods. A decision has been made. About what isn't clear.

Hurried footsteps echo from around the corner. He jumps to his feet, aims the gun. He takes a step back out of the light. His face is drenched in shadows. He holds his breath. His body trembles. Way too much. The footsteps get louder. Someone rounds the corner and a woman's voice yells, "Don't shoot!" but the back of the man's head blocks her face from the camera—

"Cut!"

For the sixth time tonight, Millie drops her head into her hands. God. Dammit. A two-minute take once again ruined by the actor not hitting his mark. How many times is she going to have to go over this?

While spending the last eighteen months writing her script, meticulously storyboarding and designing all the shots, saving every allowance, and asking only for money on birthdays and holidays to pay the Academy's summer-workshop fee, she never factored in that all of her hard work would rest in the hands of a plumber from Staten Island with day care issues. That's what she gets for not being able to afford a SAG actor for the lead.

"Let's take five, then we'll go again," she says.

"I gotta be on the ferry by six to pick up my kid in time, or my ex is going to shit," the actor replies.

"I'm aware."

He pulls out a vape pen and sticks it between his lips. The actress they just cast yesterday after the first two quit, whose face still hasn't been captured on camera, takes out her iPhone from a pocket in her vintage floral tea dress. They gather by the rented U-Haul van whose cargo area doubles as a greenroom. Both ignore the craft services provided: a grease-splotched bag of donuts and a Box O' Joe from Dunkin'.

Paz stares at Millie from on top of her apple box, arms crossed, pierced eyebrow raised, no doubt waiting to challenge going for another long take. Millie might try to play the intimidating director, but she knows that someone who's seventeen and looks younger, especially with her blond hair, apple cheeks, and overly big blue eyes, is hardly going to intimidate anyone. Instead, she pulls down the brim of her Dodgers cap to hide as much of her face as she can.

"That's fine, pretend I can't see you," Paz says. "But you know we're not going to get it before sunrise if we don't break up the shot."

"Just be ready with the makeup kit for touch-ups before we go again," Millie says, pushing her cap back up. "And can you darken the bags under his eyes? He's supposed to look like he's in his fifties." She slips her fingers into a pair of gloves, but that's as far as she gets before Paz asks what she's doing. "Changing out the scrim on the ARRI. The light's coming in too hot."

"Then ask me to do it. That's my job."

"Can you fix the scrim on the ARRI?"

"I think it's fine," she says, but after Millie doesn't break eye contact for a solid twenty seconds, Paz agrees to adjust the light.

Except for a passing car or an occasional homeless person asking for change, the street is quiet, buildings dark, the rest of New York City getting some sleep. Millie finishes her cold coffee, keeps the cup in front of her mouth so nobody can see her grimacing from the taste. Sleep is hours away. There's still so much work to be done if they're going to get this shot right.

At the beginning, keeping the crew down to four, herself included, so she could control every aspect of the project seemed like a stroke of genius. She had Paz with the cinematic eye, Jordan with the high attention to detail, and Devin with the up-for-anything attitude. Anyone else would've just been deadweight, an obstacle to overcome, an extra person she'd have to explain her vision to. Even so, she seriously underestimated how much of a production this would be, even if it was just a student film.

Not that she's complaining. Secretly, she's loving every second of this.

She might be physically exhausted, her muscles sore, eyelids heavy, but it's the best kind of exhausted there is. Her pulse speeds with adrenaline. Heart pounds with anticipation. It doesn't matter that she's been in New York City for the last two months; every day still feels like that first moment she emerged from the subway onto the city streets, the shortest skyscraper still five times taller than anything back in Fargo.

How many people back home could say they ever gave their dream a real shot? Millie already knows the answer. Just one, and it's her, and if that means having to work late into the night on a shoestring budget with actors who can't tell a mark from their asshole, then so what. She'll make it work.

Because she has a dream and a plan and nothing is going to get in the way.

Devin comes over with the night's shot list dutifully in hand. "It's been four hours, love. Sun's up in two. Paz is right. We need to move on."

"Striking," Paz yells. The Arri blasts right into Millie's face.

Devin guides her out of the light. "I know you wanted everything up to the gunshot in a single take, but we can break it up from when he stands and get the rest of it in a two-shot. Might look nice, and it'll be easier for the actor to hit his mark."

"Can't break it up. Has to be one shot," Millie says. "I want Ricky O'Naire as impressed with the visuals of the movie as he is with the script. Otherwise, we don't stand a chance of winning. We're going again. Jordan, how was sound?"

Halfway down the block, with the boom microphone aimed at them and listening through headphones hooked up to the sound mixer, Jordan calls out, "A little rough." He wears the headphones upside down to accommodate the height of his frohawk. "The bag makes too much noise against his coat when he runs. Have him hold it closer."

"Shit," Millie says. "Another note he won't remember."

"Have a chat with them," Devin advises. "You haven't given a single direction in hours, too busy trying to do all of our jobs." She winces, but he continues, his voice gentle. "Do another run-through. Make sure he knows his marks and see if you can get him to cry. Six takes and still nothing, and I know you wanted tears."

To prove his point, he flips to her storyboard of a stick figure crying over a duffel bag. The stick body is a little longer than it should be; Devin has given him a tiny stick penis.

"Stop doing that," Millie says.

Neither of the actors notice as she approaches, absorbed in their phones when they should be running their lines. "Hey, guys, can I talk to you for a minute?" They look up. "You're doing great. The footage is very noir, like something straight out of *Odd Man Out* or *Criss Cross*, but with color."

"Kris Kross? The kid rappers from the nineties?" the actress asks.

The actor seems equally puzzled. Millie's heart hurts a little. They didn't do the required watching she assigned.

"It's a movie, but that's not important right now." She removes her note cards from the pocket of her Academy track jacket, finds the card listing out the actor's motivation for the scene. He'll be her biggest obstacle to getting everything done tonight. *Complete and utter despair* is the last bullet point, circled twice for emphasis.

"Remember, this is the scene right after the crew has robbed the bank," she says. "Your character's just killed the guard you conned into helping with the heist. You're thinking what a sucker he was, how his wife and daughter are better off without him, how you're such a brilliant Mastermind that nothing can touch you. And then you open the bag and see that there's no money inside. Your character's been double-crossed, convinced it was a setup by the only woman who ever said she loved him. You go from arrogance to complete and utter despair."

"Effin' A," the actor says, blowing hot air laced with coffee and banana-nut-bread vape into her face. "But he gets with her at the end, right? Hope so. This one's super cute."

He eyes the actress, spending an obscenely inappropriate amount of time on her cleavage. The woman looks to Millie. It's clear that if he makes a move, she will break his arm, and Millie will just have to be cool with it.

"Actually, no," she says. "This is the end. Of the whole movie. Where you two draw your guns because you each think the other one ripped you off. Then shots are fired, and we close on a final image of you both dying on the cement, gurgling blood as we fade to black." The corners of her mouth twitch in anger. "You read the script, right?"

"Absolutely. Absolutely," the actor says too quickly. "I read the script. Totally. Most of it. I sometimes like to save the ending until we shoot. I feel it helps my performance if I'm surprised along with the audience."

Nothing about this sentence makes sense, but there's no time to unpack that right now.

Night is burning.

2

After four run-throughs, they're ready to go again. Sound speed, camera rolling, clapboard snapping shut. They botch the first take when the actor can't get the duffel bag open. The second take he completely forgets to open it. The third goes to hell when Paz backs up too quickly, running into Devin, who's guiding her. They both fall down, but thankfully the camera isn't damaged. Nobody tells Jordan they're rolling, so there's no sound on the fourth take, which would've been fine, they could've dubbed the footsteps and street noise in post, except that he walks into the shot halfway through the take to see if any donuts are left.

The fifth take is magic. The actor either connects with his character or has a nervous breakdown because he's thirty-five and has been doing the same damn shot for the past seven hours on a student film that he's only getting paid for with a copy of the film for his demo reel. Whatever the reason, it's pure cinema on Millie's video monitor.

EXT. NEW YORK CITY ALLEY—NIGHT

The man picks up the bag and turns it over. Stacks upon stacks of paper fall on neon-stained cement. He rakes his hands through the pile. It's all fake, not a single authentic piece of currency to be found. His eyes swell with tears. The pain is unbearable. He bends over the money, his chest shaking the appropriate amount with each sob.

Hurried footsteps around the corner. He wipes his eyes, listens. Is it her? He almost wants it to be. He pulls the handgun from his trench coat, holds it firmly. It's an extension of his hand, like he emerged from his mother's womb with it.

He jumps to his feet, takes a step back, perfectly positioning himself in equal amounts of pink neon and darkness. Footsteps get louder. He raises the gun. He holds his breath. He waits for what he knows is his destiny. Someone rounds the corner, perfectly hitting their mark, their face fully visible to the camera—

"Spare some change?" a homeless man asks, holding an empty bottle, the bottom of his pants soaked with piss.

3

Millie pauses the video playback. The homeless man fills the thirty-five-inch computer monitor in a freeze-frame, the darks and mids in his soiled crotch coming through in mesmerizing 4K display.

"And that's about when the actress quit," Devin finishes. "We don't have a single take we can use, unless you're willing to compromise and pick it up from when he stands."

Millie takes off her Dodgers cap and throws it onto the desk. It lands next to her open laptop. "Dammit."

"Quite right. And now is when I inform you that we need more crew."

"This again?"

"This again," he says. "Two more crew members is all we need to elevate this into the type of production you're asking for to impress O'Naire. Honestly, twenty-five is what we need, but even two would be a vast improvement. It's too late to ask anyone here, but I posted an ad on New York City Film Jobs for an assistant cameraman and boom operator this morning—"

"You did *what?*"

"—and already have twenty responses for each, and they'll all work for credit and copy."

"The school won't allow it."

"I knew you'd say that. I checked, and there's no stipulation in the rules that we can't hire outside help as long as the director is a student. If you believe the rumors, Yates is paying his entire crew. The other students on his set are just getting fat on craft services."

Millie gets up from her chair and leans against the counter of another workstation. There are eight stations in the editing suite, the overhead lights dimmed to reduce monitor glare. It feels like the inside of a surveillance van, only instead of trying to steal a rare diamond or infiltrate a bank's digital mainframe, students try to hide boom-mic slips and tweak the color of strawberry syrup to look like blood. "If we hire outside help, what guarantee do we have that they'll care about this project like we do?"

"Nobody's going to care about it as much as you," he says, "but if the short helps us win, they could potentially meet O'Naire. That's still worth something in this business. Granted, the last few films he's produced have been abysmal, but he's still considered a top-notch writer and director."

She takes a seat and scrolls through the other takes. There's got to be other coverage they can use.

"Mil, you have to understand that we can't do everything. It's okay to ask for help."

"We'll continue with the crew we have," she says. "We can make it work."

Devin throws his hands up in dramatic fashion and throws a blazer over his plaid button-up. "That's my cue then. We've got an early start tomorrow, so I'm going to get some sleep."

Millie eyes the time on the monitor. "We both know you're going to the bar before last call. Tell me, Dev, don't you ever get tired of hooking up with closeted tourists?"

"You know perfectly well I can't miss out on one more opportunity to disappoint my father." Devin ruffles his thick chestnut hair and checks his face in the reflection of one of the monitors. "It's not my fault my accent makes me uncontrollably desirable in this country, or that bartenders assume I'm at least twenty-one instead of eighteen."

"Which you would never take advantage of."

"No idea what you mean, love." Devin grins, letting his English cadence playfully shine on the word *love*. "It'd be the same thing if you came to London. Men would go gaga over the way you talk."

"I wasn't aware I talked all that differently."

"Oh, fer sure, don't ya know?" he says in a painfully clichéd and animated upper-Midwestern accent.

Millie twists in her seat and gives him a playful shove. "Don't start with that shit. I don't talk like that."

"My apologies. Let me make it up to you." He motions for her to follow.

"You know I'm not smoking up while we're in production."

"Come on, Mil. It's after midnight. You're not shooting anything between now and bed. You'll be fine, I promise. Nobody's going to stop thinking you're Wonder Woman."

4

Ricky's hands tremble as he pours himself a double shot of vodka from the town car's bar. It burns going down, his nostrils flaring with heat. Sweat dampens his forehead. His heart thunders in his ears. For a man whose job it is to run multimillion-dollar productions, he should be able to handle the stress, shrug it off, box it up, and set it aside with the other hundred and one things trying to ruin his day. He's dealt with this pressure before; there are people protecting him that'll take care of it. Why does it feel different this time?

His phone rests on the seat next to him. The screen illuminates the dark interior of the town car, a muffled voice ordering him to answer.

"Ricky, tell me you understand," his lawyer says, faking the right amount of concern for $700 an hour. "I need to hear you say that you understand what's about to take place."

"You're acting like I'm going to be hauled off in handcuffs at any moment."

"It could happen. Part of my job is to prepare you for worst-case scenarios."

Ricky leans back against the seat, ice rattling in his glass. Prison is hardly the worst-case scenario.

"I'm on my way to the Academy now," he says. "I'm picking up the financial statements you requested. I'll bring them to you first thing in the morning."

There's a long pause on the other end of the phone. "Will those numbers even be accurate? You know what, don't tell me. As your lawyer, I shouldn't know. I'm not the one who needs to be convinced you're innocent."

"Thank God for that." Ricky hangs up and pours another drink.

5

The air is hazy with late July. Work trucks spray the dank city streets. Music and neon glisten on the sidewalk from a nearby piano bar, the Academy tucked away from the center of Union Square, obscured in shadow. It's a redbrick building with columns and a roof that comes to a point. It'd be a knockoff of the courthouse from *Back to the Future* if it weren't for the nail salon and discount liquor store on the first floor.

Millie takes the joint from Devin, holds the smoke in her lungs. She tries to find a star, but it's useless; she knows this. She hasn't been able to find a star in Manhattan since she moved to New York, the night sky a dusky void until she gets out to Brooklyn.

She finishes smoking with Devin and heads up alone to the editing suite.

There she finds a man at her workstation, his back to her, hands in pockets as he watches the footage on the monitor. When the screen goes black, the man crouches down and uses the mouse to restart the video clip.

"First preview is free, but I start charging after that," she says.

Dressed in a pair of jeans and a white button-up, a casual look if the jeans weren't designer and the button-up fine linen, the founder of the Manhattan Movie Academy turns around, scratching his five-o'clock shadow before pushing up the brim of his Chicago Cubs cap.

"I'm guessing that wasn't supposed to happen?" he remarks, apple-green eyes narrowing. "Shame, really. The guy pissing himself is the most authentic thing that occurred during the take."

"Ricky O'Naire," Millie says, feeling dizzy, and not from the weed.

She leans against the counter for balance and examines him from the soles of his shoes to the top of his cap. She'd almost given up on meeting him, a moment she's dreamed about since her dad showed her *The Mark* and she learned that being a film director was an actual job. The movies he wrote and directed were always their favorites: gritty and real, action-packed, but with characters you actually gave a shit about. Intelligent thrillers that put him on the same level as Christopher Nolan, Denis Villeneuve, and Kathryn Bigelow.

It's why, out of all the film schools in the country with summer workshops for high school students, she chose the Manhattan Movie Academy. Not because it's considered the best (it's not) or because she received a scholarship or financial assistance (she didn't) but because it gave her the best chance to one day be in a room with her and her dad's favorite director.

She always fantasized she'd get called into his office, surrounded by posters of his movies, awards lining the shelves. He'd want to meet with her because he was a fan, maybe to tell her she was the best student the Academy had ever had.

Instead, she's meeting her idol ripped on sticky purple ganja. She's going to kill Devin.

"Good. You know who I am," he says. "This way we can jump right to who you are and what you're doing here after hours."

Millie dry-swallows. It feels like a lump of kitty litter traveling down her throat. "I was viewing some footage my crew shot last night, and wanted to watch it on the school's monitors. Didn't realize how late it was. Been on a vampire's schedule ever since shooting began, I guess." She rubs her dry and probably bloodshot eyes and tries to remember where she threw her Dodgers cap.

"So you are, in fact, a student then?" he asks. "You skipped over the first part of my question, so I'm having to piece this together myself."

"Right. Sorry. My name is Millie Blomquist. I'm in the high school summer-workshop program."

"Your footage looks like it belongs to a project of your own instead of a directing exercise. Are you preparing a submission for the Feature Award?"

"Yes."

"And what do you call this?" He looks back at the monitor. "Do you shoot your rehearsals? Because none of the departments are working together in this shot. Your DP is making found footage, while the actors think they're doing Shakespeare, and the director is calling it noir."

"I guess I'd call it a work in progress, then."

Ricky O'Naire stares at her. "You must be from the Midwest."

"Fargo." She hates how much her accent flares whenever she says where she's from.

"Aha. And tell me, Millie Blomquist from Fargo, does your RA know you're not in your dorm room, or at the dorms, or even in the borough of Brooklyn?"

Truth is, her RA probably isn't in Brooklyn either but out partying with her boyfriend at his place in Queens. Ratting her out wouldn't help her own case, so Millie keeps quiet and shakes no.

"I see." Now he's going to tell her to go home, either to the dorms or all the way back to North Dakota for breaking curfew: punishment for being a minor out on her own past midnight in one of the most dangerous cities in the country. Instead, he points to the Dodgers cap next to her laptop. "So this is for show, then?"

Huh? "No, I'm a Dodgers fan." She puts on the cap, pulls it down to cover her eyes. "We don't have pro teams in North Dakota. I'm an LA fan in general, I guess. Started when I was a kid and my dad took me to Hollywood. Walk of Fame. Radiance Theatre. All that touristy stuff. He loved your movies. *The Mark* was his favorite." She's talking way too much. Why is she talking way too much?

"That's flattering to hear," he says. "Why didn't you study at our LA location, then? It's right next to the Warner lot."

"You don't ever teach in LA, and I wanted to meet you." Millie looks down at the black-and-white-checkered floor. Even in the dim light, she worries he'll be able to see her cheeks flush. Could she be any more obvious? "To have you teach me, I mean," she adds.

Now it's his turn to admire the floor. "As I'm sure you're aware, this bullshit investigation over the last couple of months has taken up a considerable amount of my time."

He's talking about the allegations that last year's Feature Award winners haven't yet received their prize money, an accusation that he publicly denied. He even posted proof on Twitter of the money going through, but the winners were adamant that it was fake. Millie can't imagine what kind of lowlife would try to bleed more money from the place where they learned how to make films. Talk about biting the hand that feeds you.

He takes a seat in her chair. "Is this the master, or do you have another angle? Preferably one where the camera is level and won't induce nausea?"

Holy shit. Not only is he not busting her, but he wants to talk about her project.

After a beat with no response, he glares at her in annoyance, his lifted eyebrows telling her to get on with it.

"This is it," she says. "The whole thing is one tracking shot. I wanted to capture the desperation of the character by not cutting."

"Are you telling me you have no coverage? No master, no over-the-shoulders, no close-ups? Who's your directing instructor? Sidney?"

"Don't worry," she says, immediately regretting her decision to talk back to one of Hollywood's top-ten working directors. "I'm not going all *Victoria* and shooting the whole movie as one long take or anything." She pauses to see if he catches her reference to the obscure two-hour German heist film. He stays silent, but she hopes he's super impressed. "If you knew the story and where the character was emotionally, I think you'd understand why, for this scene in particular, I don't want a lot of cuts."

He turns away from the monitor. He's much older looking in person, a stack of wrinkles piled high above his eyebrows, deep trenches under his eyes. Still incredibly attractive. He'd be perfectly cast as the dreamy yet weathered small-town high school football coach who never gives up on his team.

"I notice you keep saying 'I' and not 'we,'" he says. "You're working with a crew, correct?"

"I am."

"And how many are in this crew?"

"Including me, four."

"Four?" he repeats, waiting for her to confirm before continuing. "Most of the other groups are between fifteen and twenty. Maybe one has around ten, but no less than that. No wonder you had someone wander onto your set. A real film crew can't even park a trailer with four crew members, and that's because the union won't let them."

"Did you ever see *Man on a Ledge*? They only had four people in their crew, and they were able to pull off a diamond heist, fake a death, and clear their family name at the same time. *Point Break*. They were kicking ass, just the four of them, until they forced Keanu Reeves to join. *Going in Style* only had four people. *Widows*."

He scoffs, but his shoulders are now square, his eyes on her. "All right. I'll bite. What's this magical story that only requires four crew members?"

She pulls out the chair next to him and sits down before the reality of the situation—*talking about her script with Ricky O'Naire*—causes her to lose her nerve. "It's a heist, a throwback to 1940s and '50s noir, where the heist is the midpoint of the film and the third act is filled with double crosses and bad luck. Really doubling down that there are no clean getaways, that fate will always intervene. Kind of like what you did with *The Mark*." She takes a deep breath. "It's about a guy who can't make ends meet and agrees to rob a bank after he's evicted from his home and he and his girlfriend and daughter have to live on the street. He's killed during the robbery, and the third act is about the rest of the crew double-crossing one another until everybody is either dead or in jail."

The words flow from her mouth, sounding like she knows what the hell she's talking about. While she's practiced some version or another of this pitch in the bathroom mirror, it's never gone this well. Must be the weed. She actually should probably thank Devin for smoking her up.

Ricky O'Naire's mouth works as if he's chewing on a thought. There's a glimmer in his eye, a spark of possibility.

"Sounds intriguing," he says. "Tough to fake, though. What does a high school student from Fargo know about failed bank robberies?"

Millie exhales. She knew she'd have to talk about this eventually but figured it wouldn't be until after the movie was made. She should've known better. It's not enough to just create a story simply for creative purposes. In today's world, authenticity is key. It's incredibly useful for marketing.

Here goes. "The script is loosely based on my dad. He used to steal cars and break into people's homes. He gave it up after I was born. I didn't know about any of this until after the bank heist." When O'Naire's face passes no judgment, she goes on. "I always thought he was this kind of dorky guy who was just really into crime movies. Because he never got caught for any big scores or anything, he was able to find work as a security guard at this small bank in Fargo. Then COVID hit and he lost his job."

He grimaces. "Please don't tell me this is a COVID movie. Audiences are sick of those."

"Of course not." COVID is a main theme throughout the screenplay, but she can fix that ASAP. "So after he got let go, we lost our house. That's when he agreed to help this crew he used to run with rob the bank. He knew all the employees' schedules. When the money got picked up, who had to sign off on the deposits, all that stuff."

"So you've turned your father's story into a 'legendary thief returns for one last job' script," he comments. Millie can't believe it—he really seems interested.

"I guess you could say that. The only reason he signed on was to try and take care of me and my mom, and he would've done it if one of his own crew hadn't killed him. He was shot three times. Everybody else got away. No suspects were found. No charges were ever made."

"I'm sorry for your loss," he says quietly, and sounds like he's not just saying it to be polite. "How long ago did he die?"

Millie swallows, the kitty-litter lumps back in her throat with a vengeance. "Just a little over three years ago."

A moment passes before he says, "You're rewriting history, then. Seeking the revenge your father never had. Pretty Tarantino of you. What's the name of the movie?"

"*The Gangster and the Artist.*"

He scratches his stubble. "'The gangster and the artist are the same in the eyes of the masses. They are both admired and hero-worshipped, but there is always present underlying wish to see them destroyed at the peak of their glory.' Stanley Kubrick's *The Killing.*"

She smiles. She knew he'd pick up on that.

"Looks like you've done your homework," he says, nodding at the laptop with her heist-film spreadsheet on full display. "*5 Against the House, Wasteland, Robot & Frank, The Thieves.* You've watched all these?"

"Over a hundred and twenty-five."

"And what are you looking for? What are you tracking?"

"Everything. How many open on a legendary thief getting out of jail; how many open on a heist; how many have double crosses, use costumes. How many are about one last job, getting the band back together, stealth versus guns blazing Dillinger-style. It's important to know your genre if you're going to make an impact on it."

"True, but it's a fine line between paying homage and letting your influences overpower the film. And there's something to be said about allowing a little improv into the mix." He gets up and makes for the exit. "I have to get something from my office. It's going to take me ten minutes. I expect that you'll be gone by the time I leave." He pauses. "Some eye drops might be good, too. When I was in film school, I wouldn't have dreamed of editing without a cup of coffee half-filled with Baileys, but I at least was smart enough to hide it from the instructors."

"Understood," she says.

"And by the way," he adds, leaning into the doorway. "There are plenty of movies with four-member crews where the heist doesn't work out. You even have them on your spreadsheet. *The Taking of Pelham One Two Three, Set It Off, The Friends of Eddie Coyle.* And of course *Rififi.* I can see its influence all over this. Only four people, and even though the heist worked, that didn't prevent everything from going to hell. Hire more help and get more coverage."

She waits until he's gone before letting her head droop. Of course he was going to bring up *Rififi.*

6

"I can't believe you talked to Ricky O'Naire," Jordan says the next morning, grinning from ear to ear. "And the fact you were stoned is hilarious."

The train rocks violently, and he tightens his grip on the plastic sound-equipment cases, muscles flexing under the sleeves of his polo.

"Aren't you listening to me?" Millie says. "Ricky said the most authentic thing about our film is the homeless man who pissed himself, and he's not even part of the story."

Jordan smirks. "It's Ricky now?"

The train stops at Third Avenue and Fourteenth Street. A crowd shoves in.

"Yo, let me get that spot right quick," a wiry guy in an oversized T-shirt tells Jordan, flashing a cheap grill that looks like crinkled aluminum foil. "My foot hurt." A cloud of booze burps from his throat. The guy doesn't walk with a limp, but his sneer is enough for Jordan to grab his audio equipment and give up the seat he's had since DeKalb, even though he has a good four inches on the guy, probably close to twenty pounds of muscle. He might cut an intimidating figure, but Millie has learned over the summer that Jordan falls firmly within the "big softy" category, his bulk more intimidating than he'll ever be.

She worms her way over and offers to hold the case with the sound mixer.

"Well, he did really pee his pants," Jordan says when the train gets moving again. "Even from where I was sitting, I could smell it."

"We've got a serious problem here. The guy who decides who gets the Feature Award thinks our film is garbage, and we've only got four weeks to do something about it."

"Aren't you being a little dramatic? He only saw one shot we didn't even finish. We hire a new actress and we'll be fine."

They get off at Union Square. Millie helps Jordan take his gear up the subway stairs, into the open space filled with flea market booths . . .

and a homeless man pissing into a garbage can. Millie does a double take; if it's the same guy who ruined her shot the other night, she wants to congratulate him on graduating to some type of receptacle.

Inside the Academy, the divide between film and acting students is almost comical. The acting students, toned and well rested, usually coming from money, are a self-absorbed breed, constantly checking their hair, their makeup, their outfits, in between updating their social media feeds, while the film students are tireless beasts, out of shape, running on fumes, decked out in their never-been-washed Manhattan Movie Academy cotton track jackets, baseball caps hiding their oily hair, over half of them in black-framed glasses, chewing the espresso grounds from the one quadruple-shot latte they can afford per day.

"Sorry, just going to sneak by you," Millie says each time she encounters a new cluster of students, she and Jordan pushing their way through to the back hallway that leads to the editing suite, equipment room, and classrooms.

Pacing impatiently, Paz spots them and pinches her mouth in annoyance, the dermal piercings in her cheeks giving her man-made dimples. She raises a middle finger coated in purple polish that matches the streaks in her dark bob. "Before you even ask, that's for saying to be here by three and not showing up until after four."

"Devin here?" asks Millie, unfazed.

"Getting the room ready."

Paz and Jordan go in for a kiss, keeping it brief, either for Millie's benefit or because they're fighting again. Millie has stopped trying to figure it out. As long as their relationship doesn't interfere with the shoot, she has no problems, a fact she went over with them numerous times before they started production.

"Yates is being a dickhead about the Steadicam," Paz tells her. "Says we can't use it because we didn't include it in our initial equipment request. Why do we need the Steadicam, anyways? I thought you wanted a more natural feel to this scene."

"She's taking O'Naire's advice," Jordan says.

Paz's mouth opens in surprise. "No shit? You talked to Ricky O'Naire?"

"Last night in the editing suite," Millie says. "We discussed heist films. He watched some of the footage. It was . . . rather enlightening."

Jordan laughs. "She was stoned." Paz cracks up.

Millie sighs and starts heading toward the equipment room. "Let's go talk to Yates. We're really going to need the Steadicam and the jib."

"The jib?" asks Paz. "You didn't say anything about the jib in your text. We don't have any crane shots."

"We do now."

7

Millie rings the equipment room check-in bell, drums her fingers on the counter, rings the bell again.

Two rings later, Yates Elliot, a spoiled rich kid by way of California with an aggressive tan and muscular build to make up for his lack of height and proper social skills, emerges from behind the shelves. Next to him is his stout stooge, Sammy Chen. Even though they're in the yearlong eighteen-and-over program, they smirk at Millie like a pair of twelve-year-olds who just caught the babysitter changing.

"Check it out, it's the Long Shots," Yates says. "Heard you guys are giving Alejandro Iñárritu a run for his money. Don't forget to thank us during your Oscar speeches."

"Shut up," says Paz.

Millie leans on the counter. "A long shot is the same as a wide-angle shot. It has to do with depth of field. If anything, we'd be the Long Takes. At least get the term right if you're going to insult us."

"Who's insulting anybody?" Yates says, clutching his chest. "I think it's inspiring that you guys are trying to pull off something so large with such a tiny crew, tiny budget, and tiny amount of talent. Go big or go home, that's what I always say."

"Do you guys know if Devin is around?" Sammy says. He pushes his wavy black hair away from his bloodshot eyes. "I need more bud for tonight's shoot. It's freaking boring watching the vans."

"You made him a teamster?" Jordan asks.

"How dare you minimize his contribution to our project," Yates replies in that poser-artist-bullshit manner only he can successfully execute. "Sammy has been with me every step of this cinematic journey, from conceptualization to writing the script, establishing character arcs and themes, the film's mise-en-scène, when to move the camera, and with what purpose and intent—"

"I also get the coffee and muffins," Sammy chimes in.

"Can we get back to my equipment request?" Millie says.

Yates's face lights up. "Right. The Steadicam. Can't do it."

"Who's got it next?" If there's anything worse than a rich film student with Hollywood connections, it's one who works in the film-equipment office solely to wield power over everybody else.

He leans against the counter. "What does it matter, *Fargo*?" He draws out *Fargo*, and his bad fake accent sounds like it belongs to a hick from Mississippi rather than a Norwegian from North Dakota. "It's not like you're going to win anyway. A high school student from bumfuck nowhere? Yeah, right." He snorts. "There's twenty crews vying for this prize, and some of us have worked productions before."

"Stop trying to sound like you're an old pro at this," Paz says. "Everyone knows the only industry experience you have is handing out popcorn at the last Shyamalan premiere."

Yates's mouth twists into a sneer. "Whatever. The Academy only opened up the Feature Award contest to the summer high school students so that it'd attract more gullible losers looking to part with their money for a shot at fame."

"What's the problem, Yates? Feeling threatened?" Millie asks. "Mad that I don't have to hire outside help like you do? We all know your rich daddy is paying a whole crew to shoot your film."

"Yeah, I'm getting some outside help," Yates allows, "but that's only because I've seen pornos with better production value and shot selection than I've seen in our directing classes."

"Nobody doubts that," Jordan says, and Paz low-fives him.

Yates squares up. "All right, wiseass, let's see some of your footage. I can't wait to check out this formulaic heist bullshit. Or let me guess, you conveniently don't have your laptop with you?"

"Matter of fact, I don't. Battery died last night when I was editing with Ricky O'Naire," Millie says casually. She ignores the astonished looks from Paz and Jordan. "He wanted to see a rough cut, check out the coverage."

Yates clears his throat, losing some of his cockiness in the process. "You don't know O'Naire."

"Hate to burst your 'I'm the only one with Hollywood connections' bubble, but I do, and he'll back me renting the Steadicam. In fact, he said I could also use the jib tomorrow and Saturday night."

She's not used to lying this much, but there's something about Yates she can't stand, the rich entitlement that gets under her skin. She's not naive. She's aware that making it in this business has just as much to do with who you know as with how much talent you have. Doesn't mean she has to like it.

"The jib?" Yates says. "Now I know you're messing with me. Only instructors have access to the jib."

Millie inspects her cuticles for a moment. She has no idea what they're supposed to look like, but figures she's due for a manicure. "We can call him now, if you'd like. I'm sure he'd love to be bothered by you while trying to run the Academy. Or you can ask him tonight at the screening." Her voice is dry. "You've never met him, right? What a great opportunity for you to become acquainted."

It's a bold move, and for a moment she wonders if she's still feeling the effects of last night's weed. She's about to back down when Sammy claps his hands to his face, not quick enough to hide the laughter and spit spraying from his mouth. Yates gives him a light punch to the gut, which gets Sammy coughing deeply, his face turning red as he waves goodbye and goes for some water.

"So two nights with the jib?" Yates asks.

Millie leans against the counter, chin in her hands. The hell with it. If you're going to lie, might as well go all in.

"Better make it three."

8

The Academy's rehearsal room is drab, its overhead lights yellowing the white walls. Framed posters of Hollywood classics hang every five feet: *The Extra Girl*, *Sunset Boulevard*, *A Star Is Born*.

Paz spreads out the sticks on the tripod; Jordan hands her the camera. Millie and Devin set up a folding table and chairs along the scuffed black wood floors.

"The Long Shots isn't such a terrible name," Devin says, putting the sides for the actresses to perform out on the table. "The other groups are calling themselves stupid things like the Reel Crew or Salty Dawgs, whatever the hell that means."

"He's saying we don't stand a chance and still using the wrong term," Millie says. "I'm not calling us that." She picks up the top page of the stack. "What are these sides? What happened to the 'same sob story' scene from *The Burglar*?"

"We used it for the last two rounds of auditions . . . nobody's ever heard of that movie." Devin takes his place behind the desk. "Thought I'd change it up a bit. Give the actresses something they might be familiar with."

"So we're using the 'I'm not good enough' scene from *La La Land*?"

"Why not? It's about an actress tired of auditioning. They'll totally relate."

Millie looks to Paz and Jordan for backup. "A bit on the nose, isn't it?"

"If you're going to make it a big deal," Devin says, "I don't have *The Burglar*, but I have the 'hard and boring' scene from *An Education*."

"Are coming-of-age dramas and romantic comedies the only movies you watch?" Paz asks.

"Don't forget musicals. And this from someone whose submission for the Feature Award was a horror script about a girl eating her own body to keep from starving."

"One location. One actor," she replies. "Perfect for a student film."

Jordan jumps in. "It was *disgusting*, Paz. The word you're looking for is 'disgusting.'"

"You're one to talk, Fischer. Yours was about a world where all women over the age of eighteen can't stop getting pregnant, whether they're sexually active or not."

"It's a reverse *Children of Men*! It would've been great."

"It would've meant working with children, which was why we chose Millie's script," Devin says. "The correct call, no doubt, only I still say it could do with a musical number."

Millie laughs. No way they're having that conversation again. "And for the thousandth time, I'll say that it doesn't fit with the rest of the film."

"But it's the best if it's unexpected. Like when Bette Midler puts a curse on all the parents by singing in *Hocus Pocus*, or when Joseph Gordon-Levitt starts a flash mob in *500 Days of Summer* after he finally sleeps with Zooey Deschanel. That's what's key, if the emotional state of a character can only be expressed in song. That's why *La La Land* and *Whiplash* end with musical numbers and jump-started Chazelle's career, and *First Man* was a dud."

"*First Man* ends with IMAX cameras recreating mankind's greatest achievement of putting a man on the moon," Millie says. "It was amazing."

Devin shrugs. "More people remember Michael Jackson's moonwalk than Chazelle's."

It's moments like these that have been the biggest surprise. Sure, even a place like Fargo has a few film nerds to talk movies with, but the conversations at the Academy are different—they're with people from not only across the country but across the world, all drawn to New York City to make movies. It takes guts to admit you want to dedicate your life to not just telling stories but creating visceral experiences for people you'll never meet. Here, they're all the weird dreamers with the unrealistic ambition to do more with their lives than work normal nine-to-fives.

She remembers that first week, meeting Devin, Paz, and Jordan. There were one hundred high school students in the summer workshop; the Academy open to anyone as long as space was available. The requirements for the Feature Award were to provide a two-minute concept trailer of your project, plus completed short and full-length scripts. Most of the students, Millie included, had spliced together scenes from existing movies to show the mood and atmosphere they hoped to achieve.

She had gone full noir, relying heavily on black-and-white clips from the forties and fifties, intercutting with modern heist favorites like *The Lookout* and *The Mark*. It had been enough to not only get the green light from her instructor but to attract Devin, Paz, and Jordan.

That first working lunch, the four of them eating burgers in Union Square, felt like destiny already committed to celluloid. Paz was an amateur photographer and videographer with a modest fifty thousand Instagram followers, looking for a chance to shoot a project that would provide an impressive demo reel. Jordan, a computer whiz and amateur music tech who loved manipulating audio files, absolutely geeked out when Millie started discussing multilayer soundscapes. As for Devin, she got the immediate impression that he was like her, someone for whom movies were a way of life, an integral part of existence, like breathing. Up for anything and ready to commit to her vision for the project, he made an excellent second-in-command.

The perfect crew.

The rest of that afternoon was spent back in the dorms, Millie sharing all the videos on her YouTube channel, most of them made for the three bands at her high school, as well as some stop-motion stuff she'd made in her bedroom.

"And you did all this by yourself?" Paz asked after the fourth music video, a static shot of a North Dakota prairie in winter sped up over the course of three days, the sun and blue sky in constant rotation with the moon and night filled with stars. "Didn't you get bored just sitting there?"

"This was shot on my grandparents' farm in Medina, so I just set up a GoPro and checked it every few hours to make sure it didn't tip over or get covered in snow," Millie told her. "A lot of people don't want to do stuff like this, but I didn't mind."

"Well, never again," Devin jumped in. "You've got a crew now that'll sit with you."

"That's right," Jordan added. "Though please tell me none of our project has to be shot in North Dakota. Think I'm experiencing frost-bite just looking at it."

"They don't have winters like that in Kansas?"

Jordan shook his head. "I don't think they have winters like that on Hoth," he cracked—the frozen planet from *The Empire Strikes Back*.

Millie laughed and promised she'd never make her crew shoot in a North Dakota winter, relishing the words as they left her mouth. *Her crew.* She'd found the people who could help make her dad's story. Who could help her win the Feature Award.

It was going to be perfect.

9

Hours later, Devin writes in a notebook at the rehearsal room table while Jordan plays games on his phone. Paz sits next to the tripod, reading a copy of S. A. Cosby's *Blacktop Wasteland* borrowed from Millie. Millie stands alone by the open front door, the sign for a casting call clearly displayed on a stand in the middle of the hall. She sticks her head out for the twentieth time and sees the same thing again.

Nobody is waiting. Nobody seems to be coming.

10

Students and faculty clutter the aisles of the Academy's theater, most of them near the back table with free beverages and cheese. A single direc-tor's chair and microphone sit onstage in front of the screen.

"Let's try not to get discouraged," Devin says, handing Millie a cup of some sort of punch. "If there's one thing New York has plenty of, it's actresses who are willing to work for copy and credit. I'll put something online tonight. I can pay extra and have the notice emailed to those who sign up for that sort of thing."

"How much does that cost?" Millie asks. "We're barely scraping by with the budget as is, and even if we could get people to come, there are no free rooms tomorrow. Where are we supposed to hold this casting call? The dorms? They can read in my living room slash bedroom slash kitchen while we watch from the bathroom?"

"Be serious. Your bathroom is too small to fit all of us and a camera."

She sets the cup on the floor between them without taking a sip. "The acting students are supposed to be begging to be in our films so they have stuff for their reel. Is there something else going on right now I don't know about?"

Devin shrugs, but it's too animated, unnatural, a performance for the guy sitting in the back row of the balcony.

Millie narrows her eyes. "What is it?"

"Okay, but don't shoot the messenger. There's been chatter—"

"Chatter?"

"Chatter, among the acting students, that you're a bit difficult—"

"Difficult?"

"Difficult to work for, and that the production is a disaster—"

"Disaster?"

"Disaster, and that despite a great script it's not worth their time. I mean, we've gone through three actresses already, and none have even been on camera. People talk." His face softens. "I'm sorry to be so blunt, but it's what we're facing. We can't be naive and think that just because you wrote a decent script, people will be begging to work with us. Doesn't happen that way, love."

Millie simmers internally and looks across the theater at the other students—the ones in the filmmaking program who lack vision; the acting students without any character, the camera picking up their innocence and lack of life experience in sharp high-def.

They won't work with *her*?

The theater lights flash on and off. People take their seats.

A spotlight flares on.

Ricky enters from stage left and squints at the audience. "Little dramatic, yeah?" he says into the mic. "Can we cool it with the spotlight and bring up the house lights? Thanks.

"Welcome, everybody. Glad so many of you could take time away from your projects. As you'll find, you don't normally get a night off when shooting, especially if you're on a low budget or away on location, but tonight's special because we're halfway through the shooting schedule and only four weeks away from final screenings. Give yourself a hand."

The theater breaks into applause. The other groups seem to welcome the deadline, while Millie's crew sees it as a death sentence. Even Yates and Sammy, the two biggest clowns to ever stand behind a camera, are clapping like they've already won.

"I was going to show *The Mark* tonight," Ricky continues, "but I've changed my mind." He pauses, warming to his subject. "You know, it's such a unique program we have here at the Manhattan Movie Academy. No other film school in the world is set up like we are, where students can submit their short films and a feature-length script in a competition for a grand prize of half a million dollars to turn that short into a feature. Chump change to the studio system, sure, but a healthy budget to make a splash on the festival circuit. That's only the beginning, too." He strides across the stage while acknowledging the crowd, visibly proud of what the contest has accomplished. "Most of our past winners have been able to use the prestige of winning this award to attract additional investors, ballooning their budgets north of ten to twenty million dollars and attracting such talent as—"

Ricky name-drops Netflix-level celebrities on the way up, his voice getting lost in the applause.

Millie reviews. Only one film, *The Way You Move in the Shadows*, was able to attract the kinds of millions Ricky is talking about, not to mention that nine-minute cameo from Florence Pugh that earned her a Best Supporting Actress nomination. While the other films have floundered around the two-to-three-million range, Millie feels confident that hers will stand out—like *Shadows*, it will be the exception, not the rule.

"And I'm even prouder now that we've started inviting the summer high school students to participate," Ricky continues, which gets the applause to spike again. "It's truly amazing," he adds as it settles down, "and to be part of this competition and the films that have won in the past has been a highlight of my career."

He sits down in his director's chair. Removes his cap and wipes his brow. "But honestly, I think it's easy to get too focused on the money. So instead of *The Mark*, I'm going to show you Chris Smith's *American Movie*.

"For those who haven't seen it, it's a documentary about a filmmaker living in Milwaukee who tries everything he can to make a feature and just can't get his shit together. It's heartbreaking and funny, and above all else it's authentic. I wanted to show something that reminds us that filmmaking is a gift. And I don't mean it's a gift in the sense that you're born to do it or not. I mean it's a gift that filmmaking even exists in the first place."

Something distracts Ricky. He reaches into a pocket for his phone, scans it. He swallows, the microphone catching the sound. A loud gulp echoes across the theater.

"When I think about all the other things we could do to make a living, I'm thankful that the medium exists," Ricky says, his tone slightly different. More serious. "I came up with this competition to hopefully inspire you and your crews to make the best short films possible—but in reality, I hope you're soaking this up, because some of you won't make another film after you've graduated."

"That's not what the website said," Devin whispers into Millie's ear.

Ricky goes on. "It's a hard truth, I know, but that's reality." He gets out of the chair, paces across the stage. "It's a business where loyalty gets you nothing. Absolutely nothing, and you'll always only be as good as your last film. Remember that. For the two percent of you who are lucky enough to carry someone's monitor on your back after you graduate, remember what I'm telling you." His voice carries an edge. "It's a fucking gift, and you should be nothing but grateful for every second of it."

The doors to the theater burst open. The abruptness of it, metal slamming against drywall, sends Millie's heart racing. Someone screams. Sounds like Yates.

Cops fill in the rows, the exits. A policewoman with a bullhorn says, "Ricky O'Naire, you're under arrest. You have the right to remain—"

The audience members, almost in unison, pull out their phones and hit record. It's a theater of filmmakers ready to go viral, faculty not excluded.

Millie is the only one who doesn't film Ricky dragged out in handcuffs, his eyes cast down as he passes. The phones stay in the air long after he's gone, some of the students interviewing each other about what happened, while the rest scramble to be the first to post.

11

HOLLYWOOD DIRECTOR
CHARGED WITH TUITION FRAUD

By Madeleine White *America Today* | July 28, 2023

NEW YORK CITY—Ricky O'Naire, best known as the writer and director of the Academy Award–nominated *The Mark* and producer of the ill-fated remake of *Dunston Checks In*, was charged this morning with thirty-seven counts of fraud, with more expected to be filed soon. O'Naire is suspected of embezzling over nine million dollars from students of his Manhattan Movie Academy, which has locations in New York, Los Angeles, and Austin. O'Naire also has a production company, Hitting the Mark Productions, which operates out of Chicago.

O'Naire was arrested last night at the Manhattan Movie Academy location in Union Square after turning in falsified financial statements to authorities who had requested documents linked to the case. During the arrest, O'Naire allegedly started weeping and yelled for the students to turn off their phones and stop recording him. Over sixty videos can currently be found on various forms of social media.

Investigators state that for over six years O'Naire has allegedly been adding hidden enrollment charges and fees that were either completely false or drastically over-priced. One example, filed in the complaint, was that students of the acting school were charged inflated fees for headshots, acting reels, and casting profiles. The filmmaking students were also overcharged for equipment rentals. There are many more examples: everything from housing to meal plans, laundry services, and MTA passes.

Founded in 2016, the Manhattan Movie Academy offers one-year programs and summer workshops for aspiring filmmakers and actors, high school age and up, but does not provide any type of college credit. To attract students, the Academy offers a film competition during the summer courses in which students divide into crews and shoot a short film. A faculty panel, led by O'Naire, rates the films, and the winner receives a modest budget of $500,000 to turn the short into a feature-length film. Most of the recipients, though not all, use the award's prestige to attract additional investors. Past films have included *The Long Tomorrow* and *Drop the Gun, Charlie*; the acknowledged breakout was *The Way You Move in the Shadows*, which was a hit both critically and financially.

However, recent winners have had little success selling their finished films to distributors or streamers, and last year's recipient, the noir comedy *Dying in the Filth: AKA My Weekend Home in New Jersey*, has yet to start production, citing issues with not yet having received the prize money. O'Naire was already under investigation for these accusations.

O'Naire's first court appearance is scheduled for next week. The New York Department of Commerce's Fraud Bureau led the investigation of his alleged embezzlement.

INSTAGRAM MODEL *CLAPS BACK* AT RUMORS SHE'S CHEATING ON TROUBLED HOLLYWOOD DIRECTOR

By Kitty Collins @KittyCBiz Celebbiz.com | August 10, 2023

Model **Lexi Wells** released a statement Tuesday denying she's cheating on her fiancé, fallen Hollywood director and accused embezzler **Ricky O'Naire**, with up-and-coming social media influencer **Flowers Romero**.

"Over the past few weeks I've been asked countless times to comment on reports of an alleged sexual relationship with my friend Flowers," Wells read from a statement at the Slay Classy Model Agency, killing it in a backless blazer and curve-hugging pants.

CLICK HERE TO GET THIS LOOK FOR UNDER $200!

"I'm one hundred percent committed to Ricky, especially now with all the craziness going on. He was there for me when my private photos and emails were hacked, and like back then, this experience has brought us closer than we ever have been before. I'm his rock. I won't roll away."

Her denial comes after photographs surfaced last week of Wells leaving Romero's Malibu hotel room in nothing but a sexy pair of cutoffs and bikini top.

"Those pictures of me are misleading," Wells insists. She had shared two of them on her Instagram page, where they each received over 300,000 likes before being deleted. "I was there to support Flowers on his shoot and fell asleep, which is why I left so late and my hair was a mess. We're just friends."

Nothing from the alleged shoot has surfaced at this time, though there has been a surprising turn of events regarding her bikini top. According to the manufacturer, the bikini was sold out hours after the photos appeared online.

"I don't know what she was doing there, but it's really helped our sales," said Teddy Bass, owner of Boo-Bikini. "It's kind of cool knowing it might've been our top crumpled on the floor while she was jumping his bones."

CLICK HERE TO ORDER "THE AFFAIR" BIKINI!

Rumors of trouble in the Wells-O'Naire relationship have been constant since his arrest in New York last month. Distance has reportedly been an issue. O'Naire is currently unable to leave New York City due to a judge's restriction, while Wells works primarily out of Los Angeles for her modeling jobs.

As a result, O'Naire has been frequently spotted drinking alone at nightclubs over the past few weeks. Friends close to the director say he's "blowing off steam," but an anonymous source, who claims to be in O'Naire's inner circle, told us, "Ricky's a freaking mess. The dude lost everything and he's about to lose his girl. I love the guy, but he's done."

POST WORKOUT #SELFIES— CLICK HERE TO GUESS THE SWEATY STARS!

O'Naire could not be reached for comment.

HWD | NEWS | SPORTS | **VIDEOS** | PHOTOS | CELEBS | TOURS

RICKY O'NAIRE IN DRUNKEN BAR FIGHT!

Exclusive video of Lexi Wells' ex-fiancé getting his ass beat in New York City!

Graphics for HWD Live *run across the screen. Ricky O'Naire paces down a New York City sidewalk. His shirt is torn, face red and puffy. He holds a wad of napkins against his lip with one hand; his phone is in the other. A cameraman with a thick Brooklyn accent yells at Ricky. O'Naire turns toward the camera, seeing it for the first time.*

RICKY O'NAIRE

Bleep me. Not now.

(*into phone*)

No, I can't see you anywhere.

CAMERAMAN (O.S.)

Ricky. Ricky. What happened, bro? Looks like you got into a situation back there?

RICKY O'NAIRE

Give the man a prize. Regular genius on our hands.

CAMERAMAN (O.S.)

You okay, pal? You need us to call an ambulance or anything? Looks like he got the jump on you pretty good.

RICKY O'NAIRE

(*puts the phone down, staggers a bit as he looks right into the camera*)

The *bleep* he did. That *bleep* started running his *bleep* mouth so I offered to put my *bleep* in it and apparently he's a *bleep* homophobe because next thing I know he's throwing punches. Little *bleep*. *Bleep* him and his mother. On a Ferris wheel.

CAMERAMAN (O.S.)

Damn, dude, you're really going after him. Speech a little slurred there, Ricky. Had a few drinks tonight?

RICKY O'NAIRE

What about it?

(*into the phone*)

Yeah, I'm still here. Been here five minutes.

CAMERAMAN (O.S.)

Nothing, bro. Just making conversation. Not like you
don't deserve a drink or two. What with the DA threatening a trial and rumors that Lexi's moving in with
Romero. That's some two-timing *bleep* if you ask me.
Better off single than with a girl like that.

RICKY O'NAIRE
(looks past the camera,
toward the guy holding it)
The *bleep* did you say?

12

Devin holds up his phone so Paz and Jordan can watch over his shoulder.
"Don't tell me he's going to pick another fight after losing the last one,"
he says. Normally he'd be too embarrassed to check out *Hollywood Daily*,
but the rest of the rooftop of the bar and grill is packed with students,
what faculty is left, and friends and family who had already paid for
plane tickets and hotel reservations and couldn't cancel with such short
notice, all glued to the same video. Countless tiny speakers amplify the
wet thud of fists smashing O'Naire's face.

"This cameraman might be a dick," Paz says, "but it's impressive how
he's keeping the shot with one hand and beating on O'Naire with the other.
Honestly, that's a solid Dutch angle. Even De Palma would sign off on it."

"I can't watch anymore," Jordan says, eyes on the screen. "Turn it off."

Devin waits until their former dean gets a foot in the mouth before
taking Jordan's advice. No one expresses concern for O'Naire.

This is not at all how he imagined the end-of-summer dinner. On
the Academy website, photos show past blowouts at elegant hotel ball-
rooms, ritzy jazz clubs, air-conditioned tents in Central Park. It feels

silly, but he thought of the dinner the same way he thought of prom night in his treasured coming-of-age movies, a night when his life might change forever. It'd at least be better than his real prom night, he figured, a drunken mess of an evening spent sneaking pulls from a flask in the toilet while watching his crush stick his tongue down Isla Green's throat. Wouldn't have been all bad if his mates had been there for him, though that would've required having some mates.

Instead, all he had were old movies to comfort him.

To the anger of Devin's father and medicated indifference of his mother, there were no plans to attend university, no plans of any sort, really. He'd bombed his A-levels, so no university, and he didn't see himself qualifying for any kind of employment. It wasn't until Mr. Gardner's ultimatum that Devin pick something to occupy his summer or be forced to intern at Gardner Architects that he'd chosen the Academy. Since Devin's birthday was in July, he was just under the wire for the summer workshop; this way, he could see if he liked filmmaking before committing to the full-year program.

Devin didn't actually have a strong desire to make movies, though if that was an accidental outcome, then great. He was more interested in meeting people whose lives, like his, were made better by watching the scripted.

The summer was everything he'd hoped for, and then it all came crashing down, thanks to O'Naire. Now, instead of attending an exquisite private party, he's spending four to six p.m. on a rooftop lined with cheap patio lights over some dive on Amsterdam. Cash bar. Cheese and crackers. Meat tray from a local deli.

But he's making a stand: while everyone else is in casual summer wear, he sports a navy Aristocracy London suit, custom fit. There was no way he wasn't going to wear it. He'd purchased it the same day he'd received the acceptance email from the Academy. He goes to the bar to put a bottle of wine on a credit card already at its limit. The hell with it. Getting sloshed tonight will be worth the transatlantic argument with his father tomorrow.

On the exterior of the building next door, a projector plays one of the ten completed short films that would've been in competition, had there been a competition to win. The Academy's board fought the banks to stay open for the remainder of the summer, a move that had less to do with fulfilling its promise to the students and more to do with minimizing the number of parents who would sue.

Some of the crews had decided to finish their projects. The students that didn't had the option to work with those crews or go home. Most stayed, because either way they weren't getting a refund.

With the Feature Award no longer an option, and Millie's dogged insistence that O'Naire was innocent—an absurd argument that no one else would rightly listen to—the crew promptly disbanded. Devin, Paz, and Jordan got on a period piece shoot in Central Park and spent most of their time holding bounce boards to reflect sunlight onto horse-drawn carriages, careful not to literally step into piles of shit.

Millie joined some basketball story shot near the dorms in Brooklyn, but Devin heard that she only showed up for a couple of days. He had no idea what she was really doing, because she blew off his texts and calls.

Devin takes a look at what's currently being screened. It's Yates's movie: a man in a Wall Street–looking suit, completely drenched in blood, walking across the main deck of the Staten Island Ferry. The skyline of the financial district fills the shot behind him. He stops at the railing and stares down at the water. After a beat, he lifts a bloody tomahawk into frame. Bits of flesh dangle from the blade. The man throws the tomahawk into the water and weeps. Devin can't help but crack up, remembering how Yates said his film was "a metaphor for the plight of the Native American in today's society." His actor looks Italian, for fuck's sake.

After he comes back, Devin half listens to Paz and Jordan debating the best John Carpenter–Kurt Russell film. Jordan's for *Escape from New York*, Paz for *The Thing*. Devin's always been partial to *Big Trouble in Little China*, himself.

He knocks back some wine. Paz and Jordan have always been an interesting pair: she the pierced badass in all black with a chain wallet, he the wholesome boy next door in khaki shorts and a polo. Jordan's tried to bridge the gap—the frohawk surprised everyone—but they'll both leave the city within a week, her back to Miami, him Kansas, and Devin doesn't see it working. The frohawk will grow out, FaceTiming will become less frequent, and then it'll only be texts. He gives it less than a month.

Someone next to him says, "Don't worry, Gardner. You can always come work for me. I'll let you carry my monitor. You can even wear that monkey suit. How's that sound?"

"Like a living nightmare. Caught your film. Thanks for that. We all needed a laugh."

"Eat shit," says Yates mildly. He's dressed LA in the worst possible way: patterned designer jeans and a too-tight polo paired with a thin scarf and aviators. He's the walking definition of why Devin never tells anyone he comes from money. "Where's Fargo? Haven't seen her around."

"She's not here." Devin looks around and comes to the conclusion that nobody, not even Yates's parents, would mind if he dropped the little bastard off the roof.

Yates grins up at him like a schoolyard bully. "That's right. Heard the band broke up because of O'Naire. She really thinks he's innocent, huh? Was looking forward to seeing some of that footage. Probably best-case scenario for you guys that everything fell to shit. It's easy to say how great something is without having to provide any proof."

"Thanks," Devin says dryly, "but I'm not interested in how you pick up women."

Yates storms off. Devin lifts his glass to Paz and Jordan, but it seems to be empty. "I have a fix for that," he says, pouring himself a refill. Shadows blanket the busy city street, the small brick buildings with their zigzagging fire escapes, the rooftop water towers, as the sun's rays puncture the alabaster sky.

"It's a beautiful sunset," he remarks.

After a moment, Jordan says, "I wish Millie was here. At least being together one last time would've helped us feel like this whole thing wasn't a complete waste."

Devin knows what to say but has a think on the best way to say it. "It wouldn't have helped Millie. Witnessing what this night was reduced to would've been too painful for her. She really thought her dreams would come true."

13

The sun shimmers across the East River, glinting off the steel cables of the Brooklyn Bridge. The sky is a brilliant orange and pink. Men with food carts, happy-go-lucky tourists, and a diverse blend of couples line the bridge's walkway. A video camera on a tripod captures it all.

After a while, Millie adjusts the 4K she borrowed from the Academy equipment room. This is the last city footage she'll be able to shoot; she's spent the past month capturing as much of New York as she can.

Midtown Manhattan fills the frame, the sky smearing color across the Empire State, the Chrysler, buildings she's seen on screen for as long as she can remember. She looks up and takes in the view for herself. Notes the smell of lamb from the gyro cart, the conversations of people passing, the steady hum of the cars under her feet, the cool breeze off the river. Things people back home won't know when they look at a photo, when they watch a movie set in Manhattan.

Things only she'll know. Details that'll prove she was actually here. Memories that have the heavy burden of needing to last her a lifetime.

14

Seven Months Later
FARGO, NORTH DAKOTA

The parking lot is a lumpy ice rink half-covered in twelve-foot-high piles of snow with dirty gray-black peaks. Millie gets out of her stepdad Wade's rusted F-150. It takes a few tries for her boots to grip the glazy, knobbed surface. The wind strikes her face, cuts through her jacket to her bones. There's nothing to slow it down except one-story warehouses with vinyl siding, spaced far apart with large parking lots and sky in between. It wasn't until she got back that she realized just how many parking lots there are in North Dakota, all oversized and taking up twice as much room as the buildings they serve.

Carefully inching her way across the frozen lot reminds her of how Dad used to call her his "little penguin" when she was a kid, the way she'd waddle to keep from falling.

She was fourteen when he was killed. Afterward, Millie drowned herself in movies and screenplays, watching every special feature on YouTube on how they were made. She had unsupervised time; her mom was trying every kind of church under the Fargo sun.

This is the latest, and different from the others. For one, it's in a warehouse. The space is still very industrial—concrete floors, exposed HVAC in the rafters—but the church has embraced it. The overhead lights have metal buckets for shades; the grille of a car and some street signs hang on the walls near the large cross. The pews are metal bleachers. They hurt Millie's ass and back equally when she sits to talk with the pastor.

A part-time pharmaceutical rep by day, Pastor Rod wears his nonministerial weekend duds: baggy jeans and a Fargo RedHawks Double-A baseball cap. Reading glasses hang from a chain around his neck, over the T-shirt that reads *C.O.F.F.E.E.—Christ Offers Forgiveness For Everyone Everywhere.*

He beams as he watches Millie's demo reel on the sanctuary's big screen, above the monster-truck-tire pulpit. It's hard to tell if it's because he likes what he sees or because of the frozen chocolate cake with coconut sprinkles her mom made for him. He licks the plastic fork after every bite.

The screen fades to black and returns to the main menu. Pastor Rod rests his paper plate in his lap and claps with his fork in his mouth.

"'That was wonderful," he says. "You are obviously very, very talented. I can't believe you're only a senior in high school and have already accomplished so much. I've played around on my computer with some of the stuff we recorded last year during our mission trip to Omaha by adding some cool swipe transitions and playing Thousand Foot Krutch in the background, but it wasn't nearly as good as this."

Millie rubs the back of her neck, hoping he's not fishing for compliments. Her mom has shown her the videos: they're terrible.

"Those last scenes are from *The Gangster and the Artist*," she says. "Which would've been completed if the Academy hadn't gone under."

"Disgusting. That man should've gotten twenty years for what he did."

She still has the urge to defend Ricky but waits for it to pass. As with most things in life, people think what they want to think, facts be damned. He was acquitted of all charges. The courts decided that all blame fell to the Academy's accounting firm, now declaring bankruptcy to cover their fines. Ricky issued a public apology to all his students, taking full responsibility for practicing poor judgment in trusting the firm, the result of spreading himself too thin.

If anything, people should be blaming the accountants, not Ricky. All he wanted to do was provide an opportunity for talented people who otherwise wouldn't have had a chance to break into Hollywood. How does that make him a criminal?

"The courts found him innocent, but thank you," she says to keep things friendly. "I appreciate that." She reaches into her backpack and pulls out her investor packet. "I think the demo reel displays a strong sense of the film's noir elements and the type of movie I'm hoping to make, once I've secured enough capital to go back into production."

Pastor Rod gives an encouraging nod. She can tell he's impressed with her presentation. Adults are suckers for advanced teen vocabulary.

"Now, is this to finish the short one or make the long one?"

"To make the long one, a feature, yes. The hard parts—writing the script and preproduction—are over. All we have left is to finish shooting and edit." She says this like it's no big deal, even as her guilty conscience reminds her how monumental a job it really is.

"And you have people to help you make the film?" he asks. "I know that stuff can get pretty expensive. Will you be making this with your friends from the film camp you went to?"

Millie tucks her hair behind her ear. Draws a steady breath.

She hasn't spoken with Devin, Paz, or Jordan since before leaving New York. As soon as Ricky was arrested, they agreed with everyone else that he was guilty. They wouldn't listen to the other side, even when she sent them articles that disputed most of the facts.

That hurt, but what hurt most of all was their quitting *The Gangster and the Artist*, because what was the point without the Feature Award? It was as if they were saying she wasn't worth the effort, the energy, if there wasn't something in it for them. They'd rather goof off and play production assistant on someone else's stupid project than help a friend achieve her vision.

They abandoned her and didn't even care enough to say they were sorry.

"Why don't you open to page three?" she replies, not answering his question. "Take a look at those films and tell me what they have in common."

Pastor Rod puts his empty plate and fork next to him on the pew and slips on his reading glasses. "Let me see here. *Fast Five, National Treasure, Now You See Me, Gone in Sixty Seconds*." He ponders for a moment. "I know some of them star Nicolas Cage."

"They sure do." A fact that's been brought up every time. "But do you know what else they have in common?"

Pastor Rod says he doesn't, eyes like an eager child's waiting for the reveal of a magic trick.

"They're all heist movies. And they all made over a hundred million dollars."

He whistles. "I'll be darned."

"Did you know the best Christmas movies are heist films? *Bad Santa, Reindeer Games, Home Alone, How the Grinch Stole Christmas, Trapped in Paradise*. There's another Nicolas Cage movie for you."

"Christmas should be about Jesus," Pastor Rod tells her.

"Of course." Not an argument she's going to win here. "Now, I've watched over a hundred and fifty heist movies—actually, I'm close to one sixty by now—and I've included stats on the first hundred and how they compare to my film. If you'll turn to page fifteen."

Pastor Rod closes the packet. "Sorry, Millie, but this is starting to overwhelm me a little bit. I can tell you're very passionate about this. That's fantastic. It's important to have passion in your life. It's just that, for as much as you're focusing on this film project, I wonder how much time you're giving the other aspects of your life." He takes off his cap, scratches his head. "I've never seen you here before today, and you've never come to a service. Now, why is that?"

Here we go. The way Millie's mom pushes church, she should've known she wouldn't get through this particular pitch without a literal come-to-Jesus moment.

"I've been meaning to get here," she ad-libs. "It's just, you know, so much going on and—"

"Relax, Millie. I'm not trying to force anything on you, just like you're not trying to force anything on me. But your mother says you're unhappy, you're lonely; that since you got back, you spend all your free time in your room watching movies; that you never go out with friends or to any school dances or events."

"My mom sure likes to share," Millie says sarcastically. "And here I don't know anything about you. How's your love life going, Pastor? Meeting any girls on the spiritual circuit?"

Pastor Rod gives an amused smile. "She's just worried about you, that's all. Normal for mothers with daughters your age, and I think partaking in your community could help. So I have a proposal."

If she weren't doing her pitch, Millie would've left by now, but what her mother said isn't the worst thing she's heard from a potential investor.

"I'm all ears."

Pastor Rod smiles again. She sees the kindness in his eyes, now that he's not wearing a cap. "I'm trying to reach and attract a larger congregation. It's North Dakota. There are more churches here than gas stations. People have a wide selection of where they can worship, and most haven't heard of us or even know there's a church in this building. I mean, come on, we're in a warehouse, for Paul's sake. So what I'm proposing is to have you record my sermons and put them online, and in exchange I'll give you three hundred dollars for your film."

She rubs her chin, stalling for dramatic effect even as she knows she's going to accept. It's the first pitch in months where someone outside of her extended family has been interested. "How many sermons?"

"Ten."

"I'll do two."

"Eight."

"Six. Final offer."

"For three hundred dollars? I'm preaching in a warehouse with buckets for lampshades."

He's got a point there. "Fine. Seven."

She stands up and puts out her hand. Pastor Rod, delighted, stands and shakes it.

"But I get to pick my crew," she says.

15

Wade leans back in his chair to watch TV, the bottom of his Carson Wentz NDSU jersey pulling up in front to reveal a wild patch of black hair on his doughy, pale belly.

"Wade, honey," her mother giggles. "We're trying to eat here."

Wade laughs. "Sorry, babe," he says, blushing as he pulls his jersey down.

Millie makes a faux gagging sound as she pushes away her plate of venison walking tacos, one of the various venison dishes Wade makes on his night to cook. An avid hunter who spends the fall filling the Deepfreeze, his skills have improved since they first met two years ago. Back then, when he had just started dating her mom, his only recipe was venison-sausage gravy, which he'd make on Sundays, after the two of them got back from church. A year and many stomach cramping venison concoctions later, Wade and her mom got married.

"I got Chippers for dessert," Wade says during the commercial break and waggles his bushy eyebrows. "But I'm only sharing with members of the Clean Plate Club."

"I'm not very hungry," she says. "I'm still full from the leftover meat-loaf I had for lunch."

"Surprised it's not your conscience upsetting your stomach," Mom says. She's still in her church clothes: ankle-length skirt, argyle turtleneck, and a cardigan festooned with an oversized brooch. She's dressed like the grandmother she'll never be, if Millie has any say.

Mom pours herself another glass of white wine from the handled glass carafe on the table, decanted from the cheap box chilling in their fridge. Her mom wasn't always this way—not wanting to appear high class or anything but adding nice little touches here and there. She used to plop the KFC bucket on the table, let the winter boots collect in a pile by the front door, go months without searching for where they kept the vacuum.

That all changed after the eviction and her parents' separation, just weeks before her dad agreed to the bank job and was killed. A year spent in a crummy apartment across from Reese Lanes Bowling and Bar made her mother long for a house, and after she married Wade and they moved in, Millie could tell her mother would never take what she had for granted again.

Mom sets the glass of wine back on the table, ensuring the base is on the cloth place mat so it doesn't leave a ring. "First you don't go to church, and then you make poor Pastor Rod give you three hundred dollars to video-record him." She shakes her head. "That's a sin. For sure."

"You set up the meeting for me. What did you think I was going there for?"

Mom drops her fork. It rattles against her new tangerine Fiestaware. "I thought you would see how great a guy he is and be inspired by the mission of the church and do it for free." She gives Millie a searching look. "Weren't you inspired?"

Millie stalls. "I don't know. There was a car grille on the wall. It was kind of weird."

"That's a fun story, actually," Wade says. "That came from an old Ford Mustang Bruce Bigalke was restoring but for one reason or another decided not to."

The women are silent.

Millie says, "And?"

"That's it. Now it's on a wall. Funny, huh?"

Mom keeps looking at Millie. "I don't suppose that money is going toward tuition for next year?"

Millie gives up playing with her food. "Of course not. The pastor gave me that money for the movie. If I used it for something else, that'd be called fraud."

"I understand, but that workshop and you living in New York for a summer took a pretty good chunk of the money we saved for college tuition, money you said you'd pay back by working a part-time job this year. Only instead of looking for a job, all you've been doing is trying to raise money for a movie you shouldn't be making in the first place."

"Don't go there," Millie warns. "Not tonight."

"It's just not right making a movie about what your dad did, like you're honoring the fact that he was a criminal."

"He was trying to provide for his family. That's what you told me. I didn't make it up."

Mom pinches the bridge of her nose. "What was I supposed to tell you, Millie? You're a smart girl. You know by now there are other ways to provide for your family that don't include robbing banks. Your father could've done what I do and worked at the grocery store or hung drywall like Wade here. It's not healthy spending all your time on this."

When she looks at Wade for confirmation, he's too busy pretending to be interested in ESPN. He's learned over time to just stay out of the way when the two of them go at it.

"Have you even looked at colleges?" Mom says. "An ACT score of twenty-four is pretty good, hon. You're so smart. It'd be a shame for you to throw your life away by—"

"*Throw my life away?* Are you for real right now?"

Her mother presses on. "All I'm saying is that I know it's too late for most universities, but we could look at tech schools or perhaps community college. Just for the first year, so you don't fall behind on credits."

"No, wouldn't want to fall behind on credits."

"What about West Fargo State? Their media-arts program looked pretty good."

Millie bites the inside of her cheek to keep from yelling. They're having this conversation again? If she had her way, she wouldn't go to college. Maybe she wouldn't even try film school again. Why would she, if she gets cash to make the movie herself? Tons of directors never went to film school: Nora Ephron, Paul Thomas Anderson, David Fincher, Jordan Peele, Lilly and Lana Wachowski . . .

"I'm confused," Millie says once the urge to yell has passed. "Are we starting off my spring break by fighting about me getting a part-time job or picking a college?"

Her mom scrunches her face in thought. "Both."

"At least we're on the same page now." She takes a gulp of water, preparing her throat for battle. "Let's see, West Fargo State. The cameras aren't 4K, the students are mostly stoners and YouTube rejects." She raises a finger each time she makes a point. "The head of the media department's claim to fame is shooting commercials for the Mattress Princess, and after completing their two-year program, I'll have learned exactly what I learned in *one week* at the Manhattan Movie Academy. That's why I went there. It'd be a waste of my time if I went to West Fargo." She drops her hands to her lap. "I want to make movies, Mom. That's why I went to New York. That's what I'm going to do with my life."

Her mom waves her off. "You've made your point. And by the way, I've always known you wanted to make movies. I can't remember a time when you didn't want to. Your dad always filling you up with these fantasies. But until you figure out how to make a living from movies, and if you're not going to college, then you need a job. What about asking Uncle Aaron for something at Howard Security?"

Millie almost chokes on her Diet Coke. "Uncle Aaron? Now I *know* you're out of ideas."

"What?" her mom asks with faux innocence. "I might not love the guy, but he was your dad's best friend. I know how much he matters to you. I also know he'd love to have you work for him on the weekends or part-time once you turn eighteen next month. Could go full time once school's done. Didn't you say you thought it looked like a cool place to work?"

"I said it was a cool place to get intel for my script, not to make my career."

"You don't have to work there forever like he has, for crying out loud," Mom says, exasperated. "I don't want to be the bad guy here. I'm sorry it didn't work out last summer, but you need to get over it, because you're not living here for free next year. That wasn't part of the deal when we said you could go to New York."

Millie throws down her napkin. She can't do this tonight. The last seven months have been devastating, one disappointment after another: seeing her Academy dreams go up in smoke, losing touch with her film friends, having to stomach sitting in boring classes all day while her classmates obsess over TikTok and color coordinating their prom attire, shit that won't mean anything after graduation.

Not like her movie. A great movie is timeless. It becomes part of pop culture, defines a generation.

So yes, finally, someone has agreed to invest in her film, and it's been too long since she's had cause for celebration, and she's not going to let her mom ruin it.

"I know it wasn't part of the deal, but neither was me not being able to finish my film because the guy I banked on changing my life got arrested. I'll figure something out." Millie pushes back her chair and gets up. "Just give me more time."

16

Light from the Fargo Theatre's winking marquee dances across barhopping college kids. Through the theater's storefront, Millie can see the register and snack bar. She's in luck. The guy selling tickets is new, a pimply lowerclassman who seems overwhelmed by the four-person line in front of him. The assistant manager working the snack bar is the one who's trouble. Millie pulls down the brim of her Dodgers cap and opens the theater door.

The Fargo is the same as when she came here as a kid with her dad. The ticket line is closed off by frayed nylon rope, the concession stand glass smudged with fingerprints, the walls lined with thumb-tacked single-sheet posters. The one difference is Millie's blown-up yearbook photo behind the register. Under her name, in red Sharpie, are the words *No Admittance!*

She stays close to the couple in front of her and, after they pay, moves quickly, indicating she needs one ticket, keeping her eyes on the floor. The boy holds the cash for a moment. Millie looks up. He's squinting at her.

"Did you want a ticket for Theater One or Theater Two?" he squeaks. Puberty is years away for this poor guy.

"One."

The boy punches a few register keys . . . and then the assistant manager comes over and whispers something in his ear. He winces and looks at her photo behind him. "Sorry, I forgot," he mutters and goes to take over popcorn duty.

The assistant manager opens the cash register. She takes out the ten and gives it back to Millie. "We've been through this."

"Oh, come on. That was over two months ago."

"It's for the safety of the other customers."

She raises her eyebrows. "Safety? Give me a break. I never hurt anybody."

"Not physically," says the woman, "but you verbally assaulted at least ten people and scarred the Solversons. They're friends with my grand-parents and still bring it up at church."

"They were talking loudly the entire movie, practically shouting. If you had some ushers, I wouldn't have had to say anything."

"They're old," the assistant manager replies, slipping into the dialogue they've run through a hundred times. "They couldn't hear what some of the actors were saying, so they were asking each other. If you'd talked to one of us, we could've handled it. Same with people on their phones. You have no authority to take someone's phone and hold on to it until the end of the movie."

Millie's eyes narrow. This is bullshit. "I'm supposed to suffer through a movie with a spotlight blinding me or miss part of it to tattle on people being assholes?"

The language is the final straw for the assistant manager. "You need to leave, or I'm calling the police."

17

In the slanting moonlight, Millie trudges through the shin-high snow behind the theater. A chunk slips into one of her boots. Within a few steps, her sock is soaked.

All this effort probably isn't worth it; she's not even that excited to see the *Logan's Run* remake, even if it is directed by Ava DuVernay, but she really doesn't want to go home, and it's not like she can try Century or West Acres. She's banned there, too.

The Fargo dates from the 1920s. It's been renovated a few times since—they added a second screen in 2009—but it's an old theater, and not everything is up to code. Millie stops in front of the fire exit, a black door in an old brick wall, easy to miss unless you're looking for it. The door doesn't sit flush; the edge sticks out about four inches too far. She crouches down and wedges her house key in the bottom corner. After some wiggling and rocking of the key, the door pops open.

The audience is seated, the theater's sconces half-dimmed. On screen is a trailer for the new Zendaya rom-com, counter-programming to her drug-addict role on *Euphoria*, the gist being that she'll finally find happiness and a wife once she gets her pet bakery business off the ground.

Normally, Millie would sit in the balcony, but the only way to get there is through the lobby, the assistant manager's kingdom. She takes a moment to assess and picks a spot in the middle of the theater, at least two rows away from anyone who might talk or play with their phone. She sinks into the familiar worn padding of the chair. The armrest is plastic. It wiggles when she touches it with her elbow. She puts a ten-dollar bill in the cup holder. Hopefully, whoever cleans up after the show will do the right thing and give it to the box office.

The next trailer is for a film starring Chris Pratt as a war veteran who's lost his arms and legs in combat, directed by Eli Roth, best known for the torture-porn horror film *Hostel*. The movie's an obvious attempt for an Oscar by all parties involved. The one after that is for a remake of *Armageddon* starring Dwayne Johnson and directed by J. J. Abrams, the trailer filled with lens flares and Dwayne Johnson in tiny tank tops. On paper, it's something she'd skip, but by the end of the trailer, she's all in.

Then the screen flashes green once again, saying that the following PREVIEW has been approved for ALL AUDIENCES by the Motion Picture Association of America.

Against a black screen, heavy breathing, deep gasps. Fade in on a dark alley. Steam rises through sewer grates. Dramatic violin music begins to play. Shown from behind, a masculine figure kneels at the end of the alley. He's hunched over something, his black clothes bathed in red light. The camera slowly tracks in, passing through steam, moving past a dumpster.

> WOMAN (O.S.)
> *It's foolproof. All we need is a way in.*

> MAN #1 (O.S.)
> *It's basically a mom-and-pop-type bank. The guard can be bought. Everyone has a price.*

> MAN #2 (O.S. Latino accent)
> *We get this right, and we're set for the rest of our lives.*

The man wears a black trench coat and fedora. The camera moves slowly around him. He's shaking. His shoulder is covered in lurid purple dye. So is the front of the coat, the brim of the fedora. There's an open suitcase in front of him, its edges sprayed purple. He lifts his hands from the suitcase, and we see stacks of soggy purple cash. The music gets louder, more dramatic. Police sirens scream in the background. The man looks up—it's Flowers Romero, face splattered purple, chest rising and falling.

MAN #1 (O.S.)
All you have to do is trust me.

The screen cuts to black. The music reaches its crescendo. The title card fades in:

The Art of the Gangster
a Ricky O'Naire Film

It doesn't register right away.

At first Millie assumes she's dreaming, a long nightmare in real time that started with the trip to the church. Or maybe it started before then? Maybe her whole life has been a bad dream, and she just needs to wake up and start over.

The lights dim to black. The feature comes on the screen.

Her neck and ears flush with heat; there's a queasiness in her stomach so intense she wraps her arms around herself.

It's real. What she saw was real, and no matter how much she doesn't want to admit it, she can't deny what she saw.

That bastard stole her movie.

18

Millie sits in an uncomfortable brown pleather chair, having opted for the one without any padding in the seat, as opposed to the one with springs that poke you in the back. Her older cousin, Doris, watches *The Art of the Gangster*'s trailer on her desktop, eyes widening behind her horn-rimmed glasses. Hearing the heavy breathing and the dialogue and visualizing the images on screen are enough to get Millie going again, and by the end of the trailer she's up and circling the tiny law office.

"I have a case, right?" Millie asks. "You saw the footage I shot. It's almost identical, and it matches what's in my script."

"It certainly does. Can't argue with that." Doris takes off her glasses and fiddles with her hair.

"But?"

"Buuuuuuuut." Doris stretches out the word. "A lot of this is circumstantial. All we have to go on is an image of a man in an alley with a bag of money. I haven't watched nearly as many movies as you, but I doubt that's a completely original idea. And your version had fake money and didn't include a dye pack."

Millie drops down on the chair, her ass sinking through the seat frame. "What about him using my title? That's got to count for *something.*"

"Wellllllllll," Doris practically sings. "*The Gangster and the Artist, The Art of the Gangster.* It's kind of your title, right? But there are plenty of movies that have 'gangster' in the title, and then there's"—she searches her notes—"*The Art of the Steal,* a Canadian heist movie with Kurt Russell. They probably have a better case for O'Naire ripping off their title. Are you familiar with it?"

Doris has clearly done her research. Unwillingly impressed, Millie says she is.

"Annnnnd."

"Spill it already."

"I've read over your agreement with the Academy. Part of the stipulation of your entering the contest is that you gave all consent, one hundred percent, to the Manhattan Movie Academy, to use any footage or written materials as they see fit."

"That's only if you're the winner. Then they control how the film is marketed and get final say on the edit."

Doris clicks her tongue against her teeth. "It isn't, actually. It means that, by your entering the contest, they own your idea and can do whatever they want with it. Did you turn in a copy of your script?"

"Yes," Millie says softly.

Doris offers a sad smile. "Then I hate to tell you, but this is all legal."

Millie's stomach twists. "He long-conned us."

"Is that, like, a type of heist?"

She stands to grab the agreement and flips through it, even though she has no idea what she's looking for. "Are you sure there's nothing I can do? Check it again."

"I've read it three times. The contract is clear, Mil. I'm sorry. This is too big for you to win on your own."

"What do you know? You're in environmental law." Millie sits in the other chair. A spring stabs her in the ass.

"Doesn't change what's written here. You can't be all that surprised, right? O'Naire went to trial for this type of thing."

The back of Millie's neck grows hot. "That's it, then? I'm completely screwed?"

"Not completely. They own the movie and have every right to release it, but according to this they need to give you credit for the script. Or depending upon how many changes they've made, at least story credit."

"He steals my idea, and all I get in return is my name buried in the credits?"

"Wellllll—"

"Stop that!"

"From what I read this morning, O'Naire is hoping this will be his big Hollywood comeback, and the studio is, too. They're doing a whole huge marketing push to get it out two weeks from Friday. They're calling it 'a secret movie nobody knew about,' like those *Cloverfield* movies."

Millie's jaw aches from clenching her teeth so hard. Sure, secret movies can be a great way to stir up some buzz. Fanboys went into a frenzy at the post-credits scene for the horror film *X* announcing that a prequel, *Pearl*, had already been filmed and would be released later that year, but she has no doubt about Ricky's motives.

"It's a secret because he *stole* it and doesn't want anybody interfering with it being released."

"That too, probably. The thing is"—Doris puts her glasses back on, the professional once again—"O'Naire reconciled with his fiancée, he moved back to Chicago to be closer to his family and production company, he's sober, and he's been exonerated for the tuition thing. He's got a lot riding on this. He's not going to want it ruined with a scandal about stealing the idea from one of his students, especially if it's based on something that actually happened to her family."

"What's your point?"

Her cousin shrugs as if she's indifferent to having either Italian or Chinese for lunch. "You can probably get some hush money out of it."

19

The next morning Millie lies in bed, surrounded by what looks like the aftermath of a tornado: dumped-out boxes of props from last summer's shoot, storyboards, shot lists, script notes, and production budgets scattered across the carpet, evidence of a night spent rummaging through Academy stuff with no idea what she was looking for.

Her phone rings, plays itself out. There are notifications for over thirty missed calls and twice as many texts. Most are from Devin, then Paz and Jordan. Even her lead actor, the plumber from Staten Island, left a voice mail. Millie hasn't listened to them. She knows what they say. They want her to have a plan, a way to fix this. What is she supposed to tell them? What is she supposed to do?

She tosses the phone onto her nightstand, and it knocks over the framed photo next to her lamp. Millie picks it up.

There she is with her dad in front of the Radiance Theatre in Hollywood, on their one trip to LA. She's nine, bucktoothed and freckle faced; her father's strong fingers proudly grip her thin shoulders. She can almost smell his Old Spice aftershave. Hear the way he'd laugh with his whole body.

Millie, are you going to give me back my phone anytime soon, or are you planning on only experiencing California through that lens? Look around you. There's palm trees everywhere. You're never going to see these in Fargo.

Dad, I told you. I'm making a movie so I can show Mom how much fun we're having.

That's sweet, kiddo. Your mom just has a bad headache right now. I bet your movie will cheer her up. Maybe someday you'll make a movie that'll have its premiere here. You know they show all the big films.

Maybe. But this movie is so Mom won't be mad at you anymore and she'll come with us to the beach tomorrow.

I'm sure she will. Your mom's upset right now because she thinks we can't afford this trip, but you know what I told her? I told her I'd rather spend my time being happy with my two beautiful girls than worrying about money. Do you remember that movie we watched the other night? The Mark?

Yep! My favorite part was when the good guy took on all those bad guys at the end. He got shot like a million times and didn't die. There was gallons of blood!

Ha! Yeah, well, that might've been one reason your mom got mad. She didn't like you seeing that. But remember what happens right before? When everybody double-crosses the good guy and they leave him for dead? Remember you started crying because you thought that's how it was going to end?

I didn't cry!

Of course you didn't. My mistake. But the reason the end of the movie is so great is because you thought the good guy, the hero of the movie, was never going to recover after that, but he did. You see, Millie, everything has to go to hell sometimes so that the hero can show what they're worth. Right now, your mom thinks we're down, but that's not how it's always going to be. I promise you, honey. Someday she'll see what I'm worth. Now come here.

Dad, stop kissing me!

Fine, fine. Tell you what. Let's ask that man dressed like Jack Sparrow if he'll take our picture, and then we'll get some ice cream. Sound good?

Millie sets the photo down on her bedspread, her dad's image blurred through her tears. She can still remember his hearty laugh thundering down Hollywood Boulevard. That's how she always remembers him: a sweet guy with a big heart who loved her.

She hadn't know a thing about his past, the jobs he pulled. It was only on the day he died that she learned he was a criminal. There had to have been some kind of misunderstanding. Her dad loved movies about robberies, but he would never actually commit one.

Until her mom came home from identifying the body, collapsing outside their apartment door and crying tears that looked as if they would never stop, Millie refused to believe the cops had the right guy.

They had to cremate the body. The funeral director said they couldn't have an open casket: too much damage to his face. Millie deliberately doesn't think about that; it hurts too much to think of her dad—with his friendly, infectious personality, the kind of guy who could make friends with anybody—shot to death like a rabid animal.

Her body still tenses whenever someone is shot in a movie. Took over a year before she'd even think of watching anything by Tarantino or Scorsese or Peckinpah or . . .

Her mother kept the funeral to just immediate family: her and Millie; Grandpa and Grandma Blomquist; Aunt Ann; Cousin Doris; and "Uncle" Aaron and his fiancée, Carol. Her mother's parents refused to attend. Her father's past had been news to them, too.

"Nothing but a despicable hood!" Millie heard Grandpa Ellsworth yell over speakerphone the night before the funeral, right before he hung up on her crying mom. Millie's never forgiven them, but at the same time she kind of understood. Things might've been desperate. Dad lost his job, they got evicted, and then her mom kicked him out of their new apartment, but why did he have to try to rob a bank?

As the years passed, the despair she felt began to fade. The more crime movies she watched, the more she understood why he had loved them so much. He'd point out the criminals' mistakes, cheering extra loud when they pulled off the surprise twist the audience hadn't seen coming, but he had.

They connected him to the life he had almost successfully left behind. He couldn't ever fully let it go. He hadn't been perfect—nobody is— but he'd loved Millie and her mom the best way that he could. That was what she needed people to know about him, why she started writing her movie. They needed to know that Bobby Blomquist wasn't just some "despicable hood," some piece of trash, but a complicated man who simply made a wrong decision for the right reasons.

Her despair slowly became anger, directed at the man who had pulled the trigger, the man who had stolen her dad from her.

Mom swore she had no idea who else had been involved in the robbery. Aaron said the same, that Dad had never told him about any of it.

The rage festered inside her.

And then, two and a half years after his death, during the spring of her junior year, she saw an ad on Snapchat for the Manhattan Movie Academy's summer workshop, where she learned about the Feature Award competition.

She saw a chance to tell her dad's story—with Ricky O'Naire producing.

Her anger and grief were transformed into creative vision. First there were flash cards on her bulletin board, then an outline, and then the newest version of Final Draft downloaded onto her computer. Within a month, she had the first draft of the script.

She used the medium her father most loved to tell his story, to show the world the good man he really was.

At the same time, it was her way of sending the triggerman a message.

She would never take someone's life willingly. Real-life revenge, à la *Kill Bill*, isn't her way. But showing what a decent man Bobby Blomquist was, how much he'd sacrificed for his family, would tell his killer what he had taken from the world. It'd be a front-row seat in a dark movie theater showing him why he'd burn in hell.

It would be Millie's way of saying, *I see you. I know what you did, and I'll never let it go.*

That was her through line, the motivation that kept her going. And now all of her sacrifices—all that time, all that money, all those hopes and that energy—are for nothing, because Ricky O'Naire is able to steal her work on a legal technicality.

Hope is gone. Grief has returned.

It's like losing her dad all over again.

20

With the check from Pastor Rod and her relatives' Christmas gifts, Millie's raised $694.35. Nowhere near the amount needed to produce a feature, but certainly enough for gas money.

She goes to the kitchen and puts together a few peanut-butter-and-potato-chip sandwiches. From the cupboard, she grabs a box of granola bars and dried fruit bars, checks the expiration dates, puts back the fruit bars. A pot of Folgers brews while she looks up the best route. It's close to eleven a.m., so she'll need to hurry if she's going to avoid hitting rush hour in Minneapolis.

Her only choice is to go straight to the source. She never did register her script with the Writers Guild, an amateur mistake she won't soon forgive herself for, but she's got an email trail of sending it to Devin, Paz, and Jordan and the footage they shot at the Academy. Not enough evidence for her to take legal action, but it'll get her a sit-down with Ricky.

Now what to say or do during that sit-down is another matter, one she hasn't yet figured out, but Chicago's a ten-hour drive. That's a lot of time. Certainly a plan will come to mind, one that will make him understand, give her full credit at least.

"Going somewhere, then?" Mom asks when she enters the kitchen, eyes on Millie's backpack and travel suitcase.

"Lois invited me to her family's cabin in Detroit Lakes for a few days," Millie says, ready with her alibi.

"Lois Taylor?" Her mom sounds in shock. "Been a long time since I've heard you say that name around here."

That's because her family moved to Spearfish, South Dakota, two years ago, Millie thinks. "She's really involved in band, but we still hang out at school. She's been asking me to come to the cabin for a while now, and according to Pastor Rod, I need to get out more."

Mom goes hot pink, the guilt working like a charm. "I'm sorry. I shouldn't have shared that with him."

"Got that right," Millie says and lets it rest there. She makes her voice conciliatory. "But you're also right about needing to focus my energy on more than just making the movie. So I'm going to give nature a try. See what the big deal is."

Instead of praising her, Mom says, "You'll be home tomorrow, then."

"Well, uh, since it's spring break, I think they're planning on being up there for most of the week. I was thinking I'd spend at least three nights up there. Maybe more."

"No, you misunderstood me," her mother says flatly. "I'm *telling* you to be home tomorrow. I set up an interview for you with Bob Gustafson at the store. Got an opening in the deli. Part-time, but there's a possibility to pick up hours."

Millie sharply zips her backpack closed. "I'm not working in a grocery store deli."

Her mom crosses her arms and braces her legs: battle stance. "I know you think you're a lot better than the life you've been dealt. You're a lot like your dad that way. He had the same problem, and it got him in the end." Her face softens a little, tenderness Millie hasn't seen for years. "It's okay to be ordinary, Millie. Not everybody can lead an adventurous life. I want to support you, but I also need you to support yourself. You can't throw everything away just to tell his story." Back to battle stance. "Interview is at four. Be there half an hour early. Make sure to dress nice."

This moment has been a long time coming, but now isn't the time to argue. Millie knows that when her mom's mind is made up, there's no changing it.

She shoulders her backpack. "I gotta go."

21

CHICAGO

They've been over it a thousand times in a thousand arguments, and he knows he's supposed to understand it's her job. He's in the business— longer than she's been alive, come to think of it—and he knows sex sells. But as Ricky O'Naire watches his fiancée strut around in a black lace thong and bra, the Willis Tower and downtown Chicago filling the windows behind her while some jerk-off from LA, who flew here first class on Ricky's dime, takes her picture, Ricky can't help but think this is going a bit too far.

"Maybe we could try one with the dress?" he suggests mildly, pointing to the little red number crumpled near the bed, only to be greeted with dismay by Lexi, the photographer, and Flowers Romero, who inform him that the makers of the red dress are not a tier-one sponsor and therefore don't get the privilege of having Lexi photographed in their apparel.

Flowers comes over with a flute of champagne. He flashes the brilliant smile that's landed him deals with Pepsi and Nike, abs rippling under his tight designer T, his jawline built from brick. Part of Ricky and Lexi's re-engagement agreement is that he needs to be more accepting of her friends, even the ones she'll never admit to sleeping with.

Wanting to show her he was willing to try, Ricky offered Flowers a bit part in the new film. A few lines of dialogue, nothing major, just something to help the guy transition from influencer to actor without embarrassing anyone, including Flowers himself. Instead, the investors insisted that he play the lead villain. The only acting experience Flowers had up to then, Ricky noted ironically, was pretending he hadn't slept with Lexi.

"Don't worry, Rick. Instagram doesn't allow full nudity," Flowers says now. "Marcos will blur out her nipples if it's an issue. Have a drink. It'll take the edge off."

He knows full well that Ricky isn't supposed to drink. The reason he's suggesting it has nothing to do with "taking the edge off." Flowers is making a point: Ricky is another lame, washed-up, boring celeb fresh out of rehab. Calling him Rick is to make him feel old.

It works.

He's supposed to be feeling better. He *is* feeling better, obviously, compared to how he felt when he was hauled off to jail, was abandoned by Lexi, lost the Academy, suffered considerable damage to his reputation, and then was arrested again on drunk-and-disorderly charges for hitting that pap.

Things are starting to get back on track, though. He's put the charges in his rearview, concentrating solely on fixing his reputation as one of the best working Hollywood directors. All he needs is one big hit, and all his problems will go away. He's off to a good start. The movie sites dig the teaser; advance ticket sales are steady. Experts are forecasting opening numbers around thirty million; not Marvel numbers by any means but pretty damn solid for a noir heist starring an influencer. It'll be enough to get him back on the A-list, which he never should've been off in the first place.

Yet things feel flat. There's no excitement, no electricity buzzing through his body like when *The Mark* was a smash hit at Sundance or when his follow-up, *Minutes to Redemption*, debuted at number one at the box office. Partly because the film is only half-finished, his editor working slave hours trying to piece it all together.

The other part he's not allowed to talk about.

The apartment's landline rings. There's a guest in the lobby who'd like to come up but who isn't on the approved list. Probably a friend of Flowers, some star banger with a bag of treats for the photo shoot. Perfect. Now he's going to have to play it cool while the rest of them snort their dinners. He asks for the name and almost drops the phone when he gets his answer.

"I'm sorry," Ricky says. "Can you repeat that?"

22

"Millie Blomquist," Ricky says as soon as the elevator doors open right into the apartment. He reaches out to shake her hand. Millie gives it a long stare, then looks around.

The place is immaculate: mid-century modern furniture, high-end decor, a crystal chandelier. A woman giggles from the bedroom, accompanied by a clicking camera, flashes of light, men applauding her beauty.

Ricky pulls back his hand. He offers her the choice of water, soda, or iced tea. "I was going to make a latte, if you're interested."

"I need to talk to you."

He shifts his eyes toward the voices coming from the bedroom. "Let's go in my office."

Which is more incredible than she ever imagined, like slipping back into old Hollywood. The walls are dark cherry, maybe walnut, the ceilings high with an art deco coffer pattern. It holds a masculine scent, traces of cigars and leather. On the mantel above the white marble fireplace are a variety of awards: Spirit, Emmy, and Directors Guild. Above the mantel is a framed original poster for *The Mark*.

When fantasizing over the years about this moment it was always so he'd tell her what an excellent director he thought she could be, how he'd like to personally mentor her, help make her the next Ricky O'Naire. Now that moment is a reality, and all she can think is: *What a douchecanoe.*

It's true, what they say. Never meet your idols.

Ricky sits down in a wingback chair and motions that she join him. The leather couch is so soft it's like sitting on a marshmallow, much more comfortable than the driver's seat where she's spent the past ten hours.

She says nothing. In response, Ricky crosses his legs, uncrosses, grips the armrests. "You're upset," he finally says. "And you have every right to be. I'm realizing now that we could've done a better job of explaining how the contest works."

"I don't remember reading anything that said you could make my movie without my involvement, or consent, really."

"We did have your consent. It's not my fault you or your parents didn't hire a lawyer to review the contract and explain it to you." He slides forward in the chair, close enough now that their knees almost touch. "You see, it's a highly unusual contest. To give a group of beginning filmmakers—high school students, minors, in your case—with little or no experience a budget to make a feature. I have investors—*nervous* investors, I might add—who have never felt entirely comfortable with that arrangement. They're handing over a large sum of money with no guarantee they'll turn a profit, or even recoup their costs. So in the past I have served not only as a producer of the winning project but also as a kind of second director, if you will. Guiding and mentoring the crew as we go, making the film together. And I don't take any credit for that."

Her eyes narrow. "Aren't you a saint."

"That's not the point I'm trying to make. I'm sorry about what happened with the Academy. I really am." He almost sounds sincere. "The whole thing was a billing error that I never paid serious attention to, and I should've. I hired and trusted people to handle it, they didn't, and now I'm paying the price. The Academy was my pride and joy, and its reputation, like mine, is now tarnished. I'm trying to fix that."

"By stealing a student's script and shooting it without her?" Her voice is harsh and bright, laced with disdain. Is he really trying to morally justify stealing from her?

"No," he says, his jaw tightening. "I'm trying to reestablish my name in the Hollywood community. By doing that, I can bring back the Academy and continue educating and mentoring future generations of filmmakers. It's a beautiful script." His voice is kind once again. "I could tell from our first conversation that you knew the heist genre and really cared about your characters and their story arcs. And because of the personal connection to your father, you've been able to make sure that the audience really understands his motivation. It's perfect, and I wanted the best possible version of it on screen."

"Why didn't you just ask me? I would've jumped at the chance to work with you. You're the whole reason I went to New York and blew through most of my college fund."

"You would've asked for a screenplay credit." He sits up, lets go of the armrests. "I've never directed a film that I didn't write, and the critics would have had a field day saying that I'd lost my edge. It needs to appear that I did this on my own, for the sake of my reputation, for the Academy, and for the film."

Millie is glaring at him now, and it apparently registers, because he quickly changes course. "That is to say, I did a lot of work on this myself. Yes, it started with your script, and the essence is still there, but large sections have been changed. You'll know once you've seen it." He goes on, sounding a little smug. "Why, just a few days ago I watched a working print, and I'm confident that once it's complete, this film will be the best thing I've ever done. I believe, now more than ever, that I'm the only one who could have done the story justice."

The impact of his words crushes her like a ten-ton safe.

It's too late. He's not going to listen to her. He's not going to give her proper credit—*any* credit, not even in a tiny font buried in the crawl. She was completely wrong about him in every way. Her friends, family—hell, even Pastor Rod—saw it.

"That's bullshit," she snaps. "You think because you have more experience, you're capable of making a better movie? What about *Bottle Rocket, Thief, Reservoir Dogs*—"

"I get your—"

"*Bound, Lock, Stock, and Two Smoking Barrels*—"

"Enough! Point taken."

"All first-time directors." Anger swells in her chest. He really thinks he can do a better job of telling her own dad's story? Is he serious? "You might have the connections and the technical skills, but there's no way you have the passion I do. From the trailer alone, I can see that all you did was make another corporate, soulless movie starring a fucking *influencer*, no less. What, you couldn't get one of the Kardashians to do it? Jake Paul wouldn't return your calls?"

She catches her breath. O'Naire's eyes have gone dark; his lips are curled in a sneer. Beaten-down high school coach with a heart of gold? This fuckbag would've robbed a bake sale disguised as the team mascot and gotten away in a driver's ed car.

He leans forward to rest his elbows on his knees. "I'm tired of wasting my time. You signed the contract. I own the rights, meaning I can do whatever I want. You think you could've done a better job than me? Get real. I saw your footage. Sloppy, uninspired, no real understanding of how to move a camera. You might've watched a lot of films, but that doesn't mean you know how to make one. In your hands this would've been a straight-to-Redbox piece of trash that circled out of rotation in a week. You want to fight me? Go ahead. I very much doubt you have the money to put together a legal team that can do anything. My lawyers will tie this thing up for years."

There's an ache in the back of her throat. A shiver down her back. Shit. Can he really do that?

"I can go to the press," she tries. "I, um, I'll show them my script, the footage I shot. I have all the proof I need."

"You think anyone will believe you? One of a thousand students who hold a grudge because of something I was acquitted for? Or will they believe me, a recently sober, wrongly accused Hollywood icon on the brink of a comeback? Come on, Millie. You know how this works. They'll side with me, and you'll face consequences. Or are you too inept a storyteller to see the big picture?"

The question hangs in the air.

He's right. It hurts to admit, but he is. The world isn't set up to take down guys like him. He's an asshole, but it's not like he's Harvey Weinstein. If she exposes him, he might suffer some bad press, but all that will do is entice even more people to head to the theater to see what all the fuss is about. And when *The Art of the Gangster* became a box office success, public opinion would be that he was within his rights to make the film and that she, a seventeen-year-old with a barely watched YouTube channel, should be considered lucky he did.

Her pulse begins to slow; vision goes fuzzy around the edges. All the nervous energy built over the last ten hours drains from her body, exhaustion flooding her senses.

She's about to leave when he gets up and takes down the framed poster for *The Mark*. There's a steel combination safe. He opens it and removes several stacks of bundled cash.

"That's ten thousand dollars in exchange for any and all footage of your film. And your silence." He piles the money on Millie's lap. "Don't be an idiot about this. I don't have to be the good guy here. I'm doing this because I like you, and I'm sorry for the way things shook out."

The money rests on her lap. Five stacks of hundred-dollar bills. She's never seen this much cash in person, yet it seems like very little. Nothing but pocket money to him.

He kneels in front of her, furrows his brow. He lightly pats her knee. Here he is again. That kind high school coach.

"Go home," he says. "Go to college. Forget about this business, this kind of life. It's not for someone like you."

Millie gathers up the money with trembling hands. He's right. He doesn't have to do this. The smart thing is to take the cash and run before he changes his mind.

"Make it twenty and you have a deal," she says.

23

March is still too cold for the balcony, but Ricky can't stand having to listen to the borderline porno shoot going on in his bedroom.

He could have stayed in his office, but that felt like returning to the scene of the crime. He shouldn't have ridiculed Millie. Should've controlled his temper, found a solution that didn't include making her feel two inches tall.

He reminds himself that this is better than the alternative. He had to be cruel so she'd abandon any plans to expose him. It's for her own good, really. If she'd gone to the press, jeopardized the film's success, the investors would find out about her . . . and if *that* happened, it wouldn't end well, to put it mildly, and nothing he could do would prevent it.

This is the better of two bad options. He can deal with her hating him forever. At least they both get to live. Sucks it cost him twenty grand, though. That was the last of his emergency-fund cash. Now everything he has is tied to the investors.

Ricky sets Millie's hard drive on the cement. Through the floor-to-ceiling window, he can see Lexi crouched on all fours on the bed, her bikini-covered ass pointed toward Marcos and Flowers. She smiles and waves at him, which causes her to lose her balance and face-plant, her ass going higher in the air, a fact that's not missed by Marcos as he furiously snaps his camera.

Ricky stomps on the metallic exterior of the hard drive and, when it doesn't break, picks it up and slams it against the cement, over and over, until it's in pieces.

24

Millie sits on the hood of her Chevy Metro, crammed between a Mercedes and a BMW, vehicles owned by people who can actually afford the thirty-dollars-per-hour parking-ramp fee. The night carries a chill, but it barely registers.

Her attention is squarely on the open backpack full of money in her lap.

Twenty thousand dollars. Cash.

She shouldn't have handed over the hard drive, but what other choice did she have? According to Doris, all of this is legal. Millie has no case. Giving her footage to the media might have embarrassed O'Naire, but that's not the endgame here.

Despite what he said, she could see the big picture, and it's so much bigger than he knows. This is no longer an attempt to get story or script credit. Maybe it never was.

Since the moment Doris mentioned hush money, another idea has been taking shape at the back of her brain, waiting to come to life.

Maybe her dad was right all along. Maybe stealing is the only option.

She zips up the backpack, jumps off the car, gets inside, slams the door, locks it.

You don't watch and document over one hundred and fifty heist films without learning a thing or two. Every good heist needs a backer, someone to fund the caper. *Seven Thieves* had Theo Wilkins. *The Town* had the Florist. *Cruel Gun Story*, Yakuza boss Matsumoto. *Grand Slam*, Professor James Anders.

As she pulls out of the lot, joining the taxicabs and Ubers on the crowded city street, she wonders if Ricky O'Naire has any idea that he just became her backer.

PART TWO

GETTING THE BAND BACK TOGETHER

1

CHICAGO

Heist movies have taught Millie that there are three solid ways to obtain information on a place you're planning to rob.

1. The Inside Man. No easier way to get the layout of a building than to know someone who works there. Options include either bribing a current disgruntled employee or having a member of the crew get a job. Neither of these are solid choices since she doesn't have the time to properly vet the staff, nor the work experience for even the most entry level type of position.

2. The Maintenance Routine. This job falls to either the Hacker or the Gadget Guy, depending upon the size of the crew. Whoever it turns out to be typically disguises themselves as a maintenance worker (painter, phone repairman, etc.) who is allowed into the building because they "need access." This sometimes lends itself to sneaking through heating vents, although that option requires the building's blueprints ahead of time and, typically, someone in a wired van a half block away feeding you information in case you get stuck in a tight spot (literally and figuratively).

Since she's a crew of one, there's no doubt in Millie's mind that she'd slip inside a heating vent, break her neck, and not be found until months later, when the smell of her rotting corpse was unbearable. Pass.

3. Seduce the Mark. This job falls to the Femme Fatale. First step is to determine who makes the most useful Mark. You don't want to waste your time seducing twenty guys, or girls, who don't have the information needed for the heist. Why screw twenty when you only need one?

In this case, Millie knows exactly who the Mark should be.

On a shaded city bench, Eric Schumer—designer glasses, thick vest over a tight sweater, scarf almost engulfing his nonexistent chin—burns the roof of his mouth on a mouthful of gyro, reaches for his iced tea, and winds up spilling lamb and tzatziki sauce onto his skinny jeans.

Millie spent five and a half hours of her morning outside the Oakwood Arms Building, hoping that at some point he'd come down for a break. Sloppy recon, but it was all she could manage with such a rushed timeline.

Could she really see herself making out with this dope? Doubtful, but yes, if needed, though screwing him is absolutely off the table. Her virginity might not be some precious thing she's holding on to, but she'd at least like to lose it to someone who won't go to jail for touching her.

She'll be the first to admit she doesn't have the traditional characteristics of a Femme Fatale. She's thin and flat in the areas that are usually soft and curvy, soft in the areas that should be flat. And since she can't risk him seeing her face, she'll need to seduce him in disguise. Some research into the neighborhood around the Oakwood Arms has provided one, though it's hardly cloak-and-dagger.

Millennium Park swarms with tourists—children running around, their parents chasing behind; buses of European and Asian tourists unloading, posing to get pictures in front of Cloud Gate—a.k.a. the Bean.

Millie checks her makeup one last time, fully comprehending what a colossally bad idea this whole thing is.

2

"Excuse me."

Eric Schumer looks up from wiping his unfortunately positioned crotch stain. A woman—uh, girl—no older than eighteen or so, stands in front of him, winter jacket tied around her waist, ratty sweater, backpack pulled tight against her shoulders. For some reason, her face and neck are a smudged alien green, and he wonders if she works for that RPG company half a block up, the reason why people in full costume are always clogging the sidewalk outside Dandy Donuts. The Midwest—such low standards for entertainment. He can't wait to get back to LA.

"Yes?" he responds.

"Sorry to bother you, but do you mind taking my picture?" She holds out her phone. "Can't seem to get the whole Bean and me in the shot."

He makes a dramatic show of tossing the napkins aside before he stands. He'll take her picture, all right, but she's going to know how inconvenient it is.

The girl backs up a few feet, cocks her hip, throws her hands up in the air. She's cute when she smiles, for an alien, though her teeth could be whitened. He snaps a couple and hands back the phone.

"Thank you so much," she says. "I've passed this thing a million times but never, you know, in costume. Thought I'd capture the moment."

"Not a problem. Take care."

"I work for Today's Adventure," she says, apparently feeling the need to explain her outfit. "It's a company that other companies hire out for—"

"I'm aware of what you do. I work in the same neighborhood." He reaches down to pick up his trash and book. "Have a good day."

He heads toward the gyro truck but balks at the long line; probably for the best, now that he thinks about it. He'd be too embarrassed if Jake saw what a mess he's made of himself. He's probably the only one who thinks of the guy who runs the gyro truck as Jake Ryan from *Sixteen Candles*. That in itself makes him feel his age. The guy probably doesn't even know what *Sixteen Candles* is.

"Can I trouble you for a cup of water and some napkins?" he asks the woman working the lemonade stand. When she doesn't respond, he gestures at his stained jeans.

"Excuse me?"

Someone clears their throat behind him.

He turns to see the green alien girl.

"Sorry," she says in an accent that makes him think of *Strange Brew*. "Really hate to keep bothering you, but are you Eric Schumer?"

"Uh, yeah?" he says. This has never happened to him before, and he wonders if he's about to be served, though he can't imagine what for.

"I'm a big fan of your work. The editing you did on *Minutes to Redemption* was incredible. I was stunned when you didn't get a nomination."

"Oh. Why, thank you, uh—"

"Elizabeth Lipp. You can call me Lizzie." They shake hands. "I'm a student over at the Art Institute. Film program. I want to be an editor someday."

"Not an Orion from *Star Trek* full-time, then?"

She laughs and playfully brushes her fingers against his chest.

They make conversation, mostly about what she's studying. It's refreshing to talk shop with someone still full of optimism, not beaten down with the realities of working in the industry. She's a bad flirt, though. Always trying some way to touch him, laughing far too loudly at his lame dad jokes. She mentions that she'd love to see how his studio is laid out and gives him a stagy wink.

He tries the subtle approach when letting her know she's barking up the wrong tree by asking if something's wrong with her eye.

"No," she says, frowning. "Think there was some dust in it." She rubs it once. "Better now."

Eric spots Jake running over.

"Hey, bro, what happened?" Jake points to the stained jeans. Eric's stomach flips; he becomes light-headed. Jake acknowledged his crotch.

"Minor accident. Nothing that will stop me from coming back for more." He almost smacks his own mouth. What the hell did he just say?

"Hope not. Here, don't want the stain to set." Jake pulls a stack of wipes from his apron and smiles, his gorgeous dimples making an appearance.

They talk a moment longer, Eric fumbling with his words and trying to finesse a sexy way to hold cleaning towelettes. After Jake waves and jogs off, Eric turns back to notice that the girl—Lizzie, was it?—is still standing there.

"Sorry, that was rude of me," he apologizes. "I see him every day, so I didn't want to be impolite."

"Perfectly fine." It's weird, but she almost sounds relieved.

3

The river flows out in front of them, still green from its Saint Patrick's Day dye job. The last thin sheets of melting ice wet the sidewalks and streets. The girl seems more relaxed now that she's stopped the obnoxious flirting. They reach the front doors of the Oakwood Arms Building, and he says he should probably get back to work.

Her eyebrows go up. "You work here? I bet you have quite the view."

"Not really," he says. "The movie I'm working on has a high level of security, so I'm stuck in a closed room most of the day. Sucks, but I should be done by next week. Well, let's say I better be, or it's my ass."

"Can I ask what movie you're working on? Something I've heard of?"

He shouldn't say anything, but screw it. Job is almost over, and everybody else he knows here is working on the same project, so it's not like they're going to be impressed. And what's the point of working eighteen hours a day, strung out on Red Bull, if you can't brag every now and then?

"I bet you have." Might as well make it exciting for her. He looks around as if someone might be listening, then leans in close and whispers, "I'm actually the lead editor for the new movie by Ricky O'Naire."

4

Three scrubbings with the lousy hotel soap, and Millie's skin still has a faint green tint. If anybody asks, she'll just say she has food poisoning. The headboard bangs against the wall when she jumps onto the bed. The mattress has the softness of a picnic table.

The backpack with the money from O'Naire is in the bottom corner of the closet, buried under the rest of the bathroom towels. She made sure to lock the door, dead-bolt it, and use the portable door lock her mother insisted she bring to the Academy.

She pulls back the lurid bedspread and slides in, sheets prickly against her damp skin. A nicer room would have been great, but the hotels downtown needed a credit card. The Knightsbridge was the only one she found that took cash, leaving no digital footprint that she was in Chicago.

Not that it matters much anymore. From what Eric told her, breaking into the editing suite sounds like something out of *Mission: Impossible*. Security access cards, passcodes, thumbprint protection, and voice activation.

"Only me and Ricky O'Naire can get in," Eric told her, rocking back on his heels, thumbs tucked into his front pockets, smug as a teenager who lost his virginity before all his friends. He didn't seem the type to be bought off, certainly not with the budget she has. The only other option she can think of is to force him at gunpoint, but there's no way she could do that, even if she had a gun.

After what happened to her dad, there's not a chance in hell she'd ever go that route. Guns get people killed. Happens every time in a heist.

It's probably for the best. Solo jobs never work out. There are only a few cinematic examples. Kim Basinger in *The Real McCoy*, but she gets caught in the opening bank heist. Catherine Zeta-Jones fares better in the opening art heist in *Entrapment*, but Millie doesn't have the resources or the spandex to pull that off.

As soon as she takes her phone off airplane mode, it chimes with multiple voice mails and texts from her mom. Shit. She was too busy planning a felony to remember the interview at the store.

"Millie?"

"Greetings from beautiful Detroit Lak—"

"Where the heck have you been?" snaps her mother. "I've been calling all day looking for you. You missed your interview at the deli. Now Bob Gustafson thinks you're another one of those good-for-nothing millennials. I told him he was wrong, but he refused to listen."

"I'm sorry," she says, looking down in shame as if her mom were scolding her in person. She's actually Gen Z, but now doesn't seem like the time to bring it up.

After a big inhale, Mom starts her usual, predictable rant about how trust isn't something that's just given, it has to be earned, and Millie can't keep pulling these kinds of things if she wants to be taken seriously in the real world. To keep herself from falling asleep, Millie puts the phone on speaker and starts scrolling through the photos she took today.

The first one is her, green as a pea in front of the Bean. Next, the photo of Eric Schumer going back into the building. Something catches her eye. She brings the phone closer and looks at a small sign she didn't notice before, in the bottom right corner of one of the building's windows. Something that tells her she might actually have a shot at pulling this off.

"Millie? Where'd you go?"

"Right here. Sorry. Got distracted." She checks her tone, makes sure she hits the right note of sincerity. "I should've called Mr. Gustafson. You're right, Mom. I'm going to be graduating high school in a few months, and it's time I got my act together."

"Excuse me?" her mom says, in disbelief that her daughter is conceding, let alone so quickly. "Honey, are you feeling all right?"

"I'm fine. Just hear me out."

"I'm all ears."

Millie sets the phone down and gathers her hair back into a ponytail. Pulling off this next part is critical to the plan. Spring break gives her until the end of the week, but after that she has school to deal with. She might've seen a lot of heist movies, but none explain how to pull off a heist in Chicago while attending high school in Fargo.

If this doesn't work, the whole thing is sunk.

She takes the phone off speaker. "I've been talking with Lois and her parents," Millie says, "and hearing about her plans next year for college got me thinking that maybe you're right—that I'd be missing out if I didn't try it. So I called up the head of the West Fargo State media-arts program."

"You did?" Her mother sounds skeptical.

"Just to see if maybe I could sit in on a class or something to see what it'd be like, and he said with my experience at the Manhattan Movie Academy that I could join them on a commercial shoot if I wanted. He's taking some students to Minneapolis next week and invited me to come with. Get a real firsthand experience of what the school's like. I know that means I'd miss a week of school, but I'm a senior, so it's not like my grades really matter much right now, anyway. He basically said with my demo reel I'm a shoo-in."

Silence on the other end of the line. "So he's seen your work, and he thought you showed potential?"

Mille inhales. "He did."

She can almost hear the smile in her mom's voice when she says, "Of *course* he did! I'll have to talk with Wade. I'm not saying yes, Millie. Hear me on that. But I'll think about it."

Millie exhales. Mom doesn't "think about" things unless she's seriously considering them. Might take a little more pressure, but for the most part, she's golden.

And then, of course: "What about paying for all this? That's something we have to figure out, you know. Maybe you should call Mr. Gustafson, then. Take the job in the deli."

Millie thinks of the second photo and says: "Actually, I was thinking about Uncle Aaron. Seeing if maybe I could work at Howard Security."

5

FARGO, NORTH DAKOTA

A security alarm screeches, a shrill *whoop-whoop*. Strobing white light dances along the beige walls, taupe linoleum, drab break room furniture—the world's most boring disco.

Like the rest of the lower-level Howard Security employees in khakis and yellow polos huddled around the small circular tables, Aaron is used to the interruption, a normal part of his shift, something he tunes out like an air conditioner on the fritz. A security company that can't control its own faulty emergency exit or fire alarms; a bad joke he's heard too many times.

He peels his hard-boiled egg and pretends to read the captions for the twenty-four-hour news channel on the TV, his eyes shifting left every twenty seconds or so to catch a glimpse of her.

Gabrielle.

She has the most seductive name. He didn't learn it by asking her, even though they've been having lunch together—at separate tables, but still— for almost five weeks now. Instead, last week he finally worked up the nerve to stand near her at the vending machines in order to see her name tag.

She flicks her lighter with one hand and drums the blue-polished, diamond-studded nails of the other against the table. She smooths her raven hair. Her smoky eyes flick up at the clock, counting down the minutes until she can go out and smoke. He wonders if her friends call her Gabby, even though that sounds like someone's kid sister or a gawky teenager. In a way, she reminds him of Ali MacGraw in that movie Bobby always loved, the one with Steve McQueen.

The clock moves to a quarter after and she gets up to have her smoke, her Howard polo and khakis hugging her curves in the most wonderful way.

There's not a chance in hell anyone calls her Gabby.

She walks toward him, her eyes catching his. He's been staring for too long.

Normally, a woman this attractive would intimidate him, but he reminds himself that's the old Aaron, the Aaron who Carol left, the Aaron before Food Patrol helped him lose twenty-three pounds, the shortage of fast food clearing up his skin—a little, at least—and allowing him to wear his first size-large polo since eighth grade.

He sets down the egg, conscious of its odor. He checks his sitting posture. *Project confidence and you'll be confident* is what all the self-help books say. But what approach should he take?

How's it going? In case I forget to ask later, what do you like for break-fast? I'm unbearably lonely, please marry me?

Aaron makes his move just as the alarm shuts off.

"Hiya!" he shouts into the silent void.

Heads whip around; phones are ignored. His face flushes with heat. Gabrielle doesn't acknowledge, doesn't say a word.

She doesn't even slow down as she exits the break room.

6

A ringing phone jars him from his stupor. Aaron looks up from a desk littered with fresh candy-bar wrappers and an empty bag of potato chips. His tongue is desert-dry.

The sound of fuzzy speakers and employees calling on alarms fill in the background outside his cubicle walls. His work phone rings again, but before he checks it, he pulls out his cell. No missed calls. Usually the bank tries his cell first before calling at work. It's only a matter of time before they start showing up in person.

It's never clear what he's supposed to tell them. He didn't have the money last week, and unless he gets the manager job, he won't have it this week. They have his statements. They know he can't afford the trailer now that Carol's left.

He finds his headset under a stack of papers and answers. It's his boss, Ethan. He'd like to have a word.

The walls of Ethan's office are lined with framed photos of skylines: Austin, San Francisco, Saint Louis, Chicago, some of Howard's other locations. He's focused on his work, typing with an assertiveness Aaron has never known. It's later than Ethan usually stays. Does this mean he wants to talk about the manager job?

Aaron lightly taps twice on the door.

"Sit down," Ethan says. He doesn't stop typing. "James had a miss yesterday. Freezer alarm at Spokane Meats. Company caught it in time, but another few hours and they would've had a freezer full of worthless T-bones."

Not the discussion Aaron was hoping for, but that's fine. Maybe better. *Always look for opportunities to impress.* Instead of telling Ethan what a good manager he'd be, he'll show him.

"What was the action plan in the account?" Aaron asks.

"To call site management, but James just cleared it from his screen. When I asked him why, he stated that this particular freezer alarm comes in every night, and every night he calls the night supervisor, and every night the supervisor tells him to ignore it. Said it's common knowledge on the floor that it's a faulty alarm and has been due for service for the past few months."

Past few years, actually, Aaron thinks. Everyone on his crew knows the night supervisor for Spokane Meats, a short-fused curmudgeon whose voice has turned to gravel over the years. Could be from cigarettes or yelling at Howard Security staff.

"I know the account," Aaron says. "Their management needs to call and schedule a service repair. If I'm remembering correctly, we've even had the tech department call them a few times during business hours to see if they'd like us to come out and fix it. I'd have to check with tech, but I don't think they've called us back."

Ethan waves it off. "Regardless, the action plan states to call the night supervisor."

"Did the alarm come back in again?"

"Oh, yeah." Ethan stops typing and leans forward. His hands are clenched. "It came in a total of *thirty-five times* over the last three hours of James's shift. And every time he cleared it from his screen." He slams his open hand on the table. "*Every time.* Now tell me what you would've done, what you train your employees to do, because if it's to ignore alarms, then we've got a problem. Now, would *you* have cleared that alarm thirty-five times?"

"Of course not," Aaron murmurs. He would've cleared it twice and then bypassed it for the night so it never came in again. Any of his employees would have done the same, and he wouldn't have blamed them for it.

Ethan smooths his striped tie. "I didn't think so. Effective immediately, James no longer works here."

Something turns in Aaron's stomach, and it's not the chocolate and chips from his binge. A manager would agree and fire James. Difficult responsibilities are part of the job. "He has tomorrow off. I'll talk to him first thing Saturday and let him know we're letting him go."

Ethan jabs a finger toward Aaron. "You're going to call him tonight and notify him that his personal belongings will be waiting at the security desk for him. He has forty-eight hours to claim them before we chuck everything into the dumpster. I don't want him to ever set foot on the monitoring floor again. Understood?"

Aaron nods, but Ethan doesn't divert his gaze. He's going to make him say it.

"Understood," Aaron says.

"While I have you here," he goes on, voice back to normal, "I wanted to see if you could come in early next Friday. I know you work nights, but I'd like to get started on the manager interviews, and I'm busy the rest of the week. I was thinking we could start around one. Okay with you?"

Wow. Usually HR schedules these things. They must be fast-tracking him for the job. He might not lose his home after all.

"One? Yeah—no—sure. I mean, that'd be great. Yes. I can be there. Here, I mean."

Ethan scrunches his forehead. "For your sake, I hope you're a little more articulate on Friday. I'm thinking we'll be done by five or so, depending upon how Lisa in HR schedules. There are three of them."

"What do you mean, 'three of them'?"

"Three interviews. God, maybe this is a mistake."

"No, no, no. I'm just confused. I figured I'd be interviewing with you. Are there two other people I need to meet with?"

Something in Ethan's face relaxes, making him look almost sympathetic. "I guess we're talking about two different things. I was asking you to come help me conduct the interviews. The person we select will be your boss, and HR suggested that you should have a say in who that is, which is why I'm inviting you to sit in. I'm not considering you for the position."

7

Aaron walks to the back row of cars, the snow crunching under his feet competing with his pounding heart. Even in the cold, his skin buzzes with heat.

He should have quit right on the spot, told Ethan to take his prized Director of the Year award and go screw himself with it. But who is he kidding? New or old Aaron, he'd never have the courage.

When he gets to his rusted '91 Plymouth Sundance, he opens the door, throws his lunch box onto the maroon passenger seat, and is about to get in when he hears someone call out his name.

8

Millie takes a drink from her second cup of pop; it's flat, and it takes two packets of sugar to pass as drinkable. About what you'd expect from a place called the Duck Tape, a bar and grill with wood paneling, neon beer signs, posters of girls in bikinis.

She waits for the caffeine to kick in. Her eyes are heavy. Body sore. Everything aches. She's driven twenty hours in two days. How is she going to pull this off?

Not that she's had much of a chance to get a word in. Aaron's mouth is going a hundred miles a minute, topics tumbling over one another like he hasn't had someone to talk to in months. She listens patiently, waiting for her opening, and jumps in when he complains about having to fire someone over the phone for ignoring a stupid freezer alarm.

"That's awful," she says, and attempts to give it a humorous spin. "Next time have your staff dispatch police right away. Any type of freezer alarm immediately results in rolling out SWAT."

"I like it." Aaron takes a generous gulp of beer. "You know, your dad would've been so proud of you. I heard about what happened at that film camp you went to. I'm sorry it didn't go as planned, but don't sweat it. I know that things will work out."

Millie blushes. "Why do you say that?"

"Because you *do* things. It's amazing how many people talk about wanting to do something but never actually go through with it. Takes guts to try something like what you did, and at your age? I know you took a bath on the money, but in the long run that won't matter. We're going to see your name in lights across the gold screen."

She smiles. "It's the silver screen, but thank you."

So much has changed, but Aaron hasn't. He's still the same guy she remembers from when she was a kid. The same wispy walnut-brown hair in a widow's peak, the same moon face patchy with stubble, the same big heart. No matter how much life beats him down, he still wants others to make it. That's the main reason why he and her dad stayed best friends since they were five. No matter how much Millie's mom complained, Aaron was always invited over on holidays, birthdays, and the Super Bowl. He was family, even though Mom didn't really want him to be.

It wasn't until after her dad died that Mom came around. Now she keeps in touch with him, she says, for Millie's sake, because it's important to know people who saw the good in her father.

Now or never. "Remember my script?" Millie asks.

Aaron nods into his beer. "The one about Bobby? Of course. That was a great script. Well, not that I have anything to compare it to, but I remember really liking it."

The anger comes roaring back. "Ricky O'Naire stole it. He made it himself. It comes out two weeks from tomorrow, and I'm not getting any credit."

"You're kidding me." He furrows his brow, wipes his mouth. "He can't be allowed to do that, right? Can't you do anything?"

Millie lowers her voice. "There is something."

9

The success rate for crews of two is split. On one hand, you have playful comedic capers like *How to Steal a Million* and *After the Sunset*, where the stakes are never that high and everything works out in the end. On the other, you have gritty white-knuckle thrillers like *Good Time* and *The Silent Partner*, heists that end with crew members either in prison or shot and killed. It really is a crapshoot.

However, if she has to add to her crew, she could do a lot worse than Aaron. Unlike the men who betrayed her dad, Millie doesn't have to worry about any kind of double-cross. He's been loyal to her dad since the sandbox. It's that loyalty that she's banking on. Some might say she's using or exploiting him, but she's not going to force him to do anything he doesn't want to. She's only a teenager. He's the adult here. Just an extremely agreeable and down-on-his-luck one who will be easier to convince than most.

This is the first time she's ever been to Aaron's place, and it's no wonder why he always came to their house. The trailer is sparsely decorated with hand-me-down and thrift-store furniture. Flower prints from the seventies. Lace curtains. Despite how small it is—living room only five feet from the kitchen, bathroom next to the fridge, next to the accordion bedroom door—it feels almost spacious.

Maybe that's because four months ago his ex, Carol, took half of what they owned.

They'd gotten married soon after her dad's funeral, the only time she'd met Carol, in fact. The two of them had hooked up through a dating app during the COVID shutdown.

"I don't know about this," Aaron finally says after minutes of thinking it over.

"Of course you don't. I'm asking a lot. I know that. But don't you want more . . ." She's about to say *than this* but doesn't want to kick him while he's down. "It's an easy job, and I'm taking all the risk. You won't even be there."

"Where will I be?"

"At work, probably. Pretending like it's any normal day. And if you're not scheduled to work, go to the movies, grab some food. Credit card transactions that prove where you were. Go out with friends or something. In fact, it's better if you're seen with people. But if you're not, that doesn't matter. What I'm asking for could technically come from anyone, and if I'm caught, there's no possible way I'll let the cops trace it back to you. I promise you that."

He shakes his head. "Yeah, right. Like I'm going to let Bobby's little girl go to jail. Do the responsible thing here. Take that money and put it toward college. Twenty grand? That's probably like two years' tuition at State. And your mom would agree with me. I should call her right now. Nip this thing in the bud before it even begins. A heist? What are you, nuts?"

Her pulse quickens. Aaron telling her mom was a risk she knew going in. "If you do that, then nobody is ever going to know that this movie was inspired by a really great guy who just made some mistakes. You know how important it is to me. It's my future, and your best friend's legacy, at stake. Doesn't that mean something?"

He examines the peeling linoleum floor. "Why me? If anyone can do it, why are you asking me?"

"Because you're the one with the most to gain if this works. No offense, but the bosses at Howard are never going to appreciate you. How long have you been there?"

"Nine years," he replies.

"*Nine years?* Aaron, that's almost a decade, and you're still just a second-shift supervisor? Dude, screw them. Help me, take your share, and get out. With the money we're looking at, you could get a house. A real house, without wheels."

"Tiny houses are in fashion now," he counters. "There's TV shows about 'em and everything."

"Not like *this*." So much for not kicking him while he's down. "Don't you want to be one of those people who does something instead of just talking about it?"

"Making me eat my own words, huh? You really are Bobby Blomquist's daughter."

Clearly, her words have stung, because he gets up from his chair, knocking into the pullout table behind him. A stack of bills falls to the floor. Millie can see red warnings across white envelopes: *Overdue. Final Notice.*

"What if I gave you two thousand dollars?"

Aaron whips his head around. He couldn't have looked more surprised than if she'd started speaking fluent Hungarian. "What?"

"Two thousand dollars," she says again. "A little seed money until we get paid for the film." Her eyes drift toward the overdue bills on the floor. "Take some pressure off you until the job is done."

He hustles back into the living room. "Are you bribing m—"

"Yes," she says.

Before he can utter another word, she pulls off her backpack, unzips it. Aaron's eyes bloom at the sight of the cash. She peels off twenty hundred-dollar bills and smacks them into his hand.

Neither speak for a moment, both staring at the money spread across his palm. Aaron laughs a little, scratches his shoulder. "Well, shit. You really think you can pull this off?"

The back of her throat itches. She swallows a little louder than she'd prefer. "There's no doubt in my mind."

He takes an audible breath, visibly tearing his eyes away from the money.

"I'm not saying I'm in," he says. "But for argument's sake, what would I have to do if I was?"

10

Aaron taps his finger against his desk as if he's sending a Morse code distress signal. His eyes twitch. Sweat dampens his neck, pools down the back of his polo.

His mission is to access the Oakwood Arms mainframe, where Hitting the Mark Productions is housed, and obtain a copy of the office layout. Half his staff is on dinner break, so now's the time, but two women from HR have been chatting in the hall right outside the monitoring area for over twenty minutes. If they see what he's trying to do, it'll be his job and probably conspiracy charges. He picks up the third cup of coffee he's had since they started talking. It's empty.

When he gets back from the break room with a refill, the women are gone, but only five minutes remain until two of his employees come back from dinner. He navigates the corridor, keeping his eyes on his overfilled cup, making sure he doesn't spill. He doesn't even realize who he runs into when they collide, the coffee splashing up and burning his neck, staining his clothes.

Gabrielle glares at him. Her polo and khakis are a soggy disaster. "What the hell, man? Watch where you're going!"

His breath hitches. She *talked* to him.

"Hiya," he says.

11

It was never going to be as easy as she imagined. Millie knew that going in, but like so many before her, she's relied upon wishful thinking and crossed fingers. And in her case, a spreadsheet.

She sits opposite Aaron in his living room. The account information she asked for lies across the coffee table. "You're sure this is the most up-to-date copy?"

Hands folded in his lap, his coffee-stained polo shirt reeking of hazelnut, Aaron says, "That's all I could find."

"Nothing about an editing suite? Voice activation or needing a thumbprint?"

"If there is such a thing, it's not monitored by Howard. I could call the building management and ask."

"Is that a normal question, or would that draw attention after the robbery?"

He ponders for a moment, says, "They'll probably just think it's a coincidence."

She looks back at the layout. "The police won't. There's no such thing as coincidences when it comes to heists. Don't ever forget that." According to this, she'll be able to get past the front desk and onto the elevator, which will take her to the eleventh floor that houses Hitting the Mark Productions.

Her access ends there.

"Why would someone have two different companies monitor their property?" she wonders. "It doesn't make sense. None of this makes sense. Either this is wrong, or my source was lying to me. Either way, I have conflicting intel, meaning I have no clue what to do next."

She sags back in the chair, presses her palms against her eyes. "Stupid. This whole idea was stupid, a pipe dream that only a dumb teenager would think up. What the hell was I thinking? O'Naire was right. There's no way I could've made this movie. I can't do anything."

"Hey, hold on a second, don't talk like that," Aaron says.

That's when she realizes she's crying. "Dammit," she says, wiping her wet hands on the leg of her jeans. Some great criminal mastermind she is.

Aaron comes over and kneels next to her chair. "You're not a dumb teenager, all right? You're a lot smarter than most folks. A lot smarter than me, that's for sure. A lot braver, too." He rubs her shoulder, a comforting gesture that makes her miss her dad even more. "You just don't know security like I do, which is why you were smart enough to bring me in."

That makes her laugh. "Genius move, huh?"

"Absolutely," he says as he sits back down. "Now the way I look at this, if there's supposed to be another room that requires additional security checks, then I don't think it'd be monitored by two companies."

"What do you mean?"

"Well," Aaron says, "there's a lot of do-it-yourself security systems these days. Sales at Howard have been on the decline for years because of it. I'm speculating, but if I'm this O'Naire dude and I'm betting my whole future on a movie I stole from someone else, then I want to be in charge of everything, and I mean *everything*. Maybe he didn't want anyone from building security to have access, so he either hired some-one to install a separate system or did it himself."

"He could've done that? Voice activation, too?"

"Sure. I mean, I don't think he bought the equipment off Amazon, but it wouldn't have been that hard to do. My guess is he's using this room here." On the schematic, he points to a corner room that juts out onto the main floor. "No windows. No other exits. All access can be controlled by one entrance. That's what I would've done."

Assuming he's right, there's no pulling this off with only the two of them. Millie looks again at the layout, the single-entry corner room, accessible only by Schumer and O'Naire. She leans back in the dingy recliner as another idea starts to hatch.

12

OLATHE, KANSAS

The army recruiter is a no-nonsense dude. Short-cropped hair. Face freshly shaved. Full camo. A row of alternating United States and Kansas flags takes up an entire wall of his cramped office.

"Your agility test scores are phenomenal," the recruiter says, thick finger running down some paperwork. "Speed. Strength. All top scores. You're in remarkable condition. But what's really impressive are your aptitude results. Your computer skills are off the charts. I'd like to see you out in the field, but someone like you would also really excel in intelligence. Probably as an analyst or in surveillance. You'll have your pick of what kind of soldier you want to be."

Jordan Fischer, in his Sunday suit, checks his posture. "Yes, sir. Thank you, sir." His stomach clenches. It's going to be hard getting used to saying that. "An analyst, more likely. I don't see myself as someone who'd do well in combat."

The recruiter scoffs. It's clearly not the first time he's heard that from a potential recruit. "That's what basic training is for. Just wait until you feel that M4 carbine in your hands. It changes a man. Your mama won't even recognize you once you graduate, and I'm not talking about how you'll look after we get them shears on you," he adds with a grin.

Jordan reflexively touches the top of his frohawk, doing his best not to wince at the thought of losing his hair. His mother scowls at his knee-jerk reaction. He tries to give her a reassuring smile that he's on board, but his mouth won't cooperate.

"Were his scores really that high?" she asks, probably so she can hear the recruiter brag about her son again.

The recruiter obliges. "Let me put it this way, ma'am: if we had someone with Jordan's skills after 9/11, we would've found bin Laden right away and avoided the entire Iraq War."

The statement is complete bullshit. He's a decent coder and a below-average hacker, but it serves its purpose. His mother squeezes his arm and preens.

"Can I ask why you waited so long to enlist?" the man asks. "Most seniors signed up last fall. From what I understand, you come from a military family. Father, was it?"

Jordan's mother proudly confirms that's right and squeezes his arm again. She's in a floral dress she's been saving for this occasion, the day she's been waiting for. "His father was a chief warrant officer before he entered the public sector. Uncle, a lieutenant. Grandfather, a captain in the navy. Serving our country is in his blood."

"Outstanding," says the recruiter. "What was the holdup?"

"Had another passion I wanted to consider," Jordan says. "It didn't pan out as expected, so I took some time to reevaluate my options and landed on the army."

His mother clears her throat. Her face sours. *Don't ruin this for me*, it reads.

"And happy I did so, sir," Jordan adds.

The recruiter sets some paperwork down on the desk. Jordan signs his name in two places, flips to the last page. His cell beeps in his pocket.

"Sorry," he says to both of them. "Thought it was off."

He takes out the phone. There's a text from Millie Blomquist. *Check your email. Heist Project.*

Millie? He hasn't spoken to her since August. What could she possibly want?

"One second," Jordan says and gets up before signing the final page. "This might be important."

13

MIAMI, FLORIDA

Paz Delgado looks down at the common area from her family's tiny balcony. Little children play in the shade of palm trees. Some junior high–aged girls in tank tops and shorts braid each other's hair. The hot sun glares off her laptop screen. With the AC down, it's too hot to be inside. She'd leave if she could, but her dad has the car and isn't due back from work until late. Not that there's anywhere she'd want to go. That always involves money.

She drags her cursor down the list of local film-production jobs. Associate creative director, project manager, senior multimedia producer, and video production specialist, all of which require three to five years of experience and a reel providing the proof. Her fifty thousand Instagram followers don't count. She knows. She's tried.

With so many followers, why doesn't she just try to attract sponsors? That's what her brother and her friends want to know. *Yeah, thanks, already thought of that.* There's a big difference between the money offered to a teenage videographer like her and that thrown at the buxom bikini influencers bouncing around Miami. Sponsors don't just care about followers, they care about how good you look, how short your shorts are, how much skin they can see. Fuck that.

The rest of the jobs are freelance: wedding videographer, editor, miscellaneous crew—on her last few gigs, she learned that meant *coffee bitch*—and they only pay fifty to a hundred dollars per job. She hits the main Miami page. The office positions are mostly secretarial, eleven dollars an hour. They all require a bachelor's degree. No one's going to be impressed by her GED and uncredited workshop hours from the Manhattan Movie Academy.

It's official: she's not qualified to do anything.

She's about to close her laptop when an email chimes its arrival, a confirmation from Delta Airlines: MIA to MSP.

"The hell is this bullshit?" she mutters. She must have gotten hacked. But there are no withdrawals from her bank account, and when she checks her credit card, she finds the same thing.

There's a second email waiting for her.

Subject: Heist Project

Dear Paz . . . If you would care to earn back the money stolen from us, and probably a great deal more, please read the attached script at once and have dinner with me at 7 p.m. on Sunday at the Café Royale in Minneapolis. If all goes well, you will have no further financial worries.

—Millie

14

NEW YORK CITY

The script blurs in and out of focus on Devin's phone. He's too drunk for this, but what choice does he have? If he's going to accept, he needs to read the script first, and he only has—he checks—twelve hours before he needs to leave for LaGuardia.

Christ, has Millie gone completely mad?

He gets up from the bed, careful not to create too much movement and wake the bloke hogging the covers. What's his name again? John? Jake? Jack? Hard to keep them all straight. Devin laughs. He must be drunk if he's making puns.

He brews an espresso, smacks himself awake while he waits for the machine.

In the seven months since the debacle at the Academy, he's spent his time either at the movies or with handsome American men who can't get enough of his accent. Seven months spent hiding from his father across the Atlantic, pretending to be building his reel by taking on production-assistant work. He makes sure to say that it's free PA work so his father keeps putting money into his bank account. Seven months of lying to himself that everything is fine.

He's embarrassed to admit how good it is to hear from Millie, even if it's only because she wants something from him.

A little more sober now after the espresso, he rereads the email, questions what she means by *the money stolen from us*. Does she mean what they lost at the Academy because of O'Naire? The script she's attached is for a short film. Minimal dialogue. Heavy visuals. Only two locations. That's good. Production's still going to cost a pretty penny. Lots of extras means lots of makeup and wardrobe.

The real question is why Millie didn't simply call him and say she wrote a script and found some funding. He thought they were friends. Close ones, actually.

But she left town without saying goodbye and ignored his texts and calls. Yes, it hurt. After a while, he gave up. He's given up on Paz and Jordan, too, their tight crew relationship dwindling to liking one another's posts on social media. Has Millie reached out to them as well? Seems like she would, considering the skills they bring to the table. But if this is a reunion of sorts, why the secrecy?

Why would she pay for a plane ticket, not knowing if he'd accept?

15

MINNEAPOLIS, MINNESOTA

The proposal of a heist is a delicate thing. It's not like the locker-room pep talk a coach in a sports movie gives a team of underdogs right before the big game. You don't feed a heist crew inspiration, or say they'll always wonder if they could've done better, or remind them that it's only a game and the important thing is to have fun.

The stakes are too high for that. You need them desperate. You need them angry. To do that, you break them down. You point out how shitty their lives are. You show them how life has screwed them over, and when they are at their lowest and angriest, you provide a solution: one job that'll change their lives.

If you do it right, they'll be begging to join.

Inside the Café Royale, Millie sits at her four-top in the private room she's reserved for the night, keeping an eye on the door. The whole thing—the vague emails with a script attached, the private dinner to suggest the heist—is inspired by the 1960s heist move *The League of Gentlemen*, about a disgruntled group of veterans who rob a bank. A good choice for a disgruntled group of film students performing a heist of their own.

Of course, in *League*, the Mastermind is a rich British guy who treats his crew to a deluxe meal at a posh restaurant. All Millie can swing is a hipster burger joint that serves decent Jucy Lucys. She's got this upstairs room for free until 9:00 p.m., when the place becomes twenty-one plus and they have drag-queen karaoke.

None of the three confirmed they were coming, but their flights have all landed at Minneapolis–Saint Paul. Now it's just a matter of waiting. She looks down at her note cards and mouths her opening lines.

There's the creak of someone ascending the wooden stairs. She stands. Her heart beats wildly. She straightens the bottom of her sweater, runs her hands down the front of her plaid skirt. Stockings and the fedora from *The Gangster and the Artist* complete the look. She's channeling Anna Karina from Godard's *Band of Outsiders*, but she's doubtful anyone will make the connection.

The footsteps stop shy of the doorway, just out of her sight. Silence. She imagines whoever it is gathering . . . courage? She's about to go check when Devin rounds the corner.

"Hello, love," he says.

She clenches her hands. Feels her chest rise and fall. She removes the fedora. It seems silly now. "Hi," she replies.

And then runs to greet him, throwing her arms around his neck. She didn't realize how much she'd missed him. He laughs and embraces her.

"Not the type of greeting I was expecting, to be honest." he tells her. "You were so mad at me about the whole O'Naire fiasco. Left without saying goodbye. Haven't spoken to me in months."

"I was wrong," she mutters into his shoulder. "I can't believe I stood up for that prick."

He steps back and wiggles a finger in his ear. "I swear I just heard Millie Blomquist admit she was wrong about something. Must be my imagination. Maybe my ears need to pop." He looks around, his cashmere sweater and gray chinos a stark contrast to the surroundings. "Well, this is bit of a dump, yeah?"

"A lot of the budget went to flights and hotels. Have to cut corners where we can."

"Understood. So you raised the money yourself then, or did you find funding?"

"Both, but yeah, I have a backer. Producer, I mean." He raises a brow. "Someone in the business." She sits down in her chair, palming the note cards. "Have a seat. I'll explain everything when everyone gets here."

Devin stands behind the chair across from her but doesn't sit. "Millie, what is this?"

"What do you mean?"

"Last-minute flights, promises about getting money back with no explanation. A script that's, forgive me, one big heist scene with no real character development."

"There's a love story." It's in her nature to defend her work.

"A bit, I'll give you that. But it doesn't feel right, now does it?"

Millie glances up at the clock. Seven fifteen. Where are Paz and Jordan? "It's a heist project, like the email said. Can we wait for everyone before I explain? It's kind of complicated, and I don't know if I'll have the energy to go through it more than once. Catch me up until the others get here. How's your dad? Has he visited you in the city?"

Any happiness to see her vanishes from his face. "My father is a miserable old dog who emails every week to let me know what a disappointment I am compared to my Oxbridge-attending brothers and sisters and how I've accomplished nothing except for slipping into the cliché role of a spoiled rich kid who relies on his parents to handle everything." He splays his hands palms up as if to say, *What can you do.* "To avoid thinking about it, I've completely proven him correct and spent the last seven months lying to him while in a drunken fog with American tourists when I should've been using that time to make films, or at least talking to the only true mate I've made here . . . only she skips town and avoids me like the plague.

"Then one day she sends me a script and a plane ticket and tells me I have less than twenty-four hours to decide if I want to fly seventeen hundred miles to work on a heist project that I think we both know isn't going to be a film. Now, I've missed you like mad, and it's brilliant to see you, but I want to know what you're up to, Millie Blomquist, and I want to know right now."

16

The Uber stops in front of an old, vine-covered brick building. The sidewalk is slick with hard ice that Paz has to navigate carefully. Small piles of snow glow red from the neon *Café Royale* over the awning. What did the driver call this area—Nordeast? *Nord?* What is this, Minneapolis or Middle-earth?

It's March, already spring, but it's so goddamn cold. Paz's only warm clothes are the leather jacket she's wearing and her Academy hoodie. Millie better buy her a winter coat.

She gives Millie's name to the bartender and is directed upstairs to a private room. On her way to the stairs, she passes the bathroom that Jordan Fischer exits.

He doesn't say a word, just looks at her with those gorgeous brown eyes.

"Looks like we've both been recruited," Paz finally says.

"Both gluttons for Millie's punishment." He gives her a once-over, and she notices her heart speeding up. "She's lucky I'm on spring break right now, otherwise I wouldn't have come."

"Yeah, lucky."

She opens her arms to go in for a hug, but he takes a step back. "Probably didn't think you'd ever see me again," he says.

"I didn't." She knows she should say something more, but what? Fact is, she really didn't think they'd ever see each other again, which was why she stopped FaceTiming. They live in different parts of the country, and they're too young for a long-distance relationship. "I probably owe you an explanation."

"You don't owe me anything." Jordan's voice is casual. He squares his shoulders. Hair included, he clears six feet five, easy.

"Wasn't sure you'd keep the hawk," Paz says. "Could never tell if you liked it."

"I wouldn't have kept it if I didn't." She must have made a face of disbelief, because he adds, "Don't even start, Paz. My hair has nothing to do with you."

Paz mock-surrenders. "Not a word."

Jordan rolls his eyes, but he's smiling now, and the curve of his full lips makes Paz's skin tingle. He puts his hand on her arm. "Let's go see what this heist project is."

17

Devin waves his hands like an orchestra conductor, spouting off all the reasons why he thinks this is an enormously bad idea. All Millie can do is shake her head and hope he tuckers himself out soon, otherwise this is going to be a long night.

The stairs creak. Footsteps outside the door, then silence. Devin continues yelling as Millie goes to investigate.

Jordan and Paz are in a full make-out session at the top of the stairs. Millie clears her throat. Paz is the first to pull away. Jordan, on the other hand, starts kissing her neck.

Paz at least has the grace to look embarrassed. "We, um, heard you inside and didn't want to interrupt."

"It'd be nice if you felt the same," Jordan mumbles, and pries himself away.

As soon as Devin sees the two of them, he starts in again. "The script's not for a heist film," he says. "It's a heist. Like an *actual heist*. Like a we-could-all-go-to-jail type of heist."

Millie gestures toward the table. "Care for some pop?"

"What are you talking about?" Paz asks.

"It's what we call soda here."

"She means, what is Devin talking about?" Jordan clarifies.

Devin comes out from behind the table. "She brought us here," he announces, "to convince us to steal O'Naire's film before it's released into cinemas and hold it for ransom."

"Technically, it is our film," Millie interjects. "He just made it before us."

Jordan asks, "And how do we do that? Steal a bootleg of it or something?"

"No." Devin starts to gesture again. "She wants us to—"

"Hey, can I tell it? It is my plan, after all. Let me find where we're at." She pulls out her note cards.

Devin steamrollers on. "She wants us to break into Ricky's Chicago editing studio and steal the master, the working print, the raw footage, everything, so that the studio and Ricky have no choice but to pay us for it."

"That's crazy," Jordan says.

Millie slumps into her chair. "It is how he explained it."

"How much is the ransom?" asks Paz.

Jordan's eyes go wide. "You're not seriously entertaining this?"

"Two million," Millie tells them. "That's enough to recover our Academy fees and what I feel we should be paid for developing the project, with enough to make our next movie. Honestly, we deserve more, but I don't know how to move it."

"Our next movie?" Devin asks.

The three of them look more than dubious. Millie stands. "Of course. If we'd won the contest, *The Gangster and the Artist* would've gotten studio attention. And I know we would have won that contest."

Paz looks at Millie like she's out of her mind. "How? What makes you think we possibly could have won? We were the youngest group; we had the smallest crew, the least amount of footage in the can. Shit, we couldn't even get an actress to work more than a day, and you think we were going to walk away with the grand prize? Why?"

Because there's no other option for me, Millie thinks but would never say out loud. She doesn't have a backup plan. Doesn't have anything original to say outside of her dad's story. She just never realized it until now.

Or maybe she did but didn't want to admit it.

She takes a deep breath. "The project might've had its hiccups, but I know we would've produced something spectacular. O'Naire stole that opportunity from us twice. First, when the Academy closed, and now, by making the movie himself. And before you ask, yes, I tried to reason with him. Even went to Chicago, but all he did was throw me twenty grand to shut me up and then slam the door in my face. Everything he's doing is legal. It's unfair, but it's legal.

"So instead of us fielding offers right now, we're back home, doing the same shit we did before the Academy. This is our chance to take what we learned and use it against him. I've watched over a hundred and—"

"We know!" the others cry in unison. There's a moment when all four exchange looks. Then they burst out laughing.

And just like that, for the first time in months, Millie feels as if she's herself again. She's back with her friends, her crew. Sure, they might be planning a felony instead of debating movies, but she'll take it.

Maybe she should have tried harder to make things work before leaving New York. Maybe if she'd just explained her side better, it would have been okay. Maybe they even would have helped her finish the short. Hindsight really is a bitch.

"I'm just saying I know what I'm talking about," Millie says when the laughter dies down. "If you'd all sit, I'll tell you more. I wouldn't have brought you here if I didn't have a plan. A good plan. Where nobody gets hurt and, if we do it right, nobody will even know the four of us were there."

"No, thank you," Devin says flatly, back in argument mode. "I'm not listening to this. They'll reopen Guantanamo Bay if we're caught. It's not worth the risk."

Paz looks at Jordan. He smooths his mustache with his thumb and first finger. "What do you think?" she asks.

"I don't know," Jordan says slowly. "I've never done anything illegal. But I also know Millie's never half-assed anything in her life." His voice strengthens. "When the girl sets her mind to something, she attacks it with everything she has, even to the point of being extremely annoying about it."

Millie shoots him an annoyed side-eye, yet refrains from starting an argument. It looks like Jordan might be leaning toward her side, and she needs all the help she can get, even if his help does come with back-handed compliments.

"She's proven she's committed to this by flying us here, putting us up. And we all can agree what O'Naire did is reprehensible. We could at least hear her out."

"For fuck's sake," Devin says.

Paz sits down. "Mil? Start talking."

18

Empty plates smeared with melted cheese and ketchup sit in front of them. Millie looks at her last note card and wishes she'd been able to deliver the proposal the way she'd wanted to right from the beginning. Stupid Devin. He slurps his coffee, probably needing the caffeine to regain his strength. She thought Paz would be the biggest challenge, but now she's the only one Millie thinks will agree. She has no idea which way Jordan will go.

"And this . . . Inside Man," Jordan says, the first words he's spoken in an hour, "will be able to get us upstairs?"

"Up to the production offices, yes."

"But we can't meet him?"

"I promised he'd stay anonymous. It's better for everyone. That way, if we get caught, you'll have no idea who he is. Only I will, and there's no way I'll ever give him up. I'm minimizing risk as much as possible. That's why the crew stays at five. *Inside Man, Bandits, Now You See Me* are all examples of five-person crews who pulled off successful heists."

She gives it a moment to see if anyone's going to call her bluff, possibly mention *The Ladykillers* or *Triple 9* or *The Usual Suspects* (which works out fine for Keyser Söze and no one else), but they've never been interested in the numbers. If they were—and had looked at her spreadsheets back at the Academy—they would know the success rate for a crew of five is 55 percent; better than some, but not overly encouraging. With five crew members, the chance of a double cross is an alarming 71 percent, which is why she's taking extra precautions.

"What about the rest of us?" asks Devin. "Can you promise we'll stay anonymous?"

"You know I can't. For this to work, you all have to be there in person. There's sound design, lighting, costumes, makeup, extras: all the things we'll need to create a fictional world. It's no different from making a movie, except for the fact that it'll be in real time. There's no yelling 'Cut.' There's no fixing it in post. It has to be one flawless take." She suppresses a smile.

That was her favorite part of the pitch she didn't think she'd get to give. "I'll take the heat if it goes wrong, but the cops will figure out that we went to the Academy together. Nothing I can do about that."

"I don't know," Jordan says, nervously drumming his fingers on the table. "It all seems too risky. Are you sure we can't just go to the cops?"

"My cousin says we don't have a case. We all signed the same authorization forms, giving him permission to do this."

"What about our footage from the Academy?"

"What about it? O'Naire's got it now. It was the only way he'd give me the cash. This is our only option unless we walk away, and I'm not going to do that." Anger flares inside her. "I can't do that."

"Look, Mil," Devin says, "we know this is hard on you because of your father, but ask yourself what he would've wanted."

Millie says nothing, only clears her throat. Given his relationship with his own father, Devin is in no position to offer advice.

He looks like he has something to add but seems to decide it's not worth the effort. Jordan glances at Paz, but she's pulling out her phone. She runs her finger across the screen and holds it out for everyone to see.

It's an image of Yates standing next to Greta Gerwig. Sammy's in the background, stoned, looking like an extra in a Seth Rogen movie.

"Yates posted this last week," she says. "He and Sammy got to meet Greta Gerwig, a hookup through Yates's dad, no doubt. They were at a house party in Malibu. He couldn't even figure out how to use a light meter, and now he's partying with Greta Gerwig while I'm stuck in Miami, getting paid a hundred dollars a day to shoot wedding videos." Her voice is edged with bitterness. "It's not fair. We were promised more than this."

"Then do something about it," Millie tells her.

They lock eyes. She's in.

"What if we get caught?" asks Jordan.

"Then we get caught. We're not carrying guns; we're not holding anybody hostage. Is it illegal? Yes, but serious prison time? Well, maybe, but doubtful. If anything, we'll just explain what O'Naire did and use whatever money we have left to hire a lawyer to fight him for the rights. Slim chance that'll work, but at least we'll know we gave it our best shot."

Great. Now she's slipped into sports-movie mode. "Look at the alternatives, Jordan. Ask yourself if you really want to join the army, because I don't think you'd be here if you did."

Millie tries to catch his eye, but he's focused on Paz again. "You're sure you want to do this?" he asks.

Paz nods.

"Then I'm in."

"You don't need to do it to protect me," she tells him.

"I'm not," he says, double tapping his chest. "My future was taken, too. Millie's right. You think I want to join the army and follow the future laid out for me before I was even born?"

"That's a good line," Devin puts in. "Someone should write that down."

Paz turns to Jordan, her look so intimate that it's clear why they couldn't keep their hands off each other earlier tonight.

"It's your life, Fischer," Paz says. "Just tell your mom you're not into it. She loves you, right?"

"You don't get it. It's about tradition with her. A sense of honor. So much of my family is military, and she'll just assume I think I'm too good for that life or something if I don't join up."

"But you've been wanting to do sound design since you were little," Paz argues. "Think about that. What kind of kid watches *Gravity* and doesn't want to be an astronaut, doesn't care about the awesome way the spaceship gets destroyed, but says to himself, *Hmm, I'm really inspired by their use of multitrack sound effects and the quality—*"

"I get it, I get it," Jordan cuts in. "And I was eight when I saw it, so I didn't think about the sound quality until I was eleven and toured Warner Brothers and saw the demo during the studio tour." She makes a face at him. "But I see your point. And yeah, I know, I've been wanting to do this for a long time. That's why I think if I'm going to tell my mom I'm going to do something other than enlist, it'd help if I could produce something tangible, something real, where I can show her I'm still using my talents. I mean, if we pull this off and get to make that next movie like Millie says, my mom might understand where I'm coming from. She might see that I'm trying to be part of something greater than myself. Or at least she might make a small attempt. So I'm in, but I'm in it for me."

Devin slow-claps. "Yeah, we got it, mate. Heard you loud and clear before your little soliloquy."

"Man, shut up," snaps Paz. "At least he's on board. You haven't said shit about which way you're leaning."

The table looks to Devin. He pulls down on his sweater collar and then scratches the side of his face. He addresses Millie. "Let me ask you something, and don't lie to me or to yourself. Be honest. You think you're a good enough director to pull this off? Because the last set I was on with you, a man literally pissed himself."

"'All film is a dream sequence that comes from following the plan you make during preproduction,'" Millie says, not even needing to look at her note card. "'The *plan* is what makes a movie.' David Mamet said that. I don't see any reason why it wouldn't apply to pulling off a heist. My plan is solid. That's why I did all the recon before bringing you three on, so I'd know exactly what we're getting ourselves into. All you have to do is show up and follow the plan."

Devin looks at the other two, comes back to her. "Right, then. Where do we start?"

This time she can't hold back her smile. Sometimes good lines just fall into place.

"The same way we'd start a movie," she says. "With auditions."

19

CHICAGO

Soft copper light glows from table lamps. A jazz trio plays in the background. They have a prime table at the Green Cat, perfectly positioned so Ricky can greet the eager eyes that make contact with his. He offers a bashful smile, a small, simple wave. Chicago is different from New York and LA. People here don't care about the media, the accusations. He's the hometown boy, back from the edge, stronger and healthier than ever.

Lexi emerges from the bathroom, her leather jacket zipped all the way up to hide her sweatshirt, her blond hair casually styled, wearing just a touch of makeup. Her insistence that she wasn't presentable for a night out holds no water; the glow from the table light sparks a glint in her hazel eyes.

"You look beautiful," Ricky says.

"I look like shit." Lexi glances around the room, frowning. "This place is fancy. The waiters are in suits, and I'm in leggings and a jacket. I'm barely dressed for Walmart." She gives him an accusing look. "You said we were going straight to the apartment after the shoot."

"I got hungry and wanted to go to dinner. Why is that a crime?"

"Don't lie to me, Rick. You like the attention we get in this town."

Of course, she's right, but come on, once in a while he wants to take some time to feel good about himself. It's not like he hasn't earned it. There's only a handful of people who can shoot, edit, and distribute a major movie in four months, and he's doing it after all he's been through.

Maybe she'd understand the pressure he's under if she'd been around more.

"Maybe," Ricky admits, shuffling the ice in his glass. "Since when do you call me Rick?"

The arrival of a waiter forestalls their brewing fight. After he takes their orders, Ricky excuses himself. It's amazing how fast club soda runs through him.

While he's at a urinal, the bathroom door opens. Noise from the restaurant—the jazz trio and lively dinner conversation—ricochets off the tiled walls. It ends abruptly when the door closes. Then there's a click—the lock?

Ricky tries but can't see who the other guy is. He shakes himself dry and zips up.

"You're out of mints, by the way," he says, assuming that it's the attendant back from break. Instead, it's another diner, a man dressed up for a night out. Ricky notices that his brown leather gloves match his jacket. "Sorry. Thought you were the guy that works here."

"No problemo," says the stranger. He wears his hair a little long, brushed over and slicked with gel. He inspects the basket of colognes and lotions on the sink. Picks up a bottle of something, sniffs it, puts it back. He catches Ricky watching him in the mirror. "You Ricky O'Naire, ain't ya?" the man says. His accent is hard to place; not local, maybe East Coast. "Of course you are, I know that. I'm a big fan of yours. *The Mark*, boy, that's a great one. Classic."

"Thanks." Ricky grabs a towel. "Always happy to meet a fan."

"How's the new movie going?" For some reason, the man smirks a little. "When does that come out? Soon, right?"

"Week from Friday, in fact."

"Wow, quick turnaround, huh? Must be a lot of pressure."

"A tremendous amount."

"I bet. Though it's hard to tell, you at a fancy place like this, showing off with your girl. Looks like you don't have a care in the world." There is something almost menacing in the way he says it.

Ricky realizes that the door is still locked.

The man removes his gloves and sets them on the counter. His hands are at odds with the rest of his appearance: battered, knuckles bald and dark, palms calloused and chalky. A scar on his left hand stretches from first finger to wrist. He turns on the faucet.

"Movies are such a complicated thing," he continues, pumping out some soap. "Most people don't get that. A lot of people need to get paid. A *lot* of people. I bet you got a ton of people counting on you. Probably more than the public realizes. I can't even imagine the consequences of not getting something this big done in time. Or even worse, if you go through all of this and it's a flop." The man dries off his hands. He steps closer. Ricky can feel hot breath on his face. "That'd be awful, wouldn't it?"

"It would," Ricky agrees.

There's a knock, a sudden bang on the door that makes Ricky jump.

The man laughs and gives him a pat on the arm. Ricky flinches at his touch. "Relax, it's probably just the guy." He grabs his gloves, works them onto his hands on his way to open the door. "Sorry about that," he tells the bathroom attendant. "My buddy's a little drunk and wanted to talk in private. Spoiler, it's not that he wants to blow me. Imagine my relief." He turns back to Ricky. "Good luck with that movie. Hope it works out for you."

Ricky can only nod.

"So serious, this guy," the man jokes as he slips the attendant a few bills. "Here's for the cologne. By the way, you're out of mints."

20

POPE COUNTY, MINNESOTA

There are certain heist movies where the crew has some type of "audition" before the main event: *The Driver, Den of Thieves, Tower Heist*. This is to ensure that they're up to the challenge, that nobody will chicken out at the last minute, like in *Dog Day Afternoon*. There, the character Stevie waits until Al Pacino's Sonny has already pulled his gun and started robbing the bank when he says he can't go through with it and wants to leave. He even asks if he can use the getaway car to drive home. Millie needs to make sure nobody in her crew is a Stevie.

Millie, Devin, Paz, and Jordan walk down a small town's main drag of darkened storefronts. They stop half a block away from the Pope County Co-Op and Convenience Store. It's a box of a building: steel siding, large windows. The wind blows sheets of snow across the ice-glazed road. The store is fifteen minutes away from closing; no one is getting gas at this hour. A wave of nausea rolls across Millie. She bends forward and spits.

"Is our Mastermind having second thoughts?" Devin says through chattering teeth. "Because I am perfectly fine saying 'fuck it' and going to a hotel."

"Yeah, I mean, I know why you want to test us," says Jordan, stamping his feet to stay warm, "but I'd rather shoplift from a mall or something to prove I'm committed. This seems stupid."

In fact, Millie thought of having all of them shoplift or steal someone's wallet; the wallets they'd mail back afterward, untouched. But it just felt too minor, like they weren't taking it seriously, as if all of this was part of some cutesy teen flick.

This is the big leagues, and she needs to act accordingly.

She takes four sets of disposable gloves from her jacket and hands them out. "If we can't rob a nearly empty gas station two hours outside of Fargo on a Sunday night, we'll never be able to pull off the job in Chicago. We need to do this."

"She's right," Paz agrees. "We need to see what we're capable of."

Devin frowns at her. "Don't be daft. We don't even have guns."

"We don't need guns," Millie counters. "Remember what Stanislavski said: 'You can kill the King without a sword, and you can light the fire without a match. What needs to burn is your imagination.'"

"How the hell does that apply here?"

"If we start trashing the place and display a real threat, the woman in there's imagination will run wild and she'll do whatever we say to get us out as soon as possible. I've been here every trip I make to the Cities, and it's always been this old woman working alone. I'm pretty sure she owns the place. She's like seventy years old and always has her nose buried in a book. She's harmless."

"Fine," Devin says, "but I'm not the one asking for the money."

"So what will you be doing?" Jordan wants to know.

"I'll be the lookout hanging by the door. I'll give you the signal if someone's coming."

From a shivering Paz: "What's the signal?"

"I was thinking I'd yell out that Millie Blomquist of Fargo put us up to this."

"You could just whistle," Millie suggests.

"I'll consider it."

She claps her hands. "Okay, folks. Masks on."

All four pull out the masks Millie bought at a liquidation store. She's a crash test dummy. Jordan is Napoleon Dynamite. Paz is Quagmire from *Family Guy*. And appropriately enough, Devin is a crying baby.

"So bloody stupid," he mutters, putting it on.

It's more difficult to navigate behind the mask than Millie thought. The eyeholes don't line up right. It's too big for her head. The inside smells faintly of beef jerky. She closes one eye to see. She was right: the old woman is working alone.

21

Deep breath, quick exhale, door swings open.

Paz is in first. With one swipe of her arm, she sends the top row of potato chips flying. Next is Jordan. He kicks over a spinning magazine rack. Millie runs inside, the mask jostling around, eyeholes shifting and leaving her in the dark.

An abrupt sound. Metallic. It's one she recognizes from Wade cleaning his rifles at the kitchen table before deer season. She pulls down on the back of her mask so her eyes line up with the eyeholes.

Standing behind the sales counter is a potbellied woman in flannel. On the counter is a half-eaten microwave burrito and a splayed-out John Sandford paperback.

She holds a shotgun. The sound Millie heard was her cocking it.

"Been watching you knuckleheads for the past five minutes," the woman says. She keeps the shotgun up so they can see it. "Not much else to do around here but wait for customers. At first I thought you might be selling the pot to each other or something, but when I seen you put the masks on, I figure you was fixin' to rob me. Now I'm going to ask you one time and one time only. You got any firearms on ya?"

The three of them shake their heads. For a second, the eyeholes shift and Millie can't see.

"Okay then. But you was fixin' to rob me? I'm correct in my assumption?"

Everyone nods.

So does she. "This is what we gonna do. You gonna pick up the mess you made. I'm closing in ten minutes, and I got a case of Keystone waiting for me at home. Ain't got time to be picking up after some knuckleheads. I reckon the police will be here by then. If you do a good job cleaning, I'll keep it to myself about the robbery part. I'll just say you came in and made a mess. Fair?"

Napoleon Dynamite and Quagmire turn to Millie. Keeping one hand on the back of her mask, Millie checks what Devin's doing. The big baby is standing outside the store, hands circling his mask's eyeholes and pressed against the glass so he can see inside. At least he didn't run.

Objective complete. No Stevies in the crew.

"Yes, ma'am," Millie says in a raspy voice like Christian Bale's Batman. Napoleon Dynamite tilts his head at her. "Let me tell our partner outside what's going on."

The clerk takes a moment to consider. "Yeah, all right. Go tell your partner. Have him come in here and help clean up too."

She sets the shotgun on the counter next to the burrito and picks up the phone. Millie's heart beats in her ears. Her fingers slowly wrap around the door handle.

"Go!" she yells, pulling back the door, the overhead chime giving her away.

Jordan and Paz dash as fast as they can to catch up to Devin. Millie looks back at the clerk. She has the phone to her ear, eyeing the shotgun.

Millie should run, but it's not a heist if they don't take anything.

The closest thing is the bread section. She sprints to it and grabs a loaf of wheat. She hears the phone drop, the metal of the gun grating against the counter. She catches the door before it closes.

A gunshot rings out.

It stops Millie dead in her tracks. She spins around. The clerk's hair, face, and shoulders are covered in ceiling dust.

"Goddamn!" the woman yells. She drops the rifle on the counter. It bounces off and falls to the floor. She reaches for it, and Millie bolts from the store.

Her heavy boots crunch against the snow. Her lungs are on fire. She pants; this is why she always cuts gym. The other three are already in the car, engine running. Thank God she gave Jordan the keys beforehand. She leaps into the back seat.

"Drive!" she yells, inches from Jordan's ear.

"Oww!" Jordan yells back. He shifts the car into gear and slams his foot down. Tires spin, catch, and launch them forward. Jordan jerks the wheel at the end of the street, merging them onto the highway. Millie pulls off her mask, as do the others. All four breathe heavily. The windows start to fog.

Devin looks at her and whistles.

22

FARGO, NORTH DAKOTA

After dropping the three of them off at their motel, Millie quietly closes her own front door. She's two steps into the hall when her mom comes out in a bathrobe and slippers.

"Hi, hon. How'd it go?"

"Went good." It takes a moment to remember where her mom thinks she was, and the cover story begins. "The school's equipment isn't as impressive as the Academy's, but it'll get the job done. Tomorrow we're testing the rest of the gear, going over the schedule, and then loading the van. So that means it'll be an early morning and another late night."

"What's that on your shoulder?" Her mom reaches out and drags two fingers across the top of Millie's ceiling-dust-covered jacket.

"Uh, yeah," she says, "it's supposed to look like ash for some type of dream sequence. They were conducting camera tests. Guess I got some on me." Millie wonders how she became so damn good at lying and hates herself for it.

"A dream sequence in an eyeliner commercial?"

Millie shrugs. "I don't question the director, Mom. I'm just crew for this one."

Her mom wipes her hand on her bathrobe. "I'd still like to talk with the professor in charge before you leave for Minneapolis. I promise I won't embarrass you."

"Right. Sorry. Totally forgot. I'll have him call you tomorrow. Just a heads-up, he's British. His accent is a little thick. Makes him sound ruder than he intends to be."

The two exchange good-nights, and Millie waits until she hears her mother getting into bed. Since she's blown the attempt to sneak into her bedroom, she hits the kitchen to get some leftovers, update her budget spreadsheet, and review the next day's schedule.

Thumbs-down to Wade's leftover venison spaghetti. She makes herself a peanut-butter-and-potato-chip sandwich and pours a glass of milk. Halfway through the sandwich, she falls asleep with her head on the kitchen table, bathed in the computer's sterile light.

23

A pack of elderly women in matching sequined swimsuits and swim caps prance in a circle, their wobbly-skinned arms high above their heads in synchrony. Beethoven's "Ode to Joy" blasts from a boom box. A woman no more than four feet tall, with lilac hair, a magenta tracksuit, and gaudy gold jewelry, holds a stopwatch while shouting encouragement.

The music ends. The women collapse creakily onto the floor. A symphony of wheezing. Pink Tracksuit tells them, "Suck it up, ladies, it'll be a hundred times harder in the pool." They're about to do another run-through when Millie, from the doorway, tells them she has the room reserved.

The Red River Mobile Homes Community Center isn't terrible. The carpet seems to have been installed in the last decade and vacuumed in the last month. Still, as she uses gaffer tape to simulate the layout of

Hitting the Mark Productions, she makes a mental note to wash her hands. And her jeans.

She pushes a few tables together in front of a corkboard. She's tacked up a picture of Eric Schumer, the schematics of the production offices, and the storyboards she finished this morning. Crude drawings, but they'll get the idea.

There's a kitchenette with an empty minifridge, microwave, and sink. She stocks the fridge with pop and water, and puts bagels and cream cheese out on the tiny counter.

Next to them she sets down the bread from last night and can't keep from swelling with pride. Stealing a loaf of whole wheat is as penny-ante as it gets—she's basically the equivalent of Aladdin—but since 41 percent of heists aren't successful, she'll take the win.

Car brakes squeal outside. Doors slam. Paz, Jordan, and Devin tromp inside, kicking snow off their shoes.

"I swear I specifically remember someone promising we'd never have to experience a North Dakota winter," Jordan says, brushing snow from his frohawk.

They stopped for coffee on their way over from the hotel, and Devin hands her a latte.

"Does this mean you're not mad at me anymore?" she asks.

"Stark raving, love," he says, "but I'm an accomplice now. Might as well get on with it."

They each grab a bagel and spread out along the tables. Paz takes a chair opposite Jordan. He watches her sit down, sighs, and folds his arms. They're definitely fighting about something.

This is why it's bad for everybody when crew members get romantically involved.

Millie stands in front of the corkboard, note cards in hand. "So . . . once again, I'd like to apologize for last night's mishap."

Jordan says, "I want to go on the record and state that I never would've gone inside if I'd known guns were involved. I followed Millie because I thought she'd done the research. Put that on the record."

"Stop saying to 'put it on the record.' There is no record. Do you see anybody taking notes?" Paz asks harshly. She doesn't look at him when she says it, and it's enough for Millie to piece together that they're arguing about last night's robbery.

"I agree, though," Devin says. "It was rather insane to go in there. Whole mission almost went tits up over a loaf of bread."

Millie looks at the corkboard, her back to the three of them. They're right. Last night was reckless and stupid. Hopefully, they won't think the next part is. She'll really need to sell it to gain back their trust.

She points to a picture of the editor. "This is our Mark. His name is Eric Schumer."

"*Minutes to Redemption* Eric Schumer?" Jordan asks.

"One and the same. He's been editing the film in Chicago for the last six weeks. From what he told me, everything is in-house—sound, color, special effects, which are minimal. His deadline is Friday. From there, it's shipped off to LA for the final mix, then sent out for distribution. The premiere is Sunday. I have no idea where it's being scored, and even if I did, it'd be too late.

"We need to get the footage, all of the footage, before it's sent out. We're going to hit them Thursday morning."

"In three days? We're going in *three days*?" Paz's mouth hangs open.

Millie nods crisply. "We are. I know it's going to be tight, but we don't have any choice. I've got copies of the shooting schedule, if you'd like to look things over."

"Shooting schedule?" Jordan asks.

"Heist schedule. Shooting schedule. Don't get caught up on the terminology. We don't have the time. We're leaving for Chicago tomorrow morning." She indicates the schematic. "Here's what we're up against. The production company's on the twenty-seventh floor of the Oakwood Arms. You need an access card to get through the turnstile to the elevators on the main floor, and a passcode to enter the production office. As I explained earlier, our Inside Man can get us both of those and Howard Security uniforms."

"But you never told us why we don't just go at night," Devin points out. "If we have a way in, why attempt to pull this off during the day, when the office is full of people?"

Millie takes a breath. This is a vital piece of information she withheld at the proposal dinner. "Because to enter the editing suite, which from the layout is probably toward the far-northeast corner—"

"Quit stalling," Paz says. "We see where it is."

"First off, there is someone there at night. Eric's been editing around the clock and said they have a guard who sits outside the suite when he's there alone. Second, entering the editing suite requires thumbprint and voice activation, which unfortunately aren't connected to Howard Security. The only way is if Eric or O'Naire himself lets us in."

Devin rubs his temple. "For fuck's sake."

"This doesn't change anything. If you read the script, you see that a block from the Oakwood Arms is a company called Today's Adventure, which specializes in elaborate team-building, role-playing exercises, everything from treasure hunts to jungle safaris to alien invasions. That's our way in. We'll pretend we're with Today's Adventure—that O'Naire has hired us for a zombie-apocalypse simulation to congratulate the team on wrapping the movie. Eric is familiar with the company. He'll buy it."

Jordan raises his hand as if he's in a classroom, eliciting an eye roll from Paz. "Why zombies?"

"Because, according to Eric's social media, he's attended multiple zombie pub crawls in the past three years and went to a special screening of *Shaun of the Dead* last Halloween. The guy is into zombies. It increases the chances he'll want to participate."

She holds up a copy of the script. "Each one of us has a role, same as on a movie set. Only difference is that everyone will be pulling double roles. Paz, what you did on *The Gangster and the Artist* was fantastic and, I think, one of the main reasons O'Naire was attracted to it. But it wasn't just how you shot it. The production value was stellar, and I need that same type of focus on this. I need us to create a world that Schumer will fully accept as reality. I'm putting you in charge of lighting, makeup, and wardrobe."

"Wardrobe?" Now it's Paz's turn to hold up the script. "This calls for like fifty extras. How am I supposed to pull that off?"

"Don't worry. We'll have them wear their own clothes, older stuff they don't mind getting covered in blood." She turns to Jordan. "Jordan, you know how much I admire your sound design. Did you see how O'Naire basically copied it for that teaser trailer?"

Jordan scoffs. "Yeah, he did. Except the wind sounded like bullshit. Anyone with any knowledge could tell it came from a standard Adobe sound effects package. And it totally overpowered the dialogue."

"I had no idea, but see, you catch stuff like that. You're amazing, and I know you can bring that same level of detail to this. You're in charge of sound design and will be working with Paz on the smoke machines. You'll have to learn the makeup, too; we're all going to have to pitch in. That's your film role. Your, for lack of a better term, heist role will be the Hacker. You'll be breaking into the server room, downloading the finished film, and replacing it with a dummy video. Paz will have to help. Then, later, when we need to reach O'Naire for the ransom, you'll create a fake IP address in case he's already contacted the authorities and they're trying to track us."

Paz looks at him, impressed. "You can do that?"

"Pretty simple, yeah. How long are you giving me for the download?" he asks.

"About ten minutes," Millie says. "Maybe fifteen, but that's pushing it."

An amused expression crosses Jordan's face. "Well, get ready to push. The file will be at least a terabyte. A transfer over USB to a drive will take almost an hour, longer if we take the raw footage, too."

The news almost knocks the wind out of Millie, and she has to set down her note cards so the crew won't see them shaking in her hands.

Every heist has unexpected complications, but an *hour* to download? They're supposed to be throwing quarters at tollbooths by then.

"I can make that happen," Millie says quickly. "No problem. Now, Dev—"

Devin grins and leans back in his chair. "Oh, I'm excited about this. I don't know why you didn't just start with flattery. Couldn't possibly have anything to do with us getting shot at by a backwoods redneck last night, does it?"

"Do you want to hear this or not?"

"Go on."

Millie sighs. "You're incredibly intelligent, dashingly handsome, witty, charming, and an invaluable asset to any production. You're going to be the AD, but most of your time will be with the extras when you're not in character."

Paz almost spits out her coffee as Jordan coughs up some bagel.

"Wait a minute," Devin says. "You never said anything about having to act."

"Who's he playing?" Paz asks.

"Kirby," says Millie.

Devin sits up. "The zombie the editor's supposed to fall in love with? Millie Blomquist, am I the fucking *Femme Fatale*?"

Jordan starts cracking up. "This is going to be hilarious."

"It's going to be fine, Dev," Millie assures him. "All you need to do is follow the script."

"How am I even supposed to play the part of Kirby? We have no idea what Schumer is going to do when we show up. What if he goes off script? Scratch that. What happens when he *does* go off script because he doesn't know there's one in the first place?"

Millie pinches the bridge of her nose. It's a habit of her mother's she swore she'd never pick up, but it does help with her rising headache. "It's called improv, Dev. You listen and then react based upon what he says, his emotions. It's the same thing you do every night when you're picking up guys at the bar. You flirt with him, get him involved in the game, and then when the timing is right, before we take the rest of the group outside for the finale by the river, you get him to let you into the editing suite. That's when Jordan and Paz follow, knock Eric out with some chloroform, and download the movie."

Paz purses her lips, says, "I don't know. Sounds kind of weak."

Jordan adds, "Yeah, Mil. Where do we even get chloroform, CVS?"

Millie sighs. "I'm open to other ideas, but I've checked this out, and unless Jordan has some voice-alteration software and we can come up with a thumbprint, it's either this or busting through the wall with sledgehammers."

She takes a seat. Her crew sits expressionless, lost in the details of the job, or perhaps piecing together the best way to tell her she's out of her mind and they'd like their plane tickets home now, thank you. Maybe she *is* out of her mind, but don't you have to be, at least a little, to try something worthwhile?

When nobody says anything, Millie picks up her script and opens to the first page. "We've got a full day, and I want to make sure we have time to talk about character objectives before rehearsal this afternoon. If everyone wants to open their scripts, we can start the table read. I'll read the narration and play the part of the editor."

```
INT. HITTING THE MARK PRODUCTIONS—LOBBY—DAY


Excitement buzzes through the office. With the deadline for
The Art of the Gangster less than a day away, employ-
ees ride high on adrenaline. They run down halls for
last-minute meetings. Yell on phones to confirm guests
for the premiere. Everyone is so busy that nobody notices
when a MAN in a delivery uniform enters and VOMITS BLOOD.
```

24

CHICAGO

Jake looks particularly handsome today, Eric decides. Must be because he's done something new with his hair. Instead of a side part, he's rocking

a "just out of bed" look, the disheveled mess that takes at least fifteen
minutes to perfect.

"Here you go. The usual," Jake says as he hands Eric the gyro and
iced tea. "Try to keep from wearing it, all right?"

Eric laughs, even though Jake has used the same joke for the past
three days. "No promises." Why does he say stuff like that? "Um, your
hair looks good. Different."

"Thanks, bro. I just ran my fingers through it a few times. Kind of
in a hurry this morning. Overslept. Hungover from watching the Blackhawks last night. Did you catch that?"

"I was working until four in the morning. No time for sports right
now," Eric says, hoping he got that right and that the Blackhawks aren't
a band or something.

After he settles in his usual spot, Eric pulls a sandwich out of
his backpack. No way is he going to choke down another gyro. He
takes a bite and thinks about what he's learned about Jake over the
past weeks—he's a sports fan, hair care matters to him, and he works
at a gyro stand. Pretty surface-level information, but that's okay. It's
a pretty surface-level crush, if he's being honest. And Jake does get
drunk on work nights, which isn't great, but that's youth. It wears
off. Should only take another hundred more trips to the food truck
to maybe work up enough courage to ask the guy his real name. Too
bad the movie will be finished soon, and he'll never get the chance.

A shadow falls over him. He looks up, squinting in the sunlight.
Ricky O'Naire stands with his arms folded.

"They told me I'd find you here," Ricky says. "You do know we
have a break room."

Eric swallows a bite of sandwich. "I've only been gone fifteen
minutes."

"That's fifteen minutes you're not working on the movie. Come on.
We need to talk about the interrogation scene. You're sticking on the
police chief too much. I need more reaction shots of Romero."

"It's the chief's scene."

"Doesn't matter. The audience wants to see Flowers Romero, not some Broadway asshole nobody's heard of because Gary Oldman passed."

"I'm doing my best. I'm working around the clock. I need breaks every now and then. Fresh air. If I had help—"

Ricky holds up a hand. "Save it, all right? We're not going over this again. The more people with access, the higher the chance it'll be leaked, and that fucks with our opening weekend. Wait here, I'm going to get Lexi."

Eric gathers his stuff, tosses the untouched gyro. Lexi's over by the Bean, taking selfies with fans, mostly men, gorgeous men at that. She wears skintight leather pants, and a top that would be a stretch to call a bra. Ricky yells at her, telling her fans the show's over. They huff back to Eric, Ricky gripping Lexi by the arm.

"Because it's embarrassing, that's why," he hisses through clenched teeth.

25

Ricky sits in Eric's chair. Eric stands behind him. They watch the dual monitors, the one on the left displaying the police chief's coverage, the one on the right Flowers Romero.

The editing room, Eric thinks, has always had a sterile science-lab vibe. White walls, no windows. A filing cabinet and a steel mesh server rack line the left wall, the rack a tower of blinking hard drives that hold all of the raw footage and, eventually, the finished product.

Ricky highlights a section on the film's timeline, hits delete, then marries the remaining footage together. The new timeline plays on the right monitor. It sticks on Romero's reaction while the police chief's dialogue is heard off screen.

"Much better," Ricky announces. He gets out of the chair and waits for Eric to take his place. "I'll be back tonight to see the finished scene and then look at the shots for the prison sequence."

"What time are you thinking? In case I run somewhere for dinner."

Ricky gives him a blank stare. "Chicago has great delivery," Eric amends. "I'll see you tonight."

Ricky turns as if he's about to leave, but instead walks over to the server tower. He runs his hand down its side. "You haven't noticed anybody snooping around lately, have you?"

The question is so random it takes Eric a few seconds. "Snooping? Not really. There are movie sites that email and call, asking if they can get a first look, but nothing besides that. Pretty normal for a project with this much secrecy."

"Nothing else?" Ricky asks. "Anybody stopping by to make claims about the movie or anything?"

"Not that I know of."

Ricky turns and pins him with an intense look. His eyes are hard, his face tight. "You would tell me if someone did, though, right? Your career, your reputation, is worth more than a few bucks?"

A chill creeps up Eric's back, spreads across his shoulders. The way Ricky's asking, he can tell this isn't a hypothetical.

Eric makes sure his voice is steady. "God, of course."

In the silence, Ricky pauses for a moment, then moves to the filing cabinet. He takes something from his inside jacket pocket—what, Eric can't see, but it's in a gray cloth bag. Ricky puts it in the top drawer with a metallic clunk. A hard drive?

"Is there something I should know about?" Eric asks carefully.

"Just that I think my paranoia is finally getting to me." Ricky closes the drawer and locks it. The key goes into his pocket. "I'm going to be on site more for the rest of the edit." Another intense look. "Stay out of this drawer. It's where I'm keeping my things."

"Okay," Eric says. The next words leave him before he's had a chance to think things through. "I don't need a babysitter."

Ricky's mouth twists. "I tend to disagree. I would've had this film in the can by now if I'd edited the thing myself. Hurry up. You're costing us money."

The door slams shut behind him. Eric turns back to his monitors.

"Prick," he says.

26

FARGO, NORTH DAKOTA

Everything hurts, especially Millie's brain. It smashes against the inside of her skull like a wrecking ball.

The rehearsals were terrible. Devin's a drama queen who won't listen to the simplest direction. It was the same with the actors in *The Gangster and the Artist*. Why can't she make people understand her vision?

She walks slowly from the community center to Aaron's trailer. There's a used passenger van parked next to his car. She sizes it up: over twenty-five years old and hardly showing its age aside from some dents and a little rust. Millie peeks through the driver's side window. Two bucket seats with worn upholstery fill the middle row. The third row of seats has been removed, allowing for more cargo room.

Not bad for $1,500, cash. At least somebody listens to her.

She's greeted by the sound and stench of frying eggs. As she now knows, the Food Patrol diet allows an unlimited number of things high in protein: chicken, turkey, nonfat Greek yogurt, eggs. The latter are Aaron's favorite and likely the cause of his excess gas, which she tries not to mention. The other day it sounded like a flock of quacking ducks in the bathroom.

"Hope you're hungry," he says when the toast is done. He makes her a breakfast sandwich of five thin slices of ham and three over-easy eggs. Yolk runs down the plate when he cuts it in half. "Eat up. Plenty more where that came from."

"You have any cheese?"

A look of pure longing crosses Aaron's face. "No. Too many units."

"Don't worry about it," she says, taking a seat. "Van looks good. Did the guy give you any trouble?"

"None. In fact"—he reaches into his front pocket, pulls out a few bills, and hands them over—"since we didn't take the last row of seats and the overall condition of the van was a little, shall we say, shittier than advertised, I saved you a hundred bucks."

"That's amazing."

"That's not all. Hold on a sec." He turns down the burner and disappears behind the accordion bedroom door, emerging with a Howard Security badge. It's for a white woman with strawberry-blond hair and glasses; she could be a pudgy Millie going through a goth-mermaid phase. On the back is a Post-it with a six-digit number.

"Is that the passcode?"

"Yep. It changes every week, but tomorrow the building is scheduled for their monthly motion-alarm diagnostic check. I'll run the check, and while I'm in there, I'll make sure the codes haven't changed. Won't raise any suspicion this way. If I do it the day before you guys go in, they're going to figure out pretty quickly that I was involved."

"Smart thinking."

He slides the badge across the table. "Now, I'm not saying this is the best idea or that I'm thrilled you're doing it, but I know if you're even a fraction of your old man, you're going to do it anyways. Bobby never was good with people telling him no. So I figure if you're going to do it, I better make sure it's done right." He clears his throat. "I've been thinking I should meet with the other people. The crew people. The crew, is what I'm saying. I need to meet with the crew."

An unexpected twist. Millie wipes runny yolk off her chin and swallows her food. "Why's that?" she asks.

"Because I have no idea who they are, and I'm taking a lot of the risk. I'm the adult here, Millie. I'm not trying to make you feel like you're not up to the challenge, but if this goes sideways, I'm the one facing real jail time. If I could meet with them and see what they're like and maybe sit in on the rehearsal—"

She drops her sandwich onto the plate. "This is exactly why you shouldn't meet them. The less you know, the better. This is for your protection. The same reason why the crew doesn't know anything about you. So if something does go wrong and the cops question you, you won't have to play dumb."

"I'll just be dumb?" he says sarcastically.

"You know what I mean. Trust me, I'm doing you a favor."

Millie pulls her laptop from her backpack and opens her spreadsheet. Earlier in the day, she booked the rehearsal space in Chicago. It was the only place that took cash, as long as she paid in advance: $1,200 for the full day, nearly twice her budgeted amount.

Aaron finishes making his own sandwich and turns off the stove. "You know," he says, sitting next to her, "if this does go south, I'm not going to let you take the blame. I'll tell them it was all my idea."

"Not if I tell them first."

He laughs. "Wouldn't that be something? The two of us fighting over who goes to jail. Wasn't that in a movie once? Feels like it was. No?" She shrugs. "Well, if either of us would know, it'd be you. But I'm serious, Millie. I'm not letting you go to prison. Bobby would pull himself up out of his grave and kick the shit out of me."

Millie quickly recaps her ever-growing list of objectives. She has to honor her dad, get back the project that was wrongfully stolen from her, and now keep her dad's best friend from going to prison over something he feels forced to do; another brick added to the pile on her shoulders.

She needs to lighten up the mood. "Like he did junior year after he caught you flirting with his girlfriend at the homecoming bonfire?"

Another laugh, rueful this time. "Oh man. Courtney Crunstedt. He told you about that?"

"Dad said he caught you buying her a hot chocolate. You had a rose hidden in your sweatshirt, and you were going to try and convince her to dump him and go out with you."

Aaron's glowing red at this point. "I had this whole thing prepared about how nobody but me knew who she really was, that Bobby just loved her for her beauty, but I loved her for her soul. I was always falling in love with Bobby's girlfriends," he says sheepishly. "He was cool about Courtney. Gave me one in the gut for it but shared his six-pack at that Friday's game. He knew I couldn't help myself. It was the only time I got to be around beautiful women. Your mom included. Though, boy, she's never liked me."

Since he's right, she decides to stay quiet and goes back to the spreadsheet.

Her inbox chimes. There's a new message, a reply to her Craigslist ad for new or gently used laser tag gear. The guy's name is Lester, and he's able to sell her twenty laser tag guns and chest shields for $3,500. The best she could find for new equipment was $3,000 for eight. "I'm going to see if this guy can meet in a few hours. Want to come with and be my muscle?"

Aaron looks up, his sandwich halfway gone. "What are we buying? Better not be guns or drugs, Millie. There's only so much I can take."

"Relax. It's neither. Laser tag equipment."

Aaron narrows his eyes. He drops the sandwich. Smacks his fist into his palm.

He says, "Now we're talking."

27

The Collins Pub has been abandoned for years, the windows smashed, dick graffiti sprayed across the front door. Aaron parks the passenger van under a cone of light.

Soon, headlights flash across the windshield. A minivan stops ten feet away.

Millie's pulse increases. In heist movies, well over half of all gun buys go wrong. There's always a setup, or a double cross, or a Wild Card who doesn't want to pay and ends up shooting everybody. This might not be an actual gun buy, but the rules are the same. And after last night, she doesn't want to take any chances.

"Let him get out of the car first," she says.

Aaron's up on the edge of his seat, looking out the back window, then through the windshield. He reminds Millie of an anxious dog ready to attack. She almost expects him to growl.

The driver's side door opens, and out steps a narrow-faced man with thin oval glasses. He's probably in his late forties, early fifties, wearing a sweatshirt and earmuffs, his balding head uncovered and shining in the moonlight. He smiles and waves.

"I think we're going to be fine," she says and gets out of the van.

Aaron strides past her, puffing himself up, sticking out his chest, keeping his chin high. He reaches the man first and shakes his hand. "Lester, good to meet you. For security reasons, I'm going to need to frisk you. Hands on the car, please."

"What's that now?" Lester's accent is as Norwegian as lutefisk. His Dilworth Chess Club sweatshirt goes with the *My Child Is an Honor Roll Student* sticker on the minivan's front bumper.

Millie's ears burn with heat. Aaron can be so embarrassing.

"He's kidding," she says quickly and shoots Aaron a look that lets him know that she'll handle the talking from now on. "Thanks for doing this so late at night. You're really helping us out of a jam."

"Oh, no, not a problem. Been in a few sticky laser tag situations myself." He laughs and gives them both a smile. "My kids don't use this stuff too often, so I've been trying to sell it for a while now. I saw your ad and thought I should at least reach out and see if you'd be interested."

"Glad you did. Twenty units, huh? That's a lot."

"Six boys," he explains. "Lots of friends." He takes his wallet from his back pocket, a move that momentarily puts Aaron on high alert. Lester flips to a picture of himself with a short, overweight woman with a bob, and six broad-shouldered boys with blue eyes and blond hair.

"Your sons are very handsome," Millie says.

"Oh, thanks. Last one moved out this past fall. Empty nest now. It's hard for my wife, but I'm enjoying the break. Finally getting to my puzzles." He stows the wallet and heads toward the back of the van. "Suppose I should show you the goods. Let you try it on. Make sure it works and all."

The storage compartment is jammed with thin boxes around three feet long. Lester removes two boxes from the top and slides one open. Inside is a plastic gun, something straight out of *Star Trek*, and a chest shield with straps. Millie picks up the gun and flips a switch on the bottom of the stock; there's the sound of a power source booting up. Green lights glow along the barrel.

"Not sure how familiar you are with this particular brand," Lester says, "but these are much better than the average laser tag guns. This is the kind they use professionally, like when you pay a place to do it. They have a five-hundred-foot range, and vibrate and flash different colors when hit. But don't take my word for it. Try 'em out."

"We're pretty pressed for time," Millie says, but Aaron grabs the second box.

Within moments, he's got the shield across his chest, lights glowing from a circle in the middle like Iron Man. "A couple of minutes?"

Soon they're both racing across the lot, blasting off hip shots, ducking behind cars for protection. Aaron slips on some ice, and his gun slides away; Millie is on him instantly.

His shield igniting red, Aaron rolls over on his back and flails his limbs. He lifts his head, hair damp from the snow. "Awesome."

"Looks like these are gonna work out, then," Lester says.

"Yeah, maybe." The guns are great, exactly what she needs, but her budget could always use some negotiation. "Price is a little high. Any wiggle room?"

Lester puts his hands on his hips, looks up at the moon. "Gee, I don't know. Let me think. It's already a good deal, but I suppose I could knock off a hundred if that gets things moving."

"Make it two, and I'll pay you in cash right now."

"Cash?" Lester's face lights up like a Christmas tree. "Ah, heck. Why not? Otherwise, this stuff will just be sitting in my garage. If you want to pop open the back of your van there, I'll load you up."

28

Guided by the small light above the trailer's front door, they unload the boxes. Aaron brings them two at a time to where Millie stands in the doorway. On his third trip, he carries four.

She braces herself for the extra weight. "Careful, I'm not as strong as you."

"Don't worry. These ones aren't as heavy."

"What do you mean?"

"They must be a different model or something. Feel." She can hold all four with ease. They barely weigh anything.

"Oh shit." She drops the boxes. Some slide down the front steps onto the sidewalk. Aaron watches, not having caught on yet. Millie tears one open and looks inside.

It's empty.

Only three boxes hold guns and shields. Millie figures the third was in case Lester had to play in order to convince them the equipment was good. The rest are filled with used phone books or garbage or are just empty.

Millie hurls a phone book into a snowbank. "Goddammit! Are you kidding me? I'm trying to rob someone in three days, and I just got ripped off?"

"No wonder he insisted on loading them all," Aaron says. "Can you call him?"

"I don't have his number. Wasn't in the email, which I'm sure he's not using anymore."

Aaron lifts the flap on his bomber cap to scratch the side of his head. "We could go to the cops."

"And say what? Did you write down his license number? Because I didn't."

"No, but we saw that picture of his family. We could give their description to the police. How many families in Dilworth have six boys who look like that?"

Millie taps her foot, pinches her lips tight. This is exactly the reason why she's put him on an information diet. "None. That's the point. It was all bullshit. A story he was selling that we bought. There is no wife. There are no kids. He saw my ad and played me."

29

A fire crackles. The Hallmark Channel runs silently on the TV. Despite it being after ten, Wade and her mom are still awake, playing their continuous game of cribbage with no scorekeeping and no winner. Wade counts their runs while Mom twists Tiffany-blue ribbons onto an Easter wreath, one of fifty she's making for the church's fundraiser to send missionaries to Detroit.

Millie's arrival draws her mom's attention to the time. She stands to give her daughter a kiss, turns to give Wade one, too. He touches her wrist, whispers something in her ear, and she's all smiles.

Her parents might have separated before Dad was killed, but that didn't make his death any easier for Mom. She battled with depression, saw a shrink, took meds, tried church. God didn't help—at least not directly—but if you ask Deb Larsen, he's responsible for bringing Wade into her life. Millie couldn't care less how Wade got to them, just that he did, a man who wouldn't stop until he found the one thing nobody else could.

He found her mom's smile. Millie has to love him for that.

After her mother goes off to bed, Wade moves to his leather recliner and switches the channel to TCM; he knows it's Millie's go-to. She walks to the couch, *To Catch a Thief* barely registering.

She sits with her spine curled, head bowed, eyes gazing down at the carpet. Thankfully the fireplace is going strong, the heat coming out in waves. It'll help disguise why her face is so flushed, why her sweater collar is dark with sweat. Conned out of $3,300? How humiliating.

Is this the universe telling her to give up? Quit now, before things really get out of hand?

Without that cash, there's no way she can run the heist she planned, and it's too carefully crafted, too good, to abandon. Even with Aaron giving her back almost half of the $2,000 she fronted him—the rest he already used to pay bills—she's still a couple of grand short. Where can she make up the difference? The money she raised on her own is gone, Devin's father has cut him off financially, and the money from O'Naire is spoken for.

Wade's voice startles her. "You seen this one?"

"A couple of times." At least.

"I'm gonna fall asleep soon. How's it end?"

Millie sees how far in they are. "Okay, the French girl with the crush on Cary Grant is the thief. Nobody suspects her because of her age, though it's pretty obvious on second viewing."

"Reminds me of someone."

Millie doesn't catch on until she looks over and sees Wade staring at her. Her stomach drops. "Me?"

"Maybe. Suddenly talking about a friend we haven't heard about in forever. Said friend inspiring you to 'see what college is like.' Just happens to be the perfect story for someone like your mom. Even if she didn't believe it, she'd want it to be true, so she wouldn't question it."

"Sounds like you're questioning it, though."

"That I am, but I'm cheating a bit." He lets her worry before continuing. "You left your laptop open this morning on the kitchen table, and I saw your schedule. I know all about what you're up to."

First rule when confronted by someone accusing you of planning a heist: Play dumb and don't admit to anything. Wait to see what they know before confessing. Same first rule when dealing with a parent who's figured out you're supposed to be in trouble.

"And what do you think I'm up to?" Millie asks playfully, keeping her eyes on the TV. It's important to not panic until there's a reason.

"A short film, obviously," Wade says. "Why else would you need a van and all those extras? And I'm assuming you're shooting this week, which is why you told us you'll be in Minneapolis."

Millie exhales, the tension in her shoulders releasing. "You got me. Only it's not a short film. It's been tough raising money for the feature, so I was going to make a fake trailer to show investors. Only it turns out I don't even have enough money to do that, so the whole thing's off. Just found out before I got home." She rolls on her side to offer her full attention. "Sorry I lied."

"Are you even working with West Fargo State? Or was that a lie, too?"

And the tension's back, now creeping down her spine. "I am. The head of the department said I could use the trailer we're making in place of an admission essay." She has to stick with the lie. She's in too deep to tell only half the truth. "He said with my experience, if I can show them that I know how to work a production, they'll look at taking some of my workshop hours from New York and putting them toward college credits. So I could skip the entry-level courses."

"That's amazing," Wade says, impressed.

Guilt slaps her in the face. "Well, doesn't matter now. Like I said, I don't have enough money to shoot the trailer the way it needs to be done, and I'm not going to half-ass it. Wouldn't be worth it."

Wade rocks forward, locking the footrest back into position. He turns and rifles through a stack of papers on the end table. Once he's found what he's looking for, he sits next to her feet on the couch.

He's holding one of her investor brochures. "Your mom might come off like she doesn't understand you, but she does. She feels bad you got taken advantage of, like your dad did."

She does? News to Millie. How come her mom's never said that?

Millie straightens up on the couch and puts her feet on the floor. "That was way different."

"Hmm, maybe," Wade says. "But to her it feels the same, and she blames herself for not doing a better job of protecting you."

"Really?"

He shakes his head like he can't believe she had to ask. "Of course. She's a parent; it can't be helped. But she's proud of you. I'm proud of you. It takes guts to go after your dreams. This world is full of people who coulda and woulda but never did, you know?" He pauses. "I include myself in that category."

The confession surprises her. "What did you want to do?"

"It's been a long time since I've thought about it. I don't really know anymore. But it was more than hanging drywall, not that I'm knocking it. The pay is steady. I get to meet interesting people, check out their homes. And it provides for me, my wife, and my stepdaughter . . . who I love very much." He looks down at the investor's packet. "Is this one of them rough movies? Like, really violent and all?"

"Not at first, but it gets there," she admits.

Wade looks into the fire, now burning down to embers. "Be careful, then. The news was saying there's been some home robberies around Valley City. Really violent people. That's only an hour from here. Minneapolis has a much higher crime rate. You don't want to be filming and have the cops think you're doing something illegal."

Millie's read about these break-ins, how they don't care if the house is empty or not. If the people are home, the robbers tie them up and sometimes even kill them. She suppresses a shudder. "I'll be careful," she reassures him.

From under the brochure, Wade pulls out his checkbook. "How much are you short to buy this here trailer?" he says, clicking his pen. "Is it for one of your stars to sit in?"

Millie chuckles. "No, a trailer is what they call a preview—what comes before the main feature—because when silent movies first came out, they were shown at the very end. You don't need to do this, though," she says. "Honestly, you've already helped me out so much."

"I know I don't, but 'need' and 'want' are two different things. Now either give me a number, or I'm going to make one up."

She settles on $2,500. It's the smallest amount that'll get new laser tag equipment and the largest her conscience will allow her to accept.

He hands her the check. "Do I get my name in the credits now?"

"Absolutely. Executive producer."

"That a good one?"

"It's the best," she says and hugs him as tight as she can.

30

The sky is still dark. Flecks of pink tiptoe along the horizon. Paz, Devin, and Jordan watch out the motel lobby window like kids waiting for a parent to pick them up from day care. As soon as Millie rolls up, they're in motion.

Paz takes shotgun. The guys take the middle bucket seats. Millie hands them each a gas station coffee, sets a box of donuts in the middle console.

Breakfast goes unnoticed. None of them talk. They're tense, on edge, squirmy in their seats. Paz's eyebrows are furrowed. Jordan looks out the window as if he thinks they're being watched. Devin appears to be holding his breath.

"It's like a ten-hour car ride," Millie tells them. "You guys can relax a little."

Nobody does.

31

Of all the things Aaron is supposed to remember between now and when they're going to steal the movie, the most important is not to change his routine. *Don't do anything out of the ordinary, anything that'll draw attention.* Millie's been extremely insistent about that. Stressed it multiple times yesterday morning before she left for Chicago. Was almost borderline rude about it. So getting a flat tire and showing up thirty-seven minutes late to work the day before Millie and her crew plan to break into the Oakwood Arms Building is literally worst-case scenario.

Aaron runs across the parking lot, kicking up slush, dampening and staining the bottoms of his work khakis. When he gets closer to the building, he sees Gabrielle. She's arguing loudly with the driver of a black Escalade with a cracked windshield and broken headlights, the exposed shards of plastic sticking down like vampire fangs.

Gabrielle's words are accompanied by accusatory finger-pointing and eyebrows drawn together in a frown. Clearly, she doesn't notice or care if anyone hears her call the driver a "redneck piece of shit."

Aaron wonders who deserves this title, and sneaks a look. The driver is a scrawny dude with some kind of bird tattoo covering his full neck. He rocks a mullet and a questionable goatee. This is the kind of guy Gabrielle goes for?

Neck Tattoo sees Aaron watching and gives him the finger. It takes him by surprise; he runs into the curb, stumbling but thankfully not falling down.

"What the hell is wrong with you?" Gabrielle yells at the driver.

Aaron doesn't hear the answer, because as soon as he opens the building door, he trips the alarm.

32

CHICAGO

The tourists start early in this city. It's barely nine a.m. They line up for boat rides down the river, clutching shopping bags from Michigan Avenue. All of them require multiple selfies with the river, the bridges, the skyscrapers. *Isn't that the building from that Wilco album down there? What's a Wilco? Does it matter?* Click.

Devin watches it all from hard concrete steps designed to resemble bleachers facing the river. An untouched old-fashioned donut in its bakery wrapping sits next to him. His coffee grows cold. The cigarette between his fingers slowly burns down to the filter. He doesn't even smoke, just wanted something to keep his hands busy. He had to bum one from an annoyed university student who only wanted to smoke and listen to her podcast in peace. He seems to be getting on everyone's nerves this morning.

It's clear now why Millie asked him to leave rehearsals. "Get some air," she said. "Clear your head." A much politer way of saying *piss off.*

He doesn't blame anyone. He knows he's been stressing everyone out with too many questions, his insecurities getting the best of him.

He never meant for Millie to think he didn't trust her or the plan; it's his acting ability he's unsure about. However, if she's confident he can handle the role of Kirby, then he needs to trust that she knows what she's doing. Giving him line readings was a bit insulting, though.

Across the river, on the city street, a limousine pulls up to the Oakwood Arms. Devin climbs the stairs to get a better view.

Ricky O'Naire, in the flesh for the first time since Devin saw him dragged out in handcuffs from the Academy's theater, emerges from the back of the limo.

Even from this distance, he looks whipped, thick five-o'clock shadow and aviators covering most of his face. Devin checks the time. Millie already knows when O'Naire arrives, but he'll report back to her anyway; show that he's willing to follow her lead.

He heads for the train station, going over the plan in his head. In a few hours, they'll be back down here in full costume and makeup. He should make sure to avoid O'Naire spotting him. They've never met, but he is tied to the movie the guy stole, after all.

He stops in the middle of the sidewalk. Somebody bumps into him, grumbles under their breath. Avoid O'Naire spotting him? But why is the guy even—

The cigarette burns past the filter, scorching his fingertips.

33

Over two dozen extras snarl and drag their feet, arms out in front of them, spit running down their chins. It's a full representation of every struggling, desperate actor in Chicago's creative scene, young and old, anyone who has nothing preventing them from responding to a day's notice to play a zombie for fifty bucks. There are improv students from Second City, as well as extras and understudies from the theater district. Out-of-work actors not ready to commit to waiting tables, and those who do but have the day off. They all lurch from side to side, inching across the rehearsal room Millie rented for the day.

"That's it, everybody, but more menacing," she calls out. She's in full zombie makeup herself to hide her identity, her face a ghastly gray green, an infected cut across her neck. "Strain your faces and roll your eyes into the back of your heads."

A blond with an upturned nose wearing a Harold Ramis Film School T-shirt stumbles into the two people next to her, causing a pileup. "When you roll your eyes, remember to watch where you're going," Millie reminds them as politely as she can. The level of talent isn't great, but she can't help but be a little stoked. At least people showed up.

They run through it again, and then she has them finish up their costumes. "Stop by the makeup station first, then fluids." The actors are responsible for putting on a green-and-gray base before Paz applies the details: scabs, welts, blisters, decay, wounds, and bruises. When she's done, they move along to Jordan, who drenches them in either fake blood, green slime, or a combination of both. The two of them are in full zombie makeup as well.

Devin, his face hidden by a ski mask, startles some of the extras when he races into the room. He signals to Paz and Jordan to go outside and tells Millie, "We need to talk."

"Now?" she protests. "We're in the middle of everything."

Devin's already halfway out the door. "It can't wait."

This part of the city is mostly deserted, away from the skyscrapers, tourists, locals who work downtown. The wide streets are cluttered with trash, the sidewalks cracked and uneven; there are few shops or restaurants. It's not where you want to be after midnight, but during the day, it's fine.

The four huddle outside the building's entrance.

Devin yanks off his ski mask. "We've got a problem. It's O'Naire. I saw him getting dropped off outside his building."

"What were you doing?" Millie berates him. Can he really be that stupid? "What if someone saw you?"

"Remind me again about the part of the plan where we trick the

Mark into leaving his own production offices so we can steal from him. Because, you know, I'm drawing a complete blank."

Jordan and Paz exchange a look, their faces question marks.

Millie's mouth has gone dry. A void opens in her stomach.

"You forgot," Paz says.

She might've.

"Shit," Millie says.

"Well, did you?"

"Fuck!"

"You *forgot* that we need O'Naire out of the building?"

She did.

"I thought he'd be on a press junket in LA or something by now," Millie admits. "Dammit. I meant to check. It was on my to-do list."

"We should call it," Jordan says. "Just walk away. O'Naire might have a lot going on right now, but he's going to remember that he didn't order an apocalyptic zombie team-building simulation. He'll shut it down right away. Our arrest will be longer than the heist. Millie," he says, turning to her, "you've done the research. I've seen your spreadsheet. What is it, like only sixty percent of all heists work?"

"Fifty-nine, but that's because in the forties and fifties British films had a code of ethics that required all movie heists fail."

"Probably to keep idiots from leaving the cinema and thinking they could pull off a heist as well," Devin mutters.

What is she supposed to do?

There's a roomful of zombies prepping for a full-on apocalypse, not to mention a rapidly shrinking window of opportunity. Aaron was very clear about the schedule: the employee whose badge he lifted works Friday–Tuesday, making this the last possible time they can get in before Sunday's premiere. And even if they could get another badge, Schumer's deadline for the film is tomorrow anyway.

It's now or never.

It burns behind the back of her eyes, but she won't let herself cry like she did in front of Aaron. They can't see her break.

The front door opens. The girl in the Harold Ramis Film School

T-shirt sticks her head out and says, "Hey, people are starting to wonder what to do next. Most of us are ready for the fluid station."

"Gross. Why do you call it that?" Devin asks no one in particular.

Millie inhales deeply, puts her shoulders back. "We'll be right there. If you can let everyone know, that'd be great."

"Sure," the girl says, then pulls a pack of cigarettes from her shirt pocket.

She's about to light up when Jordan says, "Can you go tell everyone first?"

Once the girl is gone, Paz rolls her eyes. "Actors."

Millie takes stock. Yes, giving up is the logical move, but she knows exactly what that will lead to. She'll be back in her mom's basement, working at Howard Security, her only creative outlet spotting interesting angles of the monster-truck pulpit during Pastor Rod's sermons.

And O'Naire will be flying high, his career back on track because he stole her work, because he stole her father's story.

"If we know anything about O'Naire, it's that he's desperate for this movie to be a hit," Millie says. "I think I've got a way to use that desperation against him."

PART THREE

A RELUCTANT FEMME FATALE

1

CHICAGO

A knife punches into Flowers Romero's sternum, the blade against bone cringingly loud. Flowers clutches his chest, thick blood oozing between his fingers onto his white tuxedo. There's a second stab to his neck; arterial red sprays out into the moonlight.

He sinks to his knees, fumbles for the gun in his belt, but doesn't make it in time. His eyes roll back as the third strike finishes the job.

Ricky O'Naire runs his tongue across his teeth. His eyes twinkle. It might be Eric's imagination, but the unbelievable has happened: the man appears to be happy.

O'Naire's cell rings. Eric pauses the timeline, Flowers Romero's bleeding corpse frozen on screen.

"Do you need to get that?" He's aware of the hope in his voice. Except for a couple of power naps in the corner of the editing suite, he's been at this for the last twenty-eight hours. Eric's armpits are sodden with sweat. His wrist is sore, and his eyes burn; maybe from staring at the screen, or perhaps it's the lingering stench of body odor, old pizza, peanut butter cups, and burnt coffee. If he doesn't get out of this room soon, he's going to have a nervous breakdown.

O'Naire barely glances at his phone. "Just my manager. I'll call him back. Let's pull up the crash scene next. I need the cuts to be quicker. Let's not go Michael Bay on the audience where they can't tell what's going on, but this isn't a play in real time. It's a movie. Speed it up."

Eric saves the Romero death scene and brings up the timeline with the car crash. O'Naire's phone rings again, and again he ignores it. "Go back to the different takes of Romero waking up after the car rolls down the hill."

They're going through takes again?

O'Naire's phone double-chimes with a text. "Goddammit," the director snarls, "I told him not to bother me." He checks his messages and makes a call. "They do this to me every time," he mutters.

Eric silently barters with the universe: thirty minutes away from O'Naire, and he'll talk to his mother more than once every six months. He'll even stop hanging up when she suggests conversion therapy.

". . . I can make it work. It's the *Hollywood Daily*. What choice do I have? We need all the publicity we can get." After a moment, O'Naire ends the call, stuffs his phone in his pocket. "I have to do an interview across town. I should only be gone for a few hours. Work on the crash scene and have it ready by the time I get back."

There's no goodbye, just a grunt of exasperation and a slam of the door. That's fine by Eric. Except now he has to talk to his mother.

He saves the project and stretches, cracking his back. Out of curiosity, he goes over to the filing cabinet. O'Naire's drawer is still locked. He hasn't opened it or even mentioned it since the day he told Eric to stay out. What's he hiding in there?

The office is quiet, typical for this time of day. Two writers with matching looks of button-ups, jeans, and dark stubble pitch to a group of suits in one of the conference rooms; the admin staff, all of them in their twenties and wearing the same bored, disillusioned expression, answer the phones, send emails—the mundane repetitive tasks they're forced to do.

None of them even acknowledge the man in the vestibule. Wearing khakis and a long-sleeved brown shirt, he holds a clipboard and a rather large box that needs to be signed for. That's supposed to be handled by security in the lobby; they must have changed the protocol. O'Naire would be pissed if he found out they were letting just anybody onto the floor.

In the break room, a couple of women from HR throw him half-hearted waves. Seeing them always makes him smile; in their knee-high boots and on-trend Kona capes, they look like Jedi from *Star Wars*.

He fixes himself a bagel with cream cheese, tops it off with a slice of salami, and bids farewell to the Jedi Council. The delivery guy is still waiting in the vestibule. Eric looks to the admins. Is nobody going to handle this?

Finally, he asks: "Who you here to see?"

The delivery guy doesn't say anything. His eyes dart around the room, his mouth clamped shut. He inhales deeply.

This doesn't look good. "You okay?"

The delivery guy shakes his head no. His cheeks bulge. The package and clipboard clatter to the floor. He bends forward, clutching his stomach. A yellow-brown liquid spews from his mouth and splashes on the carpet. He looks helplessly, desperately at Eric. "I thought it was safe," he gasps. "The vaccination was supposed to protect us."

"What's going on?" asks one of the admins. Of course, *now* they're taking an interest. "Should we call security?"

"Security can't help you," manages the delivery guy. "They'll be here any minute."

"Who will?" Eric asks.

"Everyone." The guy's legs give out, and he collapses to the floor.

The light above the elevator goes from red to green, indicating someone has used a security code. The elevator doors open. A man in a military uniform and a woman in a white lab coat and thick glasses rush out.

The man speaks first. "Everyone, remain calm. My name is Captain Rhodes, and I'm part of the army's Undead Safety Initiative." He's tall and dark skinned, younger than most of the admins, way too young to be a captain. Attractive, though, with nice eyes and defined arms. The mustache isn't Eric's thing, but he can see how people would go for it, even if it might be fake. "I regret to inform you that you've all been exposed to Level Two Inferi Virus, also known as the Zombie Plague."

As if on cue, which it probably is, the woman steps forward. "But there's no reason to panic. My name is Dr. Sarah Bowman. My team is on the way with enough vaccine to cure you all." She's also far too young for the part she's playing.

"Vaccine?" Eric says. At this point, he figures he should help move the story along for those who haven't caught on. "This guy said he was vaccinated, and look what happened to him." He points to the delivery guy, who's still on the floor watching everyone when he's supposed to be pretending to be on the verge of zombification.

"He was given an older version of the vaccine," Dr. Bowman says. "We've since discovered that it's missing one key ingredient."

"And what's that?" asks one of the assistants, clearly excited.

Captain Rhodes and Dr. Bowman exchange looks, their concerned expressions transforming into grins.

"Alcohol!" they yell in unison.

They remove oversized syringes filled with blue, red, or neon-green liquid from an aluminum test-tube case Dr. Bowman carries; flavored vodka, if Eric had to guess. "Don't worry. We have Shirley Temples if you don't drink," she says.

Captain Rhodes pulls out a note card and clears his throat while Dr. Bowman distributes the vaccines. "On behalf of Ricky O'Naire, congratulations on all of your hard work against the clock on *The Art of the Gangster*. We're with Today's Adventure, a company that helps you explore the very best of your team. I'm sure most of you have seen us around the neighborhood from time to time."

Everyone has come into the main space. A few people nod and smile. Others are already tipping back their vaccines.

"Wonderful," Rhodes says. "For those who don't know, we utilize costumes and special effects to create team-building exercises. Mr. O'Naire chose the Zombie Apocalypse scenario for you."

His voice becomes deep and dramatic, as if he's narrating a trailer. "All is lost as the streets of Chicago are overtaken by a terrible plague that has turned its citizens into creatures of the living dead."

Encouraging oohs and aahs circulate around the employees, but one of the admins takes it too far and screams, "Fuck yeah!" after getting a double shot of vaccine. This earns a stern look from her boss, and Eric feels a reprimand will be the focus of her next one-on-one.

Rhodes continues, "Trapped on the twenty-seventh floor of a city skyscraper, the employees of Hitting the Mark Productions must defend themselves against a horde of zombies hell bent on taking their lives." He looks around the small crowd. "To survive, you'll need to have strong leadership, effective communication, and teamwork to avoid forever walking the earth . . . between light and shadow."

"Like me," the delivery guy says, indicating his puke-covered face.

"And afterward," Dr. Bowman adds, "we'll have cake."

The elevator chimes; the doors open. Six people in full army fatigues run out. The first two steer carts loaded with long, skinny boxes. The others carry trays of vaccines.

The delivery guy rushes to catch the elevator down.

"Suit up for battle," says a woman in fatigues. She hands Eric a box. "You can kill a zombie by either shooting one of their sensors or pressing your hands against their chest guard."

Eric inspects the box. Laser tag equipment? They're going to have a laser tag zombie battle, get drunk, and then eat cake? If he didn't know O'Naire better, he'd say this was a nice gesture from a kind director, but there's no way in hell the guy did this. It must have been the producers' idea or arranged by the studio distributing the film; something to make up for O'Naire's punishing schedule.

He sets down the laser tag equipment and picks up his second breakfast. As far as Eric's concerned, it's too little too late. Not to mention the work he still has to do. Juggling his plate and coffee mug, Eric presses his thumb against the scanner on the editing suite door.

The office goes dark.

Thin blades of light cut through the blackout shades. From the four corners of the room, black light cannons mounted on C-stands shoot rays of UV light. Smoke machines cloud the air. The Hitting the Mark employees all yell in shared excitement. Chest guards and laser guns glow in various colors of neon.

Eric changes his mind about going back to work. He closes the editing suite door, leans against it, and takes a bite of his bagel. Wouldn't hurt to watch a little. Maybe that film student he talked to last week is part of the zombie crew. What was her name again?

"Look alive, people," Captain Rhodes yells out. "It's go time."

The light above the elevator goes green. The doors open. People scream. The infected run out.

2

Eric has to hand it to whoever is in charge of the zombies' makeup.

Their decayed skin texture is perfection; the rotten teeth so real it's hard to tell if they're wearing partial dentures or not. Parts of their cheeks hang down like mud flaps. Some have burn scars, or nails driven into their necks and arms; others have open wounds oozing pus. Their clothes, which range from professional attire to hospital gowns, are torn and covered in blood, puke, and some type of green slime. Some of the undead hold their guts in their hands, and Eric can even spot bone coming out of someone's clavicle. Excellent production value.

Helicopters and police sirens shriek from speakers around the office. His colleagues follow the orders of Captain Rhodes, ducking behind desks, hiding in doorways. When they fire their laser guns, a hit lights up the zombies' chest guards, sending them flailing about and falling to the ground.

The suits take refuge in the conference room, flipping the table on its side as a shield.

A hunched-over zombie shuffles up to Eric. He bares his teeth and makes his hands into claws. Eric takes a bite of his bagel and washes it down with coffee.

The zombie stands up straight and looks around. "Did you not get a gun, mate? Apologies. Let me find one for you. I think Larry knows where they are."

Eric almost chokes; you do not expect zombies to have British accents. "Larry?"

"Uh, yeah. The bloke in the military uniform. Can't recall his character's name at the moment."

"I think it's Rhodes," Eric says.

"Rhodes. Right. I should know that."

The zombie puts out his hand. When they shake, slime oozes between Eric's fingers. "Sorry," says the undead Brit. "Embalming fluid. I turned at the very last minute. I'm Kirby, by the way. I'm a day player. Hired this morning." Kirby eyes the floor. "Not that I should be explaining that to you, or that it makes up for how terrible I am. Shit. I'm totally ruining this for you, aren't I?"

"You're fine," Eric says. "I don't have a gun because I'm not playing. I'm not really into the whole zombie thing."

Kirby looks genuinely confused. "You're not?"

"I had an ex who was obsessed with this crap. He'd drag me to zombie pub crawls and endless zombie movie screenings. I got so sick of it. It's unbelievable how many there are."

"It's like the genre just won't die." Kirby shakes his head. "Sorry, bad joke." It's hard to tell through the layers of rotten flesh, but it looks like he's blushing.

"I love bad jokes," Eric says. "They're the only ones I tell." God. Is he actually flirting with this zombie? It's pretty sad, but it's the longest conversation he's had with a guy since he's been working in Chicago.

"Well, you're not going to sit by and watch everyone else have all the fun, now are you?" Kirby says. "What's the harm if you play for a bit?"

Eric pops the last bit of bagel into his mouth and swallows quickly. "I was going to finish some work before my boss got back," he says, indicating the editing suite, "but it can probably wait."

He's surprised when Kirby suddenly goes serious. "Don't let me keep you. Work is important. That's the real reason we're all here, isn't it? Hell, look at me. I'm at work right now. Let me tell Rhodes what's going on. I think he has to sign off on employees who aren't playing, or something. That doctor might have a form as well."

"No need. You're too good a salesman, Kirby," he says, this time surprising himself. If the studio wants to thank them for all their hard work, then why the hell shouldn't he participate? He's felt the brunt of O'Naire's wrath more than anybody. And Kirby is really cute, in a recently turned sort of way. "Work can wait. I'm all in."

Kirby smiles. His teeth are stark white against his moldy flesh. "Great."

Eric straps on a chest guard and charges up his gun.

When he's ready, Kirby closes his eyes and says, "I'll give you a ten-second head start. One. Two. Three . . ."

So cute.

3

Eric and Kirby trade off deaths, racing down aisles, leaping behind desks, laughing like flirty teenagers whenever one kills the other. Other zombies and staff join them, but Eric has the most fun when it's only the two of them.

When Eric pulls ahead, five deaths to Kirby's three, he stops trying so hard and lets Kirby kill him in the corner of one of the conference rooms. As Kirby stands above him, hand on Eric's chest, his soft demonic eyes and decomposing lips inches away, it takes every ounce of strength for Eric not to reach up and kiss him, but then—

"Gyro and iced tea!" exclaims Jake. "I didn't know you worked here."

He's smeared in blood, and there's an open gash across his chest, but there's no way any amount of makeup could ever hide those angular cheekbones.

"What are you doing here?" Eric says, then quickly corrects his accusatory tone. "I mean, I didn't know you were an actor."

Jake says, "I'm not, bro. Some chick came up to me yesterday at work and offered me the gig. Said I'd make a great zombie. Paid me five hundred bones, and since I'm off today anyways, I figured why not. What do you think?" Jake flexes. It's like the zombie version of Michelangelo's *David*.

"Not bad," Eric says.

"For fuck's sake," mutters Kirby. He rubs the bottom of his chin and stares at the floor.

Jake lifts his gun over his head. "Let's get back out there. I'm kicking so much ass. I've only gotten killed twice, and that's because some dude cheated and shot me while I was taking a piss and the other time . . ." He looks away. "Mistakes were made that won't happen again."

Racing out of the conference room, Jake smacks two employees in the chest for a double-kill combination. Eric picks up his gun and starts to follow, not realizing until he's at the door that Kirby hasn't moved.

"You coming?" he asks.

Kirby scratches the back of his head. "I thought maybe we could take a break. Not used to all this running around. Don't have the lung capacity. Is there a place we can sit and catch our breath for a sec?"

"I don't think so. They're using the whole floor."

"What about that room you were going into?" Kirby points at the editing suite. "Is that your office?"

"I can't let you in there. Only a few people have clearance," Eric says. "I'm going to continue playing. I guess you can hang out here until you get your bearings or whatever. It was nice meeting you."

He's almost out the door when a set of sticky green fingers takes hold of his wrist.

"Wait a minute," Kirby says. "We've had some laughs today, yeah?"

"Sure," agrees Eric. An explosion blasts through the speakers.

"Thought we could keep this going. Go in that secret room of yours and have some fun."

"Not possible. My boss would kill me if I let you in there."

Kirby holds his breath, his eyes filled with uncertainty. Poor guy is working up his courage. "Some things are worth dying for." He moves in for the kiss, his lips wet and rubbery.

Eric lets it go a moment longer than he should, then raises his rifle and pulls the trigger. Kirby's chest guard blinks in rhythmic red neon.

"We'll always have the apocalypse," Eric says.

Kirby's head drops. "Cheers."

4

The main floor is pure madness—papers flying everywhere, fake slime and blood all over the place. Eric runs into the break room, where Jake is attacking the HR ladies, the HR ladies using upturned tables and chairs as some type of fort, Jake shooting at them from behind the fridge.

Eric takes a few shots at Jake, nearly killing him before he notices. With zombie superspeed, Jake rolls across the kitchenette, springs up in front of Eric, and pushes so hard against the chest guard for the kill that Eric falls, hitting the back of his head against the cupboards.

"Give me a challenge!" Jake barks.

With a thumping head and bruised ego, Eric finally admits that Jake isn't interested in him romantically. It also dawns on him that competitive circumstances make the guy kind of a dick. He walks slowly through the chaos, leaving himself open to attacks from three different zombies. Who cares? *Sixteen Candles* is bullshit. In reality, every Jake Ryan is an asshole.

Maybe it isn't too late to find Kirby, apologize, invite him to dinner? He scans the room and spots him.

It takes a second to comprehend what's happening.

"What the fuck are you doing?" Eric yells.

Kirby freezes, his bloodred eyes wide, his hands clenching a crowbar wedged between the door and frame of the editing suite. He bangs his fist on the crowbar, one, two, three times before the frame cracks and the alarm starts wailing.

O'Naire is right. People *are* trying to steal his movie.

"Somebody call security!" Eric's shout is muffled by the sirens and sounds of the game, everyone oblivious to the robbery taking place.

The doorframe is cracked, but the door stays closed. Kirby goes at its hinges with the crowbar. The skinny zombie is midswing when Eric tackles him to the floor.

The UV lights turn off.

The office is completely black.

The overhead lights blaze on.

"What's ha-happening?" the office manager slurs, overvaccinated. "What's going on?"

"He's trying to steal the movie." Somebody still hasn't turned off the background noise. "Call security!"

Captain Rhodes is at his elbow. "Dude? We were told not to break anything. That door looks expensive as shit."

"The door," Eric snaps, "is the least of your problems." Kirby squirms, but it's no use. Eric has him in a death grip, a little surprised by his own strength.

Three security guards arrive. Two of them haul Kirby into the conference room. Eric inspects the door; a minute or two more and he would've had it. He presses his thumb against the finger scanner, whispers "swordfish" into the intercom. The sensor on the door clicks to green, and Eric turns the handle.

To his relief, the room is untouched, same as he left it before going to get coffee.

"We're going to move everybody to the fifth floor until the police arrive," the third guard says, close to Eric's ear. Her name tag reads *Laura*; she has pink-streaked blond hair, dark eyeshadow, and a pair of narrow glasses perched on her upturned nose. "There's no tenant at the moment. I've talked with Mr. O'Naire, and he's on his way. My supervisor is waiting for him and the police in the lobby. Are you Mr. Schumer?"

"That's right."

"Can you verify everything is still intact in here?"

"Best I can tell. You better hope so, or Ricky O'Naire is going to own this building by the end of the day. He's not someone who puts up with incompetence."

"I understand. We're doing the best we can, sir." She raises her voice. "Now, everyone, let's please start moving toward the elevators."

"I should stay here," Eric says. "I can give my statement to the police when they arrive."

Laura puts her hand on his back, trying to guide him away. "We'll be taking your statement, sir, but I'll need you to go with the others for now. This is a crime scene, and I need to clear it."

"But I can—"

"I'm sure you can, but I have protocols to follow. I'm keeping my two best people up here to watch everything until the police arrive. Now, let's go."

The employees line up for the elevators. Eric catches the last one down, wedged toward the front. He spots Jake toward the back, who smiles when their eyes meet.

"Fucking nuts," Jake says.

5

The fifth floor, a series of halls and small offices overlooking the river, was previously rented to a law firm whose logo still graces the reception desk. Probably easier to rip people off while they're distracted by the view, Eric cynically thinks. The Today's Adventure employees are taken to the north side, everyone else to the south.

Eric doubts all of the zombies were in on the job; there were too many to keep all those stories straight. It takes a real professional to orchestrate a full-blown scam like this. It reminds him of *The Sting*. Or maybe it's more like *Matchstick Men*? If he had to guess, probably one or two members of Today's Adventure were the ringleaders, the rest paid actors for a day gig.

Jake follows him into a corner office. "Bro, honestly, I would've thought you had special-ops training or some shit, the way you handled yourself. I mean, you took that motherfucker *down*. Balls out."

"Balls out," Eric replies, fist-bumping his zombified former crush. If he actually had any special-ops training, he'd use it to shut Jake up.

Laura sticks her head in the office. "Just got word that the police are in the lobby. I'm going to get them up to speed and bring them to the crime scene. Mr. Schumer?"

"Yes?"

"I'll need you to come speak with them in a moment. Give your side of the story."

Eric paces the room after Laura leaves. Jake rambles on about the tackle before growing bored. He looks out the window, forehead pressed against the glass. "This is what God sees," he proclaims.

"The Imperial March" from *Star Wars* plays—O'Naire's ringtone. He's probably with the cops and wants him to come up. "Hi, look, I want to start by saying that I'm so sorry for what happened," Eric says, "and assure you that they didn't get anything. I stopped him. I tackled the bastard. Are you there now? Should I come up?"

"What are you talking about?" O'Naire says. "Is this why I got a notification for the door alarm? It only came in once, so I thought you were being an idiot and forgot your code."

"No, not this time. It was a real break-in. It happened during the zombie team-building scenario that you—"

"The zombie *what*?"

"Maybe they didn't tell you what the theme was when you ordered. They said it was to reward the staff for all our hard work."

"Reward you? If anything, I should've fired all of you for your incompetence. Why didn't you call me?"

Eric's stomach begins to bottom out. "One of the security guards for the building said they contacted you. She said you were on your way."

"Nobody called me, dipshit. The only reason I'm calling now is to see if you have any messages for me. I'm in some building where I was told I'd be interviewed, only nobody's here. It's just some empty rehearsal space." Eric knows what the next question is going to be and doesn't want to be the one to give the answer. "Who's with the footage now?"

"Building security."

"The same building security that never called me?"

Eric clenches his fist. "*Fuck!*"

"About time," Jake remarks, turning from the window to look at Eric. "Been waiting forever for someone to realize the game's not over."

Eric's throat constricts. "The game's . . . not over?" he manages.

"*What fucking game?*" O'Naire yells down the line.

"Nah, bro," says Jake. "This is part of it. All of security are actors too. I got to admit, I'm not the smartest dude, but I don't really get the goal of thi—"

"Shut up," Eric snaps. Then, into the phone: "Not you. I'll call you back," he says before ending the call.

The security guards are actors. That means all of this is fake. A distraction. Kirby was meant to get caught so they could remove all of the employees and leave the floor unattended.

The blood drains from Eric's face. He grips the back of a chair to stay upright.

Did he shut the door?

6

Eric sprints out of the room and down the hall to reception, where Captain Rhodes and Dr. Bowman share a small bench, chatting with Laura and the other security guards. They're all drinking Starbucks. Captain Rhodes reattaches his mustache with some stage adhesive. Eric smashes the elevator's up button.

"Hey, all right," Dr. Bowman says. "I thought it might be you who'd figure it out. Get on up there and claim your victory."

The elevator arrives. Eric hits twenty-seven. As it ascends, he retches twice but manages not to vomit.

The production office remains a chaotic mess, but all of the equipment—C-stands, laser tag guns and chest guards, speakers, UV lights—is now gone. The edges of the editing suite door are splintered from Kirby's crowbar, but there's no new damage.

The door remains closed.

Eric remembers how to breathe. Air in. Air out. He tries the handle and cries out with happiness when it won't budge. He laughs, a little at first, but soon he's holding his ribs. He doesn't even want to imagine what would've happened if his fears had come true. Public humiliation, some type of lawsuit; that is, if O'Naire didn't kill him outright.

He presses his thumb against the sensor, whispers the password. He enters the editing suite, his stomach twisting so hard that he almost crumples to his knees.

Turns out he didn't remember to close the door, but whoever was here last sure did. The only things left are his chair and empty desk, bearing only crumbs and coffee rings.

The server tower, filing cabinet, dual monitors, and computer are gone.

PART FOUR

NO CLEAN GETAWAYS

1

FARGO, NORTH DAKOTA

Aaron bought enough bingo cards at the VFW to play up to six games at once but abandoned the idea after only a few rounds. He's too distracted to concentrate, eyes constantly shifting to his phone.

It's been over three hours since the robbery, and he still hasn't heard from Millie or anyone at Howard Security. Howard would call only if they determined that he'd been involved . . . if they'd even call first. He half expects SWAT to roll out any minute.

A bored caller cranks the cage. G-47 lights up on the wall screen. The VFW is half-full, mostly elderly women in wind suits, each with at least ten daubers. The rest are stoned college kids and a few single middle-aged men who, from the amount of cologne in the air, must think bingo night is a good place to pick up women.

His phone rattles against the table. He reaches for it, knocking over his beer.

"Shit, sorry," he tells the others, who give him dirty looks, more likely from his swearing than from his spilling the beer. It's a restricted number. "Hello?"

"Grandma loved her cardigan," a raspy-voiced woman tells him. The line goes dead.

Beer drips over the edge of the table, into his lap, but he doesn't feel it. "Grandma loved her cardigan!" he yells. Heads turn; hearing aids are adjusted. "Whoo!"

"That's lovely, dear," says an old woman at his table, then turns to her friend. "What a nice young man."

"Kind of a dweeb," the friend says.

2

ROSEMONT, ILLINOIS

Millie hangs up the pay phone in the back of the neighborhood bowling alley, which, with only six lanes, has more customers drinking at the bar than making spares. She rests her head against the wall and closes her eyes. She'd cry tears of happiness if she weren't so damn tired.

Now that this part of the job is over, she can finally admit to herself, in no uncertain terms, how it should have failed.

Paz was right. Nothing about their time at the Academy indicated they had the ability to pull this off. Smart money would've been to bet against them, so what was different between then and now? Was it that there was no backup plan?

Some people do their best work under pressure. That must've been it, because she directed with a confidence missing on set in New York. Calling cues to the actors, keeping the crew calm and focused once Devin took a crowbar to the editing room—the moment they crossed the line from entertaining distraction to felony breaking and entering.

Thankfully, Eric Schumer did exactly what she'd predicted. Well, she hadn't known he was going to *tackle* Devin but figured he'd stop Devin from entering the suite, which allowed Paz and Jordan, the "security guards," to escort Devin to a private room while Ms. Harold Ramis Film School led everyone else to another floor, giving Millie and her crew just enough time to clean out the editing suite and escape down the freight elevator to the basement parking garage.

Her first successful short film, and nobody was recording.

The crash of pins snaps her into the present. The place smells like stale popcorn and foot deodorizer. She should go to the motel, see how the download is going. Maybe take a nap.

Instead, she sits at the bar and orders a Scotch, neat, three fingers.

"Try again," the bartender says.

"Diet Coke, please."

She pulls the Dodgers cap from inside her hoodie and puts it on, so drained that she feels like she's moving in slo-mo. In the gold-veined mirror over the bar, she catches her ashen reflection. Bedraggled pony-tail, temples still gray from lingering zombie makeup, puffy eyes. In essence, the look of a tired director after a bumpy yet successful day.

Using that guy from the gyro truck might've been a gamble, but it was clear that Devin wasn't up to the challenge of his role. In hindsight, she'd known this from the moment she cast him. So she diverged from the original plan, allowed a little improv into the mix.

What do you know? She's learned something from Ricky O'Naire, after all.

3

Even at thirty-nine dollars a night, they've overpaid for the room. The carpet's crusty, faded, stained. The wallpaper peels in spots, bubbles in others. Paz perches on the edge of the mattress, which has all the firm-ness of oatmeal. Her stomach growls. They haven't eaten since breakfast.

The filing cabinet stands next to the server tower, which hums and blinks and takes up much of the walking path to the bathroom. Jordan tries to pry open the locked top drawer with a pair of plastic ice tongs. They creak for a moment before snapping in two.

"Damn," he says, sweat beading on his forehead. "I need to get the crowbar. I'm going to the van."

"Not before we cut your hair." Paz motions to the desk chair surrounded by threadbare off-white towels. "Sit."

She wraps a towel around his shoulders and turns on the clippers they bought back in Fargo. As a joke, she puts them right next to his ear, and he flinches. "Don't do that," he says.

"Just trying to lighten the mood."

"I don't see anyone else having to cut their hair."

She turns off the clippers and crouches down beside him. "What's wrong?"

"Nothing."

"You're lying, and before you give me some bullshit that you're not, I know you are because your leg hasn't stopped shaking since you sat down. Now, let's try again. What's wrong?"

Jordan swallows and looks out their first-floor window. "Doesn't feel right, does it?"

"What doesn't?"

A vein pulses in his neck. His leg jiggles again. "All of this," he says, looking right at her. "We got lucky, Paz, but I don't think it'll last much longer. We shouldn't be here. We need to leave. Now."

"Hey, it's okay." She laces her fingers with his. "Movie's download-ing, yeah?".

"Yeah," he echoes.

"All right, then. It's just jitters, that's all, baby. Perfectly normal."

This gets a smile. "I'm 'baby' now, huh?"

"Why not? You can't be my baby?" She tastes the sweat on his lips. "Nobody knows who we are. This room's not even in our name, right?"

"Right." He slides an arm around her waist, presses his head against her stomach. She rubs her hands down the knots in his back.

"Then we finish the download and hit the road. The only thing we need to worry about from here on out is if we have enough change for those tollbooths."

4

VALLEY CITY, NORTH DAKOTA

It's a nice home they've created for themselves—a reflection of the times, what the style blogs and HGTV probably think is trendy. The living room is country chic; lots of whites with pops of gray and teal, splashes of plaid, distressed wooden furniture. Silver-framed photos of the happy couple and their friends and family grace the various rooms.

Because he's in his late forties and his eyes aren't what they used to be, Hoyt has to squint at some family reunion photo. With his irregular teeth, hair razor short on top and long and curly in the back, and fully tatted neck, he is an entirely different species from anyone in the photo.

It never used to bother him, not being part of "normal society." Not having a family. When he made the switch from banks to houses, he used to laugh at the people they'd steal from; whoever spent that much time color coordinating throw pillows deserved to be robbed.

Now he realizes that he's envious. Envious of material possessions he's never had, the photos of life events he'll never experience. Maybe that's why he'd rather spend his time robbing this kind of house than be at his apartment, arguing with Gabby about the shitty example he's setting for her son. At least here there's the illusion of love.

He saddles up on the couch and puts his feet up on a glass coffee table, letting his boot heel come down harder than it needs to, so the glass cracks. It takes a minute, but he figures out the projector. It's a shame he doesn't deal in electronics, but he's never found a good market, and jewelry nets the most cash.

There's Netflix, but all these people watch are reality shows. After thirty seconds of some pregnant women in Australia, he switches to satellite. A national news report starts, and the lead story actually holds his interest: someone lifted the new Ricky O'Naire film from his Chicago office. Hoyt watches intently, each detail more fascinating than the next.

"Norm, get up here," he yells. The house is so big that he's not sure Norm heard, so he keeps yelling out until he finally shows.

Norm's huffing, his buzzed head slick with sweat. For a brother-in-law, Hoyt could've done a lot worse; the guy's never asked for a handout. just for the opportunity to make money. He's never complained, not even during the oil boom, when they were working twenty-hour days running girls and meth to field workers in the Williston Walmart parking lot.

Norm might not be the most skilled, but he's loyal. In today's world, that's got to count for something.

Norm catches his breath. "Got a deal going on down there."

"We'll go check in a minute," Hoyt says and gestures at the screen. "Look at this. Someone ripped off that director Ricky O'Naire. They took his new movie in broad daylight by pretending to be zombies. Isn't that incredible?"

"They say that O'Naire's connected." Norm wipes his hands on the back of a throw pillow. His T-shirt is soaked. There really must be something serious going on downstairs.

"Rumors his own people probably started. Fake street cred, like a rapper who says he's been shot ten times in Compton but is really a rich brat from Scottsdale." He flips off the projector, the screen going blank. "Let's go see what's got you so out of breath." Then he realizes that something's missing. "Where's your mask?"

"That's part of the deal," Norm says. "No point in wearing one. The woman ripped it off Paul's head. She's seen him."

Hoyt makes a fist. Fuckin' Paul.

The basement is your typical man cave for the stupid and rich. A bar with four stools and shelves of high-end shit takes up most of the space. Neon beer signs line the walls, next to outdated Fighting Sioux pennants. There's another projector, bigger than the one upstairs, and five leather La-Z-Boy recliners.

The homeowners are immobilized on the carpet, which is littered with dumped-out bowls of chips, dip, and salsa. Duct tape has been strategically deployed: a single strip across the mouth to keep them from screaming, hands bound together at the wrists, legs at the ankles, again at the knees. Bungee cords strap them back to back. They're a couple of years younger than Hoyt, if he had to guess.

Paul smokes a cigarette at the bar. He's helped himself to the whiskey.

"Don't go feeling sorry for yourself," Hoyt says. "It's your fault we're in this mess. And could you use a glass? Have a little decency."

"She's a fighter, that one. And a biter." Paul lifts his right arm to show the proof.

His inability to quickly subdue the woman isn't a surprise. Paul's always been one of the more useless cousins on Hoyt's mom's side, more interested in growing pot and smoking it than helping with the family ranch or learning any type of professional skill—he's not even committed enough to be lazy. The only positive thing Hoyt can say is that he shows up. Sometimes on time.

He eyeballs the bite marks along Paul's arm. "She broke the skin, all right. A few times. Make sure to get a tetanus shot, if you're not up to date."

The woman makes an angry, protesting sound.

Paul pours more whiskey into a tumbler. "Of course I'm up to date."

Hoyt takes a knee in front of the woman. Platinum blond, no doubt from weekly salon visits. She's had some work done: forehead improbably smooth, face carved to lift her cheekbones. Her manicured fingernails are caked with skin and blood. She takes care of herself, that's easy to see, but she does it for her, because it's clear her husband doesn't notice. He's been hiding down here for years, Hoyt figures, belly growing larger from chugging beers with his buddies or getting drunk by himself. The man's actually crying, his body heaving with sobs; his wife, bound to him, shakes too.

Hoyt looks at the woman with some detachment. In her eyes there's only disgust for Hoyt and the tattoo covering his neck, his phoenix rising from the ashes.

It rises every day, every robbery a new possibility.

"You have a lovely home," Hoyt says conversationally. "I can see why you wouldn't want people like us in it. Normally it doesn't end like this, but you see, you fought back and removed my friend's mask. So now I don't have an option. You realize that, right? You can understand where I'm coming from?"

He rests a hand on her shoulder, giving it a sympathetic squeeze that still makes her whimper. Enough of this bullshit. They should get going. He silences the woman with a fist to the temple, her head bouncing against the back of her husband's skull. He cries out in pain, the tears really coming down now.

This is not one of the aspects of his profession Hoyt enjoys. He didn't get into stealing from people so he could kill them, but sometimes the decision isn't up to him. The woman got a good look at Paul's face, and if Paul gets made, all roads lead to Hoyt.

If he were only working with a skilled crew, he wouldn't be faced with these types of choices.

He gets up and says to Norm, "I promised Gabby we'd be back by ten, so let's hurry this up. Take these two to the bathroom. Put them in the tub. We can at least do the family one favor and not make them have to replace the carpet."

5

ROSEMONT, ILLINOIS

Millie lightly knocks three times, then drums her fingers on the motel room door before opening it, the secret code to let her crew know it's not the police.

Paz and Jordan are back in their regular clothes. They both look uneasy as they watch her enter the room. Neither speaks. Paz, hair still wet from the shower, points to the bed.

A gun sits on top of a gray cloth bag.

Millie's mouth falls open. "What the actual fuck?"

"It's a Glock 9mm. We found it in the filing cabinet," Jordan says. With his hair short and mustache gone, he looks like a fourteen-year-old talking about finding his dad's weapon in a sock drawer. "It's loaded. But the safety's on."

"Why the hell would they have a gun?" Paz wonders.

"I don't know," says Millie.

Jordan breaks in. "This is messed up, and for a few reasons. The first, if he has this because he's worried about you stealing the movie, the dude is mentally unstable."

"Agreed," Paz says.

"And the second?" Millie prompts.

Jordan swallows. "If this gun isn't for you, who's it for?"

"There's been rumors that he had help getting the embezzling charges dropped," Paz says. "Like Mob help, or whatever. I always thought it was bullshit. But after this . . ."

Jordan shudders. Paz puts her arms around him. The only sound is the humming server tower.

Millie picks up the gun. She's never held one before. It's heavy and feels cool to her fingers. She turns it over, not sure what she's looking for. "Jordan, you know guns, right? I want you to take out the bullets and dump them behind the motel. We'll lose the gun somewhere on the way back to Fargo."

Jordan raises his eyebrows. "Is that the best idea? Maybe we should keep it."

"Keep it?" from Paz. "Why the hell would we want to do that?"

"Were you not listening to yourself thirty seconds ago? Mob connections? Jesus, if that's true and O'Naire felt he had to be armed in an *editing suite*—then we're definitely in the kind of situation where you want a gun."

"And end up shooting ourselves or each other in the process." Paz shakes her head. "No way."

"I know how to use a gun," Jordan counters. "I've had safety classes."

A quote from *The Asphalt Jungle* pops into Millie's head—*You carry a gun, you shoot a cop. Bad rap, hard to beat.* Guns escalate everything; criminal charges, injuries, death. "Paz is right. This is asking for trouble." She slips the bag carefully over the gun and hands it to Jordan. "Get rid of it. Just do it."

A silent Jordan accepts the bag and sets it on the table.

"Where's Devin?" asks Millie.

6

Devin slumps against a paint-chipped post, a joint between his lips. Smoke clouds the air around him. He's cleaned off the zombie makeup, but there's still some green slime in his hair, now crispy from the cool night. He doesn't acknowledge Millie. They both look at the half-empty lot where they parked the van.

"Where'd you get weed?"

"Some guy outside the front office. I asked for a cig, he said he could do me one better. Relax, it's legal here."

"Not for someone on a visa. You want to risk everything for a joint?"

Devin inhales. "I needed something to calm me down," he says after a moment, words and smoke simultaneously pouring from his mouth.

"You're angry. You have every right to be."

He scoffs at this and turns to face her. Traces of black eyeliner sharpen his narrowed eyes. "Millie, I trusted you." His tone is as frigid as the air against her skin. "Imagine my surprise when I learned my trust wasn't returned. You never told me that I was going to get caught, that it was part of your master plan."

Millie takes him by the shoulders. She figured he'd get upset but didn't expect him to be this angry. "Would you have done it otherwise? Be honest."

"That doesn't justify what you did."

"The security guards were Paz and Jordan. You were never in any danger."

"But I didn't know that!" His voice echoes across the parking lot. Millie lets him go. Steps back. "Yes, you showed up after a few minutes, but from the time I was tackled to the time Paz and Jordan came, I thought I was done for."

"The only way to get into the editing suite without triggering the alarm was through Eric. He had to invite you. That was always plan A. When he didn't, I told you to use the crowbar, because it would set off the alarm, and we'd have an excuse to clear the floor." She gently rests her hand on his arm. "I'm sorry, Dev, but I was out of options."

He shakes her off and takes another hit. The joint's cherry glows. "It would've worked if you hadn't hired the gyro-stand tosser. Why was he there?"

"Because you kept telling me you weren't sure you could pull off the role. When I did my recon, I saw Eric talking to him, and it was obvious that he liked him." She pauses and says, sincerely, "I played the odds. We got what we needed. Can we move past this?"

Devin takes a final hit of the joint, and rubs it out on the post. "I'll tell you what," he says. "For now, sure. I'll put it behind me. But after this, after we get paid for the movie. Pay attention, Millie Blomquist, because I'm serious about this part. After we get paid for the movie, I don't ever want to see you again."

"Dev, I think you're being—"

Their room door opens. "Guys," Jordan calls, "get in here, quick."

The four of them stare at the ten o'clock news on the shitty TV. The chyron reads: *Zombie Heist*. The rest of the screen is video footage of the Oakwood Arms' underground parking garage. There they are, lifting the server tower off a dolly and into the back of the van.

"Oh, goddammit, we're on TV," Devin says.

Millie tries to control her breathing. She has to stay calm. These are the moments when a leader must take control; otherwise everyone's fear will spiral and render them useless. "We're moving *blurs* on TV," she says without affect. "You can't see our faces."

"Yeah, but what if they can enhance the image somehow?" Paz asks. "That's a thing, right? Jordan, is that a thing?"

"In the movies it's a thing, but I'm pretty sure not in real life," he says.

"'Pretty sure'? How can you only be pretty sure?"

"Because now I'm the blur on TV. Maybe I'm wrong?"

"For fuck's sake," cries Devin.

Millie asks Jordan, "How much longer until the download's done?"

"Less than an hour. Hour, tops. Ninety minutes at most."

"Pick a time and commit, mate," snaps Devin.

Millie knew they'd eventually pull footage of the van—it's why she stripped the plates before entering the garage—but thought they'd at least be in Minnesota, if not back in Fargo, by the time it was released to the press.

This moves their timeline up by at least twelve hours. There goes the chance of getting any sleep.

"That should be enough time to dump the van," she says. "Anybody know how to hot-wire a car?"

7

CHICAGO

Over the past four hours, Ricky's been waiting at the empty rehearsal space to be interviewed by the lead detectives. His phone has rung exactly one hundred and sixty-two times times. He only answers the numbers he recognizes—his manager, Lexi, Hitting the Mark staff. Everything else goes to voice mail, including the media, studio execs, PR, and talk show bookers. And some concerning calls from restricted numbers, the ones where there's just heavy breathing before the line goes dead.

He's listening to one of these hang-ups when the detectives finally arrive and introduce themselves.

Stark and Westlake don't look like detectives, at least not the kind he would cast. They're white, middle-aged, as Midwestern as it gets, bellies hanging over their belts from too many Chicago Red Hots. Facial hair is the only way to tell them apart: Westlake has a mustache with a half-inch gap in the middle. Stark is clean-shaven.

"This is ridiculous," Ricky says by way of greeting. "I've been here for hours."

"Let's get right to it, then," says Stark. "According to the officer who took your statement, you said you came here for an interview about your movie?"

"That's correct. Someone claiming they were with the *Hollywood Daily*. I got here, and the place was as empty as it is now. Someone was clearly trying to get me out of the production offices so they could steal my movie."

"Considering that's what happened, you're probably right," Stark says, unimpressed. "This is also the address several of the paid actors gave us as the place where they rehearsed."

The detectives walk the perimeter of the room, muttering to each other and jotting notes in their spiral pads.

"We'll have the lab come in here and take some samples, though I don't think it'll do much good," Westlake says when they've finished the circuit. "The actors say there were about thirty people in here, and building management confirmed that an individual from the janitorial staff cleaned up shortly before you arrived. He was tipped a hundred dollars to do so. He dusted, cleaned the mirror, swept, and mopped the floors." He sniffs the air. "With bleach."

Stark continues. "Makes it hard to get a print, and even if we find one, chances are it'll belong to one of the witnesses. They also say that they were paid in cash, that the people who hired them were in full"—he flips back in his spiral pad—"quote, 'zombie makeup' for the duration of the rehearsal. Nobody's able to give us a description that doesn't include rotting flesh or a blood-splattered neck. The email attached to the Craigslist post for actors looks to be a dummy account; the post's been taken down, and the email bounces. We can try to trace where it was created, but it'll take a few days. Since Craigslist is free, there's no credit card information to track."

O'Naire shoves his hands in his pockets. The lack of leads is disappointing. "Any cameras that would've caught them entering or exiting the building?"

"No cameras anywhere. Probably one of the reasons why they picked this place," Westlake says. "There's an alarm code to enter after hours, but the owner admits that he hardly ever uses it and doesn't give it out to tenants."

Stark jumps in. "He did meet with one person. Went by the name Elizabeth Lipp. Was already in her zombie getup when he met with her, and she paid in cash. There's over nine hundred Elizabeth Lipps in the US with about two hundred in the five-state area. My guess is it's a fake name. Only thing the owner could tell us was that she appeared to be very young, early twenties maybe, and that she had a slim build and bulbous eyes, his words. Their conversation was pretty short. She paid him and promised to be out within twenty-four hours."

Ricky takes it all in. Elizabeth Lipp. That's the alias Melina Mercouri's character uses in *Topkapi*.

"What's the next play?" he asks.

Westlake flips the pad close and tucks it under his arm. His bomber jacket isn't doing him any favors; a good trench coat and fedora would work wonders. "Right now, the email account is our best lead. We'll also interview more staff members at Today's Adventure and Howard Security. It appears the badge of a Howard Security employee was used in the basement parking garage and on your floor during the robbery. Today was her day off. We've talked with her, and she has an alibi."

"Maybe she's working with a crew. Have you thought of that?" O'Naire challenges. "While she's out locking down her cover story, her accomplices are pulling off the robbery."

"Maybe," Stark replies. "But there's no clear motive, at least none that we can see."

"Money isn't a big enough motive?"

Westlake pulls on his earlobe, says, "There are plenty of ways to make money that are a lot easier than this. Hell, if you want money, rob a bank. Any professional criminal will tell you that. You don't hold rehearsals to stage an elaborate production so you can steal a movie three days before its premiere."

Ricky walks around the space head down, his footsteps reverberating off the scuffed wood floor. Here, less than twelve hours ago, were close to thirty extras rehearsing how to steal *The Art of the Gangster*. Whoever did this is smart but takes chances. Crime isn't their wheelhouse, and maybe money's not their motive; otherwise, they would've robbed a bank or something, like the detectives said.

But extras, makeup, creating a sound design and light show, staging a fake heist so they could pull off a real one—a great distraction that's been used in countless heist movies. All of that would take planning, revising, creativity.

All the components that go into making a movie.

Millie.

"No fucking way," he mutters under his breath.

As soon as he realizes this, everything slots into place. She might not be a strong enough director, in his opinion, but $20,000 would be enough to pull it off, if a strict line producer handled the budget . . .

"What's that?" Westlake asks him.

"Nothing," Ricky says. "Just, the whole situation is a clusterfuck." He adds some weight to his tone. "If the email lead doesn't pan out, what'll you try next? I'm supposed to have a premiere on Sunday, and it's going to be pretty difficult if I don't have my film back."

Stark says, "We're aware of the tight deadline, and we're moving as fast as we can. We've already notified the press and released the footage of the perpetrators loading the getaway van."

Ricky frowns. "I wish you hadn't gone to the press. My phone was blowing up before you got here. The studio is livid. Would've been nice if we could've coordinated on this."

"It's not a movie release," chides Westlake. "We have to move quickly. Big story like this gets people talking. Egos of those involved will get the better of them, and they'll brag to the wrong person, or the pressure of twenty-four-seven coverage will get to be too much. Can your studio afford to put up a reward for information?"

"I'll make sure it happens," Ricky tells him.

"Good," Stark says. "Once they see themselves all over TV, the newspapers, and the media, one of them is bound to let something slip."

8

FARGO, NORTH DAKOTA

Techno music, or maybe what's called dubstep—Aaron's not entirely sure—pounds against his eardrums as he pushes his way to the bar. He assumed Fargo's only non-country-western club would be less crowded on a Thursday, but the dance floor is jammed with bodies swaying and grinding on one another, the women in minis and midriff-revealing tops, the men in tight-fitting button-ups or T-shirts, their hair full of product. In his pleated work slacks and a gray short-sleeve, he wishes he'd dressed better, owned cooler clothes. The other guys in the club are social-media ready, while Aaron looks like the founder of Wendy's.

According to KFGO, the police have little to go on despite so many witnesses. O'Naire's studio is offering a $50,000 reward for any information. Sounds to Aaron like they're desperate.

After he heard the good news at bingo, he went home and immediately began to feel antsy, the trailer stuffy and constricting. Millie's prior suggestion of an alibi made a great excuse. He needs to be around people. The rest of the crew were probably out celebrating, tossing back shots, smoking fat cigars. Setting the night ablaze. Why shouldn't he?

He orders an old-fashioned, the seventeen-dollar price tag a reminder of why he sticks to beer.

Although he's never been here before, he knows his employees frequent it, the younger ones, anyway. They don't ask him to come along, but that's because he's a supervisor and it would be weird to get drunk in front of your boss; at least that's what he tells himself. He also knows from her Instagram stories—which he's too afraid to actually follow—that Gabrielle hangs out here.

He spots her almost instantly out on the dance floor. Hard not to. She's with two other girls, swaying her hips in a short, gold-sequined dress that almost looks painted on. The classy thing to do would be to go over, tell her she looks beautiful, ask if she'd like to dance.

Aaron stays put.

At the end of the song, Gabrielle and her friends leave the floor and head for the VIP section. Now he moves, losing her for a moment when he crosses behind the DJ booth. He finds her again a few minutes later.

She's arguing with that neck-tattoo guy, the one who was idling his black Escalade outside Howard. Gabrielle's arms are crossed against her chest, warding off the barrage of words. The woman makes irate look stunning.

Do these two ever not fight?

Neck Tattoo is yelling and gesturing from one of the couches. There's a girl in his lap, younger than Gabrielle; her dress is so slinky it makes a bikini look like a poncho. The more aggressive he gets toward Gabrielle, the more his friends urge him on. They're rough-looking, more suited for a perp walk than a nightclub.

Gabrielle throws a red drink at Neck Tattoo, soaking his white T-shirt. He shoots up from the couch, dumping Slinky Dress onto the floor. Her skirt rides up. Anybody within a ten-mile radius can see that she's not wearing underwear.

Neck Tattoo yells and shoves Gabrielle hard. He's on her quick, his right fist cocked and ready, but before he can follow through, Aaron's got his arms around the guy, slamming him into a side table, the perfect tackle he was never able to perform back in eighth-grade football.

The two roll across the floor, drinks splattering on them, people shouting.

Neck Tattoo is pounding on Aaron's ribs. Aaron takes the punches the best he can, protecting his face. The guy fights dirty, aiming for the soft spots.

Pain explodes up and down his body.

A bouncer pulls Neck Tattoo away. Aaron rolls over onto his stomach and gasps for air. His vision tunnels and his head throbs. There's blood in his mouth. He gingerly checks and finds a cut on the inside of his cheek. The music has not stopped.

The bouncer must have seen the whole thing, because he lets Aaron stay. Neck Tattoo is booted. His friends trail behind, making sure that everyone in the club understands their outrage. Slinky Dress scuttles after them.

"That was the stupidest thing I've ever seen in my life," Gabrielle tells him. "Hoyt is going to murder you."

"You better have a drink with me, then," he says, cool-like, swallowing blood, doing his best to both smother his anxiety and ignore the throbbing pain. "Might be my last."

She laughs and looks up at the ceiling. "Fuck, men are stupid." Her hands smooth the bottom of her dress. "Don't tell anyone at work about this. I don't want people to think I'm some sort of club rat that starts shit with their man for no reason."

Aaron pushes himself upright, the pain in his back coming out as a grimace. "Looks like you had a reason. I was ordering a drink and heard the commotion." Commotion? he scolds himself. Really, dude? "Looked over and saw that other girl on his lap. That would upset anybody."

Gabrielle clicks her tongue against her teeth. "He was doing a lot more than just letting her sit on his lap."

"That's awful."

"It's typical, is what it is." She makes for the VIP-section exit, stops . . . and looks back at him. When Aaron realizes what's happening, his pain turns to pride. He's no longer the dork who spills coffee at work, the one who awkwardly says "Hiya!"

"Bar is this way, if you still want to buy me that drink," she tells him, cocking her hip. "Or are you gonna spend the rest of the night watching me across the room?"

9

ILLINOIS

Devin, riding shotgun, tells Millie to keep the engine running. "We don't want to get stuck out here. Wherever 'out here' is," he says. "It's going to take at least an hour to get back to the motel. Jordan better have the download done by then."

Millie slams the door of the Buick, the only car they managed to successfully hot-wire after four failed attempts. Thank God for YouTube.

The starless sky expands above them. It's an eerily empty landscape, open fields without houses or buildings of any kind. Using the glow of brake lights as their guide, Millie and Devin crunch down the gravel road to where Paz parked the van.

The three of them each grab a five-gallon gas canister—purchased at a random station in Minnesota on the way down, filled somewhere in Iowa—and get to work. The back of the van holds leftover equipment: costumes, makeup, lighting, speakers, enough laser tag garb for the best child's birthday party in the world.

Millie pours gas in the cargo area, while Paz handles the seats, center console, and dash. Devin takes the exterior.

When they're finished, the van shines in the moonlight like it's fresh from the car wash.

Paz rakes her hands through her hair. "This is absolutely insane."

"How do we even do this?" Devin asks.

"One of us is going to have to throw the lighter in the van and run away," Millie says, greeted with the enthusiastic response of a cow's distant mooing. "I'm guessing neither of you are volunteering."

Devin sweeps into a mock bow. "And deny you this gloriously badass moment? You have a lighter?"

She pats her pockets. "I thought you did."

"I do, but I'm saving it for this other joint."

"Then set something on fire. We don't have to get rid of the lighter," Paz suggests. "We could throw the other joint."

"We're not wasting my last joint," Devin says.

"Who said we have to waste it?"

When there's only a few hits left, Millie pries the joint from Devin's fingers and approaches the van.

"Don't get dead," he yells out.

She looks down the road to see if there are any oncoming headlights, listens for the crunch of tires on gravel. The smell of gasoline is so strong she can taste it. The cherry on the joint dims. She takes a hit, her first of the night. Just to stoke the flame, she tells herself, then throws the glowing roach inside the van, aiming for the front seats but not waiting around to see where it lands.

She slips on the gravel as she races for the Buick, catches herself. Paz and Devin are crouched behind it, peeking over the trunk. She dives down beside them and puts her arms over her head like in a school tornado drill.

They wait for an explosion, a blast of heat.

The world is dark, filled only with wind.

After a moment, Paz asks, "What happened?"

"I don't know," Devin says. "Why don't you go check?"

The three stand and take another look at the darkened van. "Shouldn't it be on fire by now?" Paz wonders.

Millie sighs. "The joint must've gone out after I threw it. Maybe there's an owner's manual in this car that we can light and—"

The explosion takes out the windows, followed by flames that reach out and lick the sky.

10

"How'd it go?" Jordan asks.

"Fucking brilliant, mate," Devin says, closing the motel room door behind him. "It was magnificent."

Jordan gives him a long look. "Are you stoned?"

"Like a whore in the Old Testament! Oh, I don't like that phrase. It's so slut-shaming."

"Are you serious? I'm in here sweating it with enough evidence to put me in jail for life, and you're out getting baked?"

Paz takes charge, calmly says, "It wasn't like that."

Jordan checks out her eyes. "You're blazed."

"Like a witch in Salem," agrees Devin.

We don't have time for this, Millie thinks. Every second spent arguing increases their chances of the police busting down the door. "Are we good here?" she asks Jordan.

"What? Uh, yeah," he says. "Have been for over forty minutes. All the footage has been transferred onto our hard drive and scrubbed from O'Naire's, so now only we have access. Oh, and I rerouted those transactions you asked about."

"Great. All we have left to do now is wipe down the tower and filing cabinet. That should tie up any loose ends."

"Except for, you know, the stolen car outside," Devin says.

Jordan lifts a single eyebrow at Millie.

"That's it, though," she promises.

11

WISCONSIN

Even sitting on a pile of motel towels, Millie can still feel the pebbly shards of smashed window glass. None of the hot-wiring videos had actually explained how to break into a car, a fact they hadn't realized until they were scavenging parking lots for a likely ride.

The driver's side window is completely gone. A cold wind lashes her face. She has the heat cranked, but all it does is warm her knuckles gripping the wheel.

It's been a few hours since the Chicago skyline faded in the rearview. They're surrounded by semis traveling cross-country. Millie tosses back the dregs of the crappy gas station coffee, grounds spreading across her tongue. She makes a noise like a cat coughing up a hair ball and hands the empty cup to Devin, who's trying to sleep in the passenger seat.

"I'm your rubbish bin now, too?" he says, blinking awake.

"Open the lid," she says out of the side of her mouth. "Please."

Devin pops the top off and hands back the cup. Millie spits out the grounds.

"If you'd like to avoid being thrown out of this car, don't even think about handing that back to me."

The Buick must've had an elderly owner. The front seat and glove compartment are full of cough drops, packets of Kleenex, OTC medicine bottles. A quad walking cane sits between Paz and Jordan in the back seat. They've been silent for a while, the vending machine sugar rush having crashed.

"I have to admit," Millie says cautiously, "that I thought things would go a little smoother than this, but we're going to be all right."

"I hope so, because lately it's been nothing but a comedy of errors," Devin says. "Or more accurately, a shit show."

Millie thinks about arguing but waits to see if either Paz or Jordan is going to do it for her. Wind fills the gap in the conversation.

"*Quick Change*," Jordan says after a long period of silence.

"What's that?" asks Millie.

"Devin said it's been a comedy of errors, so I was trying to decide what my favorite heist comedy is. I'd have to go with *Quick Change*. The one with Bill Murray as the bank-robbing clown."

"No way," Paz says. "Anybody with half a brain knows it's *A Fish Called Wanda*. 'Asshole!'" she says, imitating Kevin Kline.

"You're both wrong," Devin says. "Funniest heist has got to be *The Lavender Hill Mob*. It's got Alec Guinness in it. Obi-Wan in a heist!"

He turns in his seat a little to face them, letting the chip on his shoulder not weigh him down as much. It's a sight Millie didn't think she'd get to see so soon, and she's thankful for the momentary relief of tension, the break from focusing on the fact that they're fleeing the police.

She accepts the challenge. "What's your favorite heist movie, then?"

Devin: "You know I have a soft spot for American kids' flicks, so I very much doubt you'll be falling over yourself in praise for this one."

Millie: "Try me."

Devin: "*Getting Even with Dad*."

Millie: "Ted Danson and Macaulay Culkin? Now you're messing with me. That can't be your favorite heist."

Jordan: "Hey, now. I loved it. It's got that montage with Mac singing karaoke. If we're going by favorite heist movies, then mine is *Inception*."

Millie: "*Inception* isn't a heist movie. They don't steal anything."

Jordan: "Oh, come on. Fine, the main job might be to implant an idea, but it opens on a heist, which, if I remember correctly, is actually an audition. And then it's one final job to get DiCaprio back to America to see his kids. That totally makes it a heist. It has all the elements."

Millie: "Right, it has heist *elements*."

Jordan: "No, but—"

Devin: "For fuck's sake, you're not going to win here, so quit trying."

Paz: "My favorite is *Don't Breathe*. It's scary as hell. Imagine breaking into a house only to find out that the blind Mark is a murderer who has a girl tied up in the basement. The way he closes off the house and then hunts them down? It's awesome."

Millie: "That's more of a twist on the home-invasion genre, but I'll give it to you. There's three in the crew."

Devin: "Since you seem to have an opinion on everyone else's pick, what's your favorite, then?"

Millie: "There's a reason why *Heat* and *Ronin* are considered classics. And I like it when directors try different spins on the genre, like what Boyle did with *Trance* or Glazer with *Sexy Beast*. I used to love *The Mark*, but I think for reasons well known I won't be watching that anytime soon. For my favorite, though, I'd have to go with the classics, and it's hard to pick just one. *Rififi* is spectacular, but I always find myself going to *Asphalt Jungle* more. And I love both versions of Hemingway's *The Killers,* but I think I actually prefer the one from 1964."

Paz: "You say that as if it's a controversial opinion."

Jordan: "Yeah, you lost me after *Ronin*. Why did you get so obsessed with the genre, anyway? What is it? That it's all about a plan coming together? That each team member has a specific set of skills?"

Devin laughs. "Sounds like you're about to do the voice-over for a Liam Neeson trailer, mate."

Millie considers Jordan's question. "All of the above. I wanted to write a good script, and it's important to know your genre if you want to make an impact."

Paz blows a raspberry.

"What?"

"Sounds like bullshit to me."

Devin agrees. "Bet you used that same line on O'Naire the first time you met him. Oh, look, she's turning red. Totally called it."

Jordan cuts in. "But seriously. You could've worked in any genre.

Most new directors do horror. Heists are a bitch to script. Why did you choose it?"

"Obviously because of her dad," scoffs Devin.

"Yeah, but he used the word 'obsessed,'" Paz says, "and he's got a point. I mean, she's got a damn spreadsheet."

"I *am* still in the car, you know?" Millie says. "I can hear you."

Devin turns to her. "Come on now, love. You know he's not going to quit asking. What is it? Over a hundred and fifty films? That is a bit above and beyond."

Millie looks at the interstate stretched out in front of her. Clusters of stars shine against the dark night sky like bulbs in a theater marquee. She knows exactly why she can't stop watching heist movies; why they've been her obsession, as they put it.

It's something she's never talked about.

"I guess it started as research. That part's true," she says. "I wanted to know all the tropes and character archetypes. But the more I watched, the more I started trying to see them the way my dad might."

The Buick rounds a hill, the freezing wind now blowing with them rather than against. She feels heat from the vents spread over her hands, up her arms, across her face. She casts a look over the open Wisconsin woods, the leafless aspen and birch trees soaked in moonlight.

"He was, you know, a professional criminal, but until he died, I didn't know any of that. It was, like, his secret side. He hid it from us, his family. To me, he was just this guy who couldn't catch a break," she says, finally telling her own secret. "And the more heists I watch, the more I feel like I understand why he made decisions that most people would never even consider. Sure, some of the movies are absolutely ridiculous, but the best ones, the movies that last, they're about the underdog trying to beat the system that's got them beat."

She pauses. "It's weird, because even though I know he never in a million years would've condoned what we just did . . . I haven't felt this close to him since he died."

Her chest goes tight. She hadn't meant to say that last part. That was only for her.

"Oh, love," Devin says and takes her free right hand.

Soon there are two more hands on her, one on each shoulder. In the rearview, Millie sees Paz and Jordan lean forward.

"If you bastards are trying to make me cry, it's not going to work," she says with a hitch in her voice, her eyes starting to sting.

"Such a tough cookie," Devin says and kisses the back of her hand before he lets it go. Both Paz and Jordan give her shoulders a squeeze, then lean back in their seats.

The car is dark and cold and quiet.

A sudden blast of light shoots across the ceiling. Millie flinches and adjusts the mirror to see in the back seat. The screen of Jordan's iPad illuminates him and Paz. Her palm rests on his shoulder, her chin on top of her hand.

"What are you guys doing?" asks Millie.

"All this talk about heist movies, and we've got one of the best ones right here," Jordan says. "With everything that we've risked, might as well make sure we see it before anyone else."

The sound of a gunshot erupts through the iPad's speakers. This isn't the ideal way to watch the movie she spent years writing, but they do have a point. She'd be lying to herself if she said she hasn't been wanting to watch it since they drove the van out of the parking garage.

"Pause it," she says. To hell with their timeline. Some things just can't wait. "Let me find someplace to pull over. I'm not missing anything."

12

CHICAGO

Streaks of early dawn compete with deep pockets of shadow between skyscrapers. Ricky rests his forehead against his bedroom window and stares down at the streets, the cars stuck in traffic, the people lining the sidewalks, as if Millie and her crew might be among them.

If she's smart, she'll be somewhere off the grid, a town in the middle of the New Mexico desert or something. He wonders if he should call her, feel it out, see if his gut instinct is right. After a few minutes, he decides against it. Who knows if the cops are monitoring his calls.

Lexi stirs in the bed. She still wears last night's cocktail dress.

As if she knows he's watching, she opens her eyes, which are ringed with smeared mascara. He smiles and sits down on the bed, running his fingers through her messy hair. She frowns and puts up her hand to cover her eyes. "Close the curtains, it's fucking early," she murmurs and rolls over.

He spends the rest of his morning researching Millie and concludes she lives a normal and somewhat lonely life. Her Instagram feed is minimal; the last pics are from the Academy, some from a workshop, others on set. She only retweets, movie news mostly; nothing about *The Art of the Gangster*. She doesn't have TikTok. Her only Facebook posts are when someone tags her. He has to laugh at a shot from last Christmas; she and her mother, wearing matching ugly sweaters, are at the kitchen table, Millie clearly repelled by a dish of what looks like warmed-over white snot.

Her Facebook is linked to a Letterbox account, where users post film reviews. Millie's up to 243, the majority of them heist films. Only a few have earned a perfect rating, five stars, *The Mark* among them.

The girl knows her stuff, no doubt about it, and for a moment his heart aches. She was such a big fan of his, and what did he do? Stole everything she'd worked for and offered her a measly twenty grand to keep quiet. Inspired her and then ruined her.

If it weren't his movie, he'd be proud that she's out for revenge.

His phone rings. Restricted number. He lets the call go to voice mail. The phone rings again thirty seconds later.

This time he answers it.

"Things don't seem to be going well for ya," a man says. "Not going well at all. Some people, like the woman I work for, might even be tempted to say things are going *badly* for ya."

It takes a second to register, but Ricky recognizes the guy from the Green Cat's bathroom. The East Coast accent gives him away.

Throughout the years, the investors have used a variety of handlers to contact him as needed. Most of them one-and-done, a few repeats here and there. Sometimes they have great news, though most recently it's been bad. Ricky has been hoping—praying, more like it—he wouldn't get this guy again.

"It's good to hear from you," Ricky says. "Maybe we should talk in person?"

"Relax. Line's clean. You're not that important."

Ricky gives a tight smile. The guy's just trying to get under his skin. So far, it's working. "Did you check?"

"Not me personally, pal, but yeah, someone who works for us did. We have a lotta people watching you. Need to protect our investment."

His knee starts shaking. Watching him? What the hell does that mean? "Things are under control." His voice has a shrill edge, belying his words. He steadies himself and says, "They aren't as dire as they seem."

"I hope so, because right now your future ain't looking too good." There's light chatter in the background, the sound of silverware clinking against plates. Is this guy threatening him during brunch? "She wants to meet with you. Today."

Ricky sits at the breakfast counter. He's only met with the head of the investors once, back when he was in production on *The Mark* and she wanted a tour of the set. They went out to dinner afterward to discuss his future, how their arrangement would work for upcoming projects. At the end of the dinner, he was told, for the protection of their arrangement, they'd never meet in person again.

This is not good.

"Can't. Cops are involved. I'm working with them to help catch whoever did this. Have to meet up with them later."

There's a pause on the other end. "And who told you to involve the cops?"

"Couldn't be helped. An employee called once they discovered there was an attempt to steal the movie."

"Attempt? You mean they actually didn't get away with it?"

"They did get the original files, but we have backups in a different server room," Ricky lies. "Police want the thieves to think they got the only copy so they try to sell it or blackmail me for it. It's going to be a whole sting operation and everything."

"And you were okay with that? Letting them tell the press the movie was stolen?"

Ricky shrugs, physically committing to the lie even though the guy can't see him. "Someone staged a heist to steal a heist movie? It's front-page news now. Can't make up that kind of marketing campaign. Studio was all for it. People will be tripping over themselves to get a ticket."

Another pause. Slurp of coffee. "For your sake, I hope you're right. We didn't pay off the Manhattan DA to finger the accounting firm because we think you're a swell guy. Clock's ticking, my friend."

This guy has watched too many movies to be saying shit like that. Ricky should know. He's used that line himself.

"I know what I owe. I almost went to jail for it. How about cutting me some slack?"

"Not her fault you tried laundering her money with box office duds. That's not how this works. I mean, who told you to reboot *Dunston Checks In?*"

"The expected ROI numbers were solid."

"Would have to be, to go through with something that stupid." Another slurp of coffee. "I'll let her know what's going on, but keep your phone near you. I don't want to get your voice mail again. I don't care what time it is."

"I had it on silent. I'll make sure the ringer is on."

"Yeah, you do that, Rick," the man says and ends the call.

13

WISCONSIN

The crew has commandeered a picnic table and bought one of everything from the rest area vending machines. The Buick idles in the parking lot, running so they don't have to hot-wire it again. The morning air feels good after the long night on the road. The other travelers don't pay them any attention. Most are truckers with T-shirts tucked into their jeans, more interested in the restroom than in four teenagers.

Everyone is too busy eating to say much, and Millie's grateful for the silence. Gives her time to think. Put things in perspective—or attempt to, anyway.

She always knew her script would make a great movie, but if she's honest with herself, she didn't think it'd be half as good as what she saw last night. She did a hell of a job. But so did O'Naire, and it pains her to think that maybe he was right. That he is a better director than she'll ever be. Or at the very least, the right person to have told this story.

Was she simply too close to see that? Did her desire to send her father's killer a message blind her to the truth of her own capabilities? Because there's no way she could've pulled those kinds of performances, especially from Flowers Romero.

Holy shit. Now there was a breakthrough people would never forget, on par with Jennifer Lawrence in *Winter's Bone* or Oscar Isaac in *Inside Llewyn Davis*. Flowers Romero might have gotten a foot in the door as an influencer, but he's an undeniably brilliant actor, so much so that she was enthralled, actually forgetting how much she hated the character's real-life inspiration.

A mountain of empty wrappers and cans sits in front of them. Millie takes it upon herself to carry the mess over to the garbage.

When she comes back, the other three won't look at her.

"What is it?" she asks, confused.

Jordan and Paz stay silent, ceding the floor to Devin. "Mil, let me first start by saying how impressed we are that you were able to pull this off. It was a beautiful heist. One for the movies."

"And?" she says.

"And . . ." Devin looks to Jordan and Paz. "And we've been talking, and we . . . we want to give the movie back."

She puts her hands on her hips. "We are giving it back. As soon as O'Naire and the studio pay for it."

Paz clears her throat. "That's not what he means."

"We don't want to blackmail anybody," Jordan clarifies.

"Maybe it was seeing us on the news or how great the actual movie was, but this doesn't feel right anymore," Paz says. "Did you see how many people were listed in the credits? Did you see the production value? The thing cost millions of dollars."

"Fifty million, according to Box Office Mojo," Millie says.

"That's like a made-up number to me. That's like saying a hundred thousand bazillion dollars, it's so much. I mean, we could only afford to get a few scenes filmed. And I can't go to jail, Millie." Her eyes are pleading.

"Neither can I," from Jordan. "My mom wouldn't be able to handle it. Jail would destroy her."

"You didn't think about all this before the job?" she demands.

It's the Academy all over again. They're with her at the beginning, but the second things get difficult, get real, they abandon ship—abandon her and everything she's worked so hard for.

Devin folds his hands and sets them on the table, praying for her mercy. "We got swept up, okay? Your proposition was enticing, and at least for me, I wanted to be part of your crew again. I wish it had been for a proper film, but I took what I could get."

She glares at each of them in turn. "Just when did you have the time to decide this? I was gone for literally thirty seconds throwing away the trash, and now I have a mutiny."

"Last night, after you fell asleep," Jordan says. "People should know that you wrote it, yeah, but it's really good. The guy may be a dick—"

"An embezzling, lying dick—"

"But this deserves to be seen by an audience. Isn't that the ultimate goal of writing a movie? That people will see it?"

"The plan *is* to let them see it. Right after we get what's rightfully ours."

"You sound like you're out for revenge," Paz says.

"And what if I am?" counters Millie. "Is that so terrible? That I ask for someone to be held accountable? Or do we live in a world without consequences?"

"What about the consequences of what we've done?" asks Jordan. "This film is an investment of people's work, time, and money. It's not going to end well for us, Millie; you have to see that."

She's on her feet, headed toward the still-running Buick. What do they know about anything? From writing the script, to producing the short, to confronting O'Naire, to coming up with the plan to steal the thing itself—and then convincing them to be her crew—none of them have invested as much as she has.

"It's not that black-and-white," Devin calls out, the three of them behind her. "We're just talking about a film. It's not worth throwing your life away. For fuck's sake, you and Jordan are still in high school. You have class on Monday. We're too young to be facing jail time. I'm not even a citizen! We're your friends. Listen to us."

That gets Millie to stop dead in her tracks, so abruptly that Devin crashes into her, Paz into him, Jordan the caboose who almost knocks everyone down.

"You're not my friends," she says once they've all regained their footing. "You never have been. You just picked me because I had the best script and you wanted to be famous."

"You can't be serious," Paz says. "You came to us, remember?"

"Bullshit."

"Think about it. That first class for the Feature Award, when we all went around and introduced ourselves and what we wanted to do in the industry, you were practically drooling over anyone who said they didn't want to direct, that they were looking to support other projects."

"That's not true," Millie says, a little more quietly.

"It is, because I remember that I felt sorry for you," Paz continues, "going around the room, everyone you approached turning you down to work with someone older, with a bigger budget and more experience. That's the only reason I agreed to have lunch with you, why any of us did. Because we could relate to being the youngest, the ones that nobody was taking seriously, but we didn't pick you because we 'wanted to be famous'; we *agreed* to work with you so we could have the opportunity to show how talented we are."

"So you *did* use me," Millie says. "I'm not wrong about that."

Paz looks at her dead-on. "No more than you used us. Did you know that I lost a parent, too?" Millie's gut punched. She had no idea. "My mom died of cancer six years ago. And like you, that's why I want to make movies. Because when I was a kid, I used to shoot these little short films where my dad would be captured by my brother, the evil sorcerer, and my mom would be the one who rescued him." She takes a choky breath. "She was my hero, and I never saw movies where the hero was a girl who looked like me. So I made my own."

"That's honestly very sweet," says Devin with sincerity. "Way better than that pitch you had about the woman eating herself to stay alive. More sensible, too."

"I didn't know any of that," Jordan says quietly. He puts his arm around her.

"Because I don't like to talk about it," Paz says. "Because it sucks, and it's unfair, but if she were alive, all she'd want for me is to move on and be happy. So stop acting like all of this is only about you, Millie. We're all in this, and we're all facing the same consequences if we get caught. It's not worth it. Let it go."

"Don't act like we went through the same thing," Millie says. "Your mom got sick. My dad was murdered."

"It's unfair, no matter how you look at it."

Millie clenches her jaw. "You still don't get it. And that's fine. I don't need you to. Once we get back to Fargo and send the message to O'Naire, I won't need your help anymore. In fact, I only need Jordan for that, so I can drop you and Devin at the Minneapolis airport if you're dying to get away from me."

"Nobody said that," Devin tells her.

"You did. Last night. Remember? Outside the motel, you said that after all this was done, you never wanted to see me again."

Millie gets in the car, slams the door. Devin carefully leans in through the broken window. "I was upset and being dramatic. I didn't mean it. Mil, you don't have to do this."

"Apparently, I do," she says, shifting into reverse. Devin loses his balance. Jordan keeps him from falling to the ground. Millie aims the Buick toward the exit, then hits the brake. "Let's go, unless you want to hitchhike from here."

14

FARGO, NORTH DAKOTA

The smell of coffee nudges Aaron awake. The moment he opens his eyes, the hangover kicks in, a steel-toed boot to the head. Sunlight slants through the vertical blinds, onto the pile of clothes from last night. His ribs ache, his upper body spotted with half a dozen purple crescent moons when he lifts up his shirt.

The back of his throat hurts. He tries to swallow, and there's nothing there. Dry as a bone.

He hears the familiar sound of eggs sizzling and toast popping . . . and is that bacon he smells? Now he salivates. Aaron can't remember the last time he had bacon. He rolls over and drinks in the scent. It's been forever since Carol made breakfast. Wonder what the occasion is?

It takes a moment before he remembers he's no longer married.

He pulls back the accordion door between his bedroom and the kitchen, taking time to let the creak of his footsteps be heard. Marriage taught him never to spring his appearance on a person first thing in the morning.

Gabrielle stands in front of the small stove, shaking salt onto some scrambled eggs and ham. Aaron vaguely remembers her coming home with him, the two of them drinking and complaining about work until they passed out.

He's positive he didn't get lucky. No amount of alcohol could erase that memory.

Gabrielle's wearing one of his old button-ups, from before the weight loss. It engulfs her, hanging just below her butt, her smooth thighs on prominent display. His eyes linger on her bare skin until someone clears their throat.

Hoyt—a.k.a. Neck Tattoo and Gabrielle's ex—is sitting with two of his friends on Aaron's couch.

They're reviewing the Howard Security documents tied to the heist.

"You must be Hoyt," Aaron says. The words are sharp, scratching his throat raw. His heart beats wildly. What the hell did he tell Gabrielle last night?

"You can come out. We don't bite," Hoyt says teasingly, although it is clear he's not joking. "Love what you've done with the place. Who picked out the throw pillows? Wasn't you."

"Are you here to kill me?" he chokes out.

"What's that? Kill you?" The man laughs. "No. I mean, not anymore. Was thinking about fucking you up a bit. That was why we followed you two after you left the club last night. But Gabby here assures me you didn't have sex or nothing."

She makes a face of utter disgust. It nearly shatters Aaron.

"You go by Gabby?" he asks.

Hoyt stands. "Hope you don't mind that we helped ourselves. We were hungry. Found some bacon in the freezer. Didn't know if you were saving it for a special occasion or something." Then he smiles. "But from the reading materials we found while you were sleeping"—he holds up the blueprint for the Oakwood Arms—"I can confidently say that today is an excellent day for bacon." He pulls out one of the table chairs. "Take a seat. There's a lot we need to discuss."

Aaron meets his eyes. "And what if I don't want to?"

Hoyt's two friends stand up from the couch. Both ball up their fists. One wears a set of brass knuckles.

"I'm not really giving you an option," says Hoyt.

15

The Buick pulls up to the trailer, spraying slush as it parks next to a black Escalade taking up two spaces. For the first time in three states, they turn off the ignition. Aaron's car isn't there, meaning he's at work. At least somebody is sticking to the plan.

"Log in to the community center's Wi-Fi and check flight times for this afternoon and tomorrow," Millie says to Jordan as she slams the car door. "We need to spread them out."

"Sure Fargo's going to be safer than the Minneapolis airport?" Devin says, his tone thick with sarcasm. "Interpol won't be meeting with the FBI and CIA at the checkout counter?"

"I told you, it didn't feel right. Driving up in a stolen car and buying two people tickets out of town on the same day? That'd be stupid."

Paz points over at the community center. "There's people in there."

"There shouldn't be. I have all day and the weekend signed out," Millie says. "Whoever it is, get rid of them. I have to go check on something."

She uses the spare key Aaron gave her. The trailer is a warren of dirty dishes, blankets balled up on the couch, the stench of grease. The documents from the heist aren't on the kitchen table where she left them. A quick scan of the place, and she comes up empty. Where are they?

No need to panic, she tells herself. Aaron probably moved them so they wouldn't be out in the open. Maybe even hid them or destroyed them in case the cops show up. She almost admires his ability to plan ahead.

She finds her charger, locks up the trailer, and heads over to the community center. The black Escalade is still parked outside. She almost wants whoever is in there to give her grief. She's looking for a fight.

Jordan isn't on his laptop. "Is the Wi-Fi not working again," she asks, "or did you forget the password? It's on the fridge, where it's always been."

She takes her place in front of the table and notices a red mark under Devin's right eye, like a burn or the early bloom of a bruise. Jordan has a cut across his temple. Yesterday she was helping apply cuts and bruises to around thirty extras, and she can tell Jordan's isn't fake: it's the real deal. It glistens with sweat and fresh blood. His nose is puffy, the left nostril stuffed with a tissue.

"What happened to you two?" Millie says. "Did you guys have a fight? And did Devin win?"

Devin gives her a look but is without his usual sarcastic response.

The scratch of a lighter grabs her attention.

Three men stand in the kitchenette. One of them puffs on a cigarette and flicks ashes into the sink.

"Afraid that was our doing." The man with the cigarette is square built and lean, with sinewy arms. His hair is oily and long in the back, skull short everywhere else. He has a goatee and a large bird tattoo on his neck.

"And who are you?" Millie says.

"He told us to call him Bugs," says Paz.

"Like the bunny?"

The man nods, as if he expected this. "I was thinking more like Moran. The gangster from the thirties, born in Saint Paul, the one from the Saint Valentine's Day Massacre. But I can see why you'd go with the more famous Bugs." He jerks his thumbs back at the two men behind him. "These are my associates. Cobweb"—a runty skinhead with a paunch and a bull ring jutting out of his septum—"and Spider."

A tall drink of water, with his hair pulled back into a ponytail and veins as thick as shoelaces running up his arms, clears his throat.

Bugs frowns at him. "I told you we're going the insect route."

"I never agreed to that," Spider says.

"Get on board, man," says Cobweb. "It's serious."

The guy crosses his arms. He doesn't look at his partners.

Bugs sighs. "Fine. Fuck it. Correction. This isn't Spider. This is Hatchet."

Hatchet, formerly known as Spider, sniffs.

"So we're allowed to choose our own names now?" Cobweb asks.

Bugs scratches the back of his head. "Un-fucking-believable."

"It's fine."

"What do you want to change it to?"

"I like Cobweb."

"Speak, motherfucker, this is your last chance."

"I'm sticking with it."

"What can we do for you?" Millie says. "If it's the community center you want, it's all yours. We were leaving anyways."

Bugs takes a drag of his cigarette, lets the smoke walk out. Keeping things casual. "You know Aaron, right? That was his trailer you just came out of?" When Millie doesn't say anything, he tosses the cigarette in the sink, runs the water, and walks around the counter.

Cobweb sits next to Devin, smiles across the table at Jordan, and rests his hands on the table. Light winks off the brass knuckles on his right hand.

Hatchet takes his post in front of the entrance door. He stares at Paz with cold indifference; he won't hesitate to harm her if necessary. The crook of his right arm is pocked with black and purple marks, almost as if he's been bitten. Needle tracks? Millie wonders.

Bugs goes right to her.

"What do you guys want?" She psychs herself up, doing her best to keep the fear out of her voice. "And why are my friends sitting over there with fresh bruises?"

He looks her up and down, his mouth in a weirdly delighted sneer. "I know we've just met, but I like you. I can tell good people, and you are it. Kudos for sticking to your cover story. Wait to see what we know. Don't reveal anything you don't need to. Smart. I can see why you're the one in charge."

She looks purposely baffled. "I don't know what you're talking about."

"It's not too late to let us go," Jordan says out of the side of his mouth.

Let us go?

Until this moment, it hadn't registered with Millie that they were being held captive.

"Shut your mouth unless you want another love tap," Cobweb tells Jordan.

"Don't you dare touch him," Paz says. The skinhead blows her a kiss.

"Where are your manners?" snaps Bugs. The sharpness of his voice wipes the grin from Cobweb's face. "Don't treat her like that, understand? We're going to keep this civil as long as we possibly can."

Bugs lifts up the bottom of his shirt. A silver gun handle sticks up from the waistband of his Dickies work pants. She can't tell what kind it is, but it's not the one Jordan found in the file cabinet. That was small, with a black handle. She can almost hear him complaining that they should've kept it.

Bugs pulls out his gun, lets it hang from his hand. It's comically large but looks at home with him. If he were an action figure, the gun would complete the set.

"What is it you think you know?" Millie says.

"More than you'd like us to," says Bugs.

16

She was so careful.

Kept the crew to a minimum, didn't tell them more than they needed to know. But she should have known better. She knew the movies, recognized the signs, and ignored them.

Aaron is needy, unconfident, lonely—the exact traits she exploited to get him to help her. She offered him a spot on her team, then told him to watch from the sidelines. Of course he would be the weakest link. She can see that now. Can see why her dad never entertained the idea of using him for a job, why he kept his two lives separate.

She was so concerned about having a Stevie in her crew that she forgot about having a George, the sad sap from *The Killing* who blabs the whole score to his wife so she doesn't leave him, only to have her boyfriend double-cross them.

Seventy-one percent of heists with crews of five result in a double cross. Numbers don't lie. Aaron was their George.

"What I will commend you on is the way you pulled it off." Bugs sits across from Millie in a wingback chair, fresh cigarette in one hand, a cup of Folgers in the other. She had no choice but to explain the whole plan. "Maximum risk, but no guns and no casualties. Pretty clever."

It's hard not to be a little flattered. He is, after all, a professional in the field.

"So what do you want now?" she asks. "There's literally sixty bucks left from what O'Naire gave me. Take it. The movie, too. It's on a couple of hard drives. Take them and go. We won't say shit. We don't know anything about who you really are," she adds. "I don't know your girlfriend, or whatever, and it's not like we're going to go to the police. You win."

Bugs tilts his head from side to side. "We could take the movie and run, but then what? I'm a simple mask-and-gun criminal. What would I do? Bootleg it? I don't know how to get paid from that. You're all going to have to come with us. See your plan through."

Her crew—which has been ordered to sit in silence—takes notice. They look as helpless as Millie feels.

"I don't understand," Millie says. "I've told you how to do this. How to get there. How to contact O'Naire to make the switch. Basically everything except for how to spend the money."

Bugs points a finger at her. He has a skull and crossbones tattooed on the back of his hand. "Exactly. You've told me everything, and it's shown me how good at this you really are. Too much money at stake to send in the B team now. You're with us until the end."

"And if we refuse?"

Bugs moves quick, up out of his chair, his nails gouging her scalp as he grabs her ponytail. He drags Millie to the floor, the skin of her palms burning across the cheap carpet. A swift kick to the ribs and she's sucking wind, the pain spreading up her torso like wildfire.

"Stop it!" Paz screams. From the ground, Millie can see her trying to fight off Cobweb.

Jordan rushes up and seizes Bugs from behind, sinking his thumb deep into his neck. Jordan's got the height and weight but not the experience. Bugs throws a fist into Jordan's kidney. He stumbles, his eyes squeezed shut.

"Leave him alone, he's just a kid," Millie screams.

"You dumb fuck." Bugs pulls his gun. He aims the barrel at Jordan. Paz cries out. Jordan swallows, his nostrils flaring.

The entrance door opens a crack, and everyone freezes.

"Hello? Millie, you in here?" calls her mom's voice.

Bile floods Millie's throat.

"Who the fuck is that?" Bugs says.

Millie's already on her feet. "Shit, it's my mom. Go along with me here, and I'll do anything you want." She raises her voice, calls out, "Just a minute."

"You don't get to make deals with me."

"I do if you want to see any money for that film you don't know what to do with."

Jordan makes a break for the lounge area.

The gun comes up again. "The hell you going?" Bugs snaps. "I don't care who's here; I'll shoot you dead. Now stop and turn around."

Jordan follows orders. Millie wonders if he was going for his backpack, near one of the chairs.

Bugs shifts his eyes to Jordan, then to the door, then back to Millie. "Make this quick," he says, hiding the gun behind his back.

Millie shakes her head. "Keep it out."

"Keep it *out*?" Paz stage-whispers.

"Go with me on this."

Millie scans the room. Cobweb has let go of Paz, but when she tries to walk away, he yanks her back by her belt loop. Devin hasn't moved from the table. He's ashen white except for his red, clenched fists.

Oblivious to all of this is Hatchet, who's sprawled across the couch, checking his phone.

Millie takes a deep breath. "Okay, you can come in."

Her mom knocks twice on the doorjamb, even though she's looking right at her. "Is it safe? Sounds like a barroom brawl in here."

"We were just rehearsing," Millie says. "Of course you can come in."

Mom enters cautiously, Wade behind her. He nods politely to everybody before looking at Millie. His eyes are filled with excitement. "Hi, kiddo. Rehearsing, huh?"

"How'd you guys know I was here?"

"Tracked you down with one of those parental apps," Mom says. "Installed it on your phone after we couldn't reach you at Lois's cabin. Nothing for days and then, all of a sudden, here you are—jeez Louise, that looks like a real gun, don't it, Wade?"

There's a synchronized movement of eyes as everyone looks at Bugs.

"Feels heavy, too," he says.

A quick round of fake introductions is made. Bugs, Cobweb, and Hatchet are local actors. Paz, Devin, and Jordan are students from West Fargo State. Devin's smart enough to remember that he posed as Millie's professor when he talked to Mom before Chicago and uses a different accent—Texan, excruciating, earning a quick glare from Millie.

"Pleasure to meet you, Barb and Wade," says Bugs. He shoots Millie a smug grin. "You must be so proud of your daughter. She's a hell of a director. Won't be too long now before we see the name Millie Larsen up in lights."

"Actually, her last name is Blomquist," Mom says, then looks at her daughter. "Unless you changed it."

Millie shakes no, her eyes on Bugs, watching his reaction. It's small—you'd really have to be looking to see it—but deep in his dark eyes is a tiny flare of recognition. If this were a movie, this would be the one time she'd use an extreme close-up to make sure the audience caught it.

"Blomquist?" Bugs says, then repeats it a few times. "I used to know a Blomquist." He pauses. "You related to Bobby Blomquist, by chance?"

The question paralyzes Millie. "How do you know my dad?"

He gives a shrug and a smile. "Old drinking buddies. Used to run around together—barhopping, chasing girls. Stuff I'm sure your mom doesn't want you to hear about."

Millie's mom throws a dismissive wave. "Must've been before my time." She looks around the room. "Where's all your equipment?"

Paz jumps in. "We're actually shooting on iPhones. All the big studios are doing it now. It's pretty amazing what you can do with the right filter."

"And look at this makeup." Mom touches the cut on Jordan's forehead. He winces, clenches his teeth. "Now, don't make fun of an old woman." She swats him playfully. "Looks so real. It's even warm. How do you do that?"

Millie clears her throat, regains control of her body. "It was so nice that you guys swung by. A real treat." She puts her arms around her mom and Wade and guides them toward the door. "And we're going to talk about how I'm not too thrilled about that tracking app, but right now we have to finish rehearsing."

"Now, hold on." Her mom shrugs her off. "That's not why we came down here. I know that you borrowed money to shoot this thing"— she gives Wade a look—"when I specifically told you that you needed to put it behind you and focus on college. We came to tell you what a mistake you're making by throwing away your life."

Wade gently grips his wife by the shoulder. "Deb, come on, now."

"Wade, let me finish." She takes Millie by the hands. Her palms are soft from lotion, fingers calloused from braiding wreaths. "I was wrong, though. I can tell by what you're doing here that you take your work very seriously. It's all very professional. I owe you an apology." Her lower lip quivers; she squeezes Millie's hands. "I'm very proud of you, Millie."

It's almost too much.

How is it that parents love their kids, even at their worst? Millie assumes it's because they have no idea who their kids really are.

All she does is lie, every word leaving her mouth less true than the one before it. Which is how she's like her dad. Two generations of Blomquists living double lives. Keeping secrets.

Deb Larsen deserves better than this.

If only she knew how irresponsible Millie's been with not just her life but the life of anyone dumb enough to trust her, she would never have said those words.

Millie hugs her mom tight, breathing her in. She fears she may never get another chance. "I love you so much."

Devin speaks up. "You know, Mil, we don't have to finish this tonight." His words are measured, as if one slip will trigger Bugs into mowing them all down. "If you want, we could call it a night and pick things up tomorrow." He arches his eyebrows as if he's had a sudden thought. "You could go with your parents to dinner. Just need to drop the three of us off at school first."

"Hey, that's an idea," Wade exclaims. "I got some venison steaks already thawed. Been marinating in 57 Sauce all day. Nuke a bag of frozen veggies, and we're in business."

"Sounds perfect." Only being at gunpoint would make Millie long for Wade's cooking.

She eyes Bugs, waiting for his reaction. It can't really be this easy, can it?

"How about a picture before you go?" suggests Bugs, looking at Mom and Wade. "Something to remember your first time on set?"

"A picture?" Mom says, like it's a crazy idea, though she already has her compact out and is checking her hair.

"Sure!" Bugs turns to Millie. "Hey, can I have your phone?" He shows her all his teeth, a sight that would make any dentist cringe. Millie hands it over.

Where's he going with this?

"Great," Bugs says to the group. "Why don't you all stand over here. Perfect. Now, Jordan, let's show off that great bruise you've got going, and why don't you stand next to Wade. That's it. Wade, put your fist next to Jordan's face like you just clocked him one."

"Like this?" Wade says, getting into it.

"You're a natural." Bugs whistles for Hatchet and hands him the phone. "I'll get in it, too. Show off these great fake tats Paz gave me."

"They look so real," Mom says.

"Don't they?" Bugs stands next to Mom. He takes out his gun and points it at her. "We'll make it look like I'm holding you hostage."

"Fun!" exclaims Mom.

"Get it up closer to her face," Wade tells him. "We want to make sure the camera can see it clearly."

Bugs brings the gun barrel to within an inch of her mom's head. Millie's knees turn to water. "Everyone say cheese!"

Hatchet says he got the picture, but Millie doesn't hear the camera click. No photo, no evidence to tie them together if he does go through with shooting them.

"How's it look?" Mom asks. "Was I blinking?"

"I'm sure it's perfect," Bugs tells her, returning Millie's phone. "Millie, I hate to be the party pooper, but with my work schedule we really should—"

"Absolutely. We need to shoot tonight." And she needs to get her mom and Wade out of here right now, which proves difficult because any Larsen goodbye takes at least ten minutes, a series of false starts, a slow move to the door, a discussion of leaving with very little follow-through.

Mom's worried Millie isn't properly dressed for a night shoot, so Wade runs to the car to grab one of his sweatshirts, and it almost begins the goodbye process all over again.

"Break a leg," Wade says when they're finally ready to go.

"Proud of you," Mom adds, smiling big. Millie swallows and waves goodbye.

As the front door clicks shut, she hears a wet, metallic thwack and spins around.

Jordan is on his knees, hand pressed against his face. Blood leaks over his right eye. Bugs stands over him, gun by his side. "Try that shit again, and I'll put a bullet in you."

To show he's serious, he slams a boot heel down on Jordan's ankle. Jordan cries out in pain.

"Now hurry up," Bugs orders. "Get in touch with O'Naire and get things set up for Sunday. We're leaving for LA in three hours."

Cobweb and Hatchet jump to it. They grab the boys by the backs of their shirts, shoving them toward the kitchenette, ordering them to pack up whatever food they can find. Any hesitation results in knuckles to the ribs.

Paz cries out for them to stop and runs over to help, Millie close behind with the thought that trusting Aaron wasn't her biggest mistake; it was thinking this whole thing was like a movie in the first place.

It isn't. Not even close. Heist movies are intentional. They're stylized, performed by gorgeous actors delivering scripted speeches. They aren't reality, and they aren't enough to prepare someone for pulling off a heist of their own.

She didn't even watch a documentary on how criminals operate, never cracked a single book on the subject. Instead, she cast herself as the hero and blindly determined that everything would work out, because that's the way it happens in the movies.

Good defeats evil. How incredibly naive.

What is she going to do now? The only thing she can: follow along with whatever Bugs wants, so she can get herself and her crew out of this mess before anyone gets killed.

17

Hoyt lights a cigarette and decides to smoke it outside. He's still second-guessing his alias. Of course a bunch of kids would have thought he meant Bugs Bunny. And what's with Paul's insistence on being called Hatchet? Stupid.

The afternoon air is chilly against his skin. He's only been to LA twice, hated it both times, but now looks forward to the change of scenery and weather. If this job goes as planned, it might even net enough for him to retire and move there for a while, become one of those West Coast yoga assholes who only eats granola and berries and always complains about tourists crowding all the beaches with the good waves. The thought makes him chuckle.

Life is such a funny thing. If someone had told him three years ago

that the biggest score of his career would be masterminded by Bobby
Blomquist's kid, he would have laughed right in their face.

He takes another drag of the cigarette. Bobby was decent enough,
but he lacked the backbone to pull off anything really big. Always
concerned about making sure nobody got hurt. As if that were more
important than not getting caught.

It's why Bobby went for Hoyt's gun when he trained it on the bank
manager, a fat slob who refused to open the safe. Alarm had already been
hit. Police were on their way. No time to squabble. Two shots to Blomquist's
chest and one to the face ended that argument quick, the bank manager
pleading for Hoyt not to kill him too while he punched in the safe's code.

Hoyt never hesitates to pull his gun if it means a clean getaway.
Never. It's as true now as it was then.

The aliases were unnecessary, he realizes. He can't let any of them
live after the job goes down. They might not know his real name, but
Aaron does, and the kids have seen his face. They've seen Paul and Norm.

It's like the Valley City couple they shot yesterday—the same situation. He might not love the idea of killing teenagers, but there it is. It's
either him or them, and it's not a question he has to ask himself twice.

Hoyt flicks his cigarette butt into the parking lot. How about
that? He's going to have to kill the daughter of the man he offed three
years ago.

Life. Such a funny thing.

18

Subject: Fix It in Post

Mr. O'Naire,

If you want *The Art of the Gangster* returned in its entirety, bring
five million dollars cash to the premiere on Sunday. The money is to be

in unmarked bills in a black suitcase with no distinguishing features. It should match the suitcases used during the heist in the movie.

You will receive further instructions once you arrive at the premiere. At no point is the premiere to be canceled and you will show the film in its entirety once received. If you do not follow our instructions, or we see any signs of police interference, we'll destroy the footage. If you do not respond to this email within one hour, we'll destroy the footage.

Have a nice day.

Ricky pockets his phone and continues on toward the restaurant where he's meeting Detective Westlake. So Millie wants to do the exchange at the premiere? Either she's gambling on how desperate he is, or she knows about his debts and who he owes them to.

He decides she definitely has no clue about the latter or who really owns the movie; otherwise, she'd return it immediately. That means she's working off his desperation.

Does she really think he's that pathetic?

It's late in the day, hopefully late enough that the lunch rush is already over. Not that Ricky thinks Tangerine Dream, a smoothie place on the edge of downtown, would get any kind of rush, lunch or otherwise, a theory that's proven correct when he walks in the door.

A handful of customers are slouching over checkered linoleum tables. Hubcaps with glowing neon rims line the walls. A jukebox croons Dean Martin. Westlake's already working on a smoothie, some orange-green slop in a milkshake glass with half a banana sticking out the top.

"Interesting choice," Ricky says.

"Used to be a fifties diner. New owners never got around to changing the decor. Have a seat. You heard anything? Anybody tried contacting you?"

"Radio silence." He slides into the booth.

Westlake recaps the last twenty-four hours. They found the server tower and filing cabinet at a motel in the discount shopping area of Rosemont. The footage was gone. Hard drives stripped clean. There hasn't been any movement on the email address used to book the extras. They did find a van in a rural area that matches the one in the surveillance footage, about ninety minutes away from the city, torched to its metal skeleton. It'll take some time to see if they can pull any prints or find out who it's registered to.

As Westlake talks, Ricky can't help but think about what the guy on the phone said this morning, that someone is always watching, protecting their investment.

Who's new in his life? The production company's a revolving door, but no one has the access needed to check his phone. His inner circle is tight, has been for years, even more so after the Academy fiasco. The only new person is the portly man across from him. And his absent partner.

"Didn't there used to be two of you?" Ricky asks. "What happened to Stark?"

"We have a couple of active investigations going on at this time. He's following up on a lead."

"For this case?"

Westlake twirls his straw around in his smoothie. "Sure." It's a nonchalant *sure*, one that doesn't give any indication that the detective knows who Ricky owes money to, but it doesn't clear him, either.

"I have an update for you, too," Ricky lies. "We found a copy of the film. Well, footage, at least. A backup hard drive one of the assistant editors was working some sound on. It's not as complete as the files that were taken, but it'll do."

The detective lowers his brows, creating a shelf that sits above his eyes. "We've been here for ten minutes, and you're just now telling me this?"

"You called the meeting and had information you wanted to discuss. I didn't think a backup hard drive was vital."

"It is. And I'd appreciate it, the next time you have information, any at all regarding the case, if you'd notify me immediately." The detective grabs the banana from his smoothie and bites it in half. "Now, why didn't your editor, Mr. Schumer, inform me of this earlier this morning when I met with him?"

Great question, a plot hole in his lie he didn't think about. "Probably because Mr. Schumer is no longer employed by me, Detective Westlake. He doesn't know about it."

Westlake taps his pen against the table. Unlike the smoothie, he doesn't seem able to swallow this. "And remind me why you felt there was a need to have such tight security for the film? The separate room inside the studio offices. Thumbprint and voice activation. Seems extreme."

Ricky folds his hands in front of him. "There's literally hundreds of people who'd want to steal the film, Detective. Bootleggers. Rival studios. Obsessed fans. And due to the secretive nature of the way we shot and are distributing the film, we wanted to ensure it would stay under wraps until it was ready to be screened. If we work around the clock, we'll still be able to hold the premiere on Sunday."

Westlake upends the glass and downs the rest of his smoothie. A foamy green mustache lines the bristles of his real one. "Any way to talk you out of that? If the perps find out they don't have the only copy, they may decide not to work with us."

"Afraid not. My main concern was being able to move forward with the distributing studio's timeline. We have a premiere and a release date to honor. I'm going to make sure we do both." Ricky gets up from the booth. "I'm leaving for LA tonight, but if there's anything else I can do for you before then, please let me know. Oh, and Detective?" he tosses off. "You've got a little something right above your lip."

19

WYOMING

They're on the outskirts of a small backcountry town when Millie's phone chimes.

Email from O'Naire.

"We're on for Sunday," Millie tells everyone in the station wagon they stole back in Sioux Falls. "But he's asked that we add a temporary score and edit around the VFX shot that isn't finished. He says if we're capable of stealing the film and its raw footage, then we should be able to handle a little editing. He even sent the Miklós Rózsa score we should use."

She wonders if asking them to edit means he's figured out who's stolen the film. There's no indication anywhere in his response that he has, but given the circumstances, he's got to have his suspicions.

She puts down her phone and realizes that nobody has acknowledged her news.

Devin's riding shotgun. The only time he's spoken since the trailer park is to bum a smoke from Cobweb, who's driving. Jordan is carefully stretched out in the cargo area to get some rest. Millie's hardly up for small talk anyway.

She should be trying to come up with a plan for once they hit LA, but all she can think about is that Bugs knew her dad.

Of course she doesn't buy the "drinking buddies" story. Her father was one and done, most of the time never even finishing his beer, and forget the hard stuff. Bugs was lying, and she's sure it's because they used to work jobs together.

Could Bugs have been part of the bank heist that took her dad's life?

An ache in her throat becomes a pressure in her chest. Her fingers go numb.

Is he the one who pulled the trigger?

Is he the man responsible for destroying her family, walking around without a care in the world, no lessons learned, no heavy burden on his shoulders from the life he took?

This may not be a movie, but it's hard for her brain not to think that way. The whole situation holds the irony of a bad sequel—another Blomquist betting their entire future on one last job, only to be outmatched by the professional criminal who doesn't play by the same rules.

One last job. There's a term Millie sees in a whole new light. It's always going to be the last job if you die during it.

Cobweb pulls the station wagon into a Sip and Zip and stops at the pump behind Bugs, Hatchet, and Paz's stolen RAV4. Nobody says anything until he's filled up and gone inside to pay.

"How bad do I look?" Jordan asks. The cut on his temple is now a raised welt, but it's minor in comparison to the pistol-whipping. His right eyelid is a blood-filled balloon, the surrounding skin bruised red and blue, slowly making its way to purple. It took half the contents of the community center's first aid kit to stop the bleeding. Now, with his head wrapped in gauze, he looks like a coma victim in a soap opera.

"Never better," Devin tells him.

Jordan levers up on his elbows, stares at his reflection in the window, and sniffles. It has a wheeze to it. "Bullshit. Maybe if you'd helped me, instead of sitting there the whole time, my face wouldn't resemble ground beef."

Devin turns all the way around. "I'm fifty-nine kilos soaking wet. What chance would I have?"

"I guess we'll never know," Jordan says sourly.

"At least I tried getting us out of there by suggesting we go with Millie's parents."

"That worked out well," she says. "I have a nice image of a gun pressed against my mom's head for the rest of my life."

Jordan glares at her with his good eye. "Don't try to put that on him."

"Thanks, mate," says Devin.

"Not defending you, just reminding Millie that this is all her fault."

"*My* fault?"

"Come off it, Millie," Devin says, as if the words have been waiting to spring out of him for hours. "This was your plan, your heist. Me, I wanted to make a musical. Something with exquisite costumes and a moral lesson. You wanted to steal a fifty-million-dollar film.

"Now we've been kidnapped. Jordan's hurt. Paz is forced to ride by herself with two psychotic animals. We're driving across the country with stolen goods in stolen vehicles with proper crooks and no plan on how to make the exchange."

His voice turns bitter and angry. "We're screwed. We're completely and utterly screwed. I came to this country to learn how to make films, and instead I became a criminal."

"And that's my fault?" Millie argues. "You're not responsible for your actions at all?"

"I'm responsible for being foolish enough to trust you. I'll give you that. Maybe you do have the right idea: look out for number one, and don't count on others, because they'll only let you down."

"I don't have to listen to this." Millie gets out, slamming the door behind her.

There's a growing silence between Devin and Jordan, who are both looking out the car windows. Devin can see Cobweb paying for his snacks at the register.

"It's still on you, then?" he says.

There's a pause before Jordan says, "What is?"

"Don't do that. Millie might never understand, but if we're going to get through this, we have to do it together. The gun we found in the filing cabinet. You still have it, don't you?"

This time there's no hesitation. "I do."

"Loaded?"

"Half a magazine left. She's right, though. Guns aren't the answer."

Devin twists in his seat to look back at Jordan. "This time they might be."

20

FARGO, NORTH DAKOTA

Aaron wakes to a ringing phone. It's an out-of-state number.

"Millie?"

"No, sir. My name is Tiana. Is this Mr. Aaron Bodeen?"

He sits up on the couch and listens as Tiana delivers the bad news. There's no point in arguing. It's not her decision. She's only doing her job, his name on a list of many she needs to call, on a Sunday, no less.

It's not like he has any way to fix this. No way he's going to make any money from the heist, and the manager job is a lost cause. Friday was six hours straight of interviewing candidates almost a decade younger than he is, knowing that one of them was going to be his boss. Perfect end to a shitty day.

When Tiana's done, he says he understands and thanks her for her time.

"Uh, you too, Mr. Bodeen," Tiana says with surprise.

He looks around the trailer. Aside from some of the appliances and his favorite recliner, the rest of the stuff can go in the trash. Most of it's Carol's, anyway. The chipped walls, the worn carpet, the water-damaged windows—the place is a dump. He would move in an instant if he had somewhere to go.

"Who was that?" Gabrielle asks. She's without makeup, her skin naturally flawless. She sits at the foldout table, smoking a cigarette in one of his Minnesota Wild T-shirts. A coffee-cup ashtray rests in front of her. The whole place reeks.

Aaron wraps a blanket around himself to cover the rolls of his stomach his white undershirt fails to hide. He hates how he's basically been held hostage by his former crush for the past two days and somehow still cares what she thinks about him. Pathetic. "Bank owns the mortgage on this place," he says. "I have thirty days before they kick me out."

Gabrielle looks over the room. "Then they're doing you a favor. Place is a shithole. I'm going to need to schedule a tetanus shot when all this is over."

"You don't have to stay here," he tries. "Don't you have a son? I heard you talking to your mom last night. Go be with him."

She blows a slow plume of smoke up at the ceiling. "Yeah, right. Second I leave, you'll go running to the cops. It's bad enough I can't watch you all the time at work."

"I'm not going to say a word. I would never do anything to jeopardize the safety of Millie and her friends."

"Better not." She stumps out the cigarette, and heads for the bathroom. "I'm going to take a shower. Give me your phone. I don't want you answering any more calls."

Aaron hands it over without an argument. She's already got his laptop.

He lies back down on the couch, listening to the shower running down the naked curves he's been lusting over for months; his desire that has ruined everything.

Silently, he barters for Millie's safety. The bank can take the trailer; Ethan can hire someone half Aaron's age with no experience to be his boss. He'll spend the rest of his life working a dead-end job, coming home alone to an empty apartment—all he asks is for Millie and her friends to be safe.

He waits for some kind of sign that his prayers have been heard, something as simple as a truck backfiring or a chirping bird.

Nothing.

21

LOS ANGELES

Ricky comes out of his meeting with the studio president and board of directors to find Flowers Romero taking pictures of his fiancée's spandex-clad ass. Some crew members outside a nearby soundstage watch in awe.

The sky is awash in a dusty gray haze, backlit clouds hanging just above the black steel LA skyline. Ricky reminds himself that if he wants Lexi to come with him tonight, grabbing Romero's phone and smashing it against his face is not going to get her on board.

Lexi flashes a peace sign at the camera. "How'd it go?" she asks. "We still on for the premiere?"

"They bought it," Ricky says, when he realizes she's addressing him. "Took some convincing, but once I showed them how much publicity they'd be missing, they changed their tune. And I assured them if anything seemed unfinished, we'd still have time to edit the final cut before it gets distributed to theaters. By the end, they were all so relieved we'd found the backup hard drives that they didn't even mention an executive screening before the premiere." He lets out a breath he didn't know he was holding. "Thank God they didn't ask for that."

"Looks like your luck is changing," says Romero.

If it were up to Ricky, the guy wouldn't know a single thing about the movie being stolen. But he's Lexi's best friend, so he hears all her secrets, no matter how much Ricky asks her not to tell.

"I think so," Ricky continues. "I can tell they're excited to experience *Gangster* with an audience. Security's going to be tight, though. We're going to keep it down to one screening. Limit the number of people." Which will hopefully keep out any of his investors' spies, though it will make things tougher for Millie.

Lexi lays a kiss on Ricky's cheek. He can feel her heavy lipstick leave a mark. "That's amazing, baby. I'm so proud."

"Way to go, Rick," Romero says.

"Why, thanks, Flowers. Do me a favor and don't tell anyone about this. It's inner-circle stuff, all right?" His star nods. "Cool."

Ricky puts his arm around Lexi's waist and gives her ass a squeeze. Let Romero post *that* to Instagram.

22

According to the map—which they use instead of a GPS, so there's no digital footprint—it's another two miles until their destination, but Millie's already convinced they're in the wrong place. Where are the fancy storefronts, expensive cars with shiny rims, the patios with Hollywood executives in crisp suits lunching with leggy models? All she sees are strip malls, taco joints, single-story bungalows, and Honda Civics.

"What is this place?" Devin asks with concerned amazement.

"Burbank," Millie says.

They arrive at a redbrick bungalow with a detached garage. Palm trees with droopy brown leaves crowd the front yard, the roof is missing some shingles, and an old-school TV antenna sticks out at the back. It's sandwiched between Spanish-style courtyard apartments and a Mexican ranch in the middle of a renovation.

Millie gets out of the car. The sun is warm, and there isn't much humidity. The air smells equally of jasmine and skunk.

Bugs stands next to her and lights a cigarette. Power lines hum above them. "What's the play? This where your guy lives?"

"Yes," Millie answers and wishes she didn't look so puzzled about it. "He's not expecting me, and this is going to be a bit of a hard sell."

"I can help with that." Bugs grins and covertly lifts his shirt to show the gun in his waistband.

"Your answer to everything is exactly why I'm having you stay out here while I talk to him."

"No way," he says. "I'm not going to let you by yourself. I do that and I'll be surrounded by cops in five minutes."

"I can't just go in there with all of you. His parents could be home. It'll look suspicious."

Bugs takes a drag and looks up at the power lines. "Okay. Not all of us have to go in."

23

A young woman opens the door, mimosa in hand. Her nightgown shows off her long legs and fake breasts that sit up close to her neck. Her skin is singed bronze, her eyeshadow sparkly green smears, hair a shaggy layered bob with blond highlights. Millie can't tell if the woman is just waking up or has yet to go to bed. Neither would surprise her.

"Sorry to bother you," Millie says. "I'm here to see your son, if he's home. I'm a friend of his from the movie academy, and we were supposed to have a breakfast meeting that he didn't show up for."

The woman wrinkles her nose. "Ew. I'm only like four years older than him. I'm his stepmom." She arches a curious eyebrow at the man standing next to Millie. "And who are you?"

Hatchet, surveying the foyer, steps inside the house. Millie follows.

The parquet floor is chipped. Thin gray carpet runs down the stairs to the basement. Through an entryway, she can see a kitchen with Formica countertops and white appliances.

"I'm one of the producers on the project," Hatchet tells her.

The woman gives him a once over. "I know producers. You can't be a producer. Your clothes aren't flashy like you're trying to make up for inadequacies in other areas."

"Maybe I just got a big dick."

"Good Lord," Millie says.

The woman doesn't seem offended.

Hatchet asks, "What do I look like, then?"

"Like a drug dealer."

"Do you want me to be a drug dealer?"

"Would save me a trip."

"Consider me your neighbor. What do you need to borrow? Please say some sugar."

"Is Yates home?" Millie asks, trying to escape the bad porno she seems to have stumbled into.

"You got any LA Turnaround?" the stepmom asks.

"I got kibbles and bits."

"Is that Dexedrine?"

"Yeah."

"Then that's LA Turnaround."

Hatchet digs into his pocket and hands her a portion-control Ziploc a quarter full of orange pills. The stepmom tosses one in her mouth, chases it with a swig of mimosa, and then turns to Millie. "He's downstairs. I'm pretty sure he's asleep, but feel free to wake his ass up. Otherwise, he'll be out until two. It's all he seems capable of doing with his spring break."

Millie walks past her, but Hatchet stays put.

"I'm Gwyneth," the stepmom says to him. "Would you like to see the sculpture garden? All of the pieces are from my thesis project at Valley College. My professor said I have the potential to someday show promise. I know that sounds harsh, but if you knew the man, you'd know that's a hell of a compliment."

"You got anything to drink around here besides mimosas?"

Gwyneth says, "I think we can find something."

24

Yates sleeps in the fetal position. A small pool of spit darkens his pillow. His room is a painful cliché of an aspiring filmmaker without a job. Posters for movies Millie doubts he understands—*Mulholland Drive, Donnie Darko, The Machinist, Primer*—line the walls, and the floor is covered with piles of clothes. Faint traces of weed linger in the air. Blackout blinds do their job. The room is cool and dark, like sleeping in a tomb.

Millie shakes his shoulder and, when he doesn't wake, raps her knuckles on the top of his forehead. "The hell?" He smacks his dry lips and his eyelids flutter. "F-Fargo?"

"I don't have a lot of time, so I need you to listen to me." She sits on the edge of the bed, careful not to touch anything lumpy under the comforter. "There are some very bad men with me, and they're going to kill us if we don't do what they want. They already beat the shit out of Jordan, and they have guns, and I don't think they'll hesitate to use them."

"Then why the hell did you bring them here?" a pile of clothes says. Sammy Chen shakes off a bedspread of T-shirts and sits up, scratching his head. His stomach spills over the waistband of his boxers.

"Sammy?" Millie says. "Shit."

"Nice to see you, too."

Yates wipes crust from the corners of his eyes. "If what you're saying is true, then Sammy has an extremely valid point. Why *did* you bring them here?"

"I need you to sneak us into the premiere for *The Art of the Gangster*. You always said your dad was this big Hollywood exec, so I thought you could help us." She looks around the room again. "That's before I saw your house."

"It's a little underwhelming, right?" Sammy says.

"Shut up," Yates says.

"Sorry." If Millie's going to get him to help, she'll need to tone down the insults. "I'm just surprised that, for someone connected to A-list celebrities and directors like Greta Gerwig, you guys live here. I think it's cool that your dad isn't all caught up in material possessions and stuff."

Sammy's eyes widen. "Dude, you never told me your dad knows Greta Gerwig! Why did we have to sneak that pic when we could've asked him to hook it up?"

"You had to sneak that photo?" Millie says.

"Cost us our jobs with the catering company."

"Sammy, I told you to shut up!"

Millie feels a mixture of relief and panic. Relief for selfish industry reasons—he doesn't get to party with Greta Gerwig, and his career isn't being fast-tracked because of personal connections. Panic because if his dad can't help her, she's got nowhere else to turn.

She says, "Tell me it wasn't all bullshit. That your dad at least works for the studio."

"He bloody well better." Devin leans against the doorframe, arms crossed.

"Dev? What up?" Sammy exclaims. "The rest of the Long Shots here?"

"Paz and Jordan are outside. Bugs wanted to know what's taking so long," he says in response to Millie's puzzled expression.

"Bugs?" Yates asks. "What's a 'Bugs'?"

"I see you haven't gotten very far," Devin says.

"He's their leader," Millie explains.

Sammy chuckles and picks up a half-smoked bowl. "Who are the others? Ants and Fly?"

"Cobweb and Hatchet," says Devin.

"Hatchet?"

"It's a long story."

Sammy nods, as if that's all the explanation he needs. A lighter appears out of nowhere. He fires up, takes a long hit, and holds the smoke in his lungs. The other three just stare at him. "This doesn't concern me, does it?" he says, releasing the smoke. When nobody answers, he holds up the bowl. "Resin hit?"

"Hell, why not," Devin says on his way down to the floor.

Yates swings his legs over the side of the bed, his bare feet still inches away from touching the carpet, and grabs a bottle of aspirin from his nightstand. He shakes out the last three pills and dry-swallows. "Why do I need to sneak you into the premiere? I know you're a big O'Naire fan, but give it a rest. Wait until it comes out next week like the rest of us."

"That's not the reason . . ." God, where does she even begin? "Okay. You know that the movie was stolen, right?"

"I know the marketing department made it seem that way. New strategy." He puffs up a bit for the next part. "My dad helped lay some of the groundwork, not that he's going to get the credit he deserves."

"So your dad does work for the studio?" Millie asks.

"He's in marketing."

"But he's not the *head* of marketing, or the head of *anything*, like you were always banging on about back at the Academy, right?" Devin says. "That's why you worked in the equipment office? So you could pay the cast and crew for your feature project?"

Yates looks at a pile of laundry on the floor. "Yeah. That, and I used the rest of my bar mitzvah money."

"Can we focus?" Millie interjects.

"Seriously," Sammy says, waiting for Devin to take the bowl.

"Apologies," Devin says to both of them.

"Anyways, yes, I know about it," Yates says. "It's a smart move. The movie sites have been buzzing nonstop since it happened, and the premiere tonight is going to be huge."

"This next part is going to sound crazy, but you have to believe me. *The Art of the Gangster* isn't O'Naire's movie. It's really the full-length script I submitted for the feature competition." She speaks deliberately, making sure both Yates and Sammy are giving her their full attention. "O'Naire stole it and made it himself."

"No shit?" Sammy says between coughs.

"No shit. I didn't find out until I saw the trailer. I went to Chicago to confront O'Naire, and he said legally he had every right to do what he did, but gave me twenty thousand dollars not to go to the press. We took that money and used it to steal the edited movie from O'Naire, and now we're holding it ransom for five million dollars. The exchange is scheduled to take place at the premiere. That's where you come in. We need you to help us sneak past security."

Yates blinks rapidly. "You can't be serious." He studies Millie and, when she doesn't indicate she's joking, asks, "You're not really holding O'Naire's movie for ransom, are you?"

"We sure are," Bugs rasps from the doorway, his favorite accessory held loose at his side. "It's about as real as my boy Hatchet giving it to your mom right now out in that sculpture garden. She's not bad. Her work is a little stuck in the impressionist era, but she puts a modern spin on it."

Yates grimaces. "She would've been in, like, preschool when she had me. She's my stepmom." He scans Bugs up and down, taking in the crooked sneer, the tattoos, the scars. Millie can see the moment he realizes he should be scared. Yates sits up straight and flexes his arms. "Who are you?"

"I'm Bugs. I hear you're the man who can help get my money."

PART FIVE

ONE LAST JOB

1

BURBANK, CALIFORNIA

To rob a place, you need to know it inside and out: the floor plan; the location of emergency exits, fire escapes, employee staircases, and elevators; laundry room schedules; break schedules; peak times; slow times; shift changes; the thickness of windows in case you need to break one for a fast exit; what the walls are made of in case you break that window but can't have anyone in the next room hear the glass shatter. The list is endless. The best heists are the result of months or, in some cases, years of meticulous planning and recon.

Millie has less than ten hours.

Out in the living room, she faces her nine-person crew, the largest she's ever worked with: Hatchet and Cobweb on the love seat, a disheveled Gwyneth wedged between them; Devin in a dining room chair he dragged in; Jordan, Paz, Sammy, and Yates filling the other couch. Yates and Sammy nervously assess Jordan's gauze-wrapped head.

Bugs, gun in hand, stands behind all of them.

"I want to start off by saying that I'm sorry," she says, with a sad half smile.

Normally this is when she'd pull out her trusty note cards and deliver a rehearsed speech she'd spent weeks preparing. But not now. She's seen the outcome of making all of those decisions—in fact, it's baring its jagged teeth at her now, a hungry wolf ready to devour its next meal.

"I'm sorry that we're in this mess," she continues. "I'm proud of my script and the project we set out to make at the Academy, but I'm not delusional." She looks around the room to address her original crew, the three she owes more than she'll ever be able to repay. "We were never going to win the Feature Award," she finally admits, noticing the change in their expressions. "I was too controlling, and you can't make a movie without trusting your crew. Same as pulling off a heist. Or a break-in, which is what we're doing, only we're technically not stealing anything. Shit, Jordan, I'm changing my answer. You're right. *Inception* is a heist movie, and I've been a colossal dick, and I'm sorry for that. I really am."

She lets her arms hang by her sides, putting her remorse on full display. She's rambling, but fuck it. That's the downside of going off-the-cuff. At least it's genuine.

She scans the room again. Paz and Jordan—fingers interlaced on Paz's knee—both smile and give her a reassuring look.

In the dining room chair, Devin holds his arms by the elbows, face closed of emotion. If he doesn't forgive her, there's no way she can pull this off.

She needs her partner in crime. Her AD. Her best friend.

"So thank you for sticking by me . . . even if it's because you're being held at gunpoint," she says and lets herself laugh at the absurdity of it all.

Devin quietly joins in, then quickly shuts it down. Is he starting to break?

She looks straight at him. The others probably think she's nuts, but so what. Let them. There's a strong possibility that within the next ten hours her world will go to hell, and it's important to live every day like it might be her last. To say the things that need to be said.

"You need to know that I'm aware this is my fault," she says to Devin, "and if we get through this, I'm going to make it up to you."

And Devin smiles. He doesn't even cover his mouth this time.

"I'll make it up to *all* of you," she adds and laughs again, this time with the rest of her crew, new additions included.

"That's so nice," Hatchet says. "Friendships are everything. They're the family you choose."

Bugs smacks him on the back of the head. "Knock it off." Then, to Millie: "Let's get this shit over with. What's the next move?"

Millie clears her throat. Time to get real. Their lives are on the line, after all. "Okay. The first rule to breaking in somewhere is to know the layout. There are photos of the Radiance Theatre online and tours you can book, but they don't do a great job of showing where everything is in relation to everything else, and they aren't running tours today because of the premiere. They're not just going to hand over their blueprints, and even if they were, we're not dumb enough to ask them directly."

"And why not?" Cobweb asks.

"Because if we did, who do you think the cops would look for first after everything goes down?"

"So how do we get them?" Jordan asks.

"According to their website, the Radiance went through a lobby renovation last year. If we can find out who handled the construction, we can try to get a copy from them."

"Cut to the chase," Bugs orders. "How do we find out?"

"I don't know," Millie says.

Confessing ignorance is a cardinal sin when you're playing the role of a Mastermind, but she's tired of pretending she's something she's not. She doesn't have all the answers. Never did. If this is going to work, she's going to need to rely on her crew.

"I researched the Radiance's manager, but the only thing I learned is that he's kind of a sleazeball; he follows a ton of OnlyFans models on Instagram. I don't see how that helps us."

The crew contemplates their next move in silence, exchanging looks. After a moment, Hatchet raises his hand.

"Yes," Millie says, and when he doesn't answer, she adds, "Hatchet."

He straightens up on the love seat. "We could get the guy a hooker," he says. "You know, exchange sex for information."

Paz makes a face. "Gross."

"Hey, at least he's trying," Gwyneth says defensively.

"That he is," Devin says, "but they're called 'sex workers' now. Show some respect. It is the world's oldest profession." He looks at Hatchet. "And even though the suggestion is somewhat juvenile, it does give me an idea."

2

HOLLYWOOD

Spider-Man, Charlie Chaplin, and a dominatrix Minnie Mouse take pictures with pockmarked fanboys at ten dollars a pop. Street vendors sell maps to stars' homes. A double-decker bus cruises Hollywood Boulevard, the open top packed with tourists using selfie sticks to capture the action outside the Radiance Theatre.

Men and women in blue-and-white-striped shirts, khaki pants, and sunglasses are constructing a low steel barricade around a lush red carpet. Inside the box office, a portly guy in a Mötley Crüe T-shirt shuffles papers, pretending not to check out the two nubile studio employees working the press area.

"Excuse me," Cobweb asks him. "What's playing today? I didn't see any times listed when I looked online."

The manager flicks his eyes to Cobweb and Hatchet, annoyance seeping from every pore. "No showings. Can't you see we have a premiere tonight? Come back tomorrow."

Cobweb slumps his shoulders and makes an *aw-shucks* gesture with his hands. "Shoot. Was hoping to show my brother your new lobby. I saw a movie here last week and thought it'd be perfect for what we're looking to do."

"It'll be there tomorrow, I promise ya. Now if you don't mind—"

"The thing is," Hatchet says, "we won't be in town tomorrow. We'll be on our way back to Barstow. You see, we own a brothel outside the city limits and were hoping to talk to the company who did the work. See if we could pick their brain."

The man smirks a little and leans against the counter. "Brothel out in Barstow? You don't say."

Cobweb winks. "Nice place. Clean beds, clean girls. Looking to spruce it up. Give it that full gentleman experience. We'd be very grateful if you helped us."

"Grateful? I like the sound of that." The manager opens the side box office door. "I'll see if I can wrestle up the name of the construction company. Not that it'll help much. Truth be told, I'm the one who did most of the decorating. I've always had that designer's eye, you could say."

"Might have to have you come and check out our establishment," Cobweb suggests. "Have you stay a night or two. Really get the feel of the place."

The man smiles from ear to ear.

3

Across the street, in front of the Chinese Theatre, Devin watches Cobweb and Hatchet converse with the box office manager.

He sports a floppy cap emblazoned with the Hollywood sign, his nose white with sunscreen. He tucks a star map under his arm and takes pictures of the Radiance with a digital camera he borrowed from Gwyneth.

The intersection of Hollywood and Highland, a few buildings down, is barricaded with a tent and some tables. This looks to be where the cars will drop off the guests for the premiere.

Two men, clearly LA natives, dressed in heroin-chic leather, smirk at Devin. He smiles at them and says, in his excruciating Texas accent, "Big Hollywood pra-meere. How excitin'."

Later, he pads along the alley, taking pictures of the other buildings: some souvenir stores, a chocolate shop, another theater where they shoot a late-night talk show. Behind the Radiance is Hollywood High School, with a mural on the building of famous alumni, among them Carol Burnett and Brandy.

Devin sizes up the back entrance of the Radiance. There's a metal gate fifteen feet high that can only be opened with a security card.

4

BURBANK, CALIFORNIA

Jordan's found some websites of law firms specializing in construction lawsuits. All of them are corny. The worst has all of the attorneys, most of them old white men, wearing orange hard hats in their profile photos. One guy even ditched the suit for a flannel shirt, lunch cooler in one hand, briefcase in the other. A bit much, Jordan feels, for the fake law firm Millie has asked for. The least he can do is make sure their bogus website doesn't pander to the working class.

Once the site's live, he yells to Millie in the other room that it's okay to make the call.

"Get started on the movie website, please," she yells back. "And then I still need you to add the temp score to the movie."

"On it," he replies. He selects a new template, creates a drop-down menu: *News, Reviews, Trailers, Posters, Release Dates.* Since there's not time to create enough content for a full-blown movie news website, he has all the links just redirect to the homepage. That way, if someone visits, they'll just think there's a problem with the coding or something. (If only that army recruiter could see how he's using his computer skills now.) Jordan finishes up by adding some high-res photos and then styles the name across the top: *Revenge of the Film Nerds.*

5

The woman from Harwood Construction is no-nonsense. Her tone is direct, loud over the machines and men yelling in the background. Millie imagines her scrolling the website Jordan made for "Premiere

Law," phone cocked between her shoulder and ear, the other ear plugged by her free hand.

"Like I said, we didn't do anything to the bathrooms, just the lobby," the woman says, "but I'm not surprised they're facing a lawsuit. The manager is a real sleazeball. Kept trying to take me out to dinner, even though I told him I'm a lesbian." She snorts. "I think he thought of it as a challenge."

"Tell me about it." Millie plays along. "Guy is a real pig. Kept undressing me with his eyes. I had to show him a picture of my partner and our son so he'd back off."

"You guys have a son?" In five words, the woman's voice has switched from busy and semi-annoyed to sweet and, possibly, a bit envious. "We've been trying to adopt for two years. It's impossible."

"I know that story. Took us four. Hang in there. If it's meant to be, it's meant to be."

"Thanks. Sometimes I need to hear that." Poor woman. Sounds like she really did. "About the lawsuit . . . yeah, I still have a copy of the blueprints. Should I send them to your office?"

Millie does a happy dance.

"No need. I'll have my intern swing by and pick them up," she says. "She's in the area. But it would be fun to meet someday. Maybe we can even have a playdate."

She hangs up and goes to find Sammy. He's in the kitchen, stoned, slurping milk from a cereal bowl.

"I'm going to run and pick up the blueprints," she tells him. "I need you and Yates to go to a craft store. We need poster boards, markers, sticks. And two dozen balloons."

Sammy wipes away his milk mustache. "Yates is still talking with his dad to get us two volunteer passes. I can go, though. I'll just order an Uber."

Millie surveys him. "You can handle this by yourself?"

Sammy smirks and pours himself another bowl of Cinnamon Toast Crunch. "I got you. What's our color scheme?"

6

PASADENA, CALIFORNIA

Paz finds an equipment-rental facility that has everything they need on such short notice: a digital 4K camera, an attachable video light, and a microphone that a newscaster would use. They even rent out vans. The one she gets is a white Chevy, with more than enough room to hold all the equipment and multiple bodies.

"Why don't you take the van and get yourself a suit while Paz and I go shopping?" Gwyneth says to Bugs. "Unless you want to help us pick out an evening gown?"

"You two have fun." He takes the keys from Paz and hops into the front seat.

Paz still hasn't figured out Gwyneth's play in all of this. Nobody has forced her to help; in fact, neither Paz nor Bugs even asked her to come along. She must find it exciting, Paz decides, a welcome distraction from being a young, drunken housewife with little to do.

They drive to Adrian's Discount Gown Farm in Long Beach. A banner announcing *Prom Season Blowout 50% Off!* hangs from the rafters under yellow fluorescents. Teenage girls of all shapes, sizes, and complexions run around, yelling and scrambling for the limited dresses that remain, crying when their favorite one doesn't fit and celebrating the victory when it does.

Gwyneth comes out of a dressing room in a flowing, backless evening gown with a side cutout. Her boobs spill out of her bodice; there's more skin showing than fabric. She stands next to Paz, who's wearing a conservative black number with a halter neckline and trumpet skirt. Next to her is a skinny brunette with braces who has trouble filling out her top.

"Let me try a different size," the girl says to her boyfriend. He doesn't seem to hear her, his focus squarely on Gwyneth.

"You two going to prom together?" she asks after the brunette with braces is gone.

The boy shrugs. "Nothing set in stone. Plans can be broken."

"You got a car?"

Paz says, "Jesus Christ."

7

BURBANK, CALIFORNIA

Spread across the Elliots' coffee table are the blueprints for the Radiance Theatre, pencil marked with false starts and dead ends. A laptop with Devin's pics sits nearby. *The Hot Rock* plays on the TV in the background. Millie stands above the schematics, arms crossed, mechanical pencil between her teeth. She's been frozen like this for ten minutes now, unsure of their next move.

Devin comes in from the kitchen, a plate of food in each hand. "Gwyneth took some time away from testing the headboard with Hatchet to make everyone some lunch. She is rather lovely when not committing adultery."

Food breaks Millie's paralysis. She takes one of the wraps off the plate before Devin sets it on the table. Over the past few days, she's learned that meal breaks are few and far between. Best to fuel up when you can.

"Can you take a look at these?" Millie asks after she's finished half of the surprisingly good chicken-salad wrap. "I'm confused. According to this, it looks like there are two projection rooms, but why would they do that for a one-screen theater? Doesn't make any sense."

"Let me see." He runs his finger down the blueprint for the auditorium, then checks it against another page. "The upstairs room isn't original. See, if you compare the dates here, it wasn't added until the nineties."

Millie looks where he's touching the corner of the blueprint. If they get through this, she's going to take an online class on how to read schematics. Much more useful than knowing how many heist films include music montages—surprisingly, only 22 percent.

"How do you know that?" she asks.

"My father is an architect," he says. "Sometimes I listen. My guess is that at some point in the nineties they were going to convert the balcony into a separate theater and changed their minds."

"Makes sense. Ever been to a movie with one showing on top of another? It's awful. The sound leaks, the upstairs theater's always cramped, the picture's slightly distorted because of the projection angle." She points her half-eaten pickle at the blueprint. "So you're saying this room is empty?"

"More than likely. Or it's an office, but it won't be used during the premiere. The light from these windows would be distracting."

An empty room with multiple access points, secluded enough to be out of the way, but still close to the rest of the guests, so she can call out for help if needed . . .

She clicks the mechanical pencil and circles the second projection room. "That's where we're going to make the exchange."

Devin takes a seat across from her. He rubs his hands together. Nervously taps his feet.

"What is it?" she finally asks.

He stops fidgeting and gives a tight-lipped smile. "How confident are you feeling about all this? Honestly."

Millie rocks back on her heels and takes the last bite of her wrap. "Honestly?" she says after she swallows, knowing full well he's not going to like her answer.

8

In the half bath off the kitchen, Devin opens Jordan's backpack and gingerly removes the gun they found in O'Naire's filing cabinet. It's the first time he's had a look at the thing. In fact, it's the first time he's ever held a gun.

Probably a rite of passage for Americans, he figures.

He carefully wraps the gun in a hand towel and buries it underneath the hard drive in the other backpack he's taken: Millie's.

9

The crew stands on a cement slab under a retractable cloth awning. The sun splits the horizon, the moon faint in the sky as it patiently waits its turn. Gwyneth's sculptures are arrayed nearby. Calling the display a "sculpture garden" is generous; it's just five small statues of various sizes and disproportions sitting on a dying lawn. It reminds Millie of an idea conceived by Tim Burton but produced by a five-year-old.

Everyone's in full wardrobe, as is Millie, standing in front of them, trusty note cards in hand. Even though she's discovered she can wing it, old habits die hard.

"The most important thing to remember," she begins, "is that O'Naire is the best kind of Mark. A desperate millionaire on the verge of losing not only his fortune but his reputation. To someone like him, that's worth more than any dollar amount. His entire future rests on him getting his film back."

She pauses for a moment, letting what she said sink in.

His film.

Millie is shuffling to the next note card when Sammy catches her eye. He wears dark sunglasses and a white nylon bomber jacket. AirPods hang from his ears.

"Sammy, you're supposed to be in Academy gear. What the hell is this?"

"He thought we got to pick our own roles," Yates explains, "and he wanted to be the getaway driver. He's channeling *Drive* meets *Baby Driver*."

"Check it out," Sammy says. He turns around to show her a poorly drawn scorpion on the back of his jacket.

A ripple of laughter spreads through the crew. Even Millie can't help it, until she sees the gun coming out from behind Bugs's back.

"I'm glad you've all been having fun this afternoon playing heist flick, but this is serious," Bugs says. "You're not playing a fucking role. If we don't get that money, it's going to be an issue. A big one. And then we're going to have a conversation, and believe me, it will not go your way." He looks at them all. "Does *everyone* understand?"

Cobweb mimes cutting his own throat as illustration.

Everyone silently nods. Millie's breath hitches. She tries to catch Devin's eye, but he's exchanging a look with Jordan. Even though she can't see their faces, it's clear that they, and Paz, are as scared as she is.

She tosses her useless note cards into the garbage can. "Let's get going."

10

HOLLYWOOD

An hour's drive later, Devin looks up at the Radiance and a night sky striped with bright white spotlights. At the registration tent, a series of women—uniformly beautiful, all in gorgeous gowns and equipped with headsets and iPads—talk in unison, but not with each other. A fiery redhead whose name tag reads *Amber* tells someone in her headset to bring more ice to concessions, then asks Yates for identification.

"I remember you from the Zendaya premiere," Amber says. "You were late then, too."

"The office told my dad we were supposed to report to the Hollywood Hotel on Highland," Yates says in the entitled-rich-kid voice Devin knows all too well. "We waited for twenty minutes." He smooths out his suit coat, then adds, "It was hot," to express his extreme displeasure with the situation.

After Amber looks at Devin's passport, she hangs orange laminates around their necks and sends them through the metal detectors.

The Radiance isn't what he expected. The walls are green granite. The carpet is teal-and-orange paisley, and there's a mosaic mural of palm trees and flamingos with a nineties vibe on the wall leading into the auditorium.

In front of an illuminated display of famous past Hollywood premieres, Devin and Yates stand at a card table and hand out free popcorn and sodas. Once again, not the fancy night out he was hoping for. Instead of his tux, he's wearing a suit belonging to Yates's father that looks like a buy-one-get-two-free type of deal. He sighs. Who's the rich twat now?

On the upside, he's in a great position.

The front entrance is around the corner. The stairs leading down to the lower levels are on his right, stairs up to the balcony and the third level on his left. Bored security guards stand at the bottom of each—nothing his laminate can't get him past.

11

A crowd of gawkers lining the sidewalk in front of Hollywood High stares at the back of the Radiance Theatre, where spotlights circle the sky. Cobweb parks the van in front of the school. As Paz gets out, the back of her stiletto slips off her heel, causing her to stumble.

"How the hell do women walk in these?" she yells out into the night.

Dressed up, Paz looks closer to someone in her midtwenties than a seventeen-year-old. Her facial jewelry has been removed, her hair is held up by a silver flower clip, and she wears a touch of purple lipstick and eyeshadow. She immediately ruins the effect by fidgeting with her dress, pulling it down on the sides and in back, wishing it weren't so tight.

Bugs gets out of the van. The chocolate-colored suit he picked out is nice and goes well with his skinny red tie. It matches the dozen red balloons and heart-shaped box of candy he carries. "I'm going to take Selma to Cherokee, then up to the Boulevard," he says. "If we're not dead or in jail, we'll meet back here when it's over."

"Hell of a pep talk," Paz mutters.

Cobweb, dressed in all black, starts unloading equipment from the back of the van. Paz goes to help him, slinging the camera bag over her shoulder. They make their way up to the theater, Paz limping after half a block.

At the registration tent, she gives Cobweb the camera bag and checks in with the premiere staff. The good news is that the website Jordan created is on the press-pass list. The bad news is that it's online-only, meaning they have to stand in the section with the other movie websites.

Celebs generally skip online-only because, if they have to talk to the press, they at least want to do so on live television. Millie was very specific: they need a spot where they can get O'Naire's attention, and also one where Bugs can spot them when they give the signal.

Cheering and applause erupt from the fan zone. On one of the TV monitors, Paz can see Flowers Romero get out of his limo and wave at the crowd. The celebrities are starting to walk, which means O'Naire will arrive at any moment.

"Follow me," she tells Cobweb. They find a spot along the curve of the barricade, right before the final stretch to the theater entrance. She stands next to a female anchor with bleached blond hair and overfilled lips.

"Hey, watch it," shouts a cameraman from *Hollywood Daily*. "You're in my shot."

"Tighten up your shot, then," Paz retorts.

"This is our spot."

"There's plenty of room for us both to shoot here."

"This area is for *network* only," the anchor says with her nose in the air. "Your passes are for online. Get down at the end."

"There was a mix-up at check-in, and they ran out of network passes. Go ask for yourself if you don't believe me." Paz knows that this woman won't lose airtime to follow up.

"What network are you even with?"

"Telemundo."

"*Sí*," Cobweb says, like Speedy Gonzales.

"Telemundo's already broadcasting from the other side of the carpet," the anchor says, like Paz is an idiot.

"Ocho," she clarifies. "Telemundo Ocho. The studio is hoping for a big Latine following, so they sent two Telemundo crews."

"There's literally, like, only one Latine actor in this movie."

"And that's why we're here. To expose the truth."

The cameraman marches up to Paz and shoves a fat sausage finger in her face. "Fuck off and find somewhere else."

"You can't talk to me like that," protests Paz.

"The hell he can't," the anchor snaps.

The cameraman looks like he has more to say, but Cobweb grabs his arm and twists it behind his back. Then he pulls back the guy's thumb. Even over the roar of the crowd and paparazzi shouting for the celebrities' attention, Paz can hear it snap.

"Next, I'll break the other nine, then get started on your face," Cobweb says flatly. "This is our spot."

The cameraman picks up his camera with his good hand, and walks away. The anchor watches for a moment before begrudgingly hiking up her gown and following.

"Okay, then," Paz says, wobbling on her stilettos. "Give me a high-angle pan on the crowd and then tighten in on me. We should probably white-balance the camera before—"

"I don't know what any of that means," Cobweb interrupts. "You want me to actually shoot this? It could be entered into evidence if we get caught."

Paz sighs. It's a good point. Figures, though. She never gets to direct.

12

From his spot in front of the Hollywood Wax Museum, Hoyt has a clear view of the red carpet across the intersection. Behind him, in the museum's lobby, tourists take photos in front of a replica Hollywood sign, fighting over who gets to stand inside the Os.

He reaches into his jacket pocket and discovers that he left his smokes in his Dickies. Since there's time to kill, he asks people passing by if they can spare a cigarette.

"Of course, of course, happy to," says a woman with curly hair and a brand-new Disneyland T-shirt. She pulls a pack of cigarettes from a pink fanny pack. "See you got your hands full. What are the balloons and flowers for?"

"Asking a woman to marry me," he says, sticking to the cover story Millie provided. She even offered tips and tricks on how to "commit to character," as if he hasn't been running scams since he dropped out of elementary school. If there is anything he doesn't need, it's advice on how to sell a lie.

"She's working that big premiere across the street," Hoyt says. "When she's done, I'm meeting her here. She thinks we're going to grab a burger somewhere, but I'm going to surprise her and take her through the wax museum, then out to a steak dinner at Musso & Frank's." He pauses in case the woman wants to ask, *Why the wax museum?* and when she doesn't, he explains it to her anyway. "You see, everyone has always told my girlfriend—Catherynne's her name; that's Catherynne with a *y* and two *n*'s. It's confusing and takes longer to spell, but she's worth the extra time. Anyways, people have always told Catherynne that she looks like Judy Garland. Inside the museum they have a *Wizard of Oz* exhibit. Dorothy, the Cowardly Lion, the Scarecrow, the Tin Man. I think they even have a wax Toto." He pauses. "Shoot, they better have a wax Toto. It's just not going to be the same without a wax Toto."

The woman with the fanny pack pats Hoyt's arm. "I'm sure they have a Toto, dear. They're very good at what they do."

"You think?" He fakes a sigh of relief. Worrying about the wax Toto really adds a layer of credibility to the story. "Thank God."

Beyond the woman, on the red carpet, which he's been watching the whole time—a remarkable accomplishment, considering the performance he's giving—Ricky O'Naire and a pair of legs worth stabbing your grandmother for get out of a vintage Rolls convertible.

Hoyt lets one of the balloons slip from his grasp as he continues the story. "So, as I was saying, I'm going to take her through the museum, and when we get . . ."

13

A single red balloon floats into Millie's sight line.

"O'Naire's here," she announces, lowering her binoculars.

They're in front of the Hollywood Roosevelt hotel, two blocks away from the Radiance and the wax museum. The theater marquee sizzles neon in blue, green, yellow, red. Glossy limousines inch their way down Hollywood Boulevard. Surgically enhanced women in chic gowns grasp the arms of buff men in tailored suits. Their shoes sinking into plush red velvet, they carefully walk past fabricated studio backdrops, and when it's time to pose, they're swallowed by the photographers' dazzling light.

Millie remembers what her father said, all those years ago: *Maybe someday you'll make a movie that'll have its premiere here. You know they show all the big films.*

She shudders. Her chest rises and falls. The binoculars shake in her hands.

You see, Millie, everything has to go to hell sometimes . . .

". . . so that the hero can show what they're worth," she finishes.

Sammy is curious. "What's that?"

"Nothing." She kneels and sets her backpack down on the sidewalk with a thud.

"Easy," Jordan says. "Hard drives aren't indestructible." He's got the bill of Millie's Dodgers cap pushed down to hide the fresh gauze covering his bruises.

"Probably sounded worse than it is," she says, unzipping the bag to stash the binoculars. She shrugs on the backpack and takes the megaphone from Sammy. "You guys ready?"

He and Jordan each grab a sign from the stack of eight resting against a palm tree. Sammy's sign reads *Ricky O'Naire Stoll My Edumacation.* Jordan's says *Will Sound Design for Food.* Hatchet takes a battle stance, feet spread apart, double-fisting four signs. They're all wearing Manhattan Movie Academy T-shirts.

"I want to say this is the best plan I've ever been a part of," Hatchet tells

Millie. "Usually we just break people's fingers with a hammer until they agree to do what we want. It's nice that we don't have to hurt anybody."

"Thanks." It's easy to see why out of all the criminals, Gwyneth picked him to sleep with. He's the politest and has the least amount of facial scarring.

Millie holds up the megaphone. "Ladies and gentlemen, may I have your attention, please?" A crowd slowly gathers. "We are former students of the Manhattan Movie Academy. Ricky O'Naire stripped us of our education, our tuition dollars, and our futures. He's a thief, and instead of being behind bars, he's with his supermodel girlfriend, walking the red carpet for his new movie backed by a major studio."

"We won't stand for this!" yells Jordan, pumping his sign.

"The bastard remade *Dunston Checks In* and didn't even ask Jason Alexander to do a cameo," Sammy cries. "How can you not honor that man's performance?"

Some random guy in the crowd calls out, "Exactly. Like, what is Alexander doing besides waiting for Jerry Seinfeld to throw him a bone?"

Sammy high-fives him. "Stand with us, brother."

"I'm in!" the guy shouts. "We're all in!"

The crowd rushes up, taking protest signs, waving them in the air. Following Millie's lead, they march in a circle, rhythmically chanting, *"We're not back, we never left, we won't stand for Ricky's theft!"*

14

Devin would never have believed it if he weren't seeing it with his own eyes, but Yates is actually something of a ladies' man. Amber, the redhead who gave them their laminates, came to check on the popcorn supply ten minutes ago—a job someone else could clearly do—and hasn't left. She laughs at Yates's poor attempts at humor. She "accidentally" touches his hand when reaching for sodas to hand out.

The douchebag count in this town must be staggering for Yates to be considered a prize.

Amber slams a bottle of Sprite onto the table. "Dammit, are you serious?" She looks up at the ceiling. "We almost got away with it."

"What is it?" Yates's question is answered by the loud chanting that fills the lobby.

Devin shushes an irritating child who wants extra cheddar on her popcorn, giving her the entire shaker and sending her away. The chanting is his cue.

"Goddamn protesters," Amber says. "Poor Ricky O'Naire. It's like, he paid his debt to society, you know? He was basically a hermit for, like, six months."

"Totally. Those prats," agrees Devin. "Say, can I use the toilet?"

"Volunteers can't use the bathrooms until the movie has started. Can't have Jon Hamm waiting in line to take a shit because you forgot to go before you left home."

"I'll only be a minute."

"He won't be gone long," Yates reassures her.

She looks at him. Something passes between the two of them—either contempt or lust. Hard to tell.

"Hurry up," Amber tells Devin.

He doesn't waste any time. He hands over his scooper and heads down the hall toward the public staircase. When he looks back, Amber and Yates are absorbed in conversation, completely ignoring the growing line in front of them.

Which makes slipping down the employee staircase remarkably easy.

15

"What you got in there, Ricky?" one of the paps asks. "Couple of sub sandwiches for you and your girl?"

"No need. Plenty of food inside," Ricky says with a contrived laugh, then hoists the briefcase handcuffed to his wrist so all can see. "Copy of tonight's feature, staying with me until it's on the screen. Not taking any chances after the week I've had."

Another pap smirks. "Like you didn't orchestrate the whole thing."

In the past, Ricky's typically been annoyed by the bottom-feeders that are the red-carpet press pool, their desperation to exploit, their manipulation of the truth to make a quick buck. He's been a victim more times than he can count. But after months of the cold shade that comes from being out of the spotlight, he embraces the cascade of camera flashes.

It's short lived, however. He remembers he has no idea where to deliver the ransom briefcase handcuffed to his wrist, or what he's supposed to show this audience if Millie doesn't produce the finished film.

She really is taking this down to the wire. He checks his phone again.

"You want to focus up?" Lexi says out of the side of her mouth.

He slips his arm around her waist. She's a knockout in a slinky silver deco flapper dress. It shows off the soft slope of her neck, her delicate shoulders, those never-ending legs; it also pairs nicely with his white tailcoat tuxedo.

They make a perfect picture—one Ricky can't enjoy because the crowd of protesters across the street are getting louder by the second.

And then there's Flowers Romero. "Tough break, Rick," he says, sliding up to Lexi and resting his hand at the small of her back. "But no such thing as bad publicity, right?"

"Hey, that's great," one of the paps yells over the barricade. "Ricky, you wanna get out of the shot?"

Ricky denies himself the pleasure of giving this man the finger. "He's all yours, fellas," he says as he guides Lexi away. "Make sure he's in focus. Going to be a big star after tonight."

Romero flashes an appreciative smile and then says, practically in a shout, "Thanks, Rick. So you found the film? We're good to go?"

What part of keeping this information to himself does this idiot not understand? Ricky leans in and hisses, "Smile and pretend I'm saying something encouraging, you miserable shit. I told you to keep your mouth shut. There are things going on that you have no idea about, and if you fuck this up, I'll make sure they bury you. Now laugh, and pretend we're best friends."

The color drains from Romero's face, his mouth slightly open, his eyes devoid of any Hollywood sparkle.

"I said *laugh*, goddammit."

And just like that, the million-dollar smile returns as Romero slaps Ricky's back and lets out a hearty laugh. "That's great. Rick O'Naire," he announces to the crowd. "Living legend, everyone. One of the all-time greats."

The red carpet's been ruined by his errant star and this crowd of bleeding-heart protesters. Ricky directs Lexi past the media correspondents who were promised interviews. They're almost to the front entrance when a single voice rises above the cacophony.

"Ricky, that's my briefcase!"

He comes to a sudden stop, nearly yanking off Lexi's arm. *The briefcase.* He'd almost forgotten.

"Jeez, Rick, you trying to make me fall?" Lexi says.

He hears the voice again and lands on a Latine reporter—pretty, but honestly too thick to be on-camera talent—and her cameraman, a walking rhino with a bull ring plugging his nose.

"Darling," he tells Lexi, "will you find Flowers and have him escort you in?" His eyes stay on Millie's people.

"Uh, sure. I thought you wanted tonight to be about us?"

"It is, baby. It is. I'm just worried about how he's handling the press. Do me a favor and save him from himself?" He gives her a kiss on the cheek, a move the cameras capture a hundred times over.

When Lexi is gone, Ricky goes over to the reporter. "Trying to set me up?" He gestures at the camera.

"It's not on," she says. "You think I want a record of this?"

"Where's my film?"

"Money first," grunts the cameraman.

"No way," says Ricky. "Not in a million years."

The reporter throws the cameraman an irritated look. She's not the brains, but she's the one Millie's sent to do the talking. "There's a projection room on the third floor. Be there in five minutes."

"What about security?"

The reporter looks over at the crowd of protesters. "They shouldn't be a problem by then."

16

Bouquet of balloons in one hand, the fanny-pack woman's hand in the other, and with Paz, Cobweb, and Ricky O'Naire in his sight line, Hoyt speaks softly, his lip slightly quivering, his eyes glossy with tears.

"'Catherynne, people have told you your whole life that you look like Judy Garland, and even though I don't really see it, I want you to know that, to me, it's not that you look like Judy Garland but that Judy Garland was fortunate enough to have a sliver of your beauty, and if I was in charge of the world, I'd create a Catherynne wax museum so that everyone could see how lucky a man I really am.' And then I'll give her a minute to wipe her eyes, not because I think it's that great a proposal—"

"It's wonderful," the woman with the pink fanny pack says, squeezing his hand.

"Oh, thank you. It's not bad, but I think she'll cry because she's a crier in general, so I'll wait until she's done and then I'll drop to one knee, the left one because my right one isn't too good, and that's when I'll ask her to marry me."

The woman is left speechless. "That's the most beautiful thing I've ever heard. I'm so excited for you," she says, bouncing in place and flapping her arms in glee.

Ricky O'Naire disappears under the neon of the theater's marquee. Norm flicks the white light on top of his camera twice before turning it off.

"Thank you so much for your confidence," Hoyt says and hugs the woman, letting go of the balloons. He waits a few seconds before looking up and crying, "Oh no! Wait, come back! Why is this happening?"

The woman's face falls. "Sweetie, your balloons!"

17

Eleven red balloons soar high above the Boulevard, at times catching the spotlights before disappearing somewhere over the Dolby Theatre.

"She did it," Millie says. She looks to Hatchet. "You ready?"

"Rock and roll."

"Be careful," Jordan says to her. "Don't do anything stupid. If anything goes wrong, yell for security."

"I will. I promise. You good?"

Jordan looks over the chanting crowd that he'll lead into battle. He swallows hard. "We've got it from here."

18

"*We need more people out front,*" a voice blares from the security guard's radio. "*The protesters have taken over the red carpet. I repeat, they've taken the red carpet. It's a riot.*"

Over the back door hangs a monitor with a view of the Radiance's alley. The footage is in night vision mode. The security guard stands like he's guarding Buckingham Palace or the crown jewels: back straight, eyes narrowed, hand on his holster.

Devin's heart crashes against his chest. Is everybody in America bloody armed? He waits until Millie and Hatchet appear on screen before revealing himself.

"You can't be back here," the security guard says. "This is a restricted area."

"Calm down, mate. Just want to pop in the alley for a smoke." Devin displays his laminated alibi. "I can't exactly go out front now, can I? It's like the end of *Day of the Locust*." He stares at the monitor. "Holy shit. That woman's being attacked."

The guard's head snaps around.

Hatchet holds Millie by the front of her Academy T-shirt, shaking her violently as she struggles to get away.

"What are you waiting for?" Devin yells.

"Maybe they're having a disagreement," says the guard. "I don't wanna make things worse by throwing around accusations."

"A *disagreement*? He's about to bash her face in."

Hatchet cocks his arm, brings it around, connects with Millie's jaw. She falls to the ground, greeted by quick kicks from his massive boot.

"Obviously not a disagreement, as you can clearly see," Devin says. "Get out there."

"Dude, I only make fifteen an hour." The guard reaches for the radio clipped to his shirt. "Let me get some backup."

Devin's throat closes. If more security shows up, there's no way he'll be able to get Millie into the theater on his own. They'll probably do a bag check, and she'll be handcuffed in minutes.

He tosses the cigarette and takes the quivering security guard by the shirt. "She's going to have to go to the hospital, or worse, if you don't save her. You want that on your conscience?"

As planned, Hatchet flees the moment the guard enters the alley. Devin watches Millie collapse in the man's arms, still thanking him when they come stumbling in the doorway.

She's a staged mess—chin covered in fake blood, hair wild, face streaked with Visine tears. "Thank you so much for helping me," she fake-cries, showing why she's behind-the-camera talent. "I was cutting through the alley to duck the red-carpet traffic, when out of nowhere this guy attacked me."

"Let me help you with that, love." Devin removes her backpack, then helps her to one of the steps. "You saved her life," he tells the security guard. "You're a real hero."

The man grips his belt buckle with both hands. "Glad that guy was smart enough to run away when he saw me. Would've ended pretty badly for him otherwise."

The contents of the backpack have shifted. Devin can see the outline of the gun Millie doesn't know she's carrying; the hand towel he wrapped it in no longer doing its job.

"I'll need to inspect your bag," the guard tells Millie. "It's protocol. I'm sure you understand."

"Of course. There's just my hard drive, and a sweatshirt in case it gets cold."

"Look at her, mate," Devin pleads. "She's bleeding all over the place. I need to take her to get cleaned up and receive medical attention."

"There's an office on the third floor that has a first aid kit. Give me a second."

"Yeah, but she's—"

It's a quick look that Millie gives him, barely noticeable, but he gets the point. He shuts up, gripping the railing, holding his breath as the security guard rummages inside the backpack. He pushes aside the hard drive and cocks an eyebrow. He first looks at Devin, then at Millie.

"Something wrong?" Millie asks.

You have no idea, thinks Devin.

"Yeah, there is," the guard says and reaches inside.

If Devin shoves him down the stairs, the fall should be enough to knock him out.

The man pulls out a thin hooded sweatshirt.

Devin puts his hand to his damp chest to make sure his heart is still functioning.

"NDSU?" the security guard scoffs. "You must be from North Dakota, because no one would support that pack of cheaters otherwise. They're like the Patriots of Division One football."

"What's it to you?" counters Millie. "Where you from?"

He lifts his chin. "Ohio. Youngstown State, baby."

"I think I've heard my stepdad talk about that team. He usually naps when we play them. A 'practice game,' I think he calls it?"

"Is that so?" The guard is smiling.

Devin clears his throat. "Are you done, or did you save her life so she could bleed to death here on the stairs?"

With time wasting, they hurry down the hall, Devin cleaning the fake blood from Millie's chin with wet wipes while she rakes a brush through her hair. She yanks her Academy T-shirt over her head, revealing a thin white blouse underneath. Devin stuffs the T into the backpack, then helps her thread her arms through the straps.

"That feels better," Millie says. "What'd you do? There was something poking me before."

Devin urges her forward. "We need to keep moving."

19

Hoyt takes a deep drag of his smoke as he watches the chaos unfolding in front of him. Reporters, cameramen, and photographers are trying to both escape the riot and capture it for posterity. There must be at least two hundred people milling around on the red carpet, some of them in costume: Marilyn Monroe, Willy Wonka, Belle from *Beauty and the Beast*. He can see Jordan and Sammy and Paz in the thick of it, swinging their signs over their heads like battle-axes. Good for them, he thinks, finishing his cigarette and crushing it out on the Muppets' Hollywood star. Let them have their fun.

He walks casually, no need to hurry, Norm joining him near the theater's entrance.

"Cobweb," Hoyt says in greeting.

"Bugs," Norm replies.

Thankfully, some genius had the idea to place the metal detectors at the start of the red carpet instead of at the theater entrance, and since the event staff are too busy yelling into their walkies or trying to usher stranded celebrities inside, nobody frisks them, and the .45 Hoyt is carrying doesn't trigger any alarms when they reach the Radiance's doors and quietly slip inside.

20

Light seeps out from under the projection room door. A cough erupts from inside.

Millie steadies her nerves. The protest worked. There are no security officers or employees around. The hallway is quiet, the sounds of anarchy in the lobby diluted by the two levels between them. For better or worse, they're alone.

The door closes behind Millie with a tiny click.

Since the little room is used not for projection but for storage, it seems that much smaller. Yellowed movie posters cover the walls. Dusty 35mm projectors take up space in the back, next to a shelving unit packed with old film reels, some encased, others protected only by plastic shopping bags. Next to the shelves is a table with a film splicer and viewfinder.

The air is musty and makes Millie's eyes itch.

"I found a print of *The Rocketeer*," O'Naire remarks, looking up from the viewfinder as if he's at the library. "They had the premiere here. I almost forgot about that one. Great premise—brash young pilot, fighting Nazis with a jet pack. Now there's a movie begging for a reboot."

He smirks and leans against the editing table, the briefcase still cuffed to his hand. He doesn't look as angry as she thought he'd be. In fact, she realizes, he looks more pleased than anything else.

"Tell me," O'Naire asks, "did I fund the entire operation?"

She matches his lighthearted tone. "Not entirely, but you certainly got it green-lit and into production."

"The Mark is unknowingly the Backer." O'Naire chuckles. "Shit, that's good."

"You don't look surprised by any of this," Millie says slowly. "How long have you known it was me?"

"Had my suspicions once I saw the rehearsal space and heard the details. It's hard to be a criminal and pull off such extensive choreography."

21

They get looks—with their appearance, it's hard for Hoyt and Norm not to get looks—but nobody asks for identification or questions what they're doing there. Too much going on with the riot outside.

"They must think we're stuntmen," Hoyt says to Norm, then grabs a bucket of popcorn from a table where that kind-of-rich kid makes out with a redhead, both oblivious to their surroundings. Hoyt shakes his head. Even kind-of-rich people live differently.

He and Norm both shove handfuls of popcorn into their mouths and ascend the staircase.

22

Damp circles have started to form under his armpits; the collar of his shirt sticks to his neck. Devin opens his suit jacket and fans it to whip up a breeze. Everything is hot and damp and unsteady, his knees on the verge of buckling, a knot in his stomach so large it'll have to be medically removed.

He paces in front of the projection room door, breathing deep, keeping himself psyched. Now's not the time for doubts, not when everything is so close to being over.

The staircase groans as two shadows grow against its wall. He can hear Bugs's voice. Devin reaches inside his suit jacket and takes hold of the gun.

23

Through the projection room window, Millie can see that the Radiance has lavish, color-splashed, East Indian–painted walls stretching up to a high, curved ceiling. There, a grid of lights illuminates a grand stage whose heavy velvet curtains are pulled back, revealing a large movie screen.

The theater is empty.

"You've ruined my premiere," O'Naire says.

"At least you get one." Millie slings the backpack off her shoulder. "Let's just get this over with."

O'Naire takes a deep breath, then produces a key from the inside pocket of his white tailcoat. "No showdowns, then. No surprises, no double crosses." He unlocks the handcuffs and sets the briefcase in the center of the small room. "Put the hard drive on the floor, take the briefcase, and leave. And a word to the wise: don't ever come back to this town. You're finished in Hollywood."

"Thanks to you, I never got started," she says with spite.

His mouth is twisted, his eyes dark. There it is. There's the anger she was expecting from the start, the Ricky O'Naire she knows. If you strip away the prestige and the box office numbers and the awards, you're left with this—another angry rich white guy who's built a successful career on the ideas and hard work of others.

The hard drive trembles in her hands. She sets it next to the briefcase, along with a couple of cables Jordan gave her.

When she picks up the briefcase, it's lighter than she expected. Should she count it? How long does it take to count $5 million?

The door behind her opens. She and O'Naire both whip around to see who it is.

"Is that the money?" Devin asks. He's breathing hard, his face gleaming with sweat.

Something's wrong. Something is very wrong.

O'Naire squints at him. "I know you, right? You were a student of mine. Shit, you're all students, aren't you?"

"Give me the briefcase," Devin says.

Millie says, "We're almost done here. What are you—"

Devin lifts his right arm, and she sees he's holding a gun. She recognizes it instantly; the one they found in the file cabinet.

"Give me the briefcase," Devin says again.

"Goddammit," says O'Naire.

Millie pivots, putting her body between Devin and the briefcase. "You can't be serious," she says.

"I'm not playing, love. The briefcase. Be quick, now."

O'Naire makes a move for the hard drive. Devin backs up and widens his stance. The gun now splits the difference. He can shoot either of them with ease.

"Not you," Devin snaps. "I didn't tell you to move. Put your hands on the wall."

"This isn't happening." Millie sounds like a cliché, a stock character in denial, but it can't be helped.

Devin is fucking *robbing* her.

"It is," he says. "It very much is. Get on board." His chest heaves, nerves perhaps getting the better of him. He extends his free hand. "Please."

"Just do it," O'Naire tells her. He leans over the shelves of film reels, hands pressed against a poster for *Honey, I Shrunk the Kids*.

The door opens again.

Bugs and Cobweb walk in, munching popcorn, and take a moment to scope out the scene. Cobweb carries the popcorn bucket; Bugs carries his gun.

A minute ago, this was a stealth diversion job where nobody got hurt. Now it might turn into a Tarantino bloodbath.

Devin lowers his gun. "I thought we agreed you would stay outside."

Millie glowers at him. "You're working with *them*?"

Bugs works a kernel out from between his teeth and spits it on the floor. "I wanted to see how things were going in here." His eyes dart down to the briefcase clutched in Millie's hands. "They seem to have stalled a little."

24

The mere presence of police is enough for the protesters to drop the cause and rejoin the spectacle that is Hollywood Boulevard. If there's one thing people in LA have seen enough of, it's police looking for a reason.

Paz grabs hold of Jordan to keep him upright. He got carried away during the riot, and his ankle's starting to swell again. At some point she lost her heels—good riddance. Sammy's halfway down the block, talking to some guy with a sign. She hears one of them shout, "Jason *fucking* Alexander!"

"Where's your cameraman?" asks Jordan.

"Probably with Bugs." She looks across the street at the wax museum. "Who's also MIA."

"I'm sure it's all just fine," he says, voice ripe with sarcasm.

"Then so is that." Paz flicks her eyes toward the Radiance, where Cobweb pushes his way past the crowd. He's wearing Millie's backpack and carrying the same briefcase Ricky O'Naire had on him ten minutes ago. They watch as he crosses Hollywood Boulevard and disappears down the subway steps.

25

Bugs tells Millie to kneel in front of him. He wants Devin in the passenger seat and O'Naire driving the van.

"You signal to anybody or do anything to draw attention to yourself," Bugs tells O'Naire, "and I'll spray your brains all over the windshield and try my luck finding your house with a star map."

Bugs stands behind Millie in the back of the van, hunched over to keep from hitting his head. Devin keeps his gun on O'Naire. He holds it like a bowling ball, elbow propped on the armrest, the other hand steadying his wrist. He refuses to look at Millie, hasn't since they left the projection room.

Her mind is spinning. She tries to think of a movie where the double cross came from the Partner in Crime, the second-in-command. There's Ed Norton's character in the *Italian Job* remake, who double-crosses his team after the opening heist, but Donald Sutherland was the Mastermind and Mark Wahlberg the Partner in Crime. Her current situation is like an alternate ending to the 2001 *Ocean's Eleven*, one in which Brad Pitt takes the loot and bangs Julia Roberts while Clooney rots in jail.

"How long has this been in the works?" Millie asks Devin, voice dripping with contempt. "Spur-of-the-moment, or have you been planning this since Fargo?"

"Quite the turn of events, isn't it?" Bugs answers for him, breath hot on the back of her neck. "I was just as surprised when my associate and I came up the stairs to find this little one with a gun, saying that he'll let us take the money if we leave O'Naire for him, that he wants to rob O'Naire's house to recoup the money he lost. I don't know if I buy it, but it's a damn fine idea to rob the bastard twice, so I thought I'd tag along, help the little fella out, make sure he sees it through while my partner goes to count the money."

"You've got this all wrong," O'Naire says. "There isn't anything at my house."

"Don't give me that. Famous director like you. Where'd it go? Woman got expensive taste? Supporting a nose-candy habit?"

"I wish it were that simple," O'Naire says. "I owed a lot of money to a lot of bad people. I still owe money to these people, money that's supposed to be paid off by profits from *The Art of the Gangster*, only you assholes keep stealing it."

Either some acting ability has rubbed off on O'Naire or he's telling the truth, because it feels to Millie like he's genuinely scared.

Bugs purses his lips. "You might not have money stashed at your house, but a rich dude like you will definitely have something." He rests his arm on the back of the passenger seat, gun pointed at O'Naire. "Now drive."

26

FARGO, NORTH DAKOTA

Aaron unwraps his third turkey-and-cheese sandwich, the cheese bringing the sandwich up from three Food Patrol units to six, but whatever, it's a fuck-it kind of day. From the outside, it looks like the kind he's always dreamed of—sitting with Gabrielle in the Howard Security break room, the other employees checking them out, wondering how in hell a guy like Aaron Bodeen talked a girl like Gabrielle into sitting with him.

If only they knew that those beautiful raven locks, those smoky eyes, those perfectly manicured blue-polished, diamond-studded nails camouflage a heartless woman who's threatened to have Millie and her friends killed. Be careful what you wish for, Aaron thinks. You just might get it.

He's removing his snack of hard-boiled eggs from his lunch bag when the twenty-four-hour news channel they've been watching cuts to the *Hollywood Daily* broadcasting from the premiere of *The Art of the Gangster*. Gabrielle sits up in her chair.

The red carpet is full of confused-looking attendees and reporters. Some stand around, awaiting further instruction, fanning themselves in the California heat, while others pack up their gear and leave. A blond news anchor, not even attempting to hide her annoyance, continues her report.

"If it's not one thing, it's another," the anchor says. "After a group of violent protesters stormed the red carpet, theater officials are now reporting that writer and director Ricky O'Naire is no longer in the building. Right now, it's unclear if the premiere has been canceled or if this is another elaborate marketing stunt. What we can confirm is that O'Naire was seen leaving through a back entrance with some unidentified persons.

"His fiancée, Lexi Wells, is still in the theater with her BFF, one of the film's stars, Flowers Romero. As always, we'll stay on-scene to bring you the answers and more, live from the red carpet at the historic Radiance Theatre here in fabulous Hollywood, California . . ."

"Why would they leave the premiere?" Aaron wonders.

Gabrielle fidgets in her seat. She surveys the other employees and returns her attention to Aaron. "Keep your voice down. We don't know if this has anything to do with us. Maybe that O'Naire guy got food poisoning or something. It's probably just a coincidence."

Aaron can picture Millie now, irritated, shaking her head, saying, *There are no coincidences in heists.*

"I don't think so," he says. "Something's up. Either the plan didn't work, or your boyfriend's trying to pull another job. Let me call Millie. See what's going on."

Gabrielle just smiles. It's for show, for the benefit of the other Howard Security employees, suggesting that she and Aaron are good friends enjoying their dinner break together. She reaches across the table and takes his hand. Her fingers are freezing.

"You're not going to do shit. We're going to finish our food, and you're going to go outside with me for my smoke break. Then you'll go back to work like nothing's wrong, because you don't know that it isn't." She lowers her voice. "If you do anything besides what I just told you, I'll make sure the rest of your life is spent in a place where your biggest concern will be dropping the soap. Now finish your nasty-ass eggs so I can go smoke. Break is up in fifteen minutes."

She folds her arms. On her face is that exasperated look he's all too familiar with. He sees it with his boss, Ethan, anytime he brings up the manager job. He saw it with Carol almost every day before they split. Parents, friends, ex-girlfriends—damn near everyone but Bobby and Millie—have all given him that look, usually before they walked out of his life forever. It's a look that says he's worthless. It's why he overeats. Why Carol left.

But right now, instead of inspiring self-pity, the look fuels his desire to prove them all wrong.

27

HOLLYWOOD

They keep at least fifteen feet behind Cobweb, Jordan leaning on Paz, her arm around his waist. She can tell he's in a tremendous amount of pain; the limp's getting worse, and his breathing is shallow.

Briefcase clutched under his arm, Cobweb stops at the end of the platform and looks around. The station is crowded with people leaving the premiere, so Paz doesn't think he sees them, but she pulls Jordan behind one of the columns just to be sure. He shifts painfully and leans back against it to take some pressure off.

"This is stupid," he says. "I'm injured, and you're barefoot in a gown. It's a bad buddy-cop movie where one of us will be recast as white."

"We'll be fine. All he's got on him is his switchblade."

"Because it's only guns you're susceptible to. I forgot."

"I can handle myself against a knife."

"You watch too many movies," Jordan says.

"So do you. That's why you love me."

The Red Line train screeches into the station. Jordan rights himself and rests a hand on her shoulder for balance. The train's doors slide open. Cobweb gets on.

"I'll follow him," Paz says. "You try to find Millie and Devin. I'll meet you back at Yates's when this is all over."

She's about to sprint for the train when he reaches out and clasps her by the wrist. She turns back. Jordan's eyes are translucently bright. He looks equal parts excited and terrified, as if he can't wait to jump off the high dive even though he doesn't know how to swim.

"How'd you know I love you?" Jordan says, as if it's obvious but he's wondering what gave him away.

She's smiling so hard her face almost hurts. "I didn't," she admits.

Then, with one last look, she races toward the train, powered by adrenaline. She boards three cars back from Cobweb and gives Jordan a quick, reassuring glance. The PA system tells everyone to stand clear of the closing doors. At the announcement Jordan pushes off from the column, limping toward her as fast as he can.

He barely makes it, sticking his arm between the doors, forcing them open long enough to squeeze inside.

"What are you doing?" Paz says, as a few people grumble about the holdup.

Jordan grabs the rail above him, pain crossing his face as the train rocks back and forth. "I can't let you do this on your own," he says. "What's the plan?"

"No idea. Thought something would come to me once I got on."

"And?"

"Nothing's coming to me."

He sets his jaw. "What movies take place on a subway?"

"Let me think. There's the end of *Money Train*, the end of *Speed*."

"The end of *Mission: Impossible*. The nineties really used that as a crutch for third acts, huh?"

Old-school hip-hop blasts through the compartment. Paz turns to see a group of five guys roughly her age dressed in black. One sets down an iPhone synced to a Bluetooth speaker. They take turns break-dancing, one of them collecting tips in a Lakers cap.

"I think I have an idea," she says.

28

STUDIO CITY, CALIFORNIA

O'Naire drives rigidly, back stiff, knuckles white on the steering wheel. Not that Millie can blame him. It'd be difficult to look casual with a mute Englishman holding a gun on you.

He checks his side mirror, flips the turn signal. The van moves to the exit lane. "Must say I'm surprised by you, Millie."

Millie shoots a quick look at Bugs. When he makes no indication that she's not allowed to talk, she says, "Surprised I didn't take the money and keep my mouth shut?"

"No," says O'Naire. "After you showed up in Chicago, I would've been surprised if you hadn't retaliated, but I figured you'd just go to the press." He exhales. "That job in Chicago was brilliant. Great use of misdirection, costume, makeup. There are a couple of things I would've changed, but overall, extremely well done. But this? Allowing yourself to get involved with people who resort to kidnapping? Armed robbery? Feels sloppy."

"Wasn't exactly my choice," Millie says.

Bugs pipes up. "Seems to be working pretty well so far."

"So far, sure, but there's too many unknowns," O'Naire continues. "Admit it—this isn't very well thought out. It was an impulse. You saw an opportunity and ran with it." He risks an over-the-shoulder look at their captor. "I'm willing to forget all about this if you let me go. People are going to be looking for me. They probably are right now. Let me go before this becomes something you'll regret."

"I'll take my chances," Bugs says easily, not a care in the world. "We getting close or what? Starting to feel like maybe you're just driving around or going to a police station."

"Less than a mile," answers a defeated O'Naire.

They're winding through a neighborhood now, up hills, past gated houses. The plastic flooring hurts Millie's knees. She repositions herself so that her weight is on her heels. Bugs's attention is on the mansions they're passing.

"What would you change?" Millie says. "About the Chicago job. You said it was impressive but you would've changed a few things."

O'Naire looks at her in the rearview. "You want *notes?*"

"We were supposed to get feedback from you on our short films but never did."

"It was a major marketing point for the academy," Devin says, breaking his long silence.

The van stops at a red light. O'Naire thinks while the engine idles. "The getaway could have used some finessing. From a production standpoint, it would've been nice if you incorporated the river somehow. Took place in Chicago, after all. You didn't really use the city to your advantage. Remember, to a writer, nothing is ever random."

The light turns green. The van starts moving again.

"I also would've allowed enough time to download the footage, instead of having to take the entire tower. It did make a nice conclusion to the heist, I'll give you that," he admits. "End the scene with the dipshit editor stumbling into the editing suite to find it empty, but if it were a movie, I bet over half the audience would have figured it out before the door opened. Not that it's your fault," he adds. "It's hard to deliver a genuine surprise these days. Audiences have seen everything. The only genuine surprise I've ever experienced as a viewer was in *Straight Time.*"

"What's that?" Bugs asks.

"The *Taxi Driver* of heist films. One of Dustin Hoffman's best," O'Naire explains. "Highly underrated. Criminally overlooked. The highway scene with the parole officer is the one I'm talking about. Millie, do you remember that? Hoffman's breaking point."

Of course she knows the scene. After fruitlessly spending the movie's first act trying to reform himself and make an honest living, Dustin Hoffman's character—an ex-thief recently released from prison—is being driven back to his apartment after spending the weekend in jail thanks to his parole officer, who tried sticking him with a bogus drug charge. Deciding the world will never allow him to be more than a convict,

Hoffman punches the parole officer, grabs the steering wheel, and pulls the car over to the median. He cuffs the officer to a chain link fence and leaves him there with his pants down, bare ass exposed. The rest of the movie, Hoffman's on the lam, pulling off jewelry and bank heists to fund his escape.

The click of O'Naire's seat belt draws her attention. He's watching her again in the rearview. "You remember the scene?" he repeats, his voice urgent.

Nothing is ever random with writers.

Devin looks back at Millie. "Oh, I've seen that. Is that when Hoffman goes apeshit on the private detective from *Blood Simple* and drives them off the road?"

Millie says, "Yes," and leaps forward, grabbing the wheel and jerking it to the right, steering them directly into a lamppost.

29

At the Vermont-Sunset station, Paz moves along the platform, a subway map held up to block her face. Cobweb is still sitting in the second passenger car. The briefcase rests flat on his knees, the backpack by his feet.

The break-dancers are in the third car. Every station or two, they change cars, depending upon crowd reaction and tips.

A young mother and her two children—a boy and a girl, the girl a little older than the boy but not by much—get in Cobweb's car. They take the seats next to the bad man with a knife and five million reasons to use it.

Paz gets back on the fourth passenger car, where Jordan waits for her.

"Children," Paz says. "There are children sitting next to him. Little kids. Small. Shit, Jordan, I'll never forgive myself if something happens to them."

"Nothing will happen," he assures her. "I believe in you."

"Yeah?" She hates how vulnerable she sounds.

The train jerks forward. She gets up. "I'm going to head to the third car. That's where the dancers are. I'll go in with them. Should be within the next two stops."

"I'll be in position either way. Help me up before you go."

He puts his arm around her shoulder. She puts hers around his waist. They make their awkward way through the crush of passengers. Someone offers up a seat when the two of them reach the door to the next car. Jordan politely declines and leans against the wall.

They stand and feel the gentle rocking of the train until the PA announces the next stop is approaching.

Jordan says, "I'll see you in a—" but doesn't get to finish, because Paz leans in and kisses him, hard, then turns the door handle. She's gone before he can say anything to change her mind.

30

Millie rolls onto her back, legs momentarily over her head, twisting in the small space between the driver and passenger seats. Using the cup holders as a brace, she levers herself up.

Both airbags have deployed.

O'Naire watches with a dazed expression, like a boxer who hasn't yet realized he's concussed. "Fucking idiot," he mutters, out of it. "I was waiting till we were on Ventura. People could've helped us."

Millie points to a mansion visible through the cracked windshield. "Maybe someone who lives there saw what happened and will call the cops."

"Not a chance."

"Why not?"

He pushes down the airbag with both hands. "That's my house."

Devin doesn't move. His face is buried in the airbag. His gun is nowhere in sight.

"Dev—Dev, you okay?" Millie shakes him, to no response. Is he breathing? She puts her fingers against his neck, her ear close to his mouth. There's a pulse. "Devin, wake up."

"Nobody move," Bugs says slowly from the cargo area. He tries to lift his head, but it proves to be too much. "Shit," he says, closing his eyes.

Millie dives toward the sliding door, pulls the handle, and falls out hands first, her forehead smacking against the sidewalk. There's no time to acknowledge the pain, because the cargo door's opening. She jumps up, hands bleeding now, and runs down the street, the huge houses all quiet and far away, their occupants oblivious to what's happening beyond their fences and gates.

There's the crunch of broken glass—footsteps—and Millie imagines Bugs with the gun on her, one eye closed, slowly inhaling and then taking the shot, finger squeezing the trigger. She expects it any second now.

The shot never comes, but the footsteps get closer. A hand grabs the back of her blouse.

A gun barrel strikes her neck, knocking her off her feet. Bugs pulls her up, grabs the front of her blouse, punches her in the jaw.

A flood of pain. The taste of blood makes her gag. She turns and spits.

"Try anything like that again," Bugs snarls, "and I'll put three bullets in you like I did your pops. I don't need you anymore, understand? Not killing you yet has been a professional courtesy, one I never would've extended to a fuckup like Bobby."

White spots float behind her eyelids, but she knows what she heard. Barely lucid, she still comprehends. This is him. This is the man who killed her dad.

Bugs slaps her face, which startles her back toward consciousness. "Where you going? Another hour and this will all be over."

O'Naire leans against the mangled van. He holds his shoulder.

The passenger-side door is wide open. Bugs runs over to it, looks inside, then slams his hand against the roof. "*Shit!*"

The airbag's deflated. The seat is empty. Devin is gone.

31

It's been a few years since Aaron has checked an alarm log; that's for his staff. But he's doing it now, looking at the account for Ricky O'Naire's home in Studio City.

If Gabrielle's boyfriend and his crew are looking to make another score, this might be where they'd go. It's a long shot, but Aaron can't sit back and do nothing.

There are four people set up with access codes: Ricky O'Naire; his fiancée, Lexi Wells; a woman noted as O'Naire's assistant; and his manager. Lexi was the last one to input a code, and that was three hours ago, to set the alarm.

He's reviewing the contact information when a front door alarm comes in, followed by a hallway motion sensor. Since Aaron is in the account, the alarms are sent to him, even though he lacks speakers to hear the incoming audio. The O'Naire account is set up for Action Plan One: after an alarm goes off, the account holder has thirty seconds to turn it off. If the alarm is deactivated within thirty seconds to two minutes, the monitoring specialist calls the owner to ensure everything is fine. Anything over two minutes, the specialist dispatches the police.

Aaron waits. The alarm's deactivated within seven seconds. The code used is the one assigned to Ricky O'Naire.

32

Bugs waits for the blinking red light on the alarm keypad to change to green before he pushes O'Naire into the foyer, where he trips over his own feet and lands hard on the Spanish tile.

They start in the master bedroom. Under orders, Millie and O'Naire flip mattresses, pull out dresser drawers. They work their way through the other bedrooms, six in total, all bigger than any room in Millie's house. When they turn up nothing, O'Naire gets a thwack of the gun barrel to the back of his head. Bugs threatens to shoot him if he doesn't stop fucking around and tell him where the money is.

In the kitchen, Bugs pulls out a chair and shoves O'Naire into it. Millie opens cupboard doors and checks behind the appliances—for what, she's not sure, but it's good to look busy. Keeps her mind off what Bugs told her. Keeps at bay her intensifying anger.

There's a set of knives next to the stove, on the other side of the kitchen. Scenes of a daring escape—stabbing her dad's killer with a butcher knife—flash through her mind. Could she really hurt him to save herself?

It doesn't matter. The knives are too far away. She'd never reach them without Bugs getting off a shot.

Next to the French doors, leading out to the backyard, is a walk-in cooler. Two summers ago, Millie worked as a runner for a local steak house. Even they didn't have a cooler this big. Through its glass front she can see bottles of expensive wine and champagne, cases of imported beer, cheese wheels, fruit, vegetables, and an obscene amount of Reddi-Wip.

More yelling erupts, then the sound of knuckles smashing into bone. She turns. Blood drips from O'Naire's mouth. She looks away, not able to stomach any more, and that's when she spots it: the cooler's thermostat.

The bottom right corner reads *Howard Security*.

33

A cooler alarm flashes across Aaron's screen. Per the notes in the account, the cooler is supposed to stay between thirty-eight and forty-one degrees. It's now at forty-four degrees, on its way to the new designated temperature of sixty-five, the highest the thermostat will go.

Weird. It's what a person would do to defrost everything, but why would Ricky O'Naire do that right now, when he's supposed to be at the premiere? Doesn't make sense . . .

. . . unless he's not the one who did it.

Something scratches at the back of his mind, something Millie said back at the Duck Tape. Shit, what was it? He was telling her about having to fire James for not notifying Spokane Meats about their cooler alarm.

Next time have your staff dispatch police right away. Any type of freezer alarm immediately results in rolling out SWAT.

But that was a joke. Millie hadn't meant at the time for him to take it seriously. It must've just been . . .

No coincidences in heists.

Aaron picks up the phone and, after looking at the emergency numbers in the call log, dials the North Hollywood Police Department.

"Nine-one-one, state your emergency," the operator says.

"Um, hi, I don't necessarily know if this is an emergency or if I'm being paranoid, but I thought I'd call just to be sure."

"What's your name, sir?"

"Aaron. I'm with Howard Security out of Fargo, North Dakota."

"What's the situation that you're not sure is an emergency, Aaron?" the operator asks, her tone all business and slightly exasperated. When it comes to women, at least he's consistent.

"I'm calling about an alarm coming from a residence in Studio City."

"What kind of alarm is it, Aaron? Glass-break, motion, door, fire?"

"Freezer."

A pause. "Freezer?"

"Yes, ma'am. Technically, I think it's more of a cooler. The notes state that it contains expensive alcohol and cheese, but no meat."

There's another moment of silence, and then the operator says, "Aaron, I'm starting to understand why you're not sure this is an emergency. This is nine-one-one, sir. We are the police department. This line is for when someone is injured or facing a serious threat of possible injury, not for the prevention of cheese spoiling."

"I understand that. But this alarm belongs to Ricky O'Naire." There's silence on the other end. "The famous film director."

"I don't get out to the movies much. More of a reader, myself. But if he's such a famous director, I'm sure he can afford more cheese. Good Gouda isn't that hard to come by."

"But he's *missing*," he stresses. "Right now he's supposed to be at the premiere for his new movie, but the news says he left for no reason, and fifteen minutes ago his code was used to turn off his home alarm system. Now the cooler's set for sixty-five degrees, the highest it'll go, which makes no sense, because it'll spoil the food. I think someone is trying to signal for help."

Another pause. Aaron imagines the operator shaking her head. "Aaron, you must be spectacular at your job, providing such a thorough follow-up on the whereabouts of your client over a freezer alarm."

"Cooler."

"I'm going to hang up now. I suggest you try notifying Mr. O'Naire about his cooler problem, but don't try to be a hero. If he doesn't answer—from his own residence, that he accessed with his own code—I'd leave a message and then call it a night. Goodbye."

The operator hangs up. Aaron looks at his computer. It's been three minutes since the alarm came in. He switches to a new line and redials.

"Nine-one-one, what's your emergency?" asks a new operator.

"I'd like to report multiple alarms at a residence. Glass-break, hallway motion, and I have audio of a woman screaming for help."

34

The break-dancers command the subway car. People are nodding to the beat, laughing, and cheering as a man spins on his head. The two children beside Cobweb clap along. Their mother watches them, smiling.

Paz has a clear view from the opposite side of the train. Next stop is

Wilshire-Vermont. She bets he'll change there for the Purple Line downtown, and if connections in LA are anything like those in New York,
the platform is going to be packed. She'll need to hurry.

The train slows down. Brakes screech. People rise from their seats,
bracing themselves. The dancers collectively scramble to collect any last
donations.

Paz grips the overhead rail, as close to the doors as she can. "Come
on, come on," she says under her breath.

The train pulls into the station. As expected, the platform is full.

Cobweb grabs the backpack resting between his feet and stands up.

"Excuse us, excuse us," the break-dancers shout as they make their
way toward the next car. Cobweb realizes what's happening and tries to
get past them, but he's too late. They're blocking the platform doors.

The mother insists her children hold hands. She stands behind them,
ready to disembark.

The train slides to a stop.

The waiting passengers crowd the open doors. Paz has to throw her
shoulder into a spiky-haired dude to get by, hearing, "Watch it, bitch!"
as she runs down the platform. The swell of people pushes her toward
the train, where she sees Cobweb—briefcase in one hand, backpack
in the other—waiting for the break-dancers to exit before he can. She
reaches the doors at the exact moment he does.

Their eyes meet. They stand inches apart.

For a moment, neither moves. Then someone behind Paz pushes
her into the car.

She tears the backpack from Cobweb's grasp.

She's expecting him to give up and leave, turn around and disap-
pear onto another train with his $5 million. Instead, he reaches into his
jacket and pulls his knife, stealthily holding it down by his side.

"*He's got a knife!*" Paz yells and flings her arms wide, placing herself
between Cobweb and the children. The scene turns frantic: people
scream and shove each other out of the way.

The mother clutches her kids, wrapping herself around them.

Paz runs past, daring Cobweb to follow. She slings one of the backpack straps over her shoulder, glances back to see him bashing people with the briefcase, clearing the way. She stops at the door to the next car, the platform exit on her right wide open, passengers standing back but watching out of fear and curiosity. With the aisle between them completely clear, Cobweb breaks into a sprint, raises the knife over his head, Michael Myers–style. Paz braces herself against the open door as Jordan drives his shoulder into Cobweb's side, sending him off the train, down onto the concrete platform. The briefcase and knife fly from his hands. The briefcase lands first, landing at an angle that flips the latch. Monopoly money and cut-up paper scatter across the platform. The knife skids to a stop in front of a policeman with his gun drawn.

"Hands on your head, look down at the floor!" the cop yells.

"That's our cue," Jordan says.

They slip out of the train and head toward the escalators as more police arrive.

35

O'Naire slumps in a chair, his bloody, sweat-soaked head resting on the kitchen table. Fresh cuts glisten on his face. His eyes are barely open.

"What are you doing?" Millie thinks she says to Bugs, no louder than a whisper if the words escape her mouth. What's the endgame? Does he really expect to pull off some kind of score, or is he more sadistic than that? Is he here because he wants any excuse to hurt someone? To kill them?

Bugs is perched on the counter, legs dangling, washcloth and ice on his knuckles. She asks again what he's doing, this time for sure. "Time and options are running out," he says. "I'm done playing games."

"So you're going to beat him to death?"

"Of course not. I'll shoot him if I have to."

"What'll that prove?"

"I don't know." Bugs hops down, picks the gun up from the counter. "Let's find out."

It only takes a few seconds. He points the gun at O'Naire's thigh. There's a flash of fire from the barrel, a deafening pop, a spray of blood. O'Naire falls to the floor.

Bugs stands over him, the gun aimed at his face. "Last chance."

"Please stop," O'Naire begs, face contorted in agony.

Polices sirens wail in the distance. The sound is so beautiful she almost cries.

Bugs points the gun at Millie. "The cops sure work different for rich people, don't they?" he says. "One shot, and less than a minute later they're on their way? Weird, right?"

She tries to buy some time. "Someone probably saw the accident and called the police. They'll find the van in the driveway and come up to the house to see what happened. There's still time to escape if we go right now."

Bugs swallows hard. Listens for a moment. "I can hear at least five squad cars. You don't send that much heat for running into a lamppost, even if this is Hollywood and the lampposts are Louis Vuitton or some shit."

"All the more reason to go," she urges.

"Agreed, but we ain't leaving any witnesses." He aims the gun at O'Naire, who has somehow dragged himself across the kitchen, a trail of smeared blood in his wake. He sits with his back against one of the lower-level cupboards.

Millie runs to stand in front of him. "Don't!" she yells, hands up. O'Naire might be a piece of shit for stealing her movie, but this isn't what she wanted. It was never supposed to go this far. "Don't kill him. I'm begging you."

"Well, look at that." Bugs smirks. He lowers the gun. "History really does repeat itself. What is it with you Blomquists, taking on jobs but not having the balls to see them through?"

Rage flares inside Millie, so much rage that she's almost shaking.

"There's another way," O'Naire's weak voice says behind her. "You don't have to kill me, and I can get you money."

Bugs sneers. "You're just now bringing this up?"

"Situation has changed." The director swallows and lifts his eyelids. The sirens get louder. "Kill her, and I'll pay you a million dollars."

"What the fuck?" Millie steps away from him. "I've been trying to help you!"

"You shut up," Bugs orders, then looks to O'Naire. "Keep talking. What's changed?"

"Nothing yet, but public opinion sure will." His voice gains strength. "Now I have a story I can sell to the media. A narrative of an obsessed student who went crazy on the guy who ran her former school, and you, the one who stopped her. No." He swallows blood, his voice coming out clear. "The *hero* who stopped her."

"You asshole," Millie says.

Blood leaks onto the floor as O'Naire continues. "There's already enough evidence to tie her to stealing the film and setting up the exchange at the premiere. I'll tell the police that it was her idea to kidnap me and take me to my house, where she beat and shot me when I couldn't come up with any money."

"This is bullshit," Millie cuts in, telling Bugs, "How is he going to explain your presence?"

Bugs grimaces. "She's got a point."

O'Naire has an answer for that, too. "You were on vacation in LA when you saw me being held at gunpoint, and she forced you into the van. Simple. Wrong place, wrong time. Just like John McClane in *Die Hard*. And like John McClane, you stepped in and saved the day."

"You'd let that story out?" Bugs says. "Kind of makes you look like a punk bitch, don't it?"

"Not at all." A glint is back in O'Naire's eyes. "Don't you see? This makes me a *victim*. If there's anything this country rallies behind more than a hero, it's a victim. A survivor of a tragedy. Shoot her, and within twenty-four hours we'll be the most famous people on the planet, guaranteed."

The sirens blare from the front of the house, the squad cars' lights flashing through the living room windows, splashing red across Bugs's face.

He lifts his gun and points at Millie. "Always wanted to be a hero," he explains, as if this desire is worth taking her life.

Millie inhales and closes her eyes.

The thunder of a gunshot splits the room.

She's heard you go into shock after a traumatic event, because your body is protecting you from feeling pain. That must be what she's experiencing, because right now she doesn't feel anything except her heart pounding against her ribs. She exhales and looks down to find where the bullet hit her, expecting to see blood, or maybe smoke emerging from the wound like in cartoons. But there is nothing to see.

Bugs has an unfocused gaze. Red blooms on the shoulder of his chocolate-brown jacket. "The hell?" he chokes out.

"Millie, run!" Devin yells from the dining room.

Two more bullets splatter into Bugs. He tries to walk but only stumbles sideways a bit before crashing to the floor.

Devin races toward the French doors to the backyard and throws them open. "Come on! It's not safe."

Millie doesn't move. "What'd you do with the gun? We can't leave it here."

"I don't have it anymore. I lost it in the van."

"What?"

"That wasn't me shooting." He grabs her forcefully by the wrist and leads her outside. "We have to go."

A helicopter circles overhead, the sound of its spinning blades churning through the neighborhood, its searchlight scanning the front yard. The tendons in Millie's arms burn as she scales the privacy fence. At the top, she pauses and looks back at the house.

Bugs is dead. O'Naire is in the wind.

36

Each step hurts more than the last. Ricky should wait for the paramedics, but since that piece of white trash didn't shoot the bitch when he had the chance, he needs to give the cops—and hopefully the paparazzi—a decent image of him, injured and bleeding, emerging from this hell on earth a survivor.

Putting that narrative in the public's mind is his best chance at fighting the accusations Millie will throw at him.

He heads up the tiled hallway, following the light blasting through his living room windows. Blood runs down the leg of his white tux. The front door opens before he can reach for it, and he can feel his story, his spotlight, his redemption only seconds away.

"You have to help—"

Flowers Romero grasps Ricky's shoulder and thrusts a knife into his chest.

"Don't worry," Romero whispers. "This will settle all your debts. Lexi will be protected."

Then he pulls out the blade and slams it in one, two, three more times, each stab puncturing skin before scraping bone.

"You?" murmurs O'Naire.

"Don't look so surprised, Rick. You really think the investors made you cast an influencer with no acting experience if they didn't have their reasons?"

Ricky tries to talk, the metallic taste of blood getting in his way.

Flowers lowers him onto his back. Ricky fades out, and fades in again when he feels the sting of cold metal against his right hand. Like an iris shot in a silent film, everything but the 9mm fades away.

It's his own gun. Flowers Romero has returned it to him.

"I found him! Quick!" Romero yells over his shoulder. Then he leans in and whispers, his voice seeming to get farther and farther away. "You know what the most ironic thing is? Despite what you thought, I never slept with Lexi. Never had a chance. That girl loves you to the moon and back."

37

The two of them hurtle down the hilly, twisting road. People pass by, racing to see what's going on, phones and video cameras in hand. Once they're a block away, Millie's legs give out and she collapses in someone's front yard.

"We should keep moving." Devin sits down next to her on the damp grass. "It's like *Nightcrawler* out here. Everyone's got a camera."

She's still catching her breath. "He shot my dad," she manages. "Bugs. He killed him, Dev. He killed him, and I let that monster loose on everyone."

She buckles forward, sobbing, covering her face. Her body spasms. She rocks back and forth, shivering despite the night's heat. "I'm so sorry," she repeats over and over.

Devin rubs her back. "It's not your fault, love."

Millie doesn't believe him, nor does she have the strength to argue. Her father's murderer is dead—but instead of relief, she only feels guilt and shame. She took the selfish way out and almost got her crew killed, acting more like Bugs than Bobby Blomquist.

Tears blur her vision. Finally, she wipes her eyes clean. "You pointed a gun at me."

"Christ, you're still on about that?" He produces the tiniest smile. It's enough to relieve some of the pressure in her chest. "You didn't seem sure about the plan working, so I brought the gun as backup. When Bugs and Cobweb came up the stairs, I panicked. I knew I didn't have a chance, so I acted like I was on their side to help control the situation. Or at least fool myself into believing I had some control," he says. "Then the van crashed and you took off, so I ran. Made it about two houses before I doubled back to follow you. I know I should've called the cops, but I couldn't leave you on your own. If anything had happened, I would've . . ."

He looks down at his hands, nauseated, his face pale.

Millie rests her hand on his knee. "Thank you for coming back," she tells him. "I'm so happy you're okay."

A siren blips. A flashlight beam hits the curb in front of the house next door. She and Devin get to their feet as a cop car rounds the corner and begins to slow down.

Because they don't want to raise suspicion, running away from a crime scene instead of toward it like everybody else, they join the crowd making its way up to O'Naire's house, just two more concerned neighbors trying to figure out what's disrupted their community.

When they arrive, it's as if Millie's in a dream or the final shot of a Wes Anderson picture. Everything's in slow motion: the paramedics zipping the body bags shut, Flowers Romero in tears on the front steps, the photographers and reporters rushing the driveway, their flashing cameras competing with the spotlights from the two helicopters zigzagging overhead, as the Hollywood sign shimmers in the black California hills.

PART SIX

THE LEGENDARY THIEF

1

HOLLYWOOD

On top of a newspaper stand, in the midst of a crowd waiting for the light to change, sits a crumpled Chinese take-out bag. On the front of the bag is scrawled: *The Art of the Gangster. Please play for audience.*

An older woman wearing a pink fanny pack and Disneyland T-shirt picks up the bag. It's much heavier than she expects, so she opens it to see what's inside. As she does, two cops on patrol pass by. She looks up from the bag, folds it closed, and hurries over to catch them.

"Excuse me, officers," the woman says, "I think I found something."

2

Paz looks up and down Hollywood Boulevard. It's quieter here, about a mile from the Radiance: the backup rendezvous point Millie picked if they all got separated.

Parked on a bus stop bench, an exhausted Jordan nurses his leg as best he can, while Yates sits next to him. scrolling through his phone. Sammy, standing behind them, cracks up at the strip club marquee down the block.

"Do you think they got lost?" Jordan says. He turns to Yates. "Or went back to your place?"

Yates doesn't look up. "Gwyneth would've texted me if they were at the house. But shit, listen to this. The news says that O'Naire was stabbed to death at his house in Studio City."

"What was he doing there?" Paz says. "Do you think that's where Millie and Devin are?"

"If they are, then they've probably been arrested," Jordan says.

"Arrested?" Sammy turns away from the strip club. "We got to get them out. What would Millie do?"

Five minutes later, Yates's phone in hand, because hers is still in the equipment van—another thing that makes formal wear stupid, no pockets—Paz paces in front of the crew, oblivious to the annoyed pedestrians who have to move out of her way. How hard could this be, she thinks. Millie does this all the time. Just find the right movie and act it out.

"Okay, so there's like twenty different lists of the best movie prison breaks, and most of them are clickbait," she says. "I don't know; I'll just start naming them, and you guys tell me if they're helpful."

"This is so stupid," Yates complains.

Sammy tells him to shut up. "We're Long Shots now. This is what we do."

"*The Shawshank Redemption*," Paz reads. "It's number one on almost every list."

"Would take years, a rock hammer, and a poster of Rita Hayworth," Jordan says.

"*Escape from Alcatraz.*"

Yates sighs. "We'd have to make a papier-mâché model of Millie's head to fool the guards that she's sleeping, and then fashion a raft out of raincoats. Told you this was stupid."

Paz rubs her eye with her middle finger aimed clearly in his direction. "*The Great Escape.*"

Jordan jumps in before anyone else can. "We'd have to dig a tunnel system and then jump a fence with a motorcycle."

"*Cool Hand Luke.*"

"Haven't seen it, but I know it involves eating a shit-ton of eggs."

"*The Fugitive.*"

"Need a train and a one-armed man," Yates jokes, which earns another guest appearance from her middle finger.

"What about *Chicken Run*?" Sammy suggests, reading from a

different list on his phone. "Says here we just need to build an airplane out of a chicken coop and hire a cocky Australian rooster to pilot it."

Paz stops pacing to stare at him.

"What?" Sammy asks. "I didn't write it."

3

It seems stupid now, in hindsight, to volunteer to be interviewed at a police station, but Lexi wouldn't stop crying and insisted he come with. "Please, Flowers," she said, with damp, red eyes. "I don't want to be alone right now. Rick would've wanted you to be with me."

The irony was just too much. And of course, it would benefit his aunt if he could give her a summary of what the police knew. Besides, they bought his story—he'd only been at the house to check on Rick—and weren't considering him a suspect. Refusing to accompany Lexi would have been a red flag.

He caresses her arm as they both listen to the man in front of them, a Detective Stark from Chicago, one of the leads on what the media called the "zombie heist," here in LA on special assignment. The detective's battered attaché case rests on the table next to a pile of overstuffed manila folders.

"Now, this is going to sound a little crazy," Detective Stark says. "But we believe we know who stole the movie in Chicago."

"What does that have to do with anything?" Lexi sniffles, shredding a used tissue.

"I'm getting to that, miss. It's tied together, I promise." He waits to see if this is any comfort. "Should I continue?"

"Please get on with it," says Flowers.

According to Stark, an organized crime family that, for their protection, he'll only refer to as "the Organization"—Flowers loves how dramatically the detective says "the Organization," and almost wants to tell him that their preferred term is *investors*—is believed to have used

Ricky O'Naire and his films as a way to launder their money, dating back to his first film, *The Mark*. The Academy's Feature Award contest was their way of bringing in additional revenue. Money was cleaned and a healthy profit was made, but after a string of O'Naire box office disappointments, the Organization took a loss.

O'Naire owed them a considerable debt. He tried to pay it off by embezzling from the Academy, only to be arrested, his reputation in tatters. *The Art of the Gangster* was not only his way back into Hollywood; it was his last chance to pay them off.

Flowers rubs Lexi's shoulders and leans back in his chair, feigning disbelief. He hates to admit it, but he's impressed by how much the detective has figured out, although he obviously doesn't have a clue which crime family O'Naire was working with. If the FBI hasn't been able to crack it, there's no way this bumbling Midwest fool will.

And do they really know nothing about this girl Millie Blomquist? If so, then she's more remarkable than he originally thought—pulling off two break-ins just days apart, completely under the radar. If she's even half as talented a filmmaker as she is a thief, perhaps they'll be able to replace O'Naire more quickly than they hoped.

Flowers scratches the side of his face. "This is just all so unbelievable."

"It gets crazier, I'll tell ya," Detective Stark continues. "Because of his debt, we believe O'Naire is the one who staged the whole thing in Chicago."

"How's that?"

"He kept his own employees in the dark, lied to the police to get the story out, part of a media blitz. Used to be they just had billboards and ads, but I guess now that print's dead . . ." He shrugs. "My partner came up with the idea after O'Naire told him that he had a backup of the movie and was going to continue with the premiere. I have to say, it's a disappointing conclusion. I missed my niece's fifth birthday party yesterday to be here. Was going to be a clown. Been practicing my balloon animals for three weeks now."

"Getting any good?" Flowers asks, genuinely curious.

Detective Stark's cheeks grow pink. "Not really. Just a lot of wieners and swords."

Lexi blows her nose again. "And how is this tied to Rick's death? If he's the one who planned all this, then why is he dead and who was that other man killed in our house?"

Flowers is literally on the edge of his seat. He can't wait to hear this.

4

FARGO, NORTH DAKOTA

Only three times in Aaron's life has he had the attention of everyone in a room.

The first was in third grade, when he drank too much water at recess and pissed his corduroy overalls during the cursive lesson. The second, when he was still married and caught Carol with another man at the Cork n' Cleaver, which resulted in him getting his ass beat on top of the salad bar. The third is now, as everyone on the Howard Security floor stands at their monitoring stations, cheering and applauding.

"There he is!" Ethan calls out, striding across the room, his hand engulfing Aaron's when they shake. "Hell of a job. Hell of a job."

"Thank you, sir."

Ethan leans in close, breath smelling like celebratory Scotch. "Fuck that. It's me thanking you. A few days ago, we're facing a negligence lawsuit for what happened in Chicago. And now, an hour ago, we got a shout-out from some movie-studio president on the *Hollywood Daily*. It's a shame they couldn't save the homeowner, but that's on the police and their response time. We did our job." He cocks his head. "Say, how in the living hell did you know to dispatch the police department on a *freezer alarm?*"

"Something just felt wrong." Aaron shrugs stiffly. "I saw on the news that O'Naire was missing, and with the amount of grief we've been taking about Chicago, I thought I'd check his home account. All of a sudden, this alarm comes in after he disarmed the main system, saying that he manually turned the thermostat as high as it would go. Couldn't see any reason why someone reported missing would do that unless they were trying to signal for help, so I called it in."

"I'll be damned." Ethan's arm is now around Aaron's shoulders. "I know you're scheduled to be part of the debriefing on Monday about the manager interviews, but I've gone ahead and canceled that."

"You don't want me to attend?"

"You're not hearing me, Bodeen. I don't want *anybody* to attend; that's why I canceled the meeting. I'd like to interview you." He gives Aaron an aggressive pat on the back. "I know I said I wasn't considering you, but after tonight I'm going a new direction. It'd be nice to have someone with real experience in the trenches and not just another punk with a useless degree they earned while perfecting the keg stand. You still interested?"

The shrill *whoop-whoop* of the emergency exit cuts Aaron off before he can respond. Doesn't matter. The grin on his face is all the answer Ethan needs.

The follow-up paperwork for an alarm that leads to an arrest normally takes half an hour. There are questions to answer, call times to include, summaries and descriptions to give. Aaron does it all in five minutes, making sure to keep certain details vague. When he's finished, he turns off his desk lamp, says good night to the other employees, and heads down to the parking lot.

Gabrielle waits by his car.

"That was fucking stupid," she says.

"Give me my phone," says Aaron.

"Are you hearing me? The cops will figure out you were involved. Or Hoyt will turn on you and throw me under the bus, too, if he thinks he can get a deal out of it."

Aaron exhales, his whole body exhausted. He might not have liked the man, but delivering news of a person's death is never on anyone's bucket list.

He states the facts: a second body was found at the O'Naire residence—an unidentified man with a large bird tattoo around his neck. Gabrielle goes silent, her breath making clouds in the cool night air.

Finally, she says, "Thank God. That man was literally going to be the death of me. I never thought I'd get away."

And just like that, the stunned look vanishes from her face, replaced by an inviting smile. She pushes herself off his car and places a hand against his chest. "We got away with it, didn't we? You want to go back to your place and celebrate?"

It's a question the old Aaron never thought he'd hear, and his mind floods with images of the two of them together, his hands caressing her body, her soft lips exploring his.

"No, that's okay," the new Aaron says, removing her hand from his chest. "You're not really my type. Now, give me back my phone."

He waits until she's salvaged her pride by telling him to fuck off and storming halfway across the parking lot before he turns on his cell. The police only reported two bodies at O'Naire's residence. No mention of any arrests. Still, that doesn't mean Millie is out of the woods, and there's a jagged twisting in his stomach. It's not until he checks his texts that the ache begins to subside.

The first one is from Millie. It simply reads: *Can't wait to come home.*

5

HOLLYWOOD

There's a feeling that a joke is being played, that the last six hours spent hiding in backyards, keeping to alleys, and staying off the cops' radar were for nothing. That she's on some weird reality prank show and any minute a camera crew will pop out of the bushes to say *Surprise!*—she's not free at all, she's actually going to prison until menopause.

But when Millie and Devin step off the bus into the cool California breeze, a low mist clouding the streets like cannon smoke after an epic battle, all that's waiting is her crew standing at the end of the block.

"Never been so excited to see Yates in my life," Devin says. "Now I know something's wrong."

Paz spots them first. She looks them up and down, relief beaming from her eyes. She touches Jordan's shoulder to get his attention. Sammy and Yates follow her stare. It's only a matter of seconds before they're entangled in a mess of hands, arms, and elbows, the six of them hugging in the early morning light.

6

BURBANK, CALIFORNIA

Wearing an oversized T-shirt she borrowed from Yates, Millie wipes the sleep from her eyes, wanders into the kitchen, and finds everyone stuffing their faces with a breakfast feast: lemon-ricotta pancakes, thick French toast with powdered sugar, maple-glazed bacon, plump sausages, large bowls of seasoned potatoes, cheesy scrambled eggs, sliced fruit. A mountain of empty plastic take-out containers sits on the counter near the fridge.

Hatchet, wearing what appears to be Yates's father's bathrobe, brings over a fresh pot of coffee, pouring Gwyneth a steaming cup before filling his own.

Yates gets up from the table. "You can have my chair," he tells Millie. "I'm finished anyways. Gwyneth ordered breakfast. She figured it was the least she can do, since she's leaving my dad."

"How'd he take it? Where is he?" she asks as she sits next to Sammy.

"He had to go to work. He's fine with it. Honestly," Yates adds, speaking with the knowledge of an old hand, "I think he's just grateful he won't have to pay for any more art classes. It's better they split now than wait till they've been married a full year. Then it's a bigger mess with the lawyers. He learned that the hard way with wife number two."

Ten minutes later, Millie drops her fork onto her plate. She can't even remember the last time she had such a decent meal, and has every intention of returning to Yates's room for a nap, when she hears the muffled ringing of her phone, buried in her backpack.

It's got to be her mom.

It's been almost three days since the scene in Aaron's trailer. Her mom's probably thinking the worst, which, in this particular situation, would be disturbingly close to the truth. Millie unzips the bag and fishes around inside. What is she going to say? She's supposed to be at school today.

Crisis avoided—for now, anyway, because she doesn't recognize the number.

She answers the call, nearly dropping the phone when she hears who's on the other end of the line.

7

The limousine is large, sleek, and flashy. Corks pop. Champagne flows. Laughter fills the air. Paz and Jordan sneak kisses. Devin, Yates, and Sammy pass around a joint, blowing smoke out the sunroof.

Millie drinks in the elation and feels her heart speed up when the limo exits the highway and makes its way toward the studio. The driver gives Millie's name at the check-in gate, and the man in uniform replies with a kind smile. "We've been expecting you," he says and presses a button to lift the barrier arm.

They're directed to a special parking spot, one of only two near the entrance, the other reserved for the studio president himself. An intern, maybe a year older than Millie, with curly hair and a face full of freckles, greets them and asks if they'd like a tour before lunch.

As she takes it all in, Millie's head can't keep up with her eyes.

The whole thing is as clichéd and exciting as she could have imagined. They pass a wooden dojo exterior where extras in ninja shōzokus vape and check their phones. A famous actress in a large hat and cat-eye sunglasses is chauffeured by a motorized cart. A camera crew carries track for a dolly. Two stuntmen practice punching each other in the face outside a soundstage. Above it all is the famous water tower, the home of those zany characters from that one cartoon.

"Can you believe that we're here?" Paz says, her arm around Millie. "Did pretty good for yourself, Fargo. Think your dad would be proud of you."

"So would your mom," Millie says, squeezing the hand resting on her shoulder.

They reach an area of single-story stucco buildings. "These are our production offices," the intern says. "And although they might seem boring in comparison to all the other excitement happening around here, in the right context they can actually be the most thrilling part of the tour.

"Millie, this is where we're going to drop you off for your meeting today. The rest of you, if you want to follow me. We'll go have lunch."

A series of excited and nervous looks come Millie's way.

"Break a leg, love," Devin says. He leans and kisses her softly on her cheek. "And if the bastard gives you any trouble, break two."

8

Flowers Romero's office isn't what Millie expected. Simple beige walls, an empty desk, a couple of chairs. "I'm hardly ever here," he explains. "Honestly, I don't know why they even gave me an office, but it's kind of cool to have an excuse to come to the studio whenever. Do you want a water or coffee or anything?"

"I'm fine," Millie rasps and swallows.

Flowers smiles. It's not hard to see why the guy is such an internet sensation. In a loose-fitting shirt, the top buttons undone to reveal his defined chest, he's easily the most beautiful person Millie's ever encountered in real life.

He produces a bottle of water from a minifridge and sets it on the desk in front of her. "Probably wondering why I asked you here today on such short notice?"

"Was a bit curious."

Flowers sits behind his desk. "I'm here on the studio's behalf. It has come to their attention that, as it turns out, Rick O'Naire didn't write the screenplay for *The Art of the Gangster*. That, in fact, you did. They'd like to compensate you for your script, make sure proper credit is given."

"Oh," Millie says, because it's the most intelligible thing she can manage. The bottle of water shakes as she unscrews the cap. She finishes off half the bottle before she's able to speak again. "Thank you."

"You're very welcome," he says, amused. "I'm sure this comes as quite a relief. I understand that you even discussed the matter with Rick, only to be told that nothing could be done. I'm sorry this wasn't addressed earlier. I should've known Rick didn't write it. Guy hadn't had an original idea in years." Flowers looks at the window, takes a deep breath. "I shouldn't speak like that, now that he's dead, but the man was desperate." He shifts in his chair, looking once again at her. "Would have to be, to pull half the shit he did."

Something tells her he's not only talking about O'Naire's movie career.

"What do you mean?" she asks.

"Well, I'm not sure if I have clearance to tell you this, but I'm guessing it'll make the news soon anyway . . ." He shrugs as if he's just decided he might as well tell her, though Millie doesn't doubt for a second that he's planned to all along. "Lexi and I met with the police last night. Without giving too much away, let's just say that this thing goes deep. Mob connections. Money laundering. The whole shit show in Chicago.

"Apparently, the other man killed at Rick's house—Rick hired him to steal the movie. They're saying he's the one who stabbed Rick to death, but not before Rick got a couple of shots off. They were working with someone else, who was arrested last night for trying to stab people on a train."

"I heard about that," Millie says. "It's terrible."

Flowers rubs his jaw. "Fucking Rick. It was supposed to be a marketing ploy, but they double-crossed him, held the movie hostage for real, and he was too broke to pay the ransom." He raises his eyebrows. "You'll be interested in knowing that the cops have found some connections to the Fargo area—your hometown."

"Really?"

"Yeah, some guy pulling Craigslist scams. He'd promise big lots of merchandise but deliver mostly empty boxes. Big-ticket items like appliances, electronics, laser tag equipment. He was somewhere in Minnesota when they caught him. The FBI traced an email used to rent the rehearsal space in Chicago to his computer." He shakes his head. "Amazing."

Millie tries unsuccessfully to suppress a smile. Jordan's going to be so stoked to hear their plan worked. "Sounds like it'd make one hell of a movie."

Now Flowers smiles himself. It's not as warm as the one he flashes in photos, vids, and TV coverage. *Sadistic* isn't the right word—too dark, too extreme—but it's the only one that comes to mind.

"That's actually what we were thinking," he says. "I'll be honest, I asked you here today not just to tell you that you'll be receiving credit for *The Art of the Gangster*, but to see if you'd be interested in writing a new script. One based on what Rick did."

Millie tries to play it cool, but she can feel her face betraying her immediately—eyes opening wide, mouth breaking into a beaming smile.

Having spent the past two weeks planning and executing a felony-level robbery, destroying a production office, setting a van on fire, stealing a senior citizen's Buick, risking the lives of her friends and family, and then being kidnapped and forced at gunpoint to crash a Hollywood premiere and blackmail an A-list movie director, which ultimately led to his death—yesterday she thought her future was over. And now, she's being offered a job.

Only in Hollywood.

She almost jumps up to kiss him but keeps herself in the chair, closing her eyes while stamping her feet in glee. Fuck playing it cool.

Flowers says, "I'll take that as you're intrigued," his eyes crinkling at the corners.

Millie grins again.

"Uh, yeah. I think so." Now she laughs, putting her hands on the sides of her head. "Would this be for the studio?" she asks.

"Not exactly. You see, my aunt is incredibly well off. Most of her money comes from online trading, but she also invests heavily in films and television. She'd like to commission you to write the script, and then we'd be in charge of finding it a home, with either this studio or another. My aunt would also provide capital to help with the budget. You'd be paid whether or not we sell the script. What do you think?"

What does she think? A loaded question if there ever was one.

She should be thinking that her hard work has paid off, that her dreams are finally going to come true, that she's probably the only girl in the history of North Dakota who's going to be working in Hollywood straight out of high school.

Instead, she's thinking that, even though she's not in a movie, the false victory is a staple trope of the heist genre, where the hero pulls off the job at the end and is ready to go riding into the sunset, only to have the FBI or the Mob hot on their trail.

Hell or High Water ends this way. Chris Pine robs banks to save his family's ranch, but Jeff Bridges, as a US Marshal aware of the crimes, seeks revenge for his partner killed during a shoot-out. Steven Soderbergh ends both *Ocean's Eleven* and *Logan Lucky* with the crew pulling off the heist but never being able to spend the money without looking over their shoulders.

Bottom line: if it's too good to be true, then it probably is.

Plus, there are just too many unknowns. For example, what was Flowers doing at O'Naire's house last night? Lexi wasn't anywhere Millie could see. Even more alarming, how did Flowers figure out O'Naire stole her script and that she was in California in the first place? Sure, her alibi for traveling to LA was that she came to protest the movie, but how would he have learned that?

Could Flowers be connected?

O'Naire was long rumored to have Mob help, and from what Flowers just told her, the police feel the rumors are true. Is Flowers playing dumb right now? Pretending he just learned about O'Naire's criminal business deals, when in fact he's known all along—maybe even was in on it?

Is that possible, or is she being paranoid?

The smart move is to decline the offer. Take credit for the movie she wrote for and about her dad, and bolt before she gets in too deep. It's always greed that gets you caught or killed.

On the other hand, opportunities like this don't come along every day, and she's always wanted to be the next Ricky O'Naire . . .

Millie sits up straight and meets his eyes. "Here's what I'm thinking."

9

ONE YEAR LATER

EXT. NEW YORK CITY ALLEY—NIGHT

Feet slap against wet pavement. Clouds of steam puff through manhole covers. An overhead light sputters and goes dead.

A man in a dark alley looks over his shoulder to see if he's being followed, then slows. Pink neon from a diner sign bathes him in light. He takes off his fedora, kneels down to open the duffel bag. He removes a stack of dollar-sized paper cut from newspapers, phone books, and advertisements. He turns the bag over. Stacks upon stacks of paper land on neon-stained cement. He rakes his hands through the pile. It's all fake, not a single authentic piece of currency to be found. It's enough to make a man cry, but still no tears. He gives it a moment. Nothing.

Hurried footsteps echo from around the corner. He jumps to his feet, removes a handgun from inside his trench coat. It looks foreign in his hand, like it's the first time he's ever held a gun. He steps out of the light. His body trembles. Way too much. The footsteps get louder. Someone rounds the corner and a woman's voice yells, "Don't shoot!" but the back of the man's head blocks her face from camera.

"Cut!"

Bailey "Milwaukee" Magnusson, twenty-two, straw-wheat hair swept up in a ponytail so she'll be taken seriously, eyes too large and pleading for anyone to do so, drops her head into her hands.

"Cut!" Millie yells.

The fifty-person crew takes a collective breath before department heads speak with their teams and everyone returns to first positions. Paz looks up from the camera's viewfinder, says something to a grip about the dolly movement not being fast enough at the end. Jordan consults with his boom operator; they both agree the bag still makes too much noise when the actor runs. Devin gets up from his chair to talk with the head of makeup. He's concerned Bailey isn't looking pale enough for someone with a Scandinavian complexion.

"Great job, everybody. Let's take five," Millie says. "Paz, I want to change the shot a bit after we regroup. Instead of having them both in the frame, let's film Bailey in a medium close-up and stay with her after she yells 'Cut.' It'll give us some options in the editing room."

Paz shares an annoyed look with the focus puller. "How many options do you want?" she asks Millie. "We've shot this thing twenty different ways already."

"I guess this will make it twenty-one, then," Millie says and gives her friend a wink.

She wraps up the cord of her headphones, sets them on her chair, and checks her phone. It'll be another hour before the investors stop by. Flowers is bringing his aunt on set for the first time. She's been impressed by the dailies and wants to take Millie to dinner to discuss her career and possible upcoming projects.

Fueled by news of O'Naire's death and the string of unbelievable events leading up to it, *The Art of the Gangster* was a huge critical and financial success, propelling Millie and her crew into the spotlight—morning talk shows, paid speaking engagements, profiles in *People* and the *New Yorker*.

All of these things, plus the new film, make Mom, Wade, and Aaron proud, and it's always a hot topic every Sunday after church where Pastor Rod's congregation has quadrupled, thanks to a commercial Millie directed in place of those sermons she'd promised. Aaron comes over to the house, and he and Wade share venison recipes and watch the game while Mom works on her Millie scrapbook or twists together church wreaths.

It's been a hectic twelve months, and Flowers and his aunt want to make sure that Millie's got a handle on the pressure, provide any guidance they can with the next steps of her career.

It's almost humorous now, the idea of the two of them being organized crime. Millie thinks back to that initial meeting with Flowers and realizes how paranoid she was. They have way too many notes, way too many artistic opinions, to be gangsters. Most of the suggestions are things she can't include in the movie, since O'Naire's family refused to sell them the rights to his story.

Which is fine, because having to fabricate so much of the script allowed Millie to share her side of the story. The audience will never know what they think is fiction was her reality.

Of course she can't just lay out *everything* in the script, which is why seventeen-year-old Millie from Fargo is now Bailey, a twentysomething woman from Milwaukee, and so on. Even with so many changes, her crew was nervous about the whole thing, but never Millie. She knew nobody would actually believe four film students could steal a major motion picture days before its Hollywood premiere.

Just in case, she chose a title that would make it clear to the audience how preposterous the whole thing was:

The Long Shots.

Even without permission to tell his story, O'Naire's influence permeates the script. He was right. Sort of. While people prefer to rally around a victim, rather than a hero, what they love even more is to see that victim *become* a hero. Upon repeat viewings, and watching with a critical eye, Millie realized that it was the only thing missing from *The Art of the Gangster.*

Back then, she wanted to make sure her father was remembered and seek on-screen revenge against the man who had betrayed him. Now that man is dead. And the best revenge, she has come to learn, is to live a better life than Bobby Blomquist.

She doesn't have to be a victim. Her dad's memory doesn't live in a movie. It lives in her. And now it's time to tell her own story.

After a stop at craft services to get her latte from Yates—who's still bitter about not getting a more important job, especially since she hired Sammy to work in the art department—Millie rejoins her crew on the set of a New York City alley, where four actors in their midthirties play Academy students in their early twenties. Millie takes a seat in the director's chair and reads over her note cards. Paz gets in place behind the camera. Jordan adjusts the sound levels on his mixer before telling the boom operator to watch the frame line. And Devin makes sure all departments are ready to go before he gives the thumbs-up, and Millie gets out of her seat, walks past the monitors, pushing up the brim of her RedHawks cap to get a good look at the actors, and draws a deep breath.

"Action!"

FADE TO BLACK.

ACKNOWLEDGMENTS

Just like robbing a Las Vegas casino or breaking into the National Archives to steal the Declaration of Independence, publishing a book requires hours of recon, a highly detailed plan, a steady diet of determination, a massive heap of dumb luck, and, above all else, a crew of extremely talented individuals to help you pull off the job.

I'd like to thank my agent, Chip Rice, and the team at WordLink, Inc. I'm forever grateful for your support in my writing and finding *Breaking In* a home.

Thanks to Rick Bleiweiss, Josie Woodbridge, Ananda Finwall, Cole Barnes, Stephanie Stanton, Sarah Riedlinger, Sarah Bonamino, Rachel Sanders, Bryan Barney, Joe Garcia, Sean Thomas, my editor Sharyn November, the Blackstone Publishing print production team and the audiobook division. I couldn't have asked for a better publisher and I appreciate all of your efforts and support bringing my debut out into the world.

Thanks to Sheila O'Connor, Deborah Keenan, and all the faculty and students I studied with in the creative-writing program at Hamline University; Tom Brandau, Kyja Kristjansson-Nelson, Richard Zinober, Kevin Carollo, and the English and Media Arts departments at Minnesota State University Moorhead; and Claude Kerven and all my New York Film Academy friends (Salty Dawgs for life).

I'd like to thank those who read early drafts, provided technical knowledge (most of which I probably got wrong for narrative purposes), and have genuinely supported my creative ambitions over the years: Allison Wall, Jeff Grapevine, Mark Teats, Robert Kerbeck, Matt Goldman,

Roger Hanstad, James Mortner, J.J. Austrian, Caitlin Braulick, Trevor Mathew, Ashley and Rachelle Denton, Mark Wickline, Sarah Ahiers, and Nathan Wermerskirchen.

To my always supportive family. To Elyse, Rachel, and Broderick Elliott Andersen III. To our forever pup, Lola, the best little lap warmer in the game. To my parents, for realizing the works of Stephen King, Michael Crichton, and John Grisham are the best type of beach reads, even if I was in elementary school. Your love and support means the world to me. I'm lucky to have you. To Grandpa DeWayne, a cunning card shark if there ever was one, and Grandma Millie, whose laughter and smile I miss more than her chocolate chip cookies.

Finally, I'd like to thank my wife, Tess, who always believes I can achieve anything, long before I even think to give it a try. You and Lola are my home, and I never could've done this without your light in my life.